KU-006-763

Take Me Now

by

Nancy Jardine

This is a work of fiction. Names, characters, places, and incidents are either the product of the author's imagination or are used fictitiously, and any resemblance to actual persons living or dead, business establishments, events, or locales, is entirely coincidental.

Take Me Now

COPYRIGHT © 2012 by Nancy Jardine

All rights reserved. No part of this book may be used or reproduced in any manner whatsoever without written permission of the author or The Wild Rose Press, Inc. except in the case of brief quotations embodied in critical articles or reviews.
Contact Information: info@thewildrosepress.com

Cover Art by *Kim Mendoza*

The Wild Rose Press, Inc.   **FT**
PO Box 708   **Pbk**
Adams Basin, NY 14410-0708
Visit us at www.thewildrosepress.com

Publishing History
First Champagne Rose Edition, 2012
Print ISBN 978-1-61217-334-4
Digital ISBN 978-1-61217-335-1

Published in the United States of America

Dedication

My first thanks go to my husband and all my family,
who have been incredibly supportive.

~~~

Second thanks go to my wonderful editor,
Cindy Davis,
who keeps me motivated to do even more!

Other Books by Nancy Jardine

Monogamy Twist
available from The Wild Rose Press, Inc.

Chapter One

Nairn Malcolm's only applicant was the woman chugging into the cove down below. His fingers clamped onto the wrought-iron railing as he compelled himself to accept realities. Waiting for other candidates wasn't feasible; time was of the essence. He had to be mobile to do his normal work, never mind ferret out the saboteur who'd caused havoc again that morning. Yet, even if the woman below was suitable, could he involve her in something he knew was dangerous? Nairn's conscience smarted as much as his niggling wounds.

Viewing Aela Cameron's photograph had been enough to put him in a continuing state of readiness. Cantankerous rumbles from the healthy side of his mouth accompanied another cyclops squint at the boat now docking.

Shapely legs clambered from his newest catamaran. Deep-pink stilettos touched down on his floating jetty and found balance as it dipped and swayed, while tangled tresses billowed around her head in the stiff breeze coming in off the water. Nairn's tetchiness burbled at her impractical footwear, yet her allure soared when a wicked gust of wind blew up her flirty little skirt, a flash of white widening his eyes. His fingers scrunched the railing.

The woman's clothes were semi-professional for an office, but they weren't practical for sailing around the islands off the west coast of Scotland on a breezy end-of-June day.

Aela Cameron chatted with Aran, his boatyard manager. Though he couldn't hear their words, their easy conversation belied a long-time friendship as Aran secured the painter to the mooring hook. The generally taciturn Aran chuckled. How did Aela Cameron draw the man out of his usual reticence?

Her echoing laugh clinched it. Charm. Beauty. He squinted again. Sexy shape. What more did it take to encourage any man to flirt? He grumbled loud enough to startle the tern settling alongside. Nairn willed himself to be ready for the coming meeting, the dip of the wind in his favor.

"Honest. It's no problem; I'll take it with me," came her loud claim as Aran answered that he could look after it till later. Look after what? One good eye popped open and locked onto her rear as she shrugged into the laden backpack Aran passed up to her from the catamaran.

A backpack?

Nairn shook his head to dispel the peculiar image. Why wasn't she shouldering a jaunty little purse? His vision was loopy, but he wasn't imagining the monstrous bag as she straightened up. The dull wallop of a pile driver at the back of his skull had been present all day, now it pounded even more from the stress this woman engendered. And he hadn't met her yet.

Who, in their right mind, came to an interview wearing quasi-conservative business gear, bright pink stilettos, for God's sake, and sported a groaning backpack? His head reeled with the effort of processing her anomalies. First impressions?

Not startling.

Negative point two. Or was it three already? He couldn't remember. Frowning hurt like hell, so he resumed a squint instead, and tracked her movements. As if he was able to take his eyes off her anyway.

Aela Cameron's long-legged and agile skip along his undulating floating-jetty was unimpeded by the weighty luggage. When she came to a halt at his boatshed, she peered in the little side window. Her Canadian accent drifted up to him. "Hey, Aran! Cool collection. Can I have a peek at his floatplane?"

They vanished inside his boatshed. His mouth pursed with annoyance at the delay. Shifting his body to a better position he waited. And waited.

A peek?

He could have built a ruddy fishing boat by now. Nairn's teeth clenched. Unwelcome thoughts intruded as he imagined what could be taking place inside. What he'd want to be doing wouldn't be discussing technical specifications with a woman as luscious as Aela Cameron, who produced quite a startling stimulation with only a glimpse of her photograph.

What the hell took them so long?

Temper spiked along with his pulse, the exasperating waiting time cementing his decision she wouldn't suit him at all, but he owed his ex-PA, Brian, big time. At the very least he'd conduct the interview since Brian had worked his ass off to get even one candidate here so quickly. A woman of twenty-seven who looked like she did, couldn't have the experience he needed. An awkward shunt moved his aches and pains to the side of the gate, just out of view, though he still overlooked the boatshed.

Finally they exited the wooden building, chattering as though they'd been friends for years. Nairn sloped forward and watched Aela Cameron's head whip up when Aran indicated the climb, his finger-point a simple gesture to the top of the cliff. Unladylike snorts and comments—Nairn suspected uncomplimentary in nature—burst free from the woman as she tackled the zigzagging wooden stairway he'd had built onto the rock face. Part way up, a huge smile lightened her face before she quipped something down to Aran, who lugged the box of supplies. Aran's laughing answer drifted off on the breeze.

A funny woman was she? Nairn's annoyance increased as he shuffled along the wall to prop himself against a stout beech tree. The tumult in his head amplified as he prepared to meet her, his usual control as elusive as the vision he struggled to balance. The greenish-white gull-plop landing on his elbow was one more indignity, exemplifying how he felt.

Fresh horse crap. Steaming and hazy...and overheated.

****

Aela huffed. Just a bit.

Nobody had warned her about the climb. The only information given by the appointments agency was she should present herself at the marina for two p.m. where she'd be met and ferried to the island of Lanera, for a hastily organized interview with Nairn Malcolm, at his Garvald home.

Aran, pilot of the catamaran-had been chatty during the journey, though circumspect about her prospective employer and the location of his house, and of how she would get there once they arrived at the island. Not bothered over minor details, since she was already on the way, she'd reciprocated her own sailing experience as they skirted the Mull of Kintyre on their way north to the island of Lanera.

Now, a few hundred treads up, she was on the top step of the cliff staircase thankful she was fit; the climb with an overloaded backpack, wearing heels, would have killed some people. She chuckled at the ridiculous image as she unlatched the wrought iron gate set into a high grey granite wall and stepped through onto rough grass. Exhilarated by the scene she stood transfixed, breathless, for a couple moments before a throaty gurgle sputtered out.

"Holy shit, Aran! Would you look at that? Hell's bells and baubles. You said it would be worth it when I got to the top, but you never mentioned it was a cute little castle. Hey, can you hear me down there?"

Aran's amused answer echoed up to her. "The whole island can probably hear you, Miss Cameron."

So taken was she by the scenery, Aela didn't lower her volume. "This is my first visit to a real Scottish castle. Oh, my! Just look at the dinky turret up there. Hey, Aran, I could pretend to be the lonely little virgin watching my handsome knight in shining armor gallop in on his trusty steed. I'd drop my token handkerchief for him to scoop up on his lance before he fought death-defying tourneys over my honor."

Her unladylike hollers and arm gestures wouldn't have matched the weeping-willow creature she portrayed, but she was on a roll, her mind's eye taking flight in the magical setting.

Aran's voice floated from just short of the top step, the weight of his large package having slowed his climb. "Your historical references are a wee bit mixed up, Miss Cameron. We were short of that brand of champion up here in the islands. Our heroes were more likely to be uncouth, more hairy, and a lot less chivalrous."

Aela's loud chortles echoed all around as she scanned the rooftop crenellations. "Scrummy! Sounds exactly my type. Bring the hairy ones on, please. Plenty of 'em, and we'll have a big party in that dinky castle."

Fifty yards ahead, the original turreted keep had been renovated, two extensions having been added to make the whole construction form a U-shape. The facade of grey granite had dark wood bordering lots of shining windows, blending harmoniously. The windows, she guessed, had been widened from original gun-looped embrasures since a couple of these thin rectangular openings remained at each end of the center section on ground floor level.

"This has been the greatest start to an interview, Aran. I'm so impressed!" Aela whooped, unable to contain her bubble of pleasure because in no way did the castle resemble the forbidding bleak structures she'd read about in traditional Scottish tales. "Okay, Aran. So, what's next on this escapade?"

She turned back as Aran stepped through the gate. Aela's beaming smile crumpled, and her hand whipped up to slap her chest. "What the hell? Jeeze. You scared the crap out of me." Aela's heart jolted. The castle came with its very own ogre?

She released the indrawn breath. Fairy tales were abandoned as medieval images returned, her heartbeat settling. The vision alongside the wall was so unanticipated she smiled anyway; no way could she curb the burst of laughter. "Whoa! This is so amazing. I get to meet the battle-scarred champion as well? A full re-enactment deal? Yay! Glad to meet you, Sir Smash-Em-Up."

An uncomfortable throat-clearing came from Aran as he crossed the stretch of grass, and the stony stare of the other man curtailed any further gusto—Aela grasped that her glib comments weren't well received. Amusement vanished. Sir Smash-Em-Up's appearance didn't seem set up for her enjoyment.

A huge guy stood braced against a tree. Aela wasn't small at five feet ten, but this man towered over her—at least six and a half feet of him. He was attention-grabbing in the way a poster for an Accident and Emergency Department would be. It was as though he'd been downed in an earthquake and a hotchpotch of his parts thrown up in its wake.

Oh, my! Deadly dangerous. A dull throb started deep inside her, so powerful she wanted to flap her hand like a fan to cool down, but that wouldn't create a particularly good first impression.

Why was he even out of his damned sick-bed if the injuries he seemed to have were genuine?

His plastered right forearm nestled inside the waistband of his sweatpants. That wasn't so odd, but she gulped over the rest of him. The left leg of the black pants had been haphazardly hacked off at crotch level: the sturdy thigh below a mish-mash of scratches, bandages, purple-black bruises and dark leg hair. A rigid white plaster cast stretched from a little above the kneecap all the way down to his toes. Her gaze lingered at the jagged material edges before she forced her focus upward where there was a lot of unexplained stuff going on. Twitching? Dear hell!

Heat crept up her cheeks and something nice and cozy tingled way down low. A tremble at her knees had her clenching muscles very tightly together. Hot. She was hot all over. Wow! Nobody had affected her like this for years. Making love to this really big guy immediately came to mind...but that was so not like her at all. The sight of a half-undressed male never ever gave her such fantasies, but keeping her eyes from ogling was downright impossible with this guy.

The view above his waist didn't cool her down either for the short-sleeved black shirt the man wore was open, flapping in the warm breeze. White gauze was strapped on below his left collar bone, the rest of his chest splattered with deep scratches and Technicolor bruising. The trail of hair disappearing inside his sweatpants fascinated her as much as the bruising. Her head whipped up when she realized she was gawping. Again. Renewed heat boiled her to a frazzle.

The man was a mess, but what a glorious mess!
"So. Not an actor?"

Her tentative question wasn't meant to be answered. Just as well since the guy didn't look amused. His face was compelling, yet impassive. He never blinked once as she stared, no part of his shuttered face showing any emotion at all. Eyes of an intense blue regarded her, though the left one was barely open, with dark bloody bruising and puffy red inflammation around the eyelid, swelling and discoloration on the cheekbone below making his features unbalanced. Thick black hair, tousled like a blood-sticky thatch, drooped above his bruised brow. An angry gash slashed across his forehead, the wound scabbing over but not sufficiently deep to require stitching.

Mmm...definitely an ogre.

Unadulterated vigor oozed from every last bit of him—overall a dangerous concoction. Something stirred way-down-low inside Aela again. He was a real honey, and the bee in her wanted to be very sticky.

Her mind whirred. The man bore a vague resemblance to the ruggedly handsome thirty-two year old Nairn Malcolm of the internet photograph, but would the blonde limpet in the recent celebrity snapshot want to curl herself around this forbidding wreck of a man? Aela thought not. She wondered, though, if his blank expression was caused by current circumstances, or if this was his normal demeanor, since he hadn't been smiling in the photograph either.

With the high granite wall as his backdrop she could easily imagine this man lording over the castle, ruthlessly challenging any invaders to his domain. Taking any woman he wanted? Now there was a thought she was happy to entertain. A tiny smile broke free.

Tamping down her crazed imagination she reassessed him.

What had the guy been doing to get himself in such a state?

Who was he?

Chapter Two

"Nairn Malcolm."

Holy shit! Aela reeled back a little, her eyebrows puckering. It was as though he'd answered her internal question. His gruff declaration skittered down her sensitized backbone. Her gaze tracked his hand as it stretched out in salutation, though no other part of his huge body moved; he remained propped against the tree.

She jerked out of her reverie. Maybe the extreme sporting activities he marketed were a little too extreme? Her thoughts continued to whirl. Did she want to be transporting someone who looked like a walking advert for medical insurance? On the other hand, she could see exactly why he needed someone to fly his floatplane for a while. The appointments agency hadn't made any mention of his medical condition. It came as no surprise now she could see what he was like. They'd probably feared she'd turn tail and run from the daunting prospect of him.

She moved to return his gesture, but halted when one undamaged eyebrow twitched in scathing inquiry. Ah. To tender the wrong hand wasn't a great start, and neither was her right heel sinking into the soft grass. Blast and damn! Other mental curses were quelled as she entangled the fingers of her left hand with his, her genuine beam of merriment bowing up her fuchsia-rimmed lips.

"Aela Cameron. Good afternoon, Mr. Malcolm."

His hand was huge. Warm fingers clamped around hers as he pumped briskly, an awkward three times. The zing that went straight up her arm, through every sinew and cell, she disregarded as she tipped free of his grip. Unable to prevent it, she stumbled right out of her stuck-fast shoe and toppled onto the grass, her backpack bearing the brunt of the impact.

An upside down tortoise wouldn't have been any more graceless, her legs wallowing in air. Her burst of laughter was repeated when she looked up into the disbelieving gaze of Nairn Malcolm. "Upon my ass, indeed! Sorry, Mr. Malcolm. I'm sure you're always having females swooning at your feet, but I'm also pretty sure it's not good form to reveal the tighty-whities during an interview."

Aela squirmed her skirt down before attempting to straighten her face for Nairn Malcolm's good eye almost popped out. Events rarely fazed her, but she felt out of kilter as she swirled to her knees. After bearing weight on all fours she rebalanced herself, and the backpack, before rising, her amusement subsiding under his continued displeasure.

Sure, she'd fallen over, but it didn't deserve such a scurrilous attitude. Sobered a tiny bit she stared back. Body temperature was supposed to be ninety-eight point six, but she guessed she was easily topping one hundred. Unfortunately, the heat of the sun wasn't strong enough to account for the redness her cheeks must be displaying.

"I'm away round to Mariskay," Aran called from the top of the cliff staircase. "Call me when you're ready, Nairn."

Aela registered how long she must have been fixated on this beguiling giant if Aran had already been inside the castle with the heavy load he'd been carrying.

"Thanks for the deliveries, Aran." Nairn Malcolm's reply was brief...and toneless.

"Hey! Thanks for delivering me too, Aran. I

adored what you can do with that catamaran." In spite of still being locked in Nairn's gaze Aela quipped her answer, unable repress her grin. She wasn't sure she wanted to be regarded as one of Nairn Malcolm's deliveries, like a pizza order, although she supposed she almost qualified. She waved to Aran. "See you. But not too soon, I hope!"

She reviewed her circumstances while she waited for Sir Smash-Em-Up to say something, but all he did was maintain that flinty demeanor. Her smile crinkled a little for she supposed she had sort of laughed at his injuries, and inadvertently shown him her knickers. So, how much worse was it going to get? It had to be the strangest beginning to an interview anyone ever had for a job. A temporary job she wasn't really too bothered about getting. How could she not smile?

If she'd been a nervous simpering wimp she'd have skittered back down the cliff steps minutes ago, escaping from the grump of this mighty fine little castle. It wasn't the building's fault its owner was grimly po-faced. Pity was, he was also the most exciting guy ever under the disaster that was his current façade.

Nairn sighed, his mouth-edge twitching as much as his broken ribs stabbed, and that wasn't all that twitched. He closed his eyes and prayed for divine intervention to block out the image shooting through his retinas. The move didn't make a blind bit of difference; the replay was even better than the reality. No way in hell could he have avoided seeing her panties this time, and it had been no quick flash since it had taken a few seconds for her to fumble through the cover up.

Delicate shiny-white-silky-stuff, too miniscule to cover up the rounded cheeks he'd like a leisurely sampling of. Long, brown thighs. No tan lines. Bloody hell! The woman wasn't here for a quick tumble. He winced at his poor choice of thought: neither kind of tumble! Inhaling as deep a breath as possible he braced himself for what was to come.

The first thing he noted was she still grinned at him. Was she for real, assessing him in such a way and finding him amusing? The devoid of pain expression he'd been struggling to maintain collapsed. What on earth was the blasted woman doing? Wasting his time? She was here to interview for a bloody job!

She was stunning—even more beautiful than her photograph. The jet-black hair piled up on her head was sexily windblown. Some strands had escaped to loop delicate ears and pointed down to rounded breasts straining the material of her jacket. Thinking about what was under the jacket made him moan, his sexual reaction to the woman detrimental to his...? Health? Sanity? He wasn't sure which was worse.

He'd been willing himself for hours to remain upright, to retain some dignity. But here she was, not at all embarrassed about flashing him...or falling over. At his feet. And making glib comments. Finding everything a hoot.

Despite his current state of mind, the arousal strained even more under his trapped fingertips. His hacked off sweatpants were no restraint at all. He hated his unruly body; how could he get so stirred up when this potential employee was disrespectful?

Her mahogany almond-shaped eyes, outlined with dark fans of thick lashes, remained fixed on him; her jovial gaze mocking.

She had to go.

His head reeled as he peeled himself from the support of the sturdy tree. Lurching to the gate to call Aran back, he glimpsed the catamaran whiz around the cove, wondering how Aran had managed to get away so quickly. Gripping tight he steeled himself to do what was necessary, indicating the French doors.

"Miss Cameron. Those doors lead into the great room. Wait there."

The woman followed his instructions as he grasped the forearm crutch he'd stashed alongside the wall and hauled it into place wondering how he'd make it across the grass, for it now loomed like an impossible marathon.

Aela Cameron was already at the doors, twirling her man-magnet pink stilettos from one hand, her neat rear end like a beacon calling to him as she stepped inside his castle. Nairn whimpered as he made the first of many lurches toward the interview he didn't want to conduct.

Her height was a complete surprise, not something he deduced from the promotional photograph Brian had acquired. The concept of almost being nose to nose with Aela Cameron made him want to be wrapped all around her, feathering kisses across the soft skin of her cheeks. In profile, her nose was a classic straight line though quite long, perfectly aligned in a slightly tanned oval face, well-defined cheekbones matching a determined chin. It wasn't a delicate face, but it was intensely alluring with pink lips as enticing as they were sassy. All in keeping with her overall statuesque shape.

She was nothing like the small dainty women he often gravitated to.

He exhaled again. She was here to be interviewed for a job. Nothing else.

****

Aela was still laughing as she entered the room and dropped her backpack to the side of the doors before slipping her shoes back on. Once out of Nairn Malcolm's sight, the initial embarrassment over her drooling admiration was fading. She berated herself

14

for being an idiot to get all worked up about a total stranger. Mmm. She shook her head. He couldn't have been that good-looking. Nope. All bashed up as the guy was? Hardly. She reckoned she must just need a sugar boost, or something, since it was a while since her early lunch. That had to account for her dizzy imagination.

As she awaited Nairn's slow progress she admired the décor. When endless seconds passed she returned to the French doors where her grin faded. "Would you look at that dumb ass? Some bed should still have his name on it!" She didn't think her words were loud, but wasn't bothered if they were.

For every pace Nairn took he stopped to regain breath before he repositioned the crutch, followed by a reel as he forced his leg cast forward with a lumbering twist. Laughter went on the back burner. After all, how could she find humor in his predicament? The man shouldn't be interviewing at all, at least not until he was less incapacitated. Aela swore, unbecoming words a well-brought-up young lady should never entertain, but if the ass, who clearly needed to be recuperating, wanted to interview her, then so be it. She didn't need to respect the guy to work for him for a few weeks.

The great room was well named, eminently suitable for someone as large as Nairn. Comfortable leather sofas and wide armchairs framed a huge stone fireplace, the grate set with hefty logs and traditional peat blocks. Impressive landscape paintings adorned the white walls and added a kaleidoscope of color. Small bookcases flanked the French doors. She had plenty of time to examine them before he listed into the room.

"Guest cloakroom, second door on the left!" Nairn rasped at her, pointing to the internal entrance doors facing them. His face had leached every vestige of color, the lines around his pursed mouth indicating his determination. Aela's opinion remained—the gorgeous numbskull should be resting.

"Office, second right, when you're done."

Grim ogre, indeed. Whether she wanted to use the amenities or not, it appeared he'd just issued an order she needed to obey—if she wanted this job. And she'd just decided she did; it was nothing like she'd been expecting to find. Having made landfall at this cute castle, the location appealed even more, though she willed her mind to remain open regarding its disturbing owner who had such a peculiar effect on her. She could think of no good reason why his gruff demeanor was making her more determined to get the job. He didn't like her— but that was okay because liking each other didn't have to come into it. She was, however, determined to get the job.

"Got that, Mr. Malcolm." Aela acquiesced as required and gave the man the opportunity to get his beaten-up body down the hallway, amazed at his asinine foolhardiness. Did he think she was so stupid she couldn't see how difficult putting one foot in front of the other was for him? Was he just another of those super masculine guys she'd had dealings with over the years who'd never admit to failings of any kind? She had a feeling she'd find out before much longer.

After using the facilities, she gave her face a good wash to clear off the salt spray and tidied her hair with her fingers having found most of the pins holding her top knot had vanished to the wind during the boat trip. Rummaging in the pocket of her jacket she pulled out two pencils and secured her long hair into a new topknot. Better. She felt a bit tidier, if not quite business-perfect.

The hallway was impressive, many doors to either side, light and airy but also very silent.

Nobody seemed to be around. Or, they were too well trained to come and find out who wandered the corridor. Adjacent to the cloakroom was a cozy little breakfast nook, bright and welcoming, its large window overlooking the well-stocked side garden. A small arch led through to an impressive kitchen, the décor old-style wooden cabinets, yet it was filled with modern appliances. She was dying to investigate the rest of the castle, but instead headed for Nairn's office reckoning she'd given him enough time to get settled.

"Here, please!" His order was terse, his scowling focus entirely on his screen.

"So kind. Thank you." She was likewise abrupt as she sat where indicated opposite him. As far as she could tell her slight sarcasm fell on deaf ears.

Nairn gave sharp intakes of breath each time he moved. Biting her tongue, Aela waited till the interview began, thinking for the umpteenth time he shouldn't be attempting it because he looked even worse than he had outside. Technicolor bruising displaying different hues now held her fascination.

"One minute!"

His voice was hostile as he fiddled with his computer mouse while peering, one-eyed, at his screen. Having noticed he'd avoided eye contact since she entered the room her brows drew together, the first flicker of doubt stealing into her mind. Was she wasting her time even if it had been a lark so far? The office was large with an efficient setup. The L-shaped desk arrangement he sat behind was mirrored behind her; the second display angled so the desks weren't facing each other.

A thin bead of sweat trickled down Nairn's left temple and made a track on his battered face, into the heavy growth covering his jaws. He was the most unkempt prospective employer she could ever imagine. So ridiculous after the effort she'd put in to look professional in her charity shop suit with its too-short flaring skirt, and nipped-in-waist jacket. But the suit, shoes and fuchsia camisole had been the best she could find at such short notice. It had been a difficult call—come dressed for sailing, or wear more typical PA garb.

"This interview might have to be short."

Whoa! What did he mean?

Aela's smile faded as she nodded back, disappointment warring with irritation, but she made no attempt to speak. Was the dratted man admitting he was too ill to continue?

"Give me brief details about my floatplane, and then my 525b jet."

He inched two advertising brochures across the desk toward her—information on the two vehicles he'd referred to. The floatplane she'd seen in his boatshed, but she scanned the jet specifications before she lifted her gaze back to him. His skin tone was as grey as the granite walls of this castle, his deep voice like gravel as he brought his good arm across his chest to brace himself more comfortably in the chair. Stupid man...but he was also the most arresting guy she'd seen in years. The visceral impact he made on her had nothing to do with any current injuries. Oh, hell!

She'd best get on with it and ignore the hormonal rush that trembled her upper thigh muscles. Determined clearing of her throat grabbed his attention, which seemed to have strayed to somewhere to the right of her shoulder.

Talk about his planes?

Nothing would please her more. Aela loved everything about flying. Mentally rubbing her hands in glee, she licked her lips before starting.

"Your floatplane down in the cove is similar..."

Recounting her experience with comparable planes she watched his eyes glaze over, both lids lowering to slits. Surely he wasn't bored? Her eulogy hadn't been that long. Her information and experience, was as relevant as he would get from anyone, male or female.

"Although I haven't flown the last five months while on my world tour I kept myself updated on all new developments."

Only the merest disgruntled twitch of his lip broke the stern facemask, which she processed as sort-of listening. As she continued Nairn Malcolm slid further down in the chair, his head lolling back to lean on the backrest, his breathing settling to an even shorter rhythm, which drew her gaze firmly onto his chest.

Bad move.

Even though already annoyed as hell with the dratted man, there was something about him that irked and attracted, in equal measures. Though battered, there was strength and tone in that chest of his. She wanted to soothe the hurts...and maybe explore a bit further. Her voice faltered before she caught up with herself and restarted her sentence, their gazes colliding for a second as his eyes flashed open.

A deep whimper escaped him as he shunted around a bit more, and then his eyes closed again, his good hand making the tiniest of gestures she understood to mean carry on.

Aela squelched any other strange oddities—like unwanted desire. Why couldn't the damned man make proper eye contact for more than a nanosecond? Even with his one good eye?

He moaned again and pushed his body back up, his head now awkward, hanging beyond the backrest support, his gaze rolling to the ceiling, his eyelids flickering.

"Excuse me! If you're not already too bored to listen, Mr. Malcolm, I'll tell you about your jet." Her words whipped out, the patience thread twanging a little too much. She waited, till a nod indicated she should continue. "Thank you very much, sir." Her retort was full of the deepest sarcasm, exactly how she felt, but she might have been talking to a blank wall for his response was non-existent. "Hey! Are you even listening to me?"

Not a professional tone of voice, Aela knew, but she wasn't used to being ignored. Nairn struggled to open his eyes, looking like a total drunk as his Cyclops-gaze flickered before his chin flopped down onto his chest.

"For cripes sake!"

Unable to contain herself she jumped to her feet, and knelt at his side before lifting his chin into her hand, and used her fingertips to pry open his good eyelid. Mmm. A seriously dilated pupil. She let her trembling hand drop away as she reflected on his condition. Without her chin support his head wavered to the side.

"Mr. Malcolm!"

Her shrill tone jolted his eyes open as she maneuvered both hands to rest his cheek against her chest. His head turned and he snuggled right in, good and proper, no mistake as he squashed his nose against her breasts...and sniffed. A prickle of sensation made its presence known. It skittered down her back, as Aela stared down at him, wondering what the heck to do next. The thrumming pulse at her wrist beat against his cheek. Her nipples reacted instantly to his pouting mouth and begged for some notice, forming tight hard and itchy nubs. What the heck was this guy doing to her? His lids flickered, his mouth wriggled and his one good eye...beseeched?

Chapter Three

"Boats."

"What? You still want me to tell you about bloody boats when you're almost comatose?" Aela imagined her question sounded as flabbergasted as she felt, yet Nairn's expression flickered assent as he swallowed, the muscles of his cheeks rubbing into her flesh. Looking down into the battered face of the stubborn fool she knew she couldn't keep up the deferential interview stuff. "This is absolute crap! You want me to keep talking?"

"Oh, yeah!"

His growling sigh was accompanied by lolling head-rolls, as though he was clearing his brain, his pained whimper making her squirm as he whiffed on her silk blouse, the tightened nipples below it perked even more. His cheek turned into her breast to nuzzle further, a tiny twitch quirking one corner of his mouth as his eyes closed again.

He smelled startling so close up—a mixture of aromas assailed her nostrils. Dried blood still lingered on some strands of his hair, a hint of some kind of medicinal alcohol wipe and slightly stale sweat was at his brow, but most of all, it was the musky male smell of Nairn himself. Raw man. Everything inside her came alive...and prickled...and flooded...and hummed. She drew him all in as his breath puffed against her making her frisson all over.

So not what she was there for.

Holding and caressing this guy was just too much. Her knees jolted, the muscle spasms of her upper thighs telling her what was happening was something out of her normal realm.

Careful of his bruising, she released his head down onto the backrest of the chair, the sole protest from him being another tweak of his lip. His one good eye blinked at her, a sexy whisper barely there. "Love y...r voice."

Aela felt herself glow to the roots of her hair. Again. Blushing was already too frequent a response to this guy. This was an interview. She needed to remember that and forget the lusting that was already a shock to her system. Since he seemed to be sufficiently recovered to almost focus, she resolved to conquer his weird effect on her.

Returning to her seat gave her a little time to gain composure. Nairn's torso squirmed further down in the chair, the heel of his rigid cast scraping the wooden floor as his legs stretched out below the desk. His eyes flickered open, occasionally attempting to catch her eye. At least she thought that was what he was attempting, till disturbing sounds emanated from his clenched teeth bordered by lips becoming bluer by the second. She sped up the interview process.

"...but I haven't piloted a catamaran as new as the one used to bring me here today. Uncle Harris hasn't upgraded the fleet to those specifications yet."

Nairn stretched forward two fingers, wildly aiming at the keyboard, the words wrenched from his mouth. "Unca Harris?"

"My uncle, Harris Cameron, owns Cameron Transport Group."

His head dipped as if in recognition, and after taking a deeper breath he grunted, loudly. "G'd o...ld Har...ris Ca...ron. Know 'im. How's h...?" His fingers stabbed at the keys as tense seconds passed.

She waited till his gaze flipped up, though his chin remained down, his head appearing too heavy to lift. "My uncle's very well, thank you."

"H...many h...rs?" His lids flickered, still focused on her lips.

"How many hours? What the friggin' heck has that got to do with my Uncle Harris, you stupid prat!" Leaping up, she strode a few paces around the room before returning to her chair, hands clenched at her sides, composure not much better but a grim determination in place.

The whole interview had become too surreal, but she wasn't sure what to do about it.

Nairn's focus was still on her mouth. His intent stare made her feel ill-at-ease. Hot...slightly flustered, and stupidly even more aroused. The attraction was now unwanted. Well, she could at least try to kid herself, but, by heavens, it was overpowering.

"Your only job?"

His question came as though there had been no break in the conversation at all, no little walkabout for her. She wondered if the conversation might go better if she were in cloud-cuckoo-land as well. Maybe she should ferret out some of his happy pills and join him.

Biting her lip she answered, calm and collected—she hoped. "Yes, I've only ever worked for Cameron Transport Group."

His fingers randomly jabbed for he didn't look as though he was even seeing the keys. She was getting too used to his pained breaths as he struggled to raise his head from the chair, gave up, and let it slump back against the headrest. His whole torso lolled as his arms slid down to his sides, the weight of the arm cast making him perch at an awkward tilt. Yet the whine that escaped sounded gratified.

Peculiar.

His gaze was almost re-focused when it latched onto hers. "Ahh, t...'s much better. Lovely." Nairn's weak smile was the first proper cracking of his austere demeanor and totally changed him. "Br...t Wa...ker tr...ned m... Bet y... din't kno... ...at!" he mumbled, naming a colleague of Aela's at Cameron Airways, the original sector of the transport group. His head cocked to one side, his smile deepening into a slumberous sexy one, his good eye attempting a wink of sorts.

A wink? Aela didn't have a clue what to make of that. "I know Bret Walker quite well." Her answer was careful because his Cyclops expression was quite different from before. The miniscule lift at the edge of his mouth she imagined was an attempt at being agreeable.

"Bret's still Cameron Airways best training pilot, but it was my uncle who trained me."

"Wish you'd tr...ned me. Mmm. Y...re real gor...jus. D'y know that?" A lopsided grin broke free as Nairn slid down even further, and his chin settled on his chest again. "Can't have y...tho, y're—s'too dange...us." His head wobbled again, his eyes closed, his smile more of a leer.

Aela's gaze widened at the sexy tenor of his out-of-order comment. She squelched the warmth it created realizing Nairn Malcolm was determined to continue to interview.

"Lovely voice, matches...stun...face."

"What did you just say?"

Aela's concern over this strange man's behavior increased. Her personal safety didn't make her fearful, but she was beginning to feel responsible for him since she seemed alone with him in the castle. Though why she should feel responsible was the biggest mystery ever.

His eyes flicked open again. "Where am I?"

"Your office, Mr. Malcolm."

"Oh. Yeah. Office...speriens?"

His mumble just decipherable, she detailed

what she'd undertaken as Office Manager for Cameron Transport Group, once again to his closed eyes; though his little nods she interpreted as an indicator he was listening. He had to be the most stubborn man she'd ever clapped eyes on, yet she had to award him some merit for persistence. His weird allure annoyed her, but she couldn't watch him suffer any longer.

"I need water, Mr. Malcolm," she lied.

One finger flicked toward the mini-services in a corner of the room. A few seconds later she forced his attention as she waved a glass of water at his face, having pulled his chair free of the desk so she could get in front of him. Sliding his good leg to the side, she knelt between his knees and lifted his chin, her tone low, but stern. "Look at me, you stupid bast— prat! I know you're not interviewing for a nursemaid, but you need to swallow some painkillers."

Her commanding tone managed to get through, sufficient for him to rouse a little.

"If you fall down, you great lummox, I'll find it difficult to get you up, whereas if you'll just resort to the damn painkillers you're too macho to take, I might manage to assist you to bed when they've kicked in."

Having disgorged the anger, Aela waited for the fallout. Nairn's eyelids flickered; his hand gave a limp wave at a bunch of pencils on the desk, the ogle back again. A blister pack of tablets and the original package—a squashed mess of cardboard—were stuffed inside the round pencil canister. She scanned the dosage.

"Have you taken any during the last two hours?"

She waited but no answer came. All he seemed capable of was staring at her the desirous longing in his one good eye affecting her so much she almost forgot about the other malfunctioning one. Oh, cripes again! Grasping his prickly chin to lift his face, days' worth of beard growth scratched the soft pads of her fingertips. His cracked lips pouted in a parody of a kiss, tempting her to come closer and sample. Difficult to resist, but she needed his answer. An overdose looked like the last thing the guy needed.

"Have you recently taken any pills?"

"No." His mutter was so faint she had to lean closer as he repeated it.

"Tongue out!" she demanded.

"Oh...yeah."

His deep growl made her knees quake, and her pulse lurch erratically. Strong thigh muscles of his good leg nudged her closer. The readiness in his immediate response something Aela instinctively identified with as his chin reached forward and his tongue flicked out. It was agonizing to ignore the temptation of wrapping her own around it, to find out what he tasted like, but she had a more important use for it. She placed two tablets onto his tongue and brought the water to his lips. After an awkward swallow that Aela felt reverberate right through her fingers and onto her too-hot chest, Nairn gulped more water, some escaping to trickle down from the edges of his mouth. So vulnerable.

A freezing cold dip in the nearby Atlantic wouldn't be enough to cool her now. Replacing the glass on the desk, she slid her fingers to those droplets, removing them from his raspy prickles with gentle flicks. He exhaled satisfaction right into her face.

"S'good. Thanks... your...s'pretty."

How could she not respond? Still, hunkering down between his legs she determined to sort out her wayward lust for this incredibly stupid man. "Cut the inappropriate compliments you silly numbskull! Look at me!"

Nairn blinked his eyes totally disregarding any

of her censure. "Y're so bootful. All of you."

"All of me? What the…"

Again she forced him to look at her. She was unaccustomed to that particular phrase having any effect on her, though quite a few men had used it on her.

His weary pupils locked on, the drugged and hazy blue sucking her in. What sort of fate had led her to this situation where the mouthed platitudes of this wreck of a guy actually meant something to her? Once again she squelched the churning emotions that made her want to jump his bones. She'd probably kill the blasted man with her fervor for never had she felt so needy. But she wasn't in Scotland to indulge in a manslaughter charge. Summoning every bit of her usual self-assurance she went on the attack. A verbal attack.

Her condescending tone she intended, every single syllable of it, her teeth doing a really nice gritting thing that made her feel better about the ridiculous situation she seemed to have got herself into. "Good. That's good, Sir Smash-Em-Bloody-Up, keep looking at me. Now be a good boy, and while we're waiting for the painkillers to kick in, I'll tell you my duties as my uncle's main secretary, and then as office manager. After that, you dense prat, you'll have heard everything you require."

She needed him to gather sufficient strength. There was no way she could manhandle a man of his physique if he was unable to even hobble.

Nairn's chin slumped, his slit-eyed focus somewhere below the table, but the lopsided smile she found very weird—as weird as the aerial floating movements of his good hand, which at times managed to stroke her hair. A sort of soothing pat that made her feel…nice? Oh, dear me, no! Far too lame a word.

"Don' need 'em p'ncils."

Before she knew what he was about Nairn plucked the pencils out of her hair, sending a tousled mess falling round her shoulders.

"Oooohh yeah!" His happy sigh was accompanied by the clattering of the pencils onto the wooden floor. The gentle tug of his fingers tangled in her hair she couldn't ignore. She felt the tiniest of movements of his nails on the individual strands, as he appeared to relish what he was doing.

She couldn't prevent her grin—the look on his face was incredible: a mixture of satisfaction, drunkenness and...lust?

The jolt of his head slamming forward came as quite a surprise, since she hadn't thought he had the energy to manage it. It was even more of a surprise when his lips collided with hers in a bumbled kiss, his fingers clutching her breast for support.

Support? Maybe not, since the squeeze he managed was surprisingly firm—and exhilarating. Her pulse skipped as the pressure of lips, and fingertips altered to a seeking insistence. The kiss deepened as Nairn inhaled a new breath and aroused more passions. The kiss was no longer bumbled, his tongue winding around hers, sucking out any hesitation she might have had over his vulnerable state. Even half comatose the guy was lethal! She swayed into him, needing to be much closer, till the grunt of sheer agony vibrating against her lips was enough to wipe the pleasure from her face.

Oh, jeez! Yep. She was going to crush him to death if she didn't rein in her enthusiasm. Pulling her mouth away she gentled him against the chair. Eyes fast shut, and a tight grimace furrowing his cheeks, Nairn made no objection as he moaned.

"Rain check on that one, sir?" As the words popped out Aela knew that should a job offer transpire, another kiss like that could never happen.

It had been just a bit too stirring, stirring enough for the tingles to still remain on her lips. But then, again, perhaps they were just caused by the force of the collision? Whatever. She couldn't let it happen again.

The painkillers had to be strong, though. There was a dramatic change to his breathing, and Nairn's whole demeanor relaxed. She was wondering how to get him to do her bidding when his brows whipped into a frown.

"Got to go, Mz...?"

He couldn't even remember her name. And it seemed he hadn't a clue about what they'd just shared.

"'Scuse...me." Shrugging himself upright with his good leg his whole body tilted.

"Wait a minute, you reckless idiot! Where's your damned bedroom?" Jumping up, she wedged him against the desk, puffing as his whole weight bore down on her, his head plastered against her face.

His mouth quirked upward, his chuckle tickling her ear. "Oh yeah. Y wanna go bed...me?"

A disgusted huff passed her lips. "You need to be in bed. Just tell me where."

"I like you." Garbled words mumbled as his mouth settled on her ear lobe, his tongue licking the cheap fuchsia colored earring, and then her heated flesh as he moved along her jaw. "Like...woman wi... direction, not 'fraid t'ask what y' want."

"Where's your room?" Aela turned her head out of his reach, denying she liked the feel of his lips nuzzling her.

Nairn's lopsided smile beamed at her as though he hadn't a care in the world, his good hand squirming up between them, rubbing the still hard bead of her breast. "Yeah. Roused. Gor...jus...t' bed."

The slumberous gleam in his eyes got those low-down tingles going great guns again, and made her turn her cheek back to his marauding lips. What his hand was doing rocked her even more as those wicked fingertips plucked and played. Something shifted inside, desire escalated and burned Aela to furnace-hot, an inside conflagration nothing to do with the overheated body she was supporting. The earlier ogre had morphed into that truly sexy wild highlander, ready to plunder!

Now she could see how he earned the reputation as a millionaire charmer, though at that particular moment it wasn't exactly the seduction scene of her dreams. Although she undoubtedly loved the feel of the man in her arms he was a giant of a man...and no lightweight!

His lips slanted onto hers again, the kiss developing as though he was searching for something out of his reach, the light probe of his fingers stimulating Aela even more. Surrendering to the desire, her tongue did some exploring and seeking of its own.

Nobody had ever felt so good in her arms. He tasted...fabulous. Well, almost, if she could ignore the mysterious metallic element.

Nairn made a frantic angle change before the breath seemed to elude him. His face slumped against her shoulder. His pinching fingers left her breast bereft of his magic touch and drooped down to her side. His quest was over, but Aela's feelings weren't.

Her chuckle was a flattened huff into his shoulder.

"Look at the state of you, Nairn!"

The sudden voice whipped her head up.

Chapter Four

Aela's gaze flew to the man entering the room.

He chortled as he flanked Nairn from the other side. "Are you taking this lovely lass to bed already, Nairn?"

"I'd like to point out whatever you think you see isn't really what's happening here." Aela's declaration muffled to a whimper when Nairn's lips smacked loudly at her neck, making her even more embarrassed since her aroused flush had to be noticed by the older guy now standing at Nairn's other side.

A loud chuckle was the reply as the older man helped perch Nairn on the edge of the desk. "Dinna fash yersel, lass! Hold him steady a bit longer. I've a folding wheelchair outside the door I've borrowed from Mariskay Medical Centre for the next couple days. I'll just away and get it in."

Between them they lowered Nairn's sagging body into it. Aela didn't care who the man was, but the fact he was familiar, and was organized to deal with an invalid, made him a welcome intrusion.

"We'll just get Nairn along to the wee downstairs bedroom, lass. Stay with me. I can do with your help."

Aela trailed the man as he pushed the wheelchair past the cloakroom to a small room down the hall. Maneuvering Nairn wasn't simple, but they got him flat onto the narrow bed with his limbs relatively straight. Trying to lift his head off the pillow he failed, his grunt of acceptance accompanied by a drunken grin. The happy pills worked spot-on.

"G'night. Aela. It's Ruaridh." Nairn's good arm waved in the air as though introducing them.

"Hold him at the waist," Ruaridh instructed. "The shirt won't matter, but we'll ditch his sweatpants."

Remove his pants? Whoa! A lovely image warmed through Aela at the thought of the healthy flesh that would be exposed.

Ruaridh, thank heavens, was untying Nairn's waistband cord and didn't notice Aela's discomfiture.

Now, she held Nairn steady at the shoulders to prevent jarring of his ribs as Ruaridh first whipped apart the Velcro on Nairn's single sandal and dropped it to the floor. When he eased the soft cotton sweatpants past Nairn's hips she gulped. No underwear.

"Ah. You might want to look away, lass." Again the older guy chuckled like mad.

Aela knew she was a bit slow in closing her eyes, but what the hell. Curiosity killed more than cats. Hells bells and baubles again! The sudden dryness at her throat was so hard to swallow over.

"Mmm. Lovely woman. Y're hands are like velvet, yeah, touch me, lower." Nairn's good hand groped out to pull her closer. A feeble blue gaze flickered and latched onto her bent head. "You're" A hint of understanding flashed across his face as he realized she was not the one stripping him. "Ruaridh?"

"Aye! It's me."

Nairn's confusion was confirmed as the man guffawed at his feet. "Ruaridh? In't she gorgeous?"

"Just ignore his ramblings, lass," Ruaridh mouthed.

It was clear Ruaridh was taking great delight in the situation. She whipped away her gaze from the older man and up Nairn's body, the impressive bulges she'd seen earlier now well-confirmed as

Ruaridh pulled the pants free of Nairn's good foot. Heaven's above, she was ogling Nairn's nakedness with Ruaridh in the room. How perverted was she?

"Go to sleep, Nairn."

Ruaridh winked at her as he dragged a light cover across Nairn's prostrate body and motioned her outside. His creased face grinned as he held out his hand. "I'm Nairn's father, Ruaridh Malcolm. I wondered how long he'd hold out, but he was determined to do this interview. I'm pleased to meet you although it's clear I should have come back much sooner. I apologize for that. And for any embarrassment I might have caused there. You are?"

"Aela Cameron."

Her fingers were engulfed almost as much as with Nairn's hand, his father not quite so tall, but still well over six feet. "So, Nairn employed you?"

"Not exactly. My experience with planes and boats, I think, was favorable." That might be a bit of an exaggeration, though, given his lack of reaction.

"Sounds good, lass." Ruaridh's smile was encouraging. "Was your office experience acceptable, as well?"

Ruaridh, without doubt, knew about all the jobs, so Aela decided not to fudge her reply. "Sorry. Can't answer. I pulled the plug on the interview before your son could assess my office skills."

There was no way she would divulge the rest of the happenings of the weirdest interview anyone could ever have had. The lingering embarrassment she hoped Ruaridh would put down to her being so bold.

Aela's mouth twitched. Although she strove to be professional, the twinkling of his grey eyes was just too much. Succumbing, a guilty smile split her face.

"You called a halt to the interview? Wish I'd

Nancy Jardine

been spying and seen that."

Since the interview hadn't been completed, Ruaridh deemed it necessary for Aela to remain on Lanera till the following day when Nairn could continue. "Will that be a problem?"

"No problem. Is there a hotel you recommend?" Aela answered, happy to remain here for a few days.

"Och no, lass. No need to look for that. The office apartment will do just fine."

A self-contained one-bedroom suite, with a tiny efficiency kitchen was down the hall from the office, in the opposite wing from the small bedroom Nairn was using. The only thing wrong with it that Aela could see was that it was still close to Nairn's bedroom. Temptation? Absolutely. She once more squelched her wayward imagination and locked it into a little box labeled Do Not Open Under Any Circumstance.

"Make yourself at home, lass. I'll have a meal ready at seven o'clock. I'll see to Nairn. That'll give you time to walk around the grounds before dinner, or wander down to the harbor at Mariskay."

Aela needed little persuasion. Shucking off the suit, she changed into jeans, grabbed a light sweater, and donned her habitual walking boots— glad to be away from her potential employer for a while. Far too disturbing to her peace of mind. Nairn attractive? She tried to convince herself it wasn't him as she walked out the French doors—it had to be the sense of the ridiculous she'd been drawn to. But she knew better. She was lying to herself.

****

Mariskay was fascinating. The village was carved into a small curved inlet, yet bigger than she'd envisaged. An interesting range of shops, bars and restaurants catered to locals and tourists alike. At present it was full of people sunning themselves on benches surrounding the horseshoe-shaped bay,

34

listening to raucous cawing of the hovering gulls and sweeping terns, and inhaling the sea-salt smell permeating the warm air from the bladderwrack that littered the pebbled white sand. A pretty haven she'd like to experience more of-if she could manage to sublimate her lust for Nairn Malcolm, get the job, and keep it.

The harbor moored a variety of boats—some commercial fishing craft, others purely for pleasure. The catamaran that had picked her up earlier was berthed beside a large boatyard. As she got closer, Aran walked out with a number of other men, bidding each other goodbye.

"You got the job, then, Aela?" he asked.

"Not quite. I'm continuing the interview tomorrow."

A wry grin split Aran's face. "Ah! I'm guessing the stupid bugger collapsed on you."

"Mr. Malcolm wasn't able to complete the interview in one session."

"Nairn asked you to stay on for another day?" Aran sounded amazed.

"Not Nairn. Ruaridh asked me to remain till tomorrow."

"Right. Ought to have guessed that. Nairn should never have left the hospital yesterday. His plastered limbs are a painful, bloody nuisance, the rib fractures are hampering his breathing this time, but it's his concussion disorientation that's his main problem. The consultants didn't want to release him, but he insisted I brought him home so he could get back to work. Hates being tied down."

Aela didn't find that difficult to imagine. The concussion explained his almost comatose state. A real numbskull! Yet the way Aran referred to this time made it clear Nairn Malcolm was no stranger to serious injury.

"Would you like a tour of the boatyard?"

Aela jumped at the chance as Aran pulled out his cell phone.

"Give me a second while I explain to the wife."

When he'd finished she hastened to apologize. "Won't your wife mind you shepherding me around the boatyard?"

"Och, no. She's Ruaridh's secretary, but clocks off early to be home for our two kids. She knew you were interviewing today, so this time is as good as any."

The luxury crafts being built in the boatyard were impressive—small fishing vessels, a yacht, speedboat, and a few catamarans. There was another area for producing dinghies, jet-skis and kayaks. As Aran explained some technical details Aela wanted a shot in all of them, but glancing at her watch her dismay gasped out. "Hell's bells and buckets! I'm having dinner with them at seven. Sorry, got to run, but thanks for the tour, Aran."

His offer to drive her up to the castle she declined. "No need if I go now."

She could head back a quicker way via the shoreline to the cove, Aran explained, only possible during the current low tide.

Rounding from Mariskay Bay, Aela became aware of how quickly the landscape changed, the terrain rising steeply to form the high bluff. The vegetation of ferns, bushes and trees grew thick above the shoreline, protecting and concealing the top rise, the reason she'd been unable to see the castle from the water earlier. Ten minutes later, she'd picked her way around the narrow strip of silvery sand and rocks to the cove.

Skipping up the staircase, wearing boots and bearing no backpack, was a doddle. The sight of the castle was once again stunning. Regardless of her experience with its disquieting owner, the building was enthralling.

Back inside via the great room she headed straight to the kitchen calling softly, not wanting to disturb Nairn if he was still asleep.

"Punctual as well as beautiful, lass. That'll go down well with my very exacting son, Miss Cameron. Nairn's a master of time and hates wasting any, which explains why he's so frustrated at being laid up just now. The food's ready; we can eat as soon as you like. Nairn's still out cold so it'll be just the two of us."

Over mouth-watering seafood paella, Ruaridh explained Nairn's debilitated state. Brian, Nairn's recent PA, had spent the previous Friday on Lanera bidding farewell to colleagues at the boatyard. "On Saturday morning, Aran ferried them down to Glasgow with Nairn's motorbike on board. Brian headed for his flight to London, and Nairn rode off to conduct business nearby."

"His motorbike was on board?" She grinned, imagining the tricky transfer of a motorbike on and off the catamaran.

"Easy to do, lass. Nairn built a special ramp and a clamp for the bike. Sometimes he takes the bike and is ferried from Oban, on the mainland, back and forth to Lanera."

"Why didn't he fly the floatplane?"

"The simple answer is Nairn likes using all his toys. The business venue was about 10 miles from the marina in Glasgow, so it seemed convenient to take the bike."

"Seemed convenient?"

"Nairn's *accident* occurred on the famous Loch Lomond road, when his bike malfunctioned."

"So it was nothing to do with an extreme sport?"

"Nothing sporting about it at all!"

She winced at his change of demeanor.

"I'm thankful there was no collision with any oncoming vehicle. His injuries aren't minor, but neither are they as life-threatening as they could have been."

Since it was only Tuesday, Aela couldn't prevent her frown, scarcely crediting Nairn Malcolm had ferried her here three days after the accident. "Jeeze! Guy got a death wish or something, interviewing so soon?"

"Och no, lass. But my Nairn's a stubborn cuss."

"Why couldn't he wait till he could hold a meeting without collapsing?"

The food piled in as Ruaridh answered in fits and starts. "Wouldn't wait any longer. Too much going on for him to be confined to base, and he's interviewed for two weeks already for the PA job. Hasn't found anyone willing to come up to Lanera for days at a time."

"Why wouldn't they want to escape London and come to this pretty little island?" Amazement widened her gaze.

"Not everyone thinks this place beautiful in the depths of winter. You're seeing it in good weather just now." Ruaridh's ironic tone wasn't lost on her, neither was his vibrating chuckle.

"Mr. Malcolm, I'm from British Columbia. Do you think the sun always shines there?"

Ruaridh was no stranger to Vancouver. And neither, she learned, was Nairn. As he cleared away their main course Ruaridh related visits they'd made. A toffee dessert and a selection of Scottish cheese followed, and at his urging Aela had both.

"You can cope," Ruaridh laughed when she protested about the fattening aspects.

"Are you saying it won't add layers to my hips, Mr. Malcolm?" Aela felt very much at home with Ruaridh who reminded her of her Uncle Harris.

"You're not one of those willowy-thin types my son often squires around. I like to see a lass with a healthy appetite."

38

Aela wondered if he was referring to someone in particular, someone different from the tiny doll-like blonde she'd seen clinging to Nairn's arm in the newspaper rag, the notion of any stick-thin woman friend of Nairn not a happy one.

Refusing her offer to help tidy up Ruaridh popped the remaining paella onto a covered plate. For Nairn.

Hours passed as they chatted. Nairn remained fast asleep when checked on. Sipping coffee laced with Glayva liqueur she told Ruaridh of her plan to meet with anyone related to her great-grandfather who had emigrated from the island of Mull.

"So that's why you requested a short-term contract, and why you'd already organized a work permit and visa?"

She laughed at his expression for he seemed impressed. "Exactly! I'm well-planned. After I finished university I was too desperate to get back to work to take the ubiquitous year off. Too many new planes to fly since Uncle Harris had upgraded the fleet, and at that time too many of his newly acquired boats to play with for he'd expanded into other transport forms. Don't know where the time went, but January of this year, you know those New Year resolutions nobody ever sticks to? It was now or never, I told myself. Ruts be damned; big changes were in the cards."

"I don't get the impression ruts are your usual style." Ruaridh's eyes twinkled back at her.

"I managed to plan six months travel, but I'm starting an M.B.A. course at the University of British Columbia, beginning September 1st. Since it's the end of June already, I've not got long to make contact with any of my great-grandfather's family."

"You didn't expect a contract flying a floatplane?"

"Shit, no! I expected a filing job. The

appointments consultant was flabbergasted when she read Mr. Malcolm's requests for a PA, and for a pilot-cum-driver."

"Call me Ruaridh, and I'll call you Aela, if you don't mind. Saves the confusion of there being two of us called Mr. Malcolm."

"Be glad to, Ruaridh. Tell me to piddle off, if you like, but I'd love to know how you're so familiar with your son's business."

Ruaridh's answer was candid. "I was sole owner of Gale Breakers till eight years ago when the business took a nosedive. Not often a guy has his son pull him out, but that's what my Nairn did. He'd recently amassed a chunk of money, so he invested. Now it's half his, half mine. I run the operation here with Aran as our boatyard manager. Nairn does the globetrotting for client meetings, as well as traveling for his other companies."

By nine o'clock Nairn still hadn't wakened.

"I'm heading home, lass. I'll be back the morn, sometime after seven."

Chapter Five

Aela was staggered by Ruaridh's statement. "You don't live in the castle?"

"Och, no, Aela. I'm away back to my own bed. My house is down in Mariskay."

"What if he wakes up?" Aela wasn't inclined to panic, her first aid certificate covered a few scenarios, but not welding together limbs needing re-pinning!

"He'll be fine, lass. Today was far too traumatic. He only passed out because he tried to do too damn much. It'll take a couple of weeks for his ribs to feel good, but he's a determined lad, and he'll work around his problems. Always has and always will!" Ruaridh made for the back door, Aela in tow. "He'll likely sleep for hours, and when he wakes up he'll find the food I've left him."

Aela wasn't sure about him leaving her alone with a man she didn't know, a man who hadn't thought much of her, except maybe sexually, during the charade of an interview. One good thing though? Outrunning him would be a piece of cake.

"I'll set the alarms on the way out. Here's my home and cell phone numbers just in case you need them, though I'm confident you'll manage." Ruaridh's wink was blatant.

"But you're leaving your son with a stranger, I could rob him blind!" Words failed her.

"You could, but I don't think you will. You've told me enough, lass, for me to know my son's in capable hands. You'll be fine." Ruaridh left with another wink.

Staying in new accommodations was something she'd grown used to over the last five months. A few of the places during her world trek had been a tad threatening, but this beautiful castle was wonderful, so the situation didn't overly bother her.

At first.

After Ruaridh's departure she watched a movie, but was so restless she couldn't for the life of her have given details when it was over. She'd popped out into the hallway a number of times, but there had been no indications Nairn had wakened—no noise in the kitchen, office, or in the great room. Sleep would be impossible without knowing how he was, yet she didn't want to alarm him if he was already awake. Her noisy treads along the corridor made her confident he would at least be alerted to the presence of another person in the house.

He lay as though dead to the world.

Aela pushed away the dreadful thought, then it slammed back. Was he still breathing? It was more than six hours since they'd laid him on the bed. The last thing she wanted was to be alone in a strange castle with a corpse. Way too imaginative! Whoa. All she wanted was a job for a few weeks, but the darned man needed to be still alive.

"Mr. Malcolm," she whispered as she bent over, her hand tentative on his forehead.

Instinctively Nairn's arm shrugged off the thin bedcover, his hand flapped around, and the backs of his fingers hit her chest. An overpowering zing started again, and awakened every single nerve end that Aela owned. Whoa! She was straight back to wondering what exactly it was that this guy did to her, another Olympic pulse-jump gaining a gold.

"Mmm..." His murmur was drowsy as he grasped her top, and his fingers splayed out and caressed her breast.

What the heck was the guy doing? Aela's nipples

tingled, forming hard little beads against her silk camisole as she slid out of his reach, trying not to exhale too loud but wasn't sure if she managed for her heart thumped so hard.

His hand flopped down onto the light cover now wrapped around his waist; his breathing remained shallow though it didn't seem too pained. Battered as he was Nairn Malcolm was compellingly masculine, ruggedness enwrapping him, yet at present he was also vulnerable.

Aela grinned.

That imagination of hers took another nice little turn. She could do anything with him, within reason of course, till he woke up and realized what might be happening. She didn't mind him like this when he was unaware of her. Was it just sympathy making her feel hot and fluttery? She didn't think so; she'd never been swayed by circumstances before. Having seen beaten-up colleagues after accidents, or even worse after testosterone-fuelled fights, she'd never experienced her current emotional turmoil.

There was a compulsion to touch Nairn, to soothe his hurts—yes, but she wanted to do a lot more. And that was not like her at all. She wanted to find out what his powerful chest felt like to caress. The unhurt bits. She wanted to slide her soft fingers over his mat of dark hair and be caught up in it. She wanted to sample his cheeks, his lips. Kiss him. Wake him up and taste him all over.

Whoa! Crazy.

Sexual arousal had never been sparked by just looking at a man. A sleeping man. Her breathing hitched.

Aela let her hand drift over his bristly jaw. The fiery sensation from the pads of her fingers right up to her wrists she overlooked as static electricity from the stubble, and the warmth from his hot cheeks. Checking to make sure he didn't have a temperature she touched his brow with the back of her hand. About normal for a damaged sleeping person, she reckoned, but wasn't sure. Her hand trembled before she removed it. Lifting it to her nose she sampled his scent on her skin. Matchless. Male. Nairn. Just Nairn.

He looked so…kissable.

Aarggh!

Resisting became impossible. She just had to know if the heady sensations he'd produced earlier would be repeated. Had to know if he tasted as good as she remembered. Her head bent and her lips settled on his mouth, his lips a little bit cool.

"Mmm. Yeah…"

Nairn's hand flipped up and clamped her head in place. Whoa, again! The guy had quick fire reactions. His lips opened beneath hers, his tongue sneaked out seeking entry through her closed mouth as even in sleep he attempted to intensify the kiss. The man was unbelievable, but since there was no third party in the room she wasn't averse to more exploration. Letting him in she savored the textures, a combination of delicious sweetness and something less so.

A low groan rumbled from Nairn when her tongue wandered, seeking pleasure spots as she dueled with his, but it was not only a groan of gratification because, as he stretched one side of his mouth, he winced in pain. Withdrawing reluctantly she acknowledged one corner of his mouth was not yet properly healed, but Nairn could certainly kiss, even in his debilitated state. Feathering her lips on that battered side just once more she wondered what he would be capable of when he was fully awake because she was already frizzling up from the short-lived close contact with his somnolent body.

"More," he whispered into her cheek.

Maybe not quite asleep? When he gave an

unexpected yank at her camisole she knew. A nice little flutter pitched her down on top of him, his lips remained curled up in an appreciative smile till she made contact, and promptly squashed him. His arm slumped inactive onto the bedcover—a gigantic moan blasted her eardrum, his body jerking in agony.

Aela flinched away praying he'd not waken up totally. What the heck had she just done? She'd collapsed on top of his broken body. No wonder he writhed in misery. Guilt swamped as she pushed herself up and away. Nairn had subsided back onto the bed his body as tense as a bowstring, the lowest of moans wheezing out...but his eyes remained closed.

Jeeze! She was furious with herself. It was obvious the bloody man was well-practiced at seduction, even when sleeping, and with a half-broken body. It looked like he'd had plenty of experience overcoming adversity, but she didn't need to flatten him. Talk about hitting a man when he was down. Slipping completely from his grasp Aela was astounded to see one corner of his mouth still turned up as he exhaled pained little huffs. Content, or agonized? She wasn't sure, but he didn't completely waken.

She vowed she'd not touch him ever again. She was at the castle for a job interview—for a temporary job. She'd big plans for her future, and they didn't include having an affair, especially with a lothario who didn't even know she was in his house.

"Not tonight, Casanova!" Her whisper echoed as she left the room.

Walking back past the kitchen she left him a brief note on the easy-wipe board hanging near the refrigerator, and then went to bed determined to sleep.

****

A sense of wellbeing flooded Nairn as he awoke, the remnants of an arousing dream still hovering behind his closed eyelids. Trying a deep breath pain slashed across his torso. Ah. Still there, though not nearly as bad as the day before. He moved his head from side to side. And waited. About time! The persistent headache and concussion wooziness, thank heavens, seemed to have gone.

In progressive stages he opened his eyes and found moonlight filtering into the room since the curtains hadn't been drawn across the small window. Reckoning it must be the wee small hours, he flicked on the lamp beside the bed. The clock read one-twenty a.m. Amazing. He'd no memory of coming to bed.

He forced recall of the previous day. It'd been such a bloody awful morning. What with his staggering around like somebody smashed, and then the news of the bloody maniac wrecking the morning at his London headquarters. His buildings security needed a huge ruddy shake-up if it was so simple for someone to access the energy systems and shut them down. Just like it had been too easy to instigate the other incidents. But he had engaged a company to do a full security audit. Hadn't he? Starting Wednesday.

Was that today? He wasn't sure. He could tell he'd had a damned good sleep, but was convinced it hadn't been any longer than a few hours. His good hand rubbed across the fuzz at his chin. There was a good growth there, but he wasn't exactly Rip Van Winkle! He hazarded a laugh. Life was more like a damned nightmare than a fairy tale.

Ah!

The afternoon.

That was even hazier.

Aela Cameron had come to be interviewed. His

eyes popped open. Spectacular woman. So beautiful. But she wasn't right for the job. A roaring fire ignited in the grate of his groin; the merest image of her stirred an arousal. Nebulous details flashed around. He vaguely remembered asking her questions and finding the answers she'd given panned out, regarding her qualifications. He was fairly sure he remembered being fixated on her lips, though maybe that was just in the erotic dream he'd had? Was the woman he'd dreamed about Aela Cameron, Aela of the lava black hair and gorgeous cocoa brown eyes? And soft, soft pink lips...

Bloody hell!

Had what he dreamed taken place? With a woman who had come to interview for a job? Nairn groaned, his pain entirely unrelated to his broken body. Feelings of remorse flooded; guilt gripped him like a shackle for he couldn't remember what had happened. Now well awake he looked around the tiny room.

A wheelchair sat beside the bed, an object of his derision the morning before when Ruaridh suggested it, but since it was the only transport he could operate himself he reckoned he might as well try it. One-handed he wheeled himself to the nearest bathroom. A few minutes later, left-handed-splashed-water was a token gesture to cleanliness. Then he headed for some food since his stomach rebelled, loud and clear.

The dents he made in his hallway walls he ignored as he entered the kitchen. The wheelchair was infinitely better than the one-crutch-lurch he'd been trying to perfect earlier. Fumbling the paella into the microwave he waited for it to heat as he nibbled on the side salad and bread Ruaridh must have left for him. He'd consumed every last scrap of food and had scarfed a mug of coffee before the note written on the wipe-board drew his attention.

I'm staying over in the office apartment. If you need anything let me know. Aela Cameron.

Nairn's invectives would have awakened the castle ghost if there had been one. Why the hell was Aela Cameron staying the night? He tried to remember the end of the interview, but couldn't. Damn, damn, damn! Had he given her a job as pilot, captain, driver? Or what? Had he employed her as his PA as well? Surely he'd remember.

Wheeling himself to the office apartment he found the entry door wide open. Deliberate? He imagined so for it had a lock on it should it be required. The wheelchair hissed as he crossed the sitting room carpet and entered the open bedroom door.

Double-damn again.

It wasn't Sleeping Beauty of the golden hair lying in the bed, but the occupant was a dead ringer for Snow White.

Aela Cameron was stunning—his memory hadn't failed him. Long dark hair spilled across the pillow in ripples, an ethereal shine reflecting in the moonlight since she hadn't closed the blinds. Her pale face was mesmerizing, her eyelashes a black curve below each eye. She lay in total relaxation on her back, her sinful mouth closed, her chest rising almost imperceptibly, dark nipples outlined under thin material.

Bloody hell!

His pulse spiked along with another undamaged part of his body, and of a sudden the room felt like a sauna. Nairn swiped his fingers across his sweating brow and exhaled loudly. If he hadn't been seated he knew he just might have taken a bit of a lurch for the woman packed a five-star punch. He wanted Aela Cameron just as much now as when he'd had his first glimpse of her photograph. She was a knockout!

She'd kicked off the bedcover to almost her knees, the white camisole just covering her abdomen, below which tiny panties covered virtually nothing. Unfortunately for Nairn they were made of some sort of gossamer fine, light colored gauze, and even in the dim light he could make out a dark strip of hair.

She was definitely the woman he'd dreamed about. His erection strengthened despite details of the previous the day filtering through. She'd been annoyed at him, but that had been about on par with the way he'd felt about her too, at times. She'd derided his battered body. He'd felt gutted by her dismissive treatment. Though he remembered that hadn't stopped him from getting aroused. Not then...and not now.

And when the hell had he seen little strips of white panties?

His groan escaped before he could muffle it. How could he entangle such a striking woman in his troubles? There was no way he could employ her. His wheeled exit was silent, glad Aela hadn't wakened, but he was pissed off he wasn't capable of jumping into bed with her.

The end of the afternoon remained unclear. Someone had removed his sweatpants and put him to bed. He hoped to hell it was Ruaridh because it would be too humiliating if it'd been Aela Cameron. He wasn't averse to women removing his clothes but only when he was able to do something about it.

Resolute he could do nothing about the arousing Miss Cameron till the morning he entered his office, booted up his computer and went to work, needing to get to grips with everything neglected during the previous three days.

The phone bleeped. He debated not answering, yet knew it would just increase the stack of calls still to be attended to. He lifted the receiver, listened, and then made an arrangement to make contact later when his PA was available. Because the call had originated in South America the response was routine, given time differences, though who the PA would be Nairn didn't know. Having seen the virtually naked Aela Cameron he didn't think he would be able to stand having her as his PA—far too big a temptation to be in any room with, never mind his office.

He started on the stack of e-mails. A couple of hours later he was relieved to find the concussion headache and wooziness hadn't returned. His concentration should have been good, yet an erotic vision of the delectable Aela Cameron kept intruding. Her skin had looked so inviting, soft and unblemished, her hair an ebony river he wanted to thread his fingers through as she bent before him...between his knees. Startled, he'd a memory of her doing exactly that very thing, but when? And what had gone on?

Again his professional conscience cringed.

Forcing recall of the interview he remembered asking her to tell him about his floatplane and jet. Her details had indicated she knew what she was talking about, even though the effort of verbally responding had been beyond him. He remembered thinking her Uncle Harris had given her a cushy job, a sinecure, because she was his niece. However, she'd been very snippy when he'd asked how many hours a week she'd worked. Now he couldn't recollect her answer.

The image of her enticing lips popped into his head. They'd been an alluring deep-pink when he'd first seen her, so soft... Nairn groaned. He definitely had been fixated on her lips. But the pink had vanished. He'd been annoyed his battered face had merited a wipe-off of the lip-gloss, a device used to reel in the male sex. Removing it before the interview she'd snubbed him. Yet while she'd been relating her boating experience all he'd been able to think about were her glistening wet lips, deep pink or not!

He grunted, again, convinced he'd been hallucinating. Her shimmering lips had slid away from his own to mark a damp trace down the tiny cleft in his chin before they moved further down, leaving a moist pathway on his bare chest. They'd whispered tiny soothing kisses over his bruising as they'd dipped south to his straining abdomen, then lower to his belly button. Her voice had been the only calming thing in his existence, his whole body screaming in agony. Then, she'd moved her lips closer to where he'd most wanted their attention. That was the bit where her black waterfall of hair had covered his straining...

Shit!

What the hell had happened the day before? Exactly how unprofessional had he been? And how unprofessional had he allowed Aela Cameron to be? Nairn wasn't sure he wanted the answer to those questions because he now did remember he'd spoken way out of turn, even if he'd no recall of the exact words.

Ruaridh.

Yes. His father had put him to bed. Only partial relief came with the memory for now Nairn suspected it wasn't only Ruaridh who'd got him there. It appeared serious damage control hovered on his horizon.

His ribs ached like fury. Knowing it was stupid to push too much, he collected the tub of painkillers and took himself off to bed. He considered turning right instead of left as he wheeled out of the office because Aela Cameron's bed was much closer than the room he'd been sleeping in earlier.

Some thought! What exactly would he do with

two plaster casts, a bunch of broken ribs and half a breath? As he rolled his debilitated body along the corridor a certain persistent part of him was saying hello but not much else was co-operating in a cheerful manner. Sex wasn't in his near future, and not with Aela Cameron.

Swearing was ripe as he wheeled into the small bedroom, his flagrant erection telling him it was the wrong bed he'd dropped into.

Chapter Six

Six thirty-five? Shame slammed Aela. She'd intended to check on Nairn during the night. Scooting out of bed she flew along the corridor.

How on earth could he still be asleep? The cover was lying on the floor so it was easy to see his breathing was slight, but steady. Feeling his brow she found no untoward heat. Good.

Nairn's hand lashed up and grasped her fingers. "Mmm. Again..." He relaxed, trapping her hand against his cheek and made soft murmurs, his mouth softening into a little smile. Pure gold. Aela's sigh was almost as loud as Nairn's for the man was absolute dynamite at stirring up that inner heat— and the guy wasn't even awake.

Not daring to breathe, she extracted her hand. She wasn't going too close again; one burn was enough. Lifting the thin cover, she bent to draw it over his body starting from his toes. Huh? Excited? Oh, yes he was. An arousal, morning or otherwise, poked through the opening of unfastened black boxers.

Temptation was a bitch! The cover slipped from Aela's nerveless fingers as she froze on the spot. And gaped. And hyperventilated for a few seconds before an iron control returned. Shaky hands clutched the cover again. Shaky hands that wanted to stray elsewhere. She had to get the hell out of the room before she did something she might expire over, but would probably regret forever.

After a careful draping of the cover she sidled back, the heat she felt rising up her neck easily able to fire a kiln of ceramic pots. Stupid thoughts. The man had a catalogue of injuries. Forget imagining what could be achieved, though she was sorely tempted. She backed out the door still thinking on possibilities—so difficult to believe how perverted she was becoming.

A temporary job. That was all...it became a bit of a mantra.

****

Bacon was crackling and crisping under the grill. Aela had almost finished a stack of pancakes, having found some maple syrup in one of the well-stocked cupboards, when she became aware of someone entering the kitchen.

"Well, isn't this a sight for sore eyes, lass," Ruaridh's voice boomed in the near silence. "It's about time someone as beautiful as you made something smelling so good in this kitchen."

"What? No blonde bunnies cooking for your son?" The tart comment slipped out.

Ruaridh's chuckle was infectious. "Och, no, Aela. Nairn's blonde bunnies wouldn't have a clue which end of a wooden spoon to use."

She giggled along with him as he came over to the stove and inspected her gelling pancakes, the current batch blowing bubbles, just ready for turning.

"Nairn's lady friends aren't Scottish island mentality. They're more inclined to baking themselves in the sun at his Corsican villa than cooking pancakes."

Mentally filing away the snippet of information, she couldn't recall anything about it being in his bio. As if it would! A bunny lair would be a well kept secret. "Well, this is no culinary feast, but you're welcome to share if you haven't eaten yet." She avoided further banter about Nairn's women friends.

"You're tactful, too!" Ruaridh commented before

54

he asked for an update on Nairn.

Aela's hearty laugh pealed out. "I'm not too good at tact. Just the two of us again. Your son sure likes the Land of Nod."

She placed bacon slices and a stack of pancakes in front of Ruaridh as she sat with a full plate for herself. His chuckling continued as he complimented her on her cooking initiative.

"I hope you don't mind me doing this. You did say to make myself at home, and making breakfast seemed fair since you cooked for me last night."

Ruaridh answered around a mouthful of syrupy pancake. "No problem at all, lass. Glad to have you on board."

"On board what?" Nairn's voice had their heads whipping around. It was obvious neither Aela Cameron nor Ruaridh had heard the whisper of the wheelchair, but his sudden question halted their conversation.

"On board the company flagship, of course. Morning, Nairn. I see the long sleep improved your temper."

His father continued to eat as though his words held no implications at all, his mumbles coming around mouthfuls of bacon, his sarcastic wisecrack accompanied by a wink first for Aela, and then one for him.

A reaction typical of Ruaridh. What the hell did he mean? Company flagship? He must have given the woman a job, but he remembered not a blasted thing about it, and now his father and Aela Cameron—the even more beautiful awake Aela—were tucking into food at his kitchen table. He snagged her gaze. Her molasses-rich eyes were twinkling, but not at him. Ruaridh was the source of her good spirits. His gut lurched, but not in a good way.

"Good morning, Miss Cameron." Turning to

Ruaridh he ensured his voice was as saccharine sweet as his manufactured smile. "Morning, Father."

"Oh my word, lass! Do you hear that?" Ruaridh laid his hand theatrically over his heart.

Aela Cameron laughed again. The woman was far too flippant. Something about disrespect niggled at Nairn. He was sure he'd felt it the day before, as well as finding her too inclined to laugh at the state he was in. None of their current banter made him feel comfortable either.

"Somebody in this room must have got out of the wrong side of the bed."

The cozy sight of them sitting at his table aggravated him. His father's hearty laugh and a gentler tinkle of female amusement had wakened him, and though he couldn't hear what they'd been saying it was obvious Ruaridh and Aela were getting along very well.

Even with a scrubbed face and still-drying hair hanging straight down her back—a black shimmer trailing almost to her waist—the woman was striking. Tight denim shorts and a breast hugging T-shirt grabbed his attention. Aela was only twenty-seven, for God's sake! She was five years younger than he was and...years and years younger...than Ruaridh.

Ruaridh, at fifty-seven, was very popular with the local ladies even though he'd never shown signs of wanting to remarry after his divorce to Nairn's mother more than a decade ago. Yet Nairn knew Ruaridh was more than capable of taking a new woman, or wife, if he chose.

"Would you like breakfast, Mr. Malcolm? I've made plenty."

The woman had made herself at home in his kitchen? For God's sake, again! Had he given her a job as his cook as well? She'd soon learn he cooked for himself when he was home. Though, maybe not right now.

He could barely look at her since he wasn't sure what she'd be able to read on his face. Annoyance peppered with raging lust. He had to get a grip. His brows lowered his answer the best he could manage without a major blowout. "I would. Thank you, Miss Cameron."

Aela jumped up and removed a chair to make room for the wheelchair, her movements efficient, showcasing those fabulous smooth and slightly tanned legs that his downcast eyes couldn't remove themselves from. He shifted in the chair ensuring the short robe he wore covered the necessaries since there was a bit of unruly expansion going on there.

"So you're making use of the chariot, then? Just think, Nairn, with a bit of practice you'll be doing wheelies on the quay side, and you'll have forgotten your stookies!" Ruaridh's chuckled comments were interspersed by pauses, as he mowed his way through his food.

Nairn made no initial response as Aela cut the pancakes and bacon into small pieces before placing the plate in front of him. Did the blasted woman think him incapable of feeding himself? Irritation rippled again as he focused on Ruaridh's continued remarks and grins, but much as he tried he couldn't quite suppress the twitch at his mouth for his father often managed to make awkward situations lighthearted. "Thanks for fetching it, Father. Wheeling around, strangely enough, is much easier on the ribs."

"All joking aside, how do you feel this morning, Nairn?" Ruaridh flicked open the syrup bottle, added some to the residue of his pancakes then waved it in front of him.

After Ruaridh sprinkled syrup over his breakfast, Nairn picked up his fork with his less than expert left hand. "The headache and disorientation have finally gone, thank God." He sought out Aela's eyes. Eyes he thought were hiding something because they looked just a hint startled as they locked with his. "Miss Cameron will be delighted to know, like a good boy, I'll take the painkillers on a regular basis till the ribs heal and not be stupidly macho about it."

He didn't break a smile himself, but registered her mischievous smirk at the edited version of yesterday's conversation. There was no hint of remorse or embarrassment in her expression as she attacked her stack of pancakes with enthusiasm. On the contrary, she appeared relaxed, able to make eye contact with him without a single flinch—unlike he was able to do because every elongated gaze overheated his already smarting skin.

A bit of pancake was shuffled around before he managed to spear it properly. He just caught Aela Cameron's full-blown beam in his peripheral vision as he lifted the fork to his mouth. His mood didn't lighten any as he stared at his plate. The darned woman was laughing at him again, acting as though she knew something he didn't, but he'd turn the tables on her soon enough. There would be a way. Only good manners prevented him from throwing her right out on her ass. Out of his kitchen. Out of his castle.

Did he want that?

He gulped over a mouthful. Out of his jobs. Did he want that either? Out of reach of Ruaridh, who was behaving as though Aela Cameron belonged at his table, as if she'd been a fixture for ages. He definitely wanted Aela out of Ruaridh's reach.

Ruaridh must have asked the woman to stay overnight. Nairn stopped mid-chew. The sweetness of the syrupy pancake was suddenly sickening. What had happened between them last night? Before she'd gone to bed in the apartment? His plate became the most fascinating thing in the room for there was no way he could face Aela Cameron if she was ogling Ruaridh right that very moment. The woman had to go as soon as possible.

The pile of pancake and bacon pieces slowly found their way to his mouth as he deliberated how to achieve the expulsion of the woman who was a gigantic thorn in his already aching flesh. He lifted his head as she answered yet another of Ruaridh's questions. Those deep brown eyes of hers easily matched the glistening maple syrup making him want to lick and taste and savor her all over. The mere sight of her made him prickle alarmingly. Watching her mouth chew the sweet pancakes made him...stir everywhere.

He laid down his fork to fumble for the napkin Aela had set beside his plate and used it to mop the sweat from his brow. The room was so damned hot; he wished he hadn't squirmed his way into his toweling robe. Or maybe he was running a temperature. Yet when he looked at his table companions, it seemed he was the only one to feel the excessive heat. He really did have to get a better grip of himself. A sip of the coffee Aela had prepared for him made him even warmer, but at least it eased the dryness in his throat. And gave him something else to focus on for he knew he was back to staring at Aela—at her lips.

The meal progressed, Ruaridh and Aela dominating the conversation. Ruaridh chattered about sights to see in the town of Mariskay; Aela responded she'd been delighted with her short foray to the harbor. Nairn found Aela's voice husky, sexy. It stirred something, and not just what he remembered from his erotic early-morning dream. He couldn't remember any words of his reverie but he remembered far too many of the movements of those clever little lips of hers. Desperation to taste them clutched at his groin. A little bead of fiery-hot sweat trickled a pathway down from his forehead to his whiskered chin. The woman was lethal.

He had to stop fixating on her mouth and just eat his damn pancakes.

Any replies he gave were minimal as he concentrated on attacking what was left of the food, making sure it reached his mouth and not the floor.

"No, lass, I'll tidy up." Ruaridh intervened as Aela stood to clear the table. "Nairn will want to formalize your job, now."

"Formalize her job?" His comment spat out along with his last bit of pancake. The sexual haze vanished. The temperature changed from rampant heat to cool shiver, quite startling to his healing body. The erection beneath the table withered, the blood flow seemingly needing to be elsewhere—like his befuddled brain. What the hell did Ruaridh mean? He tried to interpret the statement as Ruaridh stacked the dishes.

"Aela needs to get started on the backlog of your calls as soon as possible, Nairn. You know how your inquiries build up."

"Your timely reminder is duly noted, Father. Since you're so up to date with my business, maybe you should be the one to formalize Miss Cameron's job?"

"Nairn. Appropriate documents weren't ready yesterday. You only dealt in the verbal. Do I have to remind you that you were not compos mentis? Aela needs to sign her contract."

"Her contract...signed?" Nairn's reply was a sibilant murmur as he stared at the enigmatic Ruaridh. A tense silence lingered. Ruaridh tut-tutted, as he finished stacking the dishwasher. Nairn glared at Ruaridh's obdurate back. His father was up to something, though he didn't know what.

Aela, he was gratified to see, gaped at both of

them.

He blasted his father to hell and damnation along with a few curses well-aimed at himself as he acknowledged what must be done to salvage the mess he appeared to have made. Wheeling himself out of the kitchen, he snapped, "Miss Cameron. Come to the office, please."

Aela did not immediately follow. He could hear her tight voice speaking with Ruaridh as he bowled along the corridor. That was all the better, it gave him time to summon some of his usual cool.

"We'll have to discuss the details again, the salary quoted and such," he grunted when she entered the office.

Her face was stormy as she clumped in, looking ready to do battle. He felt just as wild. He couldn't believe he hadn't documented anything useful on the damned file he'd opened for the interview the day before. How could he have been so unprofessional? He was meticulous about details.

Yet Nairn could find little, apart from some poorly spelled comments he'd listed on her flying and boating experience, and an all-too-revealing sentence stating she could drive any damn transport he had...but first those lovely lips had to learn to drive him.

Bloody Hell! Lips...again. No guessing any more. He had been fixated on her mouth and what it could do.

He couldn't believe he'd written that, and not a thing at all was listed after. He deleted it.

"Mr. Malcolm." Aela stomped up to his desk, forcing him to raise his head. "Before we go any further, may I just make clear what happened here yesterday afternoon?"

He heard the resolute tone and noted her grim determination. Was she going to lord it over him that he'd been, to all intents and purposes, insensible—like a drunk—during the interview? Were demands starting? Had he also made verbal sexual overtures like the written comment? She'd given no indications of it in the kitchen.

After a momentary closing of his eyes he braced himself for the retribution it seemed he'd merited before waving her into the seat, wincing when she didn't take up his offer. Again Aela forced his eye contact, her gaze spitting fire. Balled fists bracketed her hips. Her words zapped out like pinging little pellets. "Mr. Malcolm. We didn't get to the point where we discussed terms. I'm not even sure you were able to process any of my experience in my uncle's Head Office. You were, to be frank, incapable of making any friggin' decisions."

Nairn was confused. She was so damned snappy she had to be telling the truth. Quite magnificent in her ire, though. He watched her take a couple of deep breaths, her eyes flicking closed then opening to reveal sepia-haloed pupils. Then her unwavering resolute tone and steadfast gaze didn't falter at all, her voice calming a little as she clarified.

"Mr. Malcolm, you did not get around to offering me a job. None of your jobs, for that matter, regardless of what your father says. I don't know what the hell Ruaridh is up to, but I won't be party to it. I can't stand here and pretend otherwise."

He waited for her to continue. He hadn't given her a job? What the hell *was* Ruaridh up to? Waving her into the seat again he braced himself. Momentary relief flooded when she plopped in the chair, for her towering stance had been too much for his poor head to contend with. Concussion disorientation hadn't returned. It was bad conscience that currently plagued him. It was twisted, he knew it, but seeing that Aela Cameron was discomfited pleased him, though it shouldn't. Those fabulous eyes of hers were now distressed.

Sort of resigned.

"My experience in flying similar planes to yours, and driving the other vehicles you use, appeared favorable but..." Aela's voice almost dried up before she continued, her mouth whiffing as though making a momentous decision. Nairn liked her all the better for it, though he was unsure why. She resumed, "I haven't been a PA before, although I was my uncle's main secretary when I wasn't out flying."

"Your uncle?" He regretted his slight hesitation. It let her know he didn't have a clue what she was talking about.

One side of her mouth turned up. "Harris Cameron. Cameron Airways? I told you about him yesterday."

"Harris?" After a moment he nodded back. Nairn studied the beautiful woman who was clearly uncomfortable with the current situation. She was still absolutely magnificent in bad humor. "Yes. I do remember. I can recall some of your office experience now, Miss Cameron."

She'd soundly berated him for continuing to interview when he was so ill. Did she really say some of the things he now recalled? Ribald comments that would have been common in an airport hangar. Locations she'd said she was well used to. She was proving to be a woman who neither shilly-shallied, nor beat about the bush regarding her principles. A woman of courage to be telling him how it had been; nothing like Ruaridh's devious version.

Tingles of warmth crept back in and settled; this time desire mingled with a healthy dose of admiration. As she waited for him to continue he enjoyed recall of more inspired comments, suppressing the grin that wanted to escape. "The events of the day are filtering back in, Miss Cameron. The real version. Thank you for that."

Aela's taut expression lifted. A grateful smile made her appear happier. His blood surged even more. The woman's honesty had just notched up her attraction, again. Just lust? No. He was familiar with lust, but he also felt an unidentified anticipation in this woman's presence. Whatever charisma she exuded was unprecedented.

But could he employ her?

That was a whole new question. He needed her skills; he'd no one else to interview, and procrastination wasn't viable. He had to be on the move to sort out the mess his life was in. Hell! Brian's replacement was past critical, too. He couldn't work normally. One finger typing with his weaker hand wouldn't cut it.

He'd more than a niggling feeling he'd overstepped the boundaries of employer-employee liaison the previous day, which could have resulted in a sexual harassment case, but Aela hadn't hinted at anything. Nothing at all. In some ways the woman seemed perfect, a paragon, yet maybe too perfect?

Could she have another agenda for ignoring infringements he'd made? To hold against him later? Maybe she was only interested in getting the job to remain in Ruaridh's presence? Nairn looked closely at the woman sitting opposite, back to looking cool as a cucumber, reminding him he was very partial to nibbling the soft flesh. His eyes momentarily closed as he worked out how to respond to her.

No way was his father engaging in a flirtation with this woman. It was evident there'd been no scruples over foisting Aela on him by deceitful means. If it was because Ruaridh wanted to keep Aela close so he could get to know her better, his father would soon find out that wasn't going to happen. In no way was Ruaridh having anything intimate at all with her. But he'd deal with Ruaridh later.

The thought of sex with the mouth-watering Miss Cameron fired him hotter than a furnace, though given the state he was in, sex wasn't on the cards in the near future.

Just as well he had other pressing needs. A reliable chauffeur for one, and a competent PA for another. If she proved suitable he would engage Aela as his temporary employee, but he'd make sure neither he nor his father had any personal dealings with the woman.

"I'll just confirm some particulars with you, Miss Cameron."

For the next hour he asked questions about her flying experience, her boat handling and her experience with office duties. Aela confidently provided the answers he needed. The confirmatory email he'd just received from Cameron Transport Group corroborated her details and identity. Nairn deliberated no longer. Squashing misgivings about his ability to keep her at arm's length, he cleared his throat, knowing the words he was uttering still gave him far too many fanciful notions.

"Miss Cameron. I'd like to offer you the position, on a temporary basis."

Chapter Seven

Aela digested Nairn's words, looking for positive signs in his offer since he didn't look particularly comfortable, or at ease. No frowns, but there had been something tentative about his throat-clearing and his use of the word *position* that had put her on her guard. The awkwardness of it didn't match well with the thorough interview techniques he'd just used—techniques she'd admired, a lot. The man was such a conundrum now—he seemed like a totally different guy from the day before. Still gorgeous— always that—the difference in his focus was remarkable. But then Ruaridh had warned her Nairn was like that. She wanted the job even more now that she'd had her eyes opened to Nairn the businessman, rather than Nairn the comatose idiot. But she was no pushover; she needed to be really sure about what he was offering.

"Which job, and how temporary are you talking, Mr. Malcolm?"

Sensing the vagueness about his offer had been deliberate she didn't flinch a whit. The fumbling kisser of the previous afternoon was well gone. And she was glad of that. At least she thought she was, though it didn't diminish his attraction. That was revving up again the longer he stared, but she metaphorically took her foot off the gas.

After a moment Nairn nodded. "Four weeks for the jobs of PA and chauffeur of all vehicles I might require traveling in, with an additional clause of any other help required due to my mobility problems."

Down to business. His deadpan expression was

annoying. Still, if it was how he wanted to play it, Aela knew she'd be unfailingly polite—even when he provoked her. Forcing confidence in her reply she made her manner brisk, her nod of agreement efficient. "Four weeks shouldn't be a problem."

The remuneration package was staggering. Blithely quoting an amount for the PA job, commensurate with her business degree, he'd added substantial amounts for the other tasks, taking into account her expertise with vehicles beyond the typical chauffeur.

"I might spend a few days here, on Lanera, at first, but you do realize I'll want you twenty-four-seven?"

He'd want her? Twenty-four-seven? That was quite a concept. Aela swallowed her crazed imagination immediately because she wasn't going to indulge any of her wayward hormones. He'd just offered her a job, and she'd accepted. He was now her boss. And that spelled BACKOFF.

She forced her focus to the job again and out of her now a-little-bit damp panties, hoping any pink at her cheeks Nairn would put down to excitement about the prospective work.

Nairn abruptly broke off speaking to look out the window. He resumed after an awkward swallowing, his breathing so labored his loud sighs gained her sympathy. That was till he turned back to her. Then she wasn't so sure he merited it since there was such a smolder in his gaze for a flashing second before it was hooded. Just long enough to frazzle her on the seat.

Oh whoa! Had she just signed herself up as his jenny-do-everything for a whole month? Control would be a little bit hard to summon, but she could do it, if she put her mind to it, and nothing else.

Nairn's gaze dropped to his monitor, ignoring her, as he completed the details. That was much better when she couldn't see those sexy deep-blue eyes.

"Live-in, of course, food provided, with some time off, but that will be dictated by circumstances."

Aela readily agreed. Live-in status meant she'd bank the bulk of the earnings to use in her first student year. Her smile widened. "Won't be a problem, Mr. Malcolm. I've no specific plans for the coming weeks, and no personal demands on my leisure time."

Nairn's jaw tightened as he nodded, but the tiniest twitch at the edge of his mouth gave her pause for thought. Was he still doubtful of her expertise, or was it something else? For some weird reason she already felt tuned in to this man, tuned in sufficiently to know there was something about his decision that still made him uncomfortable.

But she wasn't. She wanted all his jobs.

"Right then, I'll expect you to transport me in the..." He reeled off his list of vehicles. "I've a yacht berthed on Corsica, but I doubt I'll be using that soon. My charter service pilots any long haul flights since I don't usually do the flying myself beyond western European destinations. I work with my PA on longer haul flights."

It was exhilarating listening but she halted him mid-flow. "Whoa there! Please stop, Mr. Malcolm. Although I've flown in a two-seater helicopter I don't have a current license for that."

"Miss Cameron! I'm not contemplating folding myself into a helicopter wearing two plaster casts."

Nairn's voice sounded almost whimsical. It was the first flicker of humor that had broken through his deadpan expression since they'd come in here. Try as she did to minimize the impact, he still stirred longings inside her.

"When would you be able to start?"

"Right now."

Nairn's brows rose. He seemed unconvinced. "I expected you'd need to go back to Glasgow, or someplace, and collect some things."

"I really do mean immediately, Mr. Malcolm. All my current belongings are in my backpack that's traveled with me these last five months. My possessions back in Vancouver aren't relevant."

"Let's get started then," Nairn declared after some contract forms had been signed. "I've already lost too much time."

Looking down at her shorts and cotton shirt made Aela smile for it was not what she'd envisaged wearing to work in an office. "Should I change into office gear?"

"Your suit of yesterday? You can ask me that when I'm wearing this, Miss Cameron?" Nairn glanced out the window before he continued, gently pulling the edges of his short black robe together. "No need for formality here on Lanera, not even when we visit the boatyard, so casual clothes are fine."

His robe. A dull flush made Aela shiver. The robe barely covered Nairn's muscular chest. And every other naked bit of him, at present concealed by the desk, was far too easy to conjure up for she'd ogled it way too well the previous day. She heard a deliberate clearing of his throat, and noted his gaze was everywhere but on her. Short shorts and dressing gowns were a little on the too casual side for daily use-though the idea made her want to grin. She hoped she managed to suppress it, yet a sneaky little muscle kept twitching regardless. Fortunately Nairn's focus was still out the window when he continued, "I never expected my ex-PA to wear business clothing here so why should you be any different?"

An hour and a half later Aela's brain was dancing a Highland Fling for she was by then conversant with how many small individual businesses Nairn owned, why he used so many vehicles, and why he needed a PA to co-ordinate his schedules.

Lanwater Whitecap, the diving school on Lanera, started while he was still at University in Edinburgh, had quickly expanded to become a fully-equipped water sports centre offering a range of watercraft courses and experiences. The success of it had led to his building other similar facilities around the globe. "That's how Lanwater Whitecaps became the name of the chain," Nairn clarified.

Aela hadn't found references to Lanwater Whitecaps while doing her quick Internet research so her notes were copious. Nairn explained his first profits from Lanwater Whitecaps had been invested in Ruaridh's boatyard allowing them to diversify from traditional yachts and fishing vessels. Gale Breakers had metaphorically risen from the waves and started producing luxury craft, very marketable in the present climate.

"Gale Breakers. Good name!" she muttered as she scribbled.

Noting what seemed most pertinent she was unaware she was parroting him. She wasn't just enjoying the necessary background particulars; she was also appreciating the dissipation of tension that had dominated their earlier interaction. Relaxed they weren't—not quite, though Nairn seemed a lot less tense than at first. However, his occasional slumberous glances were a little worrying, she was pretty sure his thoughts were elsewhere before he wiped them clear.

The stomach flips, and the little flutters of desire his glances generated she ruthlessly squelched. She had the job for a month and she wanted to keep it. She wasn't in the market for being so sidetracked by her hunky employer that she'd do anything to jeopardize it—like have a brief fling and then find herself out on her ear after a few days.

"I do initial consultations for the expensive yachts and vessels we produce, at venues of the client's choice, hence the need to travel so much. Ruaridh handles other negotiations here on Lanera."

"Okay, got Gale Breakers." Aela's mumble came after Nairn rattled off the last details on Gale Breakers.

Another of Nairn's companies used worldwide locations for providing extreme sporting experiences—water based ones like white water rafting, river tubing, canyoning and different kinds of bungee jumping.

"Adrenalinn Adventuring?" she asked, remembering the name from her initial searches.

Nairn nodded. An attempt to steeple his fingers failed and mild curses ensued when his arm cast slipped off the edge of the desk. His grumpy moans about his ineptitude made her smile. It was gratifying to know the guy could laugh at himself, and loosen up a bit, though Nairn Malcolm laughing at himself was just too unsettling.

"I'm impressed, Miss Cameron. How did you know that?"

Her answer was nonchalant. "A little internet research before coming to Lanera yesterday. Your companies have nice names, and sell exciting merchandise."

Nairn's tight smile acknowledged his appreciation of her compliment as she continued to jot.

"Adrenalinn Adventuring also provide land based experiences like tank driving, dirt buggies, quad biking, sphereing, bogshoeing," he rattled on.

"Whoa! Whoa! Hold on a minute." The peremptory, pleading tone she used stemmed his flow. She'd devised her own system for note taking, but his lecture was stretching it to the absolute limit. Smiling up at him, an apologetic grin broke free. "Got my notes in a tangle. Can you backtrack, please?"

"Do you always take such thorough notes, Miss Cameron?"

Aela looked to see if he was teasing; his infinitesimal change of tone implied it as he made proper eye contact with her. How disconcerting! There was just something there he wasn't quite masking. A flush of arousal rippled through her that she squashed, again. It took a moment to rally her thoughts enough to answer him.

"Initially, till I've got the basics," she said, changing her pencil during the lull. "Okay, so those last pursuits? Did you say sphereing?

"Rolling down a hill in a large plastic ball like a hamster," Nairn drolly supplied. A hint of a smile broke free, a marginal twinkle in both of his eyes.

Oh my! Aela's stomach flipped again. The man was definitely thawing. Why did his almost-smile have to be so appealing? She remembered the feel of those lips against her own and wished she hadn't for she wanted reruns, and more reruns. But that wasn't going to happen again. In a contrary way she didn't want him to be anything other than a detached employer. Temporary job, that was all. She determined to keep her tone light and airy. "Yeah! I know that as zorbing. Tried it in New Zealand. Fantastic fun."

"I expect you had lots of experiences on this world trip of yours, Miss Cameron."

Nairn's low husky tones rippled down her backbone: far too delicious.

"Oh, I did, sir." She decided she wasn't rising to his cryptic bait, sexual or otherwise. Her clarification sounded prim, even to her own ears.

"On my trip I experienced things I wouldn't have done at home, all equally exciting. But I've never heard of, or tried bogshoeing."

Their gazes connected for a couple of edgy moments before Nairn's throat cleared loudly. "Bogshoeing? Er... Bogshoeing is offered at our subsidiary Northern European bases. It's like snowshoeing, but on bogs in Estonia."

Aela felt hot all over as she processed Nairn's intense look. Why the heck did this attraction to a man happen now, when it had never happened before? Annoyed at her lack of control she struggled to answer. "I imagine the Baltic countries are beautiful?"

"Very beautiful."

Nairn seemed fixated on her lips as she plowed on. "Maybe you could explain about these subsidiary bases, Mr. Malcolm?"

"Some European destinations are not completely owned by me, but I hold the highest investment."

"Got that." Aela scribbled, keeping her head down to regroup her emotions. "And? What else?"

Nairn continued as though she'd not interrupted. "All my companies are based at my London headquarters."

Her well-worn pencil was changed for another super-sharp one before she asked her next tentative question. "So...sir. I've got notes now on all these companies."

"Yes?"

"Is that it, then?"

"Is what it?" Nairn sounded confused as if he was losing track of the conversation again.

Aela's little huff drew back his full attention. His good eye was twinkling, the other glistening too, as far as she could tell since it still struggled to open. The idiot was exhausted again, but so gorgeous she wanted to kiss him to bits.

"Have you fingers in any other pies, Mr. Malcolm? Not that I think you need any more, you understand."

Nairn actually laughed at her inquiry. "Sorry to disappoint you, Miss Cameron, but I do have other current business concerns."

"Jeeze!" Nairn was not meant to hear her tiny undertone, but she knew he did for his laugh rumbled even more.

"I've recently become a provider."

"A provider? What the friggin' heck is that?" Aela wondered what she'd got herself into. She'd be out in a trice if she found anything underhand about it. Nairn's full-blown laugh at her less than professional question made her wary of his humor, but she was glad to find the banter between them blew any residual tension to the four winds.

"That's what I call it anyway."

She waited patiently for more details, pencil poised over the paper—or maybe not so patient as she twirled it back and forth between her fingers. The sexual tension not gone at all. It was now simmering like a bubbling pot of barley broth. Her attempt at looking bland failed as she silently questioned.

His answer came with a lopsided smile. "My most recent venture completed an order to supply all the small craft and equipment-as one package-for the water sports centre of a brand new Malaysian hotel. It's one of a series of hotels at present being built in the South China Sea."

Her eyes widened as she processed just how many different craft she'd seen at some of the beach hotels she'd been at. Her throat cleared and her breath whiffed out in a puff of conjecture. "Small venture, huh? I'm taking a wild guess here. Gale Breakers didn't supply all the craft?"

"No. Gale Breakers only manufactured a little of

what was needed. I negotiated a good price with the other manufacturers and put a proposal to the hotel as a complete package."

Aela grinned, relieved his explanation of the word provider was legitimate. "So is that venture all done and dusted, then?"

"I'm afraid not, Miss Cameron. It appears they like me so much they want more."

Nairn's smile was as wide as he could manage, but his muscle spasm went undisguised as the bruising stretched. She empathized as his eyes flinched since she could see he was determined to control his reactions. It was hard to continue. The poor bloodied man was absolutely gorgeous! She wanted to gobble him up. "More, huh? I wonder why they like you."

Nairn's mismatched eyes crinkled again. "In fact, because of that success, I've already bid for another hotel chain who heard about my competence." He didn't sound as though he was bragging, just self-confident.

"Competence, is it? You've got a big back to pat, Mr. Malcolm, but I get the point. So you like this providing so much you're a sucker for punishment, and you're looking for more?"

Nairn grinned again, his arms cradling his ribs as he nodded.

Aela felt her eyebrows reach her hairline. The man was just too attractive. "And what do you call this providing company of yours? Twenty Five and a Half Hours a Day Enterprises?"

Nairn's hearty laugh rang out, though she regretted her facetiousness on witnessing the agony slashing across his face. It took him a moment to get his breath back, determination to complete the conversation very clear—his good hand splayed open in a warning gesture to confirm it. She waited, sensing he was building up to something she

75

wouldn't want to miss. "Sorry to disappoint you again, Miss Cameron. I was in a hurry to name it, couldn't dredge up any great ideas so I called it..." His expression was apologetic. "Malcolm Enterprises."

"You never did!" Aela was aghast, her censure blatant, an upbraiding tone peppering her response. "Mr. Malcolm. That won't do at all. It's just so dreary."

"Point taken." All Nairn could manage was a faint chuckle. His fingers soothed the ache in his ribs, and again she regretted her outspoken nature. The guy hurt, and she made it even worse. It should be her fingers doing the soothing. It was what she wanted, and she determined to be more careful of his condition-later-but for now she wasn't quite finished. Not when he was so approachable.

"One more question, sir." Aela leaned toward him and boldly clasped his good hand, her eyes brimming with humor. That little flicker started again at her fingernails and whispered right down to those on her toes. She squelched it while waiting for his nodded assent. "It's a really big question."

"Fire away, Miss Cameron."

Nairn's eyes glistened with a now blatant heat that should be forbidden.

Chapter Eight

"Do you expect me to be an insomniac, too?" Aela's bold brown eyes glistened with sass.

Nairn knew then he definitely liked the woman, a lot, as he watched her imperturbable slide back onto the chair before she picked up her pad and pencil again. The low simmer of desire couldn't stay on a peep any longer. Gas mark two was skipped and he went straight up to four...or maybe even five.

"Just to finish then, to be sure I've got your whole empire, Mr. Malcolm, can you bear with a few more questions."

"Yes?"

Nairn hadn't had such fun for ages; he couldn't remember when he'd been so diverted by any female.

"All your enterprises are coordinated at your London office and warehouses, except for the boatyard here on Lanera?"

"Not quite."

He watched her throat gulp, her eyes momentarily close and her pencil poise once again. He waited. Teasing this woman had great benefits—enjoyment for starters—and the anticipation of her next response. She didn't disappoint. Her smile, when she looked up at him with fallacious, fluttering eyelashes, was barefaced.

"So, you're going to tell me. No. Hmm. Let me guess..." Her fingernail tapped her teeth as she deliberated. "You also have offices in Paris, Rome and New York!" She finished on a flourish, her expression a wide beam, and waited for him to clarify.

"Yes, to one of those three. Am I so predictable already?" He couldn't contain his mirth although laughing was doing him in.

"Tell me it's Paris. The city of romance," Aela begged, catching his glance. "Can you believe I never made Paris on my travels? I'm so ashamed of myself. Of never experiencing the romance of the Eiffel Tower, or seeing the Seine, the Rive Gauche, or going to any of the raunchy cabarets!"

"Sorry to disappoint you again, Miss Cameron."

He found even saying her formal name aroused him, and why that should be flummoxed him. It was a formality he'd maintained on purpose, meant to create distance between himself and his too-appealing new assistant since he'd never insisted on using Brian's surname. It was a dismal failure, though, if it escalated his desire rather than diminished it.

"It's New York. I've a tiny office working out of New York which deals with bookings and orders for my North and South American venues."

Aela's smile enlarged and she actually whooped. "Way to go! I've never been to New York either. Fancy that."

Her face sobered as she made another scribble before jerking her head up, a polite inquiry hovering, now the very picture of efficiency. Nairn found he liked every way she looked.

"So, again I'll ask, is that it? The extent of your vast empire?"

"I believe so, Miss Cameron." He sobered too, remembering he was supposed to be employing the woman to do an efficient job; he wasn't employing her as his entertainment for the week, or priming her to become his lover. Her beaming smile and energized eyes appeared captivated, though, so he couldn't resist a little more repartee. "The prospect of coordinating all my enterprises, and transporting me, isn't too daunting?"

"Hardly!" Aela looked ready to rush out that very minute. "Can't wait. I'm desperate to get you going."

He was desperate to get going too, though not in the same manner as she was indicating. He squelched his wayward thoughts, but that did hee-haw for the erection strangling him, glad he was behind the desk, since his short robe did nothing to hide it. Sublimating his personal desires, back to business, he detailed the most pressing work to be attended to. "Contact my insurance company-details in the cabinet over there-and get yourself immediate cover on all vehicles."

Aela strolled off to find the information as he bent his head and forced himself to immerse in work that needed one-hundred per cent concentration. He didn't think his arousal was going to ever subside if he continued to look at her in those tight little shorts. Silent curses gave less satisfaction but that was how it had to be. The woman was such a torment.

After a while his rib ache bothered him. Wimping out wouldn't get the work caught up, but his body wasn't cooperating. Aela's intent gaze was upon him, with a little bit of the mothering hen lurking there—however, the bulk was of cynical censure.

"Mr. Malcolm, you're a numbskull again. Your grey pallor has reappeared, and you've been rubbing your temples for the last five minutes."

"Are you always so frank, Miss Cameron?"

Though he kept his face bland, Nairn enjoyed her pert attitude, enjoyed it-a lot. Aela didn't even try to hide her cheeky grin.

"Sure, I am. You might be paying me a wheen o'dollars, but it's not nearly enough for me to be a toady, sir!"

Nairn couldn't take his eyes off her no-nonsense walk as she approached him.

"Degenerating into the blithering ass of yesterday isn't the answer. Would you like something? Maybe a drink of water, coffee, a little rest?"

What would he like? Nothing he could tell her that moment. He'd been battling to keep the work going, but he also battled with the attraction she exuded. His plan to keep his hands off her was hard to maintain, even given his current limitations. She was right about the headache returning, though she didn't realize she herself added to his discomfort.

"Coffee would be fine, please."

Nairn drank his coffee and watched Aela's little sips, her focus intent on the advertising brochures he'd given her. God, those lips! That tantalizing plumper lower one was killing him. He felt he already knew the taste of them, but that wasn't the case. He mustn't think of it, or it would drive him nuts. Wriggling around in his chair he straightened his black toweling robe, a huge moan breaking free- as if he didn't have enough hurting body parts. He hoped it was covered by the chime of his cell phone as it bleeped an incoming text, a message he'd been waiting a while for. After scanning he wrestled himself into the wheelchair. "I'm going to rest for a while, Miss Cameron, before a great lummox like I am can't walk, or work properly."

Seeing his barb had reached the mark he should have felt pleased, yet he felt irked, especially when her delighted laughter echoed around the room. He had to remove himself from her magnetic orbit; the dashed woman was strangling him. "Tackle the inquiries on the answering machine while I'm away, please."

One-handed, he propelled the wheelchair out of the room...

****

Aela muttered some hearty curses at the busy the phone lines. Embroiled in the complexities of one particular inquiry Nairn's re-entry to the office stunned her so much she jumped up, pencil pinging from her grip. Baggy safari pants, one leg unzipped to above the knee, revealed none of the tantalizing hairy legs she'd been ogling.

Not an improvement.

She'd begun to get used to the muscular thighs she wanted to explore every inch of. But it was marginally better attire for the office—she supposed. A short sleeved green shirt with one button done up, covered his chest. That wasn't an improvement either; she wanted to look at his enticing abs all day long, bruised or otherwise. She hadn't realized her feet had propelled her toward him till her hand cupped his jaw, loving the smoothness she found there.

"Look at you! Oh my. You've got no stubble." Her mouth twisted in a grimace as she realized her comment had blasted out, her hand rapidly retreating. Pins and needles fired from nails to shoulder. Whoa! Just one touch of this guy was frazzling.

"Thank you, Miss Cameron! I'll take that as a compliment." Nairn's tone was polite as he caught up her fingers and pressed them against his shaven jaw as though he couldn't help himself. Sliding them back and forth the delicious rubbing did amazing things to Aela's kick-started libido as his sexy tone continued. "Courtesy of a neat little battery razor Ruaridh just bought for me which I can wield around my bruising with my left hand."

The imp inside Aela wouldn't be quelled as she stared straight into his deepening blue eyes. "Guess your usual is one of those frightening cutlasses twice a day, sir." Her breath stuttered as she inhaled his particular man musk that called to something deep inside her. She wanted to growl...or maybe purr along that smoothness? Dog or cat? Didn't matter. Just a little lick was her present compulsion. Her upper thighs trembled as she drew even closer to him.

Nairn's eyelids flickered, his breathing a shallow huff before his gaze suddenly dropped away, but not before he'd snatched the tiniest kiss at her fingertips. Drat! The devastating pirate was gone, and the sexy wild highlander? Nope. He was still there, now clean shaven and smelling even better than he had the night before.

The hot flicker in Nairn's gaze had seemed in sync with her own for a second, but then any rapport was veiled as he released her hand quite abruptly, wheeled away and hauled himself into his office chair. Though a little taken aback by his change of tack Aela couldn't help noticing his bruises were more colorful, though the swelling around his injured eye was receding. The man was even more alluring now. That gold-medal lurch she was becoming used to made its presence felt again as she retook her own chair. Her eyes shut tight to block out his image. Didn't work though, for the weakening warmth evoked by just thinking of expelling him reached right down to her toes. Her fingertips still tingled. Was the tingle ever going to go away? Or was that only going to happen if they had hot, hot sex to get rid of her itches?

She banished her errant thoughts; her job was for four weeks. No short-term affair for her, even if Nairn Malcolm was interested, though he now didn't seem to be because he wasn't even looking at her. His focus was somewhere a little above her head.

"Ruaridh's coming back to make us lunch. If you're not too hungry I said one o'clock would be fine."

His dull tone indicated none of the easy camaraderie from before. Aela mentally noted it and aped his manner, thinking maybe his absence from the office, the shaving and changes of clothing, had taxed him more than rested him. Detached was okay.

No, in fact, detached was better, and she could be detached even better than him. Her nod was professional as she brought him up to speed regarding phone calls. A grunt of acceptance and a terse dip she realized indicated his approval, so she resolved not to be put off by his cool responses.

"Brian called. His father's still poorly but is responding well to his medication, and glad his wanderlust son has eventually returned."

That got her some attention. Nairn looked interested, even a hint relaxed. She liked that much better since she wasn't used to being ignored. She waited for clarification, continuing only after his cynical smile faded. A sober expression was again the order of the day. "Brian will remain available if you need to contact him at his father's business number, or on his cell."

"Good."

She cheerily continued, ignoring his brief response. "Brian was very helpful. He's given me handy hints on how to apply myself as your PA; how to access all the relevant files."

Now she got the full force of his concentration.

"He was extremely organized, Miss Cameron, as I expect you to be. If his father hadn't had an unexpected heart attack then Brian would still be in my employ. He had to go home and take up the reins of his father's small engineering business."

Nairn's gibe seeped in though she refused to be cowed. Holding his snippy blue gaze her update was frosty. "Brian also informed me of the handover period, which is no longer going to take place. You can rest assured I'll do my best, Mr. Malcolm, in all capacities, though there may be times when I'll require patience to get up to speed with your business transactions."

Reaching for her already well-filled notepad she flicked to the page with the relevant number for Brian's father's business and jogged it over on a sticky note. Nairn's fumbling fingers touched her hand as he grasped it from her, but she was set on ignoring the jitters she got every time they made any sort of physical contact. The sudden flush she also squelched and put it down to the swift trot across the room.

A slight strain descended between them after she sauntered, on purpose, back to the desk and tackled more of her in-tray till Ruaridh beckoned them through to the breakfast nook for lunch.

****

The platter of stacked sandwiches was devoured quickly, as Ruaridh encouraged Aela to talk about her recent travels. They compared venues visited by both of them yet the strained atmosphere between father and son continued to be a trial. Aela couldn't understand it at all. Ruaridh made friendly approaches, Nairn rebuffed the good humored attempts his father made to include him. She wasn't enamored by some of the unsociable looks Nairn sent Ruaridh's way either, some when his father was looking, and others when he wasn't.

"No, Ruaridh. I've never visited the Pyramids at Giza, far less Karnak, as you well know. That little thing called client meetings ran on too long, if you remember. I didn't even get out of Cairo, unlike others of the party who literally jumped onto the ship and went off up the Nile entertaining the client's wife while I did all the negotiations."

Aela winced. Although she couldn't now deny she was sexually attracted to Nairn Malcolm, she wasn't convinced he was a nice person. His continual snapping at Ruaridh seemed to bear out a nasty streak in him. The meal was over for Nairn though as he bowled over to the door.

"Take a break, Miss Cameron, before you return to the office. Thanks for lunch, Father."

It was already obvious to Aela that Nairn only used the word Father when he was being super-sarcastic.

****

Mid-afternoon a sound interrupted them—a loud clanging that reverberated for a few seconds.

"That's the front doorbell. Go check, please." Nairn barely looked up from his set of figures.

Rhona, a nurse from the health centre had arrived to re-dress Nairn's chest wound, the local doctor having done it the morning before. "Good afternoon, Nairn. It's been a while since I've had to sort you out with anything."

Aela learned Rhona had known Nairn since he was a young lad.

"No need to go out, Miss Cameron, you're not going to see anything untoward." Rhona proceeded to lay out the necessary medical requirements.

Aela gulped. She'd seen plenty of his untoward already. But hey! She'd quite like to see more, even though he was the prime contender for the Grump of the Afternoon medal. Her lurid thoughts astounded her, no man had ever made her think that way before. She looked over at Nairn, but he seemed focused on Rhona, his polite inquiry about her family answered as the nurse did her job.

The wound was healing nicely, Rhona declared, but after checking his pulse she tut-tutted. It was far too fast. Was he taking the pain killers regularly?

Nairn's eyes swept toward her, his gaze challenging, warming her all over. Yet again. "Yes, I'm taking them on a regular basis, Rhona. I'm not such a stupid macho idiot I don't know what's good for me."

Aela was furious with herself. She'd never before been inclined to pinken about anything, yet this man made it happen so frequently. She bent her head back to her keyboard and attempted to ignore the proceedings in the room. Yet every belabored breath of his provoked the very reaction she wanted to throttle as Rhona tended to his other minor scrapes and cuts.

"And how are you coping with washing and dressing, Nairn? Since you can't have a proper shower, that is?" Rhona asked as she jotted down notes.

An extremely stressed silence followed. Nairn's throat cleared. He sounded a bit nervous, his gruff answer so quiet it was almost indiscernible. "Ruaridh's been helping me. Done a bit of shopping for things to make life easier."

"Really?" Rhona's response was accompanied by a full-bodied chuckle. "Nairn, lad, I've known you for years. I know exactly how independent you are. And how long do you expect Ruaridh to help you?" Aela was knocked for six when the woman turned to her. "As his PA I'm holding you responsible, Miss Cameron, for this man's personal hygiene. I know just what he'll damage if he tries to do everything by himself. He'll either stink for days—weeks even—or he'll break his good leg trying to wash himself in the shower."

"I'll hold Miss Cameron to that as well, Rhona. You can be sure of it." Nairn's bold stare was relentless as his mouth quirked up.

That pulse-jumping thing happened again, triple time. Aela was so dizzy she thought she might keel over. Then she remembered she'd never fainted in her life so it wasn't due to some lingering physical disorder.

Rhona's irrepressible humor lingered long after she vacated the room.

Aela couldn't face Nairn. There'd been no sense in telling Rhona she'd just met Nairn, and it certainly wasn't her job to wash her employer. Heavens! What a glorious thought. All that flesh. Um...the unbruised bits? She busied herself with the enquiry she was working on, but the warm fluttery feeling refused to dissipate. It was still there ages later. Ages while she'd avoided even asking any questions. Or looking at him.

"I'm going for a rest." Nairn wheeled himself out of the room.

His abrupt exit stumped Aela since he'd been in the middle of a complex set of figures he said were urgent for the following day. She tried to judge his mood, and failed. He hadn't been angry with Rhona, had even seemed to accept her humor with good grace, yet what had brought about his unexpected departure? Had it been because she'd almost ignored him for the last long while? She didn't have a clue, but she could already tell he was a man of moods. She plowed on with her stack of work, a bit moody herself.

Nairn returned a short while later, but was in no hurry to talk. His rest had been far too brief for a recuperating body, so no wonder he was cranky. Aela wasn't fussed, though, for small talk never interested her, and she'd more than plenty to do, especially as she'd resolved to keep her distance from him. During his absence she'd decided it was the only way she'd cope with being in his employ for four weeks.

Hours passed.

"It's well after six, Miss Cameron." Nairn's abrupt words came as Aela typed up the final sentence of the urgent report. "Do your first bit of chauffeuring and take us both to Mariskay. We'll find somewhere for dinner."

Aela wanted to try the local restaurants. Sometime, yes, but right that instant Nairn wasn't ready for such an outing. He was far too green around the gills, and had been noticeably placing his good arm across his chest as he worked at his desk. Though how not to offend, since the stupid prat sounded quite peremptory?

Polishing up tact she didn't have much of, she persuaded him there was plenty to use in the kitchen, and that she was capable of making a meal for them. Her foray earlier at breakfast made her certain of it.

Nairn's reply was tight. "I've organized my housekeeper to be available from tomorrow for feeding us lunch and dinner, but if you're sure about cooking tonight, then thank you."

"Should I make dinner for Ruaridh, too?" Aela's inquiry was tentative.

"Ruaridh? Why the hell would he be eating with us?"

Nairn's snarl indicated she shouldn't even have asked, his blue gaze a merciless inquest. But it was a fair question, and she wasn't going to be browbeaten by his bad temper. Her own temper was on a fair little simmer in reaction to his nastiness. Dear Hell! The man made all her emotions come to the fore. "It's a good enough inquiry, sir! Seeing as how your father ate here last night, and at breakfast this morning, and lunch."

Nairn's use of her name was deliberate, grittily direct. "Miss Cameron. My father and I lead separate lives. It's not normal for him to be around the castle and, as of lunchtime, I can guarantee it won't be a regular occurrence in the future either. I don't need his fussing."

The glowering ogre was back again. Biting back the response she wanted to make she turned for the door. "You've made that perfectly clear, Mr. Malcolm. I'll let you know when the food's ready."

She stomped to the kitchen to see what she could rustle up for dinner, berating herself for getting annoyed with the insufferable man. She would maintain her professional, polite attitude. She drilled it into herself as she opened and closed cupboards looking for something to produce a quick meal, wondering how to annoy him just a little bit like his tone had scalded her. Maybe there was something she could add, like a little arsenic? Nothing that would kill him of course—just something to make him feel a little bad for a while.

Jeeze! The man was already a debilitated wreck. How could she even joke about making him worse? Even if the annoying man was the most arousing she'd ever clapped eyes on...and touched...and kissed. And was also horrible! She groaned at how exciting the stolen kisses had been. It seemed a lifetime ago yet had only been hours.

A short while later she invited him through to eat, determined to remain aloof. "I neglected to ask if you have any special dietary requirements, but since this is your kitchen I rustled around in the cupboards, and reckoned I could give you anything."

The short break from each other's presence seemed to have done the trick, Nairn's snappy demeanor having vanished. "You're correct, Miss Cameron. You can give me anything."

That gleam sparked in his eyes again, nothing to do with food, his voice low and husky. Drawing in a deep breath, Aela concentrated on her task. The last thing she needed was to burn herself, literally or metaphorically. She removed plates from the warming oven then skillfully ladled food from the wok. Hot and cold. That was what Nairn Malcolm was and she was already fed up. She was also fed up with her own physiology since it too was fluctuating hot and cold far too often. Nairn was the recovering patient, not her. He was the one who should be having temperature variations.

But she found she didn't like the idea of lukewarm either, because until Nairn Malcolm she realized that was what her life had been like. Lukewarm.

Chapter Nine

Nairn imagined his last girlfriend in this kitchen as Aela moved around. His failure was spectacular. None of the women he'd associated with in recent years were in any way domestic. They'd never made him an impromptu meal since none of them had ever been to the island. When he was at Garvald Castle he came alone and cooked for himself.

The smell of food was enticing, but not nearly as enticing as the smell of Aela herself when she placed a plate in front of him. Her light scent—vanilla or something similar—had been tantalizing.

"Please." He answered her silent gesture with the soy sauce bottle.

Aela liberally sprinkled it on both meals then sat next to him. Spearing her first mouthful she indicated they should tuck-in while the food was hot.

Hot.

Aela Cameron was definitely hot.

"Thank you, Miss Cameron," he mumbled between mouthfuls. "Very tasty." He was driving himself mad watching her draw chopsticks full of noodles into her luscious mouth, fixated as he was by her wet, soft, glistening...

A month? He mumbled around the noodles he stabbed with a regular tined fork, for there was no way he would embarrass himself by failing with chopsticks he would have handled competently before his accident. Four weeks wasn't such a long time. Relatively speaking. Not nearly long enough to enjoy a woman like Aela, if his current sexual urges were any guide.

The noodles should have glided down his throat. They didn't. Every single strand reminded him of the pleasures of sucking...and licking...and tasting. His heavy grunt of frustration choked him.

Bloody bad timing. Karma sucked. How could he enjoy any woman? With the state he was in? Why did he have to meet her now? His want of her was so urgent he'd probably knock her out with one of the casts in sheer desperation. Four weeks? He'd be wearing casts for longer than that! But his groin wasn't listening. It didn't think too much about waiting for sex with her. He could make it happen; he just needed to work out the logistics.

Doggedly forking up more of the stir-fry he avoided looking at her. The woman was bad for his sanity. But his thoughts ran on regardless.

The meal was strung with anxiety. Aela was aware how much Nairn had to concentrate on eating with his left hand; aware of his almost permanent study of his plate and of how he avoided her eyes. But no matter that he seemed indifferent to her after his initial sexual reaction, awareness of his proximity bubbled, his unique male scent tempting her. It was an awareness of the obdurate strength of the man opposite and something that had no words as yet. The something else was a secret thrill. No words maybe, but the sensations he engendered were too powerful to ignore, yet she'd have to find a way to do just that.

She told herself she'd no business thinking about Nairn in anything but a professional capacity since she was only in Scotland for a few weeks. A few weeks? Jeeze. She'd been his PA for one day! Somehow she managed to keep the meal going with small talk, uncontroversial small talk, till they'd finished and she started to tidy up.

"I'd help clear away, Miss Cameron, but I'll be

more of a hindrance than a help. When you're done here though, I'll show you how to set the alarm system at the back door."

A short while later she followed him beyond his bedroom to the back door where she'd bid Ruaridh goodnight the evening before. Nairn demonstrated how to set and clear the alarm. "If you're not planning to be out this evening, we can set it just now."

Agreement was easy since Aela had no intention of wandering. Rain had begun to fall during the late afternoon, and it was now even heavier than before. Although Nairn wasn't expecting her to do any more work that night, she opted to clear some of the backlog of recorded phone messages. He also settled back to work talking only when she needed clarification on something, his gazes a constant assessment.

She'd long since come to the conclusion Nairn ought to be lying down but was dogged about carrying on, since she was still working. She thumped her way through closing down her computer, muttering and mumbling.

"You know something, Nairn Malcolm? Yesterday I called you some real nice names, and now I'm adding another few. But don't worry. They're in my head this time, since you're now my friggin' boss. I can see your butt has glued itself to that chair, but I'm through being a masochist for the evening, sir!"

Nairn's head lifted the tiniest bit to look at her, his unfathomable expression annoying as he waited for her to finish. Her sarcasm wasn't ruffling him, not even the slightest. She grew even more annoyed.

Stomping across to his desk she forced him to raise his head to make proper eye contact. "You're one of those infuriating guys, who don't leave their seat in the cinema till the very last credit has rolled, aren't you? Even when it's been the crappiest film you've ever seen! Savor the last drop of pain, won't you?"

Since Nairn did nothing but stare at her lips, she added a little more. "My pillow has a nice dent waiting for me, so I'm going to lay my tired little head down. I strongly suggest you do, too. You're way past needing it. Good night, sir!"

Though she didn't look back, she wasn't confident her irritated flounce had made any impact.

Nairn watched her disappear knowing his words were unlikely to be heard since she'd already rounded the doorjamb. "Good night to you, too, Miss Cameron."

Way past needing it? She was so right. About the whole damned lot. He was shattered—the biggest glutton for punishment. He hadn't wanted to slope off to bed. Where he'd think about her. All night long. She was driving him crazy. He'd never in his life before had a lips obsession, but he did now. Big time. And that little pink tongue of hers featured in lots of his daydreams, twirling and circling his own so realistically he could almost believe he'd had experience of that already. Backing off from Aela Cameron was proving a nightmare.

He maneuvered himself into the wheelchair and wheeled past her desk. A lingering scent of her was on the air. Or maybe her scent was just hard-wired into his sensual brain?

An organized series of sticky notes paraded themselves down the edge of her otherwise tidy desk. His mouth quirked up in admiration at the prompts. Although their conversations had been fraught with tension, and their eye contact had been full of deliberate avoidance tactics, she'd relentlessly rooted out details she needed to keep track of.

What the hell?

Next to the phone was another sticky note with

both Ruaridh's home and cell numbers on it. A sudden anger made him want to rip it to shreds. Had Ruaridh visited her while he'd tried to rest earlier that day? His hand thumped the desk dislodging some of the notes. Gritting his teeth, his swearing resourceful, he sorted them all back in order before taking himself off to his temporary bedroom.

The next morning, Aela didn't allow the drizzle to stop her from exploring the next morning after she'd breakfasted in her apartment. A fitful sleep, disturbed by erotic dreams of a totally healed and virile Nairn, resulted in a need of fresh air to clear her sluggish system. Finding the alarm already disengaged, she realized Ruaridh had paid another early visit. That was a brilliant thought. He could deal with any hygiene requirements Nairn might have. She wasn't going to think about washing Nairn Malcolm. No way. Her heart wouldn't be able to stand that!

Outside, she explored the area surrounding the castle, located the helicopter hangar, the garage block, and further on, stables, where she found Nairn kept half a dozen horses. So, her sexy wild highlander did have a trusty steed. He'd not mentioned that form of transport. A hearty laugh erupted when her active imagination envisaged a scene where she shared a horse with him in his present state. Without plaster casts and injuries, it would be another matter entirely.

"Come anytime and I'll find tack for you. Nairn won't be riding for a while, but that's no reason for you not to. Our bookings for the locals aren't too heavy just now so there's likely to be a spare mount." Angus, the young head groom, issued an invitation, deliberate in informing her he lived alone in the cottage next to the stable block.

Aela fended off his playful tactics for although he seemed nice she wasn't interested. Nonetheless, she'd ridden often as a child, and a romp was quite appealing.

Short of eight-thirty she was back in the castle. It wasn't a surprise to find Nairn already working, typing one-handed at a marginally faster rate than the day before. Start positive, she thought, entering the room. "Good morning. How are you doing?"

Her polite inquiry earned a genuine smile that warmed down to her toenails; it seemed the ogre was in hiding. Encouraging, yet she wondered what the heck had gone wrong the previous afternoon to change his mood so much. And how long would his present mood last?

"Much better, Miss Cameron." Nairn continued to smile. Darn his attraction. "You found the apartment comfortable?"

"Absolutely. The bed's a dream."

An economy with the truth; he didn't need to know he featured highly in the dreams she'd had lying on said bed. Nairn's reply was muffled as he shunted a piece of paper on the desk, a purposeful focus on his monitor rather than on her, but the smile had already slipped. No scowl, just back to the bland look.

He'd attempted some sort of hair wash, his thick black hair still damp. Thankfully all blood traces had been removed from the glistening strands, his whole person looking cleaner than the previous day. Gorgeous.

Combats flapped open at the knee on his plastered leg, a short-sleeved shirt buttoned in three places, covering his superb chest, though where it gaped at his waist the bruising was already aging to a greenish hue, the purple-black diminishing. His facial bruising was similar: the swelling around his eye and cheek barely visible.

The best way to cap her attraction would be to look at Nairn only when an absolute necessity. That decided, she settled into her chair and attacked the stack of paperwork he'd already deposited on the in-tray. Few questions needed clarification as she waded through the pile till Nairn's brusque voice jolted her.

"Miss Cameron? Call Richard, my housekeeper in London. Ask him to have my suit trousers and jackets altered to accommodate my casts, or have new ones made if necessary."

She found the number and introduced herself.

"Can you measure the circumferences of his casts for me?"

Richard's question was reasonable; but the measuring would not be impersonal. Oh dear! So close to him? Her body rippled, and she hadn't even got up off the chair.

When Nairn completed his call, she relayed Richard's request.

"Check the drafting table in the corner." Nairn turned his office chair around ready for her to comply, seemingly not wanting any time wasted over it.

Feeding the tape around his lower leg at strategic places she took the necessary measurements, unsure of how much she welcomed the sensation of being at his feet, like a willing supplicant. Nairn's labored breathing didn't make it any easier. The tape measure became a fiddle she almost couldn't handle as she wound it around the cast and re-checked the measurements. The delicate caress at her hair she put down to her fevered imagination—though she wasn't too sure since the tingles only started when his hand moved above her. When she raised her head in inquiry, Nairn looked so blameless she decided she must have been wrong.

Then his breathing hitched, the blue of his irises deepened to an intense navy, and a bond so strong snared her to him—so much her own breathing faltered. She couldn't look away. Her pulse was going like a jackhammer as she scrambled to her feet.

Taking his arm measurements was trickier since she needed to be even closer, her movements jittery. Maneuvering the arm cast she was so conscious of his attraction, only managing to record the measurements by avoiding eye contact. His muscular body wasn't the only overpowering thing she was aware of though; there was a strong citrus-like smell that somehow didn't match Nairn's personality, something she hadn't been conscious of the previous day. Her eyes lifted to his for explanation but it was a low growl that rumbled from him instead.

She didn't know whether to whoop with joy, or chastise when his good arm whipped out and locked her down in place, his lips crushing onto hers. The first slam of the kiss settled into an exploratory sortie, Aela too into it to call a halt. The same fit. Excitement flared again and set her upper thighs doing a happy dance of their own. The kiss deepened, Nairn took control of her inner softness, finding more places to make her desperate. He tasted like heaven, no coppery tang now, just his own unique flavor as his tongue slid around hers, and probed the supple tissue of her mouth.

This was Nairn at full consciousness, no sleepy response now. She was begging for more of it. The hunger rumbled and he fed her. She retreated and he followed. He gave and she...took. Shamelessly took. It may have been seconds, or minutes—Aela wasn't sure—but eventually the awkwardness of her body tilt, the numbness that was creeping into her leg muscles, reminded her what they were doing. She squirmed away. Nairn didn't look at all apologetic as she stared down at him, amazed. His small grin was of...mischievous delight?

"What can I say? Couldn't resist. You're a beautiful woman, Miss Cameron, and you were in my lap."

Those deep-space blues remained enigmatic as she processed what he'd just stated so dismissively. Her pulse steadied, eventually, after she returned to her desk, the air around also cooling down. Just as well. She avoided looking at Nairn Malcolm, and wondered how she could possibly last a whole month.

Kissing the boss was never a good idea...and she hadn't even had a shot of his floatplane yet.

The job had to last long enough for that!

She was absorbing details from a memo when yet another call shattered the peace. "Someone asking for you personally, sir," she informed Nairn as she transferred it to his line.

"Mhari!" His delighted laugh drifted across to her. "How are you?

The soft resonance in his tone discomfited Aela though all he'd done was greet the caller. They'd shared a room for hours now, and he'd been on the phone often, but she'd never heard these sinuous sounds. Her gut clenched. It was none of her business if Nairn took a private call.

"Well, not quite, though how did you know?" he said then yet another laugh burst from him. "Of course I wanted you yesterday! You've no idea. Oh yes, Mhari, your personal treatment's in urgent need."

Personal treatment? Aela wouldn't listen any more, but the confines of the room made it impossible for her not to hear his conversation.

"Yes. So clever of you, Mhari. My bedroom needs are the very problem right now!"

Jeeze! That was way too much to overhear. Aela surged up and left the room. Personal treatment? It was none of her business what Nairn said to female acquaintances. Not even after his tongue had just given her a tooth wipe. Wobbling legs sped her outside for some fresh air.

On her return a few minutes later the call had ended, Nairn's mood heartier if the beaming smile coming her way was a measure of his frame of mind. Grunting her way into the chair she attacked the keyboard, and ignored him for the rest of the morning, except when she had to interact and then she was pleasantness personified.

After the appetizing lunch Kirsty had prepared, and some surprisingly enjoyable conversation between the three of them, Nairn declared he would rest and wheeled himself out of the kitchen.

"Have you had a look around the castle, Miss Cameron?" Kirsty inquired.

"Please call me Aela. Miss Cameron is far too stodgy."

Aela laughed at Kirsty's expression when the housekeeper heard that although she'd already stayed two nights she'd only been in a few of the ground floor rooms.

"I'll give you a wee guided tour then. Nairn won't mind a bit."

A tour of the whole castle followed which to Aela's utter delight included an indoor swimming pool and gym area, located further along the same wing as the office apartment. The renovations to Garvald Castle were superb, no expense had been spared. The décor was spectacular yet not very personalized. The exceptions being the great room, the office, and the master bedroom suite on the first level, where, she imagined, Nairn's preferences had been catered to. It looked as though he wouldn't be occupying the upper floors for a while, though, since the spiral staircase was presently insurmountable. From Kirsty she learned Nairn's small downstairs bedroom had been intended for occasional domestic help.

The master bedroom suite was fabulous. Extending across the complete first level of the original square keep, its darkest navy was highlighted with soft dove grey—cool, yet seductive. A massive canopy bed festooned with piles of soft cushions made Aela want to experience its comfort. Images of Nairn occupying it flashed up, she wanted to include herself in them, but firmly put them into the dream category. Then her wayward brain recollected the earlier phone call. She categorically did not want to imagine some female called Mhari in the bed with him.

A huge custom-built shower with multiple massaging jets meant his en-suite bathroom was luxury of the highest order. She repressed lurid visions of him showering in the sensuous dark-marbled space since they brought warmth to her which could have fuelled the hot water the castle needed for a month.

Determined to pop Nairn back into that little pocket of her conscious mind labeled temporary employer she settled into her afternoon work. He returned looking well rested, and they segued into comfortable working harmony.

She ignored the tingling when she knew he was staring over the room at her, telling herself time and time again she wasn't interested, but he was so hard to ignore-every battered bit of him.

The phone rang.

"It's Robert Colby. Your security guard." Aela was unsure as she transferred the call for there was something odd about the request. "Giving you the heads up, he sounds pretty miffed. There's a problem with equipment in the London warehouse. Needs to speak to you personally."

Chapter Ten

Another malicious incident? Nairn was instantly alert. Robert Colby wouldn't call about something trivial. A few seconds later his good hand thumped the desk, startling Aela. From the other side of the room, her concerned gaze locked onto his.

"I'm going to nail the bastard's ass to the wall when I find out who's doing this! Yes, Robert, inform the police. Cordon off the whole area. Let me know as soon as the cops arrive, and get me a police contact name!"

After issuing further instructions he finished the call, so furious he could barely think.

"Can I do anything for you, Mr. Malcolm?"

Aela's question sounded cautious as she approached, yet her gait was determined. He liked that about her, but the question was difficult to answer. He cursed, all the while assessing how much she needed to know, since she was now in the line of fire too.

Diving gear for the Malaysian resort contract had one particular valve malfunctioning. On first glance that might seem a manufacturing fault, but he knew better. To ensure equipment was dispatch-ready there was a double-check system in place before delivery of all goods. The equipment in question had been received from the manufacturer just eight days before, and had been through a thorough check on arrival at his warehouse. If the goods in check had been inefficient it was easy to verify which technician had recorded it. Or, someone had gained recent access to the tanks. In view of recent happenings, Nairn veered toward the latter. Security cameras throughout the warehouses would indicate if there had been unauthorized individuals wandering around, thorough scrutiny of the tapes would take time.

Valve repairs were necessary, incurring possible delays. Nairn couldn't countenance that for he ensured his orders always arrived on time. Much worse, though, was the potential for disaster if final checks hadn't been effective.

The lethal element had reared its ugly head again. Till now he'd conducted internal enquiries, but that couldn't continue; authorities had to be alerted.

Nairn realized Aela was waiting for an answer to her request. She had to leave; he couldn't risk her being exposed to any harm. Taking as deep a breath as his lungs would allow, he thought of how to do it, since he'd no grounds to fire her. She'd done nothing to breach the contracts they'd signed the day before, her efficiency unquestionable.

"Sit here!" He tried to moderate his tone but knew he'd failed when her eyebrows flinched and her concerned expression faltered, replaced by a steely glint of resistance. After another gasp he tried again. "Please."

Aela's slide into the opposite seat was reluctant, her mouth a discontented line—those gorgeous lips that Nairn still fixated on, angry or otherwise. What the heck had he been thinking the day before when he'd drawn her into this mire of mishaps? But he had...and now she had to go. Engaging full eye contact with her he made sure there would be no misconception. "You sure you want to work for me?"

He noticed no hesitation at all. "I'm sure."

"Bet you'll change your mind when you hear what I'm about to say." He watched her expression become more wary as she contemplated his words.

"My bike spill was no accident. I'm convinced it was a deliberate and malicious maneuver designed to injure me."

Aela was shocked by Nairn's revelation as his attention strayed to the nearby window.

"There have been incidents during the past couple weeks which have harmed my business in some way or another. I didn't tell you about them either. I understand if you walk out this door right now, and go back to where you've come from, or wherever you want to be. It's what you need to do."

Nairn sounded furious, his body so rigid with tension she could see the muscles twitching at his neck, the effort to speak an enormous task.

"I will, of course, lay on any transport you might need, pay you for your efforts these last two days and an amount for the month you would have worked."

"No."

Nairn's gaze whipped back. "No?"

Aela was resolute. She didn't need to think about it. There was no way she would turn her back on him, even if it meant courting danger. "No, I don't want to terminate my employment with you. Whatever has happened doesn't change my mind. I'll deal with anything that comes."

She knew in her gut if this man had not been incapacitated by his present injuries he'd not be so frustrated, or be so vulnerable.

"Aela! Miss Cameron. I can't keep you." His voice was thready, and hoarse, as he entreated. "I can't guarantee your safety. You can see I can't even guarantee my own. Someone is causing malicious incidents which have escalated to a potentially lethal extent."

Nairn's terminology wasn't exactly encouraging, but she was determined. "I'm not one to run from adversity. I've been in hazardous situations before and survived."

"Have you ever faced down a saboteur?"

She watched the muscles spasm in his neck again, his teeth clenching as his fist tapped a furious drumming on the desk. "No, though I've been in potentially deadly conditions which could have downed my aircraft."

He looked like he was about to burst a blood vessel. Her heart went out to him for his consideration of her. Sensing she'd need to exert a good bit more persuasion to reassure him she scooted her chair forward and edged closer. So tense he could barely breathe Nairn's skin tone was ashen amongst all the other hues. "Tell me about the incidents."

She laid both her palms over his left hand still fisted at the place he'd just thumped. Ignoring the initial heat sending delicious waves of craving to her core she unfurled his fingers and stroked them free of the stress gripping them, flattening them on the desk, keeping them in place with her own. "I'm a good listener. This phone call is about the most recent of a string of catastrophes, you say?"

Nairn nodded, his gaze fixed on their linked hands, the tension in his fingers dissipated with her gentle strokes. As he related details of the current incident she hoped she kept her dismay from showing since she'd been an innocent holidaymaker hiring similar diving gear not so long ago.

Nairn backtracked. "The first incident happened thirteen days ago. Insignificant at first, it appeared to be lax processing. It annoyed me but the perplexing thing was no one seemed responsible."

"Somebody good at keeping below the radar?"

"Precisely! And has managed to continue."

Nairn's hand clenched again under her fingers. Continuing her sensual massage she acknowledged the little buzz she was experiencing wasn't going away anytime soon. Any kind of touch from this man did it for her. Their gazes locked, and remained so. The connection between them deep in a way she'd never experienced with anyone before. It was much more than normal empathy for someone in a bind. It was disturbing...hot.

Nairn took a few moments before he could speak. "A batch of kayaks, ordered for a new water sports centre in Ireland, was built here at the boatyard. It's normal to dispatch Gale Breaker Craft direct to the customer." Satisfied she was tuning in, he continued. "The last quality control was being enacted when dispatch realized something was odd—the new paddles and neoprene spraydecks had been purposely deleted from the order."

"Deleted?"

"We never send out new kayaks without paddles, though the spraydecks were on special request."

He sounded so disgusted Aela almost smiled but guessed the rest of the story wasn't so trivial. She picked up the threads. "But no one seemed to have zapped the order?"

"Bang on! A thorough check of pending orders followed. A number of them had had deletions, or irresponsible changes made to them.

"A second similar incident was dealt with expediently, but again without knowledge of who'd initiated it. Then a small fire had occurred in an area near the main dispatch doors of the London warehouses. A garbage bin housing used alcohol wipe cloths had been set alight. The fire was dealt with by an alert store man who tackled the fire with an extinguisher before the main sprinkler system kicked in."

"The fire authorities were called?"

"No." Nairn shook his head, a rueful expression clouding his face. "The fire was recorded in the incident log, but as it was found and dealt with immediately no further action was taken."

"Is that usual?" Aela struggled with the concept something might have been overlooked by that tactic.

"It certainly won't ever be usual again, Aela."

Nairn's tone was resolute; seemingly unaware he was using her first name. She put it down to his agitation over the situation. He was also unaware he was gripping her fingers so tight she thought he'd cut off her circulation, yet she wasn't pulling away. She welcomed the pain, hoping she could absorb some of Nairn's. When Nairn realized his grip was too firm his concerned apology sought her understanding...and maybe something else?

Another little flutter bothered her. Or maybe it was self-delusion yet again? Was she actually looking forward to those loaded gazes? Or in someway causing them to happen because she wanted to be as close to Nairn Malcolm as a second skin? Forcing herself to listen she convinced herself she was just giving him the reassurance of an interested colleague. Nothing else. She felt heat creeping around her neck.

She was such a fraud!

"I only found out about the fire the day after it happened when I returned from a publicity event on Corsica. By then it had been internally investigated by my security people, their conclusion being someone had accidentally chucked a lit cigarette in it. The workers have to go outside those doors if they're smokers."

"Could it have been an accident? If, say it was raining, or windy, and someone was smoking at the open door rather than all the way outside, and in too much of a hurry to get back to work?"

"Maybe." His eyes were an incredible deep blue, breathing more even as color seeped back into his cheeks. "We've thought of all possibilities. Of course nobody owned up, and the cameras revealed nothing."

"The next incident?" She dreaded to ask but sensed there were more to come from Nairn's taut grimace.

"Two days later a nasty virus was planted on our main intranet at the London office." Nairn slid his hand from Aela's grasp to rifle through his thick hair, slicking it back from his forehead. She missed the contact immediately. Like a part of her was gone. "It was intercepted by the virus checker, though not quickly enough to avoid all damage. It wrecked some software we use for ordering systems, and deleted other information."

"You fixed that?" She held her now redundant hands in her lap, away from trouble.

"Absolutely, though again it took time. The whole network was down for a day till it was resolved. Some customer orders for the previous twenty four hours had to be re-entered."

"So the saboteur is maybe someone who works in your head office, or your warehouses; someone who can come and go with ease? Someone who wanted to cause minor disruption?" Her last question was hesitant for the incidents seemed to be increasing in severity.

"You'd think so on the basis of those niggles, for that's what those initial ones were. They caused me time and money, but I've no idea who has such a grouse against me that they'd want to do this." Nairn again rifled his hair and cupped the back of his tense neck, unconsciously massaging the tight muscles there. Aela was desperate to jump up and do it for him. Massage unfortunately wasn't one of her certificated skills though, and she would hate to think she'd damage this gorgeously troubled man further than he was at present.

"Have you had unpleasant dealings with an employee in recent weeks, someone you've had to get rid of?"

His swearing was vehement, eyes flashing. "I've thought of that, and so did Brian. No. Brian's the latest employee to leave, though I'm damned sure it wasn't him."

"You can rule him out?"

Nairn looked appalled at her seeming suspicion. He groped for her hand and pulled her close again, as though he couldn't do without the connection either, his gaze intent on her. A serene wave of contentment washed through her, yet given the circumstances of his predicament she couldn't understand her body's reactions. Nairn didn't look at all calm: more like a turbulent Jacuzzi as his jaw twitched. "Brian was with me on Corsica the day the fire was started, so I think that rules him out."

"I agree. Unless he paid someone to do it." Nairn's negative gestures wiped out the possibility. "Okay. I get it! You trust Brian."

"Definitely. He had no motive for doing any of this."

Aela cringed at her next thought, releasing her fingers from his grasp though leaving her hand close by. Missing his warmth…and connection again was getting to be a habit. She made sure she'd his full attention before speaking again. "You're not going to like this question, but as a virtual stranger I have to ask it. Would you have pissed off some girlfriend to the degree she'd hound you like this?"

Her question was reasonable. Nairn looked startled though, his eyes narrowing as if the idea had never occurred to him. "I'm not aware of a previous lover being so unhappy she'd resort to anything like this. I've not had any long, or meaningful, relationships in years. Recent dates, or affairs, have been a few evenings out, not much more than that. I'm always on the move."

"Mmm..."

Aela could see how his constant business needs would make that the case. A little file opened in her brain and deposited a no-girlfriend-or-current-long-term-lover sign. It was a tough job to suppress the smirk that wanted to break free. She thought some more, her next probe careful to catch his response. "I don't suppose a previous girlfriend would have easy access to your office, or warehouse anyway-except if she was a co-worker? Have you dated...?" His hand flashing up stopped her. "You're going to tell me you don't have relationships with employees?"

"Never!"

"Okay."

Tucking away that bit of information somehow didn't please her, though it should have reassured her. Nairn didn't even seem to register that the kisses they'd shared negated that statement. He might not have been totally coming on to her, yet Aela was no dummy, she knew he was just as sexually interested to her as she to him. His vehement denial was at odds with the surreptitious banked desire she'd already intercepted, not to mention the connections she was feeling from his touch, touch she was sure was reciprocated.

Her new tack was marginally different. "Have you been harassed by any employees who've wanted more from you, and didn't get it?"

Aela was treading in deep water and she knew it. If her own reaction to Nairn was common then she could understand any woman employee wanting to be his lover.

Chapter Eleven

"What do you mean?" Nairn's brow furrowed again.

"Jeeze, Nairn. Look in the mirror. You're a studly man!" Aela's cheeky smile broke free as he gulped. "Okay, so hold back on the mirror right this minute, but you get my drift. There must have been plenty of women who wanted you to be more than their employer."

Danger signals flashed in his gaze. His hand again raked his hairline, his eyes wincing at his inadvertent skid over the bump and deep laceration across his brow, a tinge of deepened color flushing his cheeks. "Yes, Miss Cameron. I've been the target of women who've wanted to be more than my secretary, or PA, but I haven't given any of them one single signal that they were likely to succeed."

"Okay. Keep your hair on." Her ardor cooled because Nairn's expression was back to the blank stare. "I'm just covering as many angles I can think of."

A tense silence accompanied their individual thoughts till Nairn's swearing was fervid. When she didn't even flinch at the obscenities he continued. "Anyway, my little mishap on Saturday puts the cat-among-the-pigeons on the jilted girlfriend theory."

"How so?" she questioned, still ruminating over the details she'd heard so far.

"The saboteur wasn't only in my head office and the warehouses, but was also here on Lanera."

"Able to tamper with your bike?"

"Exactly!"

"Ruaridh told me you took your motorbike because you hadn't ridden it for a while?"

"Yes." Nairn looked confused by her change of direction.

"I assume you always do a thorough check before taking it out?"

"Of course—before I left the garage here at the castle."

"What caused your accident?"

"Initial investigation proved damage had been done to the brake discs."

Aela digested his information, gnawing her bottom lip. Somebody really had tried to harm him? A chill skittered down her backbone and settled like a heavy brick in her stomach. He could have died. The thought was horrific because she'd never have known him if that had been the case. A fierce protection gripped her, she wanted to ensure nobody ever harmed this man again...but more than that she wanted his assassin to be caught and strung up! If anyone had asked her two days ago what she was like she'd have said quite categorically that she was a pacifist, but not now. Now she felt quite murderous herself. What the heck did that mean?

Nairn hastily withdrew his gaze as though he wanted to escape the room...the conversation...her? Maybe her murderous thoughts had translated to her face? Summoning every bit of calm she possessed Aela continued her inquiry.

"Was your bike out of your sight on Saturday?"

Nairn seemed surprised by her question. "Sure, during the day. I drove it from the marina to the hotel underground car park while the client and I worked."

"Could the bike have been tampered with during that time?"

"I suppose so. I'd no problem driving it ten miles to the hotel, but it could also have been tampered with on Lanera before I left the island. The repair garage still has to establish if the malfunction happened where it did because the time lapse matched. They're working on tests to prove how long it would have taken for the damage to manifest itself."

"Who knew you were going to a client meeting?"

"Brian, Ruaridh, Aran, and Marsha."

Marsha? A little alarm bell signaled somewhere and made Aela wince. Who the hell was Marsha? The woman of the sexy phone call had been called Mhari, not Marsha. Yet Aela had read the name Marsha somewhere. "Why would this, Marsha, know of your movements?"

"Marsha Hilborne's my Office Administrator in London. She isn't in the office this week. She worked both Saturday and Sunday during the last two weekends so she's now having days off in lieu."

"Okay." Aela nodded her grasp of the situation, relief profound that Marsha wasn't another of Nairn's personal acquaintances.

"Since Brian was quitting on Friday, Marsha was primed to handle my appointment calendar and any correspondence on Saturday and Sunday."

"Was that normal procedure?"

Nairn appeared distracted by her question. "Not really. Brian would normally have been with me during client meetings, and would have dealt with any urgent calls, or e-mails. It was rare both of us were out of contact for any length of time."

"So Marsha knew you'd be unavailable during your Saturday meeting?"

"Yes." Nairn's interest was evident in his concentrated gaze that never strayed from her. That was good; they needed to focus on his problem and not on the overexcited hormones still flying around the room.

Aela tapped a pen on the desk beside her. "If

Marsha knew your venues then other people probably knew as well. When were the details of your meeting settled on?"

Nairn paused to recall, breaking eye contact as he scanned out the window. Aela missed the connection more than she would have believed and waited for it to return. When his head whipped back her way, the rush of heat around her body was a shocker; that damned lust again. The strong heartbeat following was a welcome reminder she should be repressing her urges.

"It would have been firmed up on the call Brian handled last Tuesday. There was no reason in between to change the details since by then we knew Brian was spending his last working day, Friday, here on Lanera, and he'd be going back to London on Saturday."

"Is your appointment diary just electronic?" A frown developed as her pencil tapped. "Or, is it also on paper?"

"Only on my computer and on Brian's—now yours."

"So Marsha was given access to that file." Aela segued into ferret mode, determined to root out some answers. "Can you confirm she was, in person, at headquarters on Saturday?" Nairn nodded. "Then someone else must also have had access to the file prior to Saturday."

Nairn appeared to consider her line of inquiry. She was beginning to like the hint of something else lurking there—maybe some admiration? She wasn't sure, but it didn't matter because they were back to being less tense. "You're thinking somebody had sufficient forewarning to be at the hotel in Glasgow and awaited my arrival. Then tampered with the brakes?"

"Or, they came to the island on the Friday." Aela felt her smile faltering as some doubt flickered in his eyes. "That's all I can think of at the moment."

Silence descended for a few moments as Nairn contemplated the possibilities. "How did you come to those conclusions?"

"Basic facts. No prior prejudices, no misleading information."

"Nothing to do with good deduction skills, I suppose?"

His admiring gaze and lazy smile lit her up inside, and yet again she squelched the sensations, as though stamping on a bug. Further questions popped into her head. "How did this person know you would use your motorbike? Where were you when you made that decision?" Instinct told her the answers were important.

"At the boatyard with Brian while he made his last farewells. We arranged our Saturday morning pick-up with Aran. That's when I decided to take the bike instead of ordering a taxi to meet me at the marina, and it saved Aran waiting for my return."

Aela had another sensitive question to ask for she'd liked Aran very much the day he'd ferried her to the island, could only think good thoughts about him. "Is there any way Aran could be a suspect? Would he have any reason to be in London at your headquarters?"

Nairn looked appalled. "Never! Aran worked with my father long before I left for university. He helped me start up Lanwater Whitecap here on Lanera. Managed it for me when I was elsewhere. He's a mainstay on the island, and he's never any reason to be in the London offices. He's no motive to do any of this!"

His thrashing arm-cast sent a tub of pencils and pens crashing to the floor, Aela quick to soothe as she gathered the fallen ones. "I'm sorry! Hey, I definitely liked what I saw of him, but I'm trying to help. I can't do it unless I ask these questions, even

if they are awkward and seem inane."

Nairn's apology was instant He grasped her hand when she'd tidied up the pen tub, and wouldn't relinquish it, pulling her in alongside as though he needed her even closer. Her chair whizzed beside him, her leg nestled next to his, sharing far too much body heat for one small point of contact. All the while, Nairn absently stroked her fingers as they lay next to his. She could hardly credit how much she relished the simple contact.

Their conclusion was that someone had to have overheard his conversation with Aran and Brian, because that's when he'd given instructions for the bike ramp to be readied for use. It was always stored in the boatyard because there was no way he could get the motorbike up and down the cove.

"So, I'm guessing your accident was the end of these incidents? Till today, that is?"

Nairn tilted his head toward the ceiling before he answered. "Unfortunately, no. Late Tuesday morning a power failure shut down my whole complex in London for more than four hours till the energy company found the problem. They got it up and running again just before you arrived at the castle."

"Damaging to a lot of your business." Aela's leg nudged again, giving another encouraging display of sympathy.

"You can imagine how much of an interruption that was. Most personnel were sent home, leaving only a skeleton staff. Just as well cell phones are used by almost everyone, though by mid-day I'd fielded so many questions for office personnel my head was reeling." Nairn's eyes popped open, caught her glance, and grinned-an apologetic rueful quirk of his lips. "You know just how much I was reeling on Tuesday!"

Aela couldn't deny it. What a ruddy awful time

he'd been having, and she'd been so dismissive about him being a prat! She was now the one who felt chagrined; ready to beat the hell out of the perpetrator on Nairn's behalf.

The kiss she planted on him surprised her as much as it did him, but he wasn't complaining. He groaned into her delving mouth. Her initial kiss of sympathy developed into sheer greed as Nairn's hand strayed to her breast. Aela's own whimpers escaped as she responded. His caresses were happily drifting south to her waist when a jangling of the phone jolted them out of their mutual engulfing. Aela was relieved when Nairn took the call, since answering professionally was impossible. Her reactions to Nairn Malcolm's touch were unprecedented, so much so it left her feeling deprived...not something she understood.

"Thanks, Robert. Yes, I'll speak to Detective Woods now." There was a slight pause before Nairn replied, "Yes, I'm Nairn Malcolm."

Aela slipped from the chair, but Nairn's plastered arm flaps indicated she should listen in as he gestured the speakerphone.

"Our expert tells me that particular valve has been tampered with, sir, on all the tanks. Now, your security guard has mentioned other incidents of a suspicious nature during the last week."

Aela listened as Nairn related everything that had happened, including his own accident that no one in the London office knew about. "Detective Woods. I'm sure you can appreciate why I don't want anyone in my London offices to know about my accident, not even Robert at present."

Detective Woods cleared his throat. "Do you have any suspicions about the integrity of your security guard, sir?"

Nairn was quick to dispel the notion. "None at all. I'd just prefer no one knows yet. Yes, detective, I did have a consultation from that security consultant yesterday."

"Was the nature of the visit with a view to improving your security measures, Mr. Malcolm?"

The detective's tone indicated the event was a little too late. Nairn's sigh before answering confirmed he too was thinking along the same lines. "Yes. He's gone off to get a quote together for upgraded cameras and a few other implementations to improve the monitoring of personnel movements, but I don't expect completion for a couple of days."

"Thanks for that, Mr. Malcolm. In the meantime we'll say nothing of your own mishap. We have employees still to interview, and I'll report on that as soon as I can." Detective Woods then explained he'd liaise with the Glasgow Police Office regarding Nairn's accident. Aela jotted down the relevant contact numbers for both police stations.

After the call she made coffee before resuming their earlier speculation over who might be a suspect. Their intense kiss had seemingly been forgotten: Aela was glad of it, yet also disenchanted, because it must have meant more to her than it had to Nairn. Her next question was sensitively phrased. "Could anyone else on Lanera have a grudge to settle? Someone who comes and goes to the London base?"

Nairn made no hesitation. "Nobody ever goes down to London from Lanera. Not even Ruaridh. He's entrenched on the island, and happy to be so."

"Okay." Aela changed the subject back to the bike. "Could someone have accessed your bike before Saturday morning?"

Nairn agreed it might have been possible, but the garage alarm system was operating as normal, so there'd been no reason for him to suspect anything untoward.

"Well, it sounds most likely somebody tampered

with the bike at the hotel in Glasgow."

Nairn readily concurred. Aela dragged her chair closer again. He looked so delighted with her decision it made that fiery anticipation start all over again. Such a tiny thing to kick-start it.

"What motive would anyone have for putting you out of action? Or would cause such pandemonium your business integrity would be questionable?"

Nairn said he'd thought of that aspect. "Or, do you mean something aside from me losing business?"

"No."

She gnawed on her bottom lip, tucked an arm under his good one and leaned up really close. The edges of his irises were a balmy blue that deepened by the second. The seat suddenly became unbearably hot. Aela whiffed a stray hair from her cheek to cool her face. When it didn't work she ignored the flush and forced herself to concentrate on the problem. "Let's stick with loss of business. What are your most lucrative propositions at present? What would you be reluctant to lose, or muck up?"

Nairn's gaze appeared riveted on her lips, his answer slow to materialize. "I've already told you this Malaysian deal is a big money venture. The first order was successful, and I'm now supplying for a second. Being a chain of hotels they could put huge amounts of future business my way. That's why this gas tank meddling has to be dealt with rapidly."

"Anything else?"

Nairn explained other commitments, his thumb absently massaging Aela's palm. "Gale Breakers has a prestige order for Prince Khalid. It's an expensive yacht, though it's more the cachet of getting orders like his that's important; good business is often generated by word of mouth."

Aela agreed since her Uncle Harris's business often had huge boosts from people of note using their services. Yet, neither of those two contracts sounded like the underlying cause of the incidents. "Have you potential business that's very competitive, that other companies might want so desperately they'd resort to corporate espionage?"

"Espionage? Nobody's tried to steal from me, Aela!" Nairn laughed at her, amused by her wording, his fingers playing with and squeezing her palm before he lifted it and planted a swift kiss on her knuckles.

Aela's stomach flipped as she laughed along with him, their eye contact thrilling as he released her hand. She wanted to climb onto his oh-so-debilitated-lap and kiss him senseless! Clamping down the passion her wayward hormones sought with some desperation was so difficult. Clearing her ragged throat she somehow managed. "Well, okay, maybe espionage isn't quite the word. Corporate sabotage or serious delaying tactics."

Nairn mentioned a proposed meeting for the following week, in the Caribbean, that he'd probably have to abandon due to his condition. "An upgrade of craft for a newly formed consortium of hotels. They're presently serviced by different American firms but the intention is to have a corporate image regarding water sports facilities."

"So, if you can't go next week, a competitor could win the bid instead of you?"

Nairn suspected at least three other companies were bidding, and although he would present a good package, it was no dead cert he'd get the work. Another silence pervaded, though it was a comfortable one as Aela wondered about the saboteur's motive.

She missed the bonding of their fingers when Nairn pulled away. Time to yank on the brakes anyway since she was getting too used to the lust-filled feelings Nairn engendered. His lop-sided smile exuded a confidence she was gratified to see, but his eyes flashed mixed signals. The respect building between them the last while was still there...but a certain reserve had returned. She sensed a different sort of pressure was creeping in, and it was grasping Nairn in an invisible stranglehold. He was backing off again.

That was good, wasn't it?

He called the Glasgow police station and was informed officers would visit the castle later that evening.

Without even touching him Aela felt waves of agitation gripping him by the time the call was over.

Chapter Twelve

"Still want to continue?" Nairn felt nauseated, but it was nothing to do with his physical ailments. Bad conscience churned his gut as he stared at the beautiful woman he'd embroiled in his troubles.

Aela's glare, he guessed, mirrored his own as she faced him down. "I don't go back on my word, Nairn Malcolm—not ever."

"Get the Range Rover! We'll see how Prince Khalid's order is progressing."

His bark might have been heard down in Mariskay and deafened even himself. It was a pathetic excuse, but he had to get out of the castle. He hated being inactive, hated being injured, and most of all hated that he could do nothing about the rising feelings for Aela Cameron. The odd kiss wasn't enough. He wanted to thrust into her delightful body and slake his lust...and maybe blast away the gripping force that drove him insane.

Since he was physically incapable, he forced a compromise—a different environment where he could keep Aela Cameron at a distance. Besides, going down to the boatyard might jog some memory of the previous Friday.

"How do I access the car?" Aela got up and approached the door.

Nairn watched Aela turn as she awaited his answer, she was cool, not ruffled in the slightest by the potential danger he put her in. Her professionalism had been exemplary. He ordered. She carried out. Hell! The woman had been his sounding board for hours, been supportive, her theories astute. Her soothing massage had kept him physically calm and rational—though it did nothing for his libido. He enjoyed her presence. That should have been enough, yet the arousal wouldn't subside. She had a firm grip on the situation, but he hadn't.

Overall he was a bloody mess.

Wheeling into the corridor, he barreled along till just short of the mudroom where he indicated a large watercolor on the wood paneled wall. In behind was a key container storing numerous keys. "Top level, first left, there should be a spare key for this back door." He reeled off the relevant keys, finishing with the garage and security gate remotes. Aela listened, selected the necessary keys and pocketed them. "The key for the boatshed is top row first right. You're not likely to need it yet, but at least you'll know where it is." Having fired out the information he wheeled along to the garage. "You can use any of the cars for personal use, though at present the only one I'm going to fold into just now is the Range Rover."

As she towed behind him Aela blithely remarked she didn't expect she'd use either of the two high performance vehicles to travel a few miles to Mariskay, but she'd like to use them to explore the island—if she ever had time off.

Nairn ignored her jibe, in no mood to respond to her banter. He couldn't quite ignore her, though, when she shunted the passenger seat back as far as it would go and reclined it.

"Your carriage awaits, sir. Fold yourself in while I fold this down." She plopped the wheelchair into the trunk.

At the boatyard, Aela trekked alongside the wheelchair since he insisted on wheeling himself. She was greeted in far too familiar a manner by some of the younger males, who all seemed to have valid reasons for being introduced to her. He could barely contain his aggression when yet another of them hovered.

"How's progress on this one, Aela?" Aran questioned as they stood by Prince Khalid's order.

"Is this a trick question?" Aela asked.

"Not at all." Aran grinned as she climbed into the hull.

Nairn listened to their repartee from the wheelchair where he sat feeling like a rat in a trap. A very irritated rat unable to rid himself of the frustration of being imprisoned in his injuries.

A moment later Aela's eager voice said, "You've added a marine GPS Chartplotter and an autopilot system. Has it been water tested yet?" Her head popped out of the hatch as she climbed back out.

Aran spoke of the full trials which wouldn't happen for a couple of days because other internal fitments needing to be added first.

Nairn's mood was sour as he noted Aela's interaction with Aran, who appeared impressed by her knowledge and interest. How could she know those systems had been added by just looking at the interior? They'd made a couple of phone calls during the morning regarding the order, but failing that, it must be she knew much more about boats than he first thought.

Or, and he liked this thought much less, had she been down here already visiting Aran?

Or Ruaridh? God forbid!

Had he been wrong to almost bare his soul to this woman? Could he trust her with his problems? She turned her charm on everyone, becoming their best friend in a matter of moments.

He'd earlier thought her concern had been personal. Maybe he was totally deluded. Yet being suspicious of everyone's motives didn't sit well with him either; he hated mistrust. He also hated what he was experiencing, feelings that seemed far too much like jealousy. Whatever her reasoning he determined he'd find the control to keep Aela Cameron at arm's length. No more confidence sharing with her. No more anything, for that matter.

"Get the car please, Miss Cameron!"

Hot and cold again. What the hell was annoying Nairn now? Aela drove back to the castle, the tense silence able to be cut with a blunt knife. She was miffed again with his tendency toward black moods, and his on-off lover-like approaches.

"You've done enough today. Take a break. I'll see you at dinner."

His attitude as he exited the car was dismissive, as though he couldn't stand her company any longer. But Aela wasn't kowtowing to that sort of rejection.

"Not sure what your problem is, sir, but you look like a piece of...dog's dirt! I suggest you have a nice lie down while I go and do something interesting. After I put the car away, of course."

Aela's words accompanied a simpering-sweet smile. The grunt she heard as Nairn lurched to the door didn't mask his rude comment about cheeky, insubordinate bloody women. Her laugh echoed around the courtyard as she unfolded the wheelchair and set it inside the door.

"Sweet dreams, your eminence." Her cheeky chauffeur salute was obviously not appreciated as Nairn's good fingers twitched in a rude gesture.

****

The pool was one place the domineering Nairn Malcolm wouldn't be visiting for a while. The water was a beautiful temperature, just right for fast laps and then a more leisurely swim before Aela splashed water onto the sauna coals and relaxed in the steamy haze. It'd been ages since she'd had a sauna—her backpacking holiday hadn't included places so luxurious.

Tranquil elegance surrounded her in the lush hydro-planting maintained by the pool attendant.

125

Soothing to the nerves it was heaven to be away from Nairn's bad temper, his indifference, and also his occasional affability. Away from his undeniable attraction. For a while.

****

"I've set the dining room, Aela," Kirsty informed her as she arrived at the kitchen door. "Nairn's already there waiting for you."

"Sorry. I didn't realize I was late."

"Och, no. You're bang on time."

Although Kirsty had chopped the beef into small chunks Aela noticed Nairn found it difficult to saw through his pastry left-handed. His sour look hadn't improved. "I'll cut it before you mangle it to a pulp. My fault, sir. Kirsty chose the menu for me, said I couldn't be here without tasting her traditional steak pie."

As she drew his plate closer he gave a grudging thank you. She avoided any inadvertent brushes of fingers or arms. No more delicious tingling.

Not what she was there for.

A strained meal followed where they discussed Nairn's plans for the coming week.

"Take the rest of the evening off. You've already put in plenty of hours, and the police will be here soon," Nairn declared after their coffee.

His terse dismissal grated, but he was the boss. "In that case I'll go walkabout."

Aela wasn't sure whether to feel glad or miffed by his abrasive attitude but she was becoming all too aware the dratted man's attraction was increasing, not diminishing. It was obvious he wanted to be rid of her, now barely tolerating her when she was in the same room.

The wander down to Mariskay was ideal. Since it was a warm June evening there were plenty of patrons of the harbor bars sitting at outside tables, enjoying the evening sunshine. Aela found a space, ordered a glass of wine and contemplated what a strange situation she'd got herself into. Within minutes a couple of the younger boat-builders she'd met earlier in the day strolled past and expressed delight in her keeping her company.

The next hours were the most relaxed she'd had for days, although she was careful to be confidential when Nairn's name cropped up. It was evident that though he didn't tolerate fools gladly he was admired in the local community for generating economy.

Jamie was full of praise for her new boss. "Aye, Nairn was born and raised here. Did a Mechanical Engineering Degree in Edinburgh, and then went tae Harvard Business School, but he nipped back to see Ruaridh and checked on Lanwater Whitecap during vacation times."

"Och, ye'd never have credited it, Aela. Four years ago Garvald Castle was jist a ruined shell wi' nae roof. Nairn brought much needed work fir craftsmen on the isle when he bought it and restored it tae how ye see the day." Colm was then happy to tell her about the boatyard's current financial viability, which gave the young locals some reassurance they'd have job in the near future.

Aela filed away the information as useful to her temporary job—nothing to do with her desire to know everything she could about her well-respected, workaholic, annoying boss. She returned to Garvald Castle warmed by the wine and the congenial company.

The door to Nairn's bedroom was shut tight as she passed. The office was empty, but at her desk she found a brief, impartial message—the police had called. She went to bed feeling very much the outsider, someone in the know, yet barely involved.

****

Professional politeness ruled from first greetings

the next day. Sometimes Aela looked up to find Nairn's heated gaze on her, then he would open an unnecessary conversation. His eyes betrayed something else before he veiled them—though she did wonder if she read more into his regard because it was what she wanted. And contrarily, didn't want.

She berated herself for being fascinated by him. What qualities were to like about the guy? He could be unfeeling, was a moody unpredictable sod at times, a workaholic...yet so attractive she wanted to weep! The inescapable fact was his rugged good looks and half mangled face did it for her every time! Something inside liquefied when she looked at him, and on the few occasions when he'd made meaningful contact, tiny snatched glances, it set off a longing she'd never before experienced. The ogre of Garvald Castle was the most stubborn, single-minded person she'd ever met, his self-discipline astonishing, but she wasn't sure if she admired him, or was just overpowered by those traits.

She determined to maintain the status quo for a few weeks, though, and suppress all libidinous thoughts. Soon she'd be home in Vancouver and Nairn Malcolm would just be someone else she'd met on her travels.

That notion didn't cheer her.

****

"Your wound's healing very nicely Nairn," Rhona declared later when she popped in. "I'm done with you. So long as someone tends to it on Sunday, you won't need me back again. A quick sterilizing and a clean dressing is all you'll need; the stitches are already dissolving. You're managing your personal hygiene then, Nairn?" Rhona's inquiry was deliberate, her statement falling into an unnatural tense silence. "You don't smell bad, but the citrus fragrance is pretty strong. Just use one or two, Nairn. No need to have Ruaridh buy up the whole island stock of baby wipes."

Rhona's chuckle reverberated long after she left.

So that was the fragrance! Aela's lips twitched though she didn't dare laugh outright because Nairn looked...so purple!

Baby wipes? Who else would have thought of using them as a temporary measure? Nonetheless, he smelled just too good for her liking. Ruaridh had said his independent son would find ways to overcome his current circumstances, and it would appear he had. She gave him full marks for ingenuity. The wipes were more successful than his hacking off the unwanted material of his sweatpants on the day she'd arrived. Aela chuckled at the memory.

Their time in the office was profitable, tandem working was even more successful than the previous day, but by late afternoon Nairn's disposition was back to remote. His rest had been short in the early afternoon, so he probably felt more pain than he admitted to.

Or, maybe his mood was due to the fact the police had come up with nothing conclusive. His London employees had been questioned; security tapes were being investigated; tapes from the Glasgow hotel car park had also been requisitioned, but were still under investigation. What could she do about his mood changes? She was his temporary employee, nothing more, she told herself for the umpteenth time.

Dinner, however, was agreeable. Not friendly, or intimate in any way, just pleasant. She still hankered after the veiled sexy looks of former days, but she also knew the lukewarm interaction was more professional. If Nairn could forget the attraction between them, then so could she. His inquiries about her background growing up in Vancouver showed a casual interest, and she in turn learned about his early years on Lanera before going off to university. She was astonished when he dismissed her afterward. She'd thought they'd been getting on fine. She would have been happy to spend the evening with him just hanging around the castle—was disappointed no end that she wasn't!

Aela was enjoying the evening sunshine outside a different bar a little while later when Ruaridh joined her. "Hello, lass!" His greeting cheered as though it was a happening every day of the week. "How are things progressing up at the castle? Nairn driven you mad yet?"

"He's getting closer." Aela laughed at Ruaridh's humor, and far too coincidental arrival. "He's trying, though I don't know him well enough for it to happen yet. I need to know people very well before I get caught in such a trap."

"You'll know him soon, lass. My son's very predictable. Just been to see him—given me my marching orders, too. Claims he doesn't need my assistance."

"Rhona told him to cut back on the baby wipes, so you won't have to go and buy any more of them." Aela grinned at the memory of Nairn's discomfiture.

Ruaridh agreed Nairn would have been mortally offended they knew what he'd been using but divulged the pack of baby wipes held much more than fiddly cleansing pads for women.

Aela's giggle was infectious. "Oh he'd be stinking now, rather than use them, Ruaridh!"

After a pleasant few hours learning about Lanera and its history, she set off back to the castle with Ruaridh in tow. Although it wasn't quite dark, it being almost the longest day of the year, there was no way he would let her walk home alone, even though she told him she'd done it the night before. He didn't come in when they reached the castle door, but he did bid her a raucous goodnight.

As Aela passed the downstairs bedroom a seriously aggravated looking Nairn blocked her way. "I see you've managed to attract an admirer already."

His acerbic jibe bit her to the quick.

"Yes, I guess I have, sir! For your information, it was your father." She noted the furious eyes sparking at her and got even more annoyed. "We met in Mariskay and, being the gentleman he is, he walked me home. What's your problem, anyway? You told me you didn't want me tonight!"

She glared at the tense set of his shoulders as he hunched over the crutch, his eyes wild and dark, an unleashed fury bubbling. "You're not in the wheelchair?"

"Glad you noticed. I don't want it anymore." The sound of the crutch clattering to the floorboards added to his anger. "But I do want you—"

Nairn's lips slammed down in a kiss, which was as explosive as it was unexpected. His tongue thrust against her closed teeth, probing till she opened to him. By degrees, the kiss turned from an insensitive demand to a thorough seeking. Nairn's lips softened, his tongue learning the insides of her sensitive mouth again, but she found she was devouring him just as much as he was her. She had gone from shock to arousal then in instants, wantonly urgent. She wanted everything this man could give; had never felt an escalation of passion like this!

Nairn shunted her against the wall, his lower body pressed into her as his hand slipped around her neck to caress the sensitive area there. His lips shifted to explore her cheekbones, her closed eyes, her temples before they surged back down and swooped onto her frantic mouth, mimicking a thrusting her body wanted echoed below. Their breaths mingled to exhaustion till he moaned her name.

His left hand slipped off the spaghetti strap of the light camisole and bared her shoulder. His lips followed, teeth nipping at her soft skin as his fingers feathered her collarbone before sliding down inside the cotton to cup her braless breast. She allowed everything, feeling herself trembling with anticipation, but it still wasn't enough!

Not nearly enough.

Nairn pushed the camisole strap down her arm, slipping it off her wrist and out of the way. She shuddered as he nudged his arousal against her.

"Nairn? What..." An enormous whimper lingered as his mouth covered her nipple. He teased and licked, flicking his tongue, bringing it to a hard round tip. A sharp throb shot straight to her womb as she gasped and held him tight in place. Passion escalated. "Oh...Jeeze...more...please more."

Men had caressed her in the past, but she'd never been charged with this sort of urgency. As Nairn continued to tease, she spiraled out of control to somewhere she'd never visited. But Aela wanted to be there. Her instinctive gasps had him tasting much more of her before his lips traced back to her mouth for another greedy kiss. The fingers of his casted hand slid up to remove the other strap, his erection rocking against her throbbing center as one fingernail hitched in to slide off the thin band. Her top slid to her waist, baring both her breasts. Nairn's hands crept forward to caress them, the rough edge on the arm cast stabbing into Aela's tender flesh.

"No! Nairn! Stop!" she cried out.

He wrenched his lips away, his look furious. His eyes darted to her reddened breast and then his plastered arm. His cursing was violent before he hobbled into the bedroom, slamming the door behind him.

It took minutes for Aela's heart to stop pounding and her mind to gain control. The whole episode had been so unforeseen, and so rapid, she wondered if she'd imagined it. Why was he so angry? She'd squealed her head off, for sure, but it had been to make him aware of where the cast was gouging her. She hadn't wanted him to stop making love to her— far from it! Although he'd taken her by surprise, she was just as desperate as he seemed to be for some reaction between them, some resolution to the overpowering sexual wanting dogging them.

In the bedroom Nairn slumped against the wall. What the hell was he thinking? He'd made her bleed! Why had he thought he was capable of making love to her even if it had stemmed from his jealous frustration? He cursed himself for being such an idiot. His passion for her had been simmering all evening. For days now. She'd been out there doing who knew what, and with whom. Being confined to the castle and not knowing had almost killed him. He wanted her like he'd never wanted anyone before.

Was his father really pursuing her? He knew Ruaridh's voice too well not to have realized who'd walked her back to the castle. But she couldn't want Ruaridh, or her instinctive reactions to his kisses wouldn't be so full of the fiery excitement that was bubbling inside him. He'd felt her thumping pulse and scented her arousal. She was on fire for him just as he was for her.

Or...was she so practiced she was trying them both out? To judge who was a better bet? And then found him to be wanting because of his current injuries?

The persistent niggle continued. Could Aela like his father more than him? A horrific thought made his stomach tighten beyond belief. Aela a potential stepmother? Never in this lifetime was that going to happen. But neither could he dare touch her again— not till he was cast free.

Chapter Thirteen

Aela woke more confused than she'd ever been in her life. Sleep had been fitful, her senses too strung out to do more than toss and turn, as she replayed that incredible encounter. What had happened the night before? The cast had hurt her, but they could surely have worked out something. Never ever did she want to see such a horrified look on Nairn's face again. It was like he hated touching her, hated kissing her.

It was unfortunate the morning had dawned almost as dismal as her mood—the weather overcast with grey, brooding skies and a constant drizzle. Rain didn't normally bother her, but it seemed all too depressing for words. Nairn had told her at dinner the night before he wouldn't need her much over the weekend, and that he was going to do what the doctor ordered and rest up more. The time was virtually her own. No going near the office where she might meet up with him.

Sipping a glass of orange juice in her tiny kitchen, she decided exercise would lift her spirits. The temptation to saddle up and explore was strong. She felt like fleeing the castle, but it wouldn't be fun with the mist shrouding the area, she'd see very little and then disappointment would set in.

The pool. Such an unbelievable treat to use on a whim. Lapping till she was tired and hungry, she headed for the railing to exit the water just as Nairn entered on his crutch. Her stomach flipped, blood rushing ferociously to her head. Her fingers fumbled on the metal grip, her knees trembling as she climbed out. Should she ignore what had happened the night before?

Yes, she could do that, yet she could hardly ignore the man in front of her. In spite of her misgivings, yet again, Nairn managed to make her grin like a Cheshire cat. Black plastic garbage bags were an awkward wrap around his casts, kept in place by rubber bands, and he wore only boxer shorts. White silk.

Hells teeth!

They were virtually see-through in the pool lighting. Aela closed her eyes and said a little prayer—though whether it was for the strength to avoid looking at his powerful body, or to bask in its glory, she wasn't too sure. Her arousal clicked up another notch. Dear Hell again!

Snatching up the towel from the lounger she covered the instant beading of her nipples, praying her racing pulse wasn't obvious. "Good morning. I hope it's all right for me to use the pool?"

Nairn, it seemed, couldn't take his eyes off her. The skimpy bikini she wore was rendered invisible as he stared. "Of course you can use the pool. I can't swim for a while, though I'm going to indulge in the briefest of saunas. Even I'm balking at the lemon smell dogging me."

Aela realized he was ignoring the encounter of the previous evening. She could ignore her feelings, too. Couldn't she? She focused on something else. "I'm going to breakfast after I shower. Would you like some?"

Nairn looked far too mesmerized by the beads of water running down between her breasts to answer her question, which had more than one interpretation. "Some? Mmm, I haven't had some...not yet." His gaze eventually looked up. "What were your plans?"

"A traditional Scottish breakfast?" she

suggested, attempting a distraction with humor. "No tartan but Kirsty's dead set on me having square sliced sausage with haggis in the middle, and black pudding. My little refrigerator is groaning with the stuff. I don't eat that kind of breakfast on a week day, but since today's Saturday, perhaps you'll join me?"

"In the apartment?" Nairn's throat clearing was so loud Aela couldn't fail to hear it. His gaze slipped away to look at the water before he answered. "How about we assemble our resources in the main kitchen instead, although you'll have to accept I'll just be the onlooker!" Glittering blue eyes locked onto hers, a whimsical smile lifted the corner of his lip.

Aela moved toward the door to exit the pool suite, but he blocked the way. "I owe you an apology for last night, Miss Cameron." His eyes sought her forgiveness yet the banked heat was unambiguous.

"No! You don't, sir. The way I see it there was equal blame, though it won't happen again." She broke the intense eye contact making sure her words were clear. "I'm sorry too. You don't date employees, I don't do flings, and I want to keep this job."

Aela stiffened her shoulders as she brought her gaze back up to face him, the small smile she produced she hoped displayed no offence. "So, how about we start again and try for professional only?" She held out her left hand for him to shake.

"Friends?" Nairn's question was loaded, as was his regard.

Aela hoped she appeared calm, but inside she was churning like a hot spring because the concept of being just a friend of this man was anathema. "No extras. Just friends!"

Their eyes locked in acceptance. She guessed neither of them truly believed it, though. And Nairn only relinquished her hand when she pulled it free.

Twenty minutes later both were dried and

dressed and in the kitchen, at least Aela was dressed. The wheelchair a thing of the past, Nairn hobbled around in the ubiquitous bath robe. It was tied securely at his waist, which was unfortunate since Aela couldn't see which boxers he was wearing. Her small groan was accompanied by a reluctant smile as she tucked such thoughts away. None of that. They'd made a pact. Heavens. She'd stick to it. Somehow she would.

Together they decided what to include in their hot calorie-laden breakfast, Aela making an effort to be unaffected by her feelings. Nairn? Maybe? But she wasn't too sure.

"Yes, fruit!" Her smile was adamant. "Peaches, mango and strawberries."

"Sure...okay." Nairn teased. "Hey, I like fruit. Just not on the same plate as my eggs, haggis and black pudding."

Aela grinned. "It's a good balance. Live dangerously."

"You don't think I'm doing that already? Looking like this?" Nairn's eyebrows almost hit the ceiling, his chortle amazingly endearing.

"Okay!" Aela beamed. "Sorry. Poor choice of words."

The words may have been too close to the bone, yet they did lighten the mood. They were comfortable with each other as Aela assembled their meal, though Nairn got in her way rather a lot as he attempted to set the table, the best sort-of-help he could manage. The occasional brushing together of their bodies she put down to his awkward movements, though she knew it was a lie. She could have moved more quickly. So why wasn't she?

The meal was amenable; she was in control of her yearnings, though they still hovered. They managed to have a decent conversation with him asking about her decision to travel the world and her future university plans. In turn she learned about his time at Edinburgh University and then his year afterward at Harvard Business School. "Whoa! Harvard. I'm so impressed. Nothing but the best finishing school, Mr. Malcolm."

"I never quite thought of it as such, Miss Cameron, but you're bang on the button." Nairn smiled. "My choice of Harvard was on purpose since it would improve my future business developments."

"Only the best on your CV?" she quipped.

"Never needed a CV. I've always been my own boss."

Her peal of laughter echoed around the kitchen. "I can see the prestige of having a Harvard qualification, though couldn't you have done your MBA in the UK? Somewhere with the same kudos?"

"Calling me a snob, Miss Cameron?"

"Would I dare?"

Her laugh faltered when his features sharpened. His good fingers drummed a short rhythm on the table as an enigmatic smile bathed his face. Aela waited, and waited. Then, a decision having been made, he carried on. "I needed to get the hell out of Scotland at the time, all the way out of Europe!"

She couldn't imagine what would have made it so important for him to ship out. He'd set up his diving school on Lanera with a legacy from his maternal grandmother. What would make him want to leave the country?

"The United States was far enough away for me to leave behind the trauma of my parents' divorce."

"Ah! Not an amicable separation?"

"Is there ever?" Nairn huffed, a rueful look flashing across to her. He paused a while before continuing, his words measured. "The Ruaridh you see now is a much more relaxed version than the one of fourteen years ago. Caitlinn, my mother, never liked staying on Lanera; hated the climate, constantly harped on about going somewhere warm."

Aela filled in the gaps as he revealed details. "Ruaridh had his boatyard business here?"

"Ruaridh wasn't a man to compromise when it came to the boatyard. He doesn't compromise on his lifestyle now either." At his intent stare, Aela wondered if he was highlighting what he regarded as his father's negative qualities on purpose. "My father, Miss Cameron, wouldn't budge his ass from Lanera even if a tsunami hit—not for my mother, and not for any woman."

"That bad?" she joked, though was curious for she didn't feel she'd had a real answer to her question. "But you still felt you had to be so far away?"

"They separated when I first went to University. Before the divorce papers were even drawn up my mother had taken up with an obscenely rich Spanish lover, a man she married at first opportunity." Nairn sounded so bitter Aela swallowed at his tone. "With future money no object, Caitlinn never lowered herself to haggle with Ruaridh over assets on Lanera during the divorce proceedings." He scrubbed his hair back before massaging his neck, a trait Aela realized highlighted his tension. "But she haggled constantly over me."

"But you were...what?" She was dumbstruck. "Nearly twenty?"

His eyes softened to a smolder when they found hers. "Caitlinn had existed for years being jealous of any time I spent with my father. After the divorce she wanted me to spend every vacation at her new home near Barcelona." Nairn appeared to shrug off unpleasant memories as he looked askance. "I wanted to be on Lanera to be at my own fledgling business. So, if I was on the island, it always appeared Ruaridh won the battle."

"Do you ever see her now?"

Nairn's eyes lightened a little as he dredged up a smile of sorts. "Sometimes...but still not as often as she'd like. But that's enough of my history for one session. Time for a break, Miss Cameron."

Aela was confused. Nairn's friendly attitude was what she wanted, what she'd suggested in the pool suite. She should be glad he was demonstrating he could maintain a control, which kept them within the bounds of employer and employee. But she didn't like it. It didn't make happy tingles. The tingles did still happen but they were somehow forlorn.

"I'm going back to work, though I won't need you. If the weather improves by midday, and conditions are favorable, you'd maybe like to take out the floatplane?"

"Yay! How do I learn a Scottish version of a reverse rain dance? Got Shamans-R-Us in your local directory?" Aela again retreated into humor to cover her chagrin.

Nairn's chuckle was her only answer as he hobbled off.

****

An occasional fluffy cirrus cloud shadowed the sky, but they were high enough not to be an issue for handling a floatplane. Heading to the key-safe she collided with Nairn coming out of the bedroom.

"Sorry. Wasn't paying attention," he laughed, looking so glad to see her the day seemed to get brighter.

Aela wasn't so sure of his apology, though. It seemed he'd just barreled himself out into the corridor, yet she wasn't quibbling since he'd just wrapped himself around her and held her tight. Heaven. Pity she didn't want the contact. What a liar she was as she snuggled into him!

"I'm heading down to the floatplane now," she mumbled at his shoulder, the lemony smell one she was getting used to. Reluctantly extracting her arms from their tangle she was pretty sure Nairn appeared as unwilling to break free as she was. She wanted to slide back into his embrace. And maybe...do a bit more than clutch? She hadn't properly touched him in ages.

It wasn't really a surprise when he told her taking out the floatplane was a great idea, but she could only do it if she took him too. Aela bristled like a porcupine; he was checking up on her flying skills. Her tone likely came over sharper than intended, but she didn't care to be an object of doubt and she took a deliberate step away from him. "Listen, you silly cretin. Those ribs of yours are not nearly well enough for a trip in a tight little floatplane. And there will be no room for that stiff cast of yours!"

To her total surprise Nairn's laugh was hearty, and didn't look too pained. Just a little squint showed his discomfort. "Don't you worry about my stiff...leg. Somehow I am going to fit." His deliberate hesitation didn't faze Aela. She glared at the offending body part...hmm...body parts, instead. His laugh rumbled even more. "I'm going stir crazy. I've checked the weather and everything's favorable."

There was no impediment to them taking out the floatplane.

Well, actually there was, but it was overcome with ease.

No way could Nairn negotiate the cliff staircase, so Aela deposited him at the boatyard, left him there to do a bit of catch-up while she nipped back to the castle and garaged the Range Rover. Afterward, she taxied the floatplane around the headland to the quayside slip, having done an even more thorough check than normal of the floatplane, to ensure no messy tampering problems. Nairn happily agreed with that strategy.

As she rounded the headland handling airplane controls again was so thrilling. Traveling had been a fun experience, but she'd missed flying so much.

With some geographical guidance from Nairn Aela flew the floatplane over the Isle of Mull, the birthplace of her grandfather, and further north over the Isle of Skye. Banking to the west took them over the Outer Hebrides, the flatter, more barren lands of North and South Uist, a huge contrast to the purple-topped mountainous Skye. Fabulous scenery. Her questions had been incessant but Nairn had seemed happy to satisfy every curiosity.

A few hours later Aela had clearly proved to Nairn she could fly his beloved floatplane.

"The jets you can prove another day, but it's time for me to give in and head home. It's time for more of those damned painkillers Sir Smash-Em-Up macho-me is taking regularly."

Aela grinned at the faces he was pulling knowing the ribs he'd claimed earlier were fine were anything but fine.

"Did you really call me that?" Though Nairn was laughing he seemed incredulous.

"Well, what was I supposed to think? Who the hell would interview looking like a train wreck? A re-enactment seemed to fit so well." Aela's hearty laugh echoed around them.

Back at the boat slip they were lucky to catch Jamie, who'd just completed an overtime shift. It was no trouble for him to organize Nairn's transport back to the castle.

Knowing her boss was in good hands, Aela taxied the floatplane back around the headland. It gave her the opportunity to check out his catamaran, the small dinghy and the kayaks in the cove boatshed. There was no way she would be taking out any of Nairn's transport without making thorough checks. One great advantage from having worked in her Uncle Harris's company meant she'd learned plenty about engines and working parts of many kinds of vehicles before she'd even been allowed to fly or drive them. By the time she locked up the boatshed she was happy all was in order with the assembled craft, but she was almost late for dinner!

Her backpack didn't run to elegant eveningwear, though she did have a couple of tops of good quality she'd bought in Italy. The one she wore to dine was already a firm favorite of hers—deep purple with sequins and overstitching. The fact that she wore it had nothing at all to do with any strategy to ensnare Nairn Malcolm. That didn't even cross her mind. Mmm. What was that thing she'd thought the day before about lying to oneself? Maybe she merited no Olympic gold spirit, but she was still buzzed from their enjoyable afternoon.

"Aela," Kirsty exclaimed when she arrived at the dining room. "You look so pretty in that color. Doesn't she look fine, Nairn?"

The whisper of sound passing Nairn's lips as Kirsty bustled out of the room was probably an assent, but since his intent look was fixed on her body, Aela was in no doubt of his agreement. After a long pause he met her gaze. His deep blue irises radiated lust. And sheer frustration.

"Gorgeous," he rasped. "But then you look stunning in everything."

"Thank you, sir. You're likely to see it often, since I don't have many alternatives." His compliment and hungry stare set up a heady anticipation, yet again. The man was lethal. The room was far too hot—weird, since the outside temperature could not be more than fifty-five Fahrenheit.

They picked up their casual banter of the afternoon, but the heightened sexual tension almost strangled her. One of his tiny glances, or the merest brush of their fingers when she helped him cut awkward parts of his pasta, intensified the tension.

"I know you're having your meal, Aela, but someone called Jed was on the castle's phone line," Kirsty informed her as she brought their next course. "When I said you were eating, he told me it was fine if you phone him back later. He said he's missed you so bad."

"I'm missing him too, Kirsty. Thanks for the message. I'll call back as soon as I can."

Aela's smile was reciprocated by Kirsty but not by her employer. He regressed to grumpy curmudgeon for the rest of the meal. "I don't need you any more tonight. Take the time off to do whatever you like!"

Aela watched his tense back muscles as he leaned on his crutch and stomped off as much as one can with a leg cast. Bloody chameleon! She felt quite the petulant child. Well, she didn't need him either.

The temptation was high to go down to Mariskay. Saturday evening might be a lively night for the locals but she wasn't feeling lively any more. Instead, in the office apartment, she decided to do more of her ancestry researching of official government records. The information she already had on her great grandfather's relatives was scant, and Ruaridh had given her some more sites to try. But before that...

"Jed!" Aela clucked. "You were checking up on me again." Her cousin always cheered her up, even if his tendency to be overprotective sometimes annoyed her.

****

Nairn succumbed. He'd forced himself to work but his concentration was shattered, he needed to know if Aela had gone out. Like the night before. Jealousy of Ruaridh, this Jed person, and maybe other unknown men, ate at his gut.

Frustration crippled him almost as much as his leg cast. Full attention from a woman he was dating was what he liked when they were together, but he'd never bothered about what the woman might be doing when he wasn't with her.

What did his feelings mean now? Was he jealous because he'd got used to Aela's proximity? Was it because they weren't just sharing a workspace but, almost their living quarters? Regardless of those answers, he missed her. Missed looking over at her; missed hearing her sexy, husky voice, yes, even when her laughter was overt, or berating his stupidity regarding his health. Missed her cheeky smile and twinkling censure. Missed her hot lust-filled glances when she thought he wasn't noticing. His frustration deepened, his sexual want for Aela Cameron was the itch he couldn't scratch under his plaster. He just plain wanted everything about her. The woman had wormed right in and had lodged herself deep inside him.

At the apartment he found the sitting room door wide open and a loud throbbing beat playing on the music system. Sitting with her back to him she seemed intent, working on the computer. She was home, and he felt like a louse for checking up on her. Relieved, but still a louse. He turned and hobbled to his lonely office.

He wanted her at her desk across the room, but he was the one who'd chased her away. As his employee, she deserved time off, but he needed to be with her. He looked down at his casts and in a miserable temper tossed his crutch away, all the while willing the ever-erect tent to collapse.

Chapter Fourteen

"Aela!"

The bellow shocked Aela as she rinsed her hair in the shower. Punching off the water she grabbed a towel wondering what on earth the matter was. The previous day, Nairn had seemed so much better—give or take his bad moods. No symptoms of concussion had returned, his ribs were causing fewer problems, and walking with his crutch was less awkward. Rushing out, tucking the towel in place into her cleavage, she found him entering the bedroom in search of her.

"What's wrong?" She took in the sight of his naked torso at once. She was shivering, naked; he was almost naked—and that's all it took for lust to rob her of breath.

"Sorry." Nairn's gaze fixed on her face as he stared at the rivulets of water she felt trickling from her hair. He looked jumpy, as though it was a great effort to keep his eyes north of her shoulders. "I didn't think before I barged in. I'll leave you to get dressed. Talk to you later."

Turning around too swiftly he hobbled away.

"No! Nairn. Wait. Mmm...sir." Aela found her voice, flustered by his regard. He hadn't been able to mask the naked yearning, even though it'd just been fractions of a second. "What did you want?"

His throat sounded rough when he turned back. "I can't get the new dressing on. I wondered if you could help me."

Aela found her own voice hoarse, her craving a strangling at her throat. "Give me a couple of minutes, and I'll be along to help you."

She stared as he lurched out of the room. It was the first time he'd asked for help regarding his injuries. Her body throbbed, and the hard beads of her breasts rasped against the fabric of the cotton towel. Nairn's chest was naked again—and what a sight to behold, even with the ragged reddening of his chest wound. Her tormented gaze dropped to the floor.

Could she manage a whole month of resistance? Another day? Now she didn't care. She wasn't going to struggle against it any more, or she'd combust. It would be the perfect end to her world travels. A no-strings affair before she went home to her future in Vancouver? Like never before?

Anticipation deepened as she taped on the new dressing, her fingers trembling so much she thought she wouldn't be able to smooth it into place. Nairn's whole ribcage was now a myriad of lighter purples, green-yellows, greyish-blacks; still bruised but pulsing with a need to be stroked and kissed. She smoothed the edges of the tape with great care. Nairn's singular male scent mingled with the citrus smell emanating around him and made her want to lick his bruising like a cat or dog might do to their own wounds. She'd never had this protective, nurturing streak before, had even thought herself incapable of deep sentiments. This man—and only this man—presently under her fingertips was unlocking that Pandora's Box of emotions.

She could feel Nairn's minute trembles, his face dipping down toward her bent head. She couldn't fail to hear the sniff when his nose drew deep of the scent of her newly shampooed hair. His hand reached up and stroked her still-wet locks.

"Aela?" Nairn sounded strangled.

"Am I hurting you?"

The lightweight combat trousers he was wearing

crinkled and moved in front of her eyes. Nairn clutched her chin and enclosed her mouth with his, his tongue urgent, the kiss deepening. Eager. Unbridled. He tasted so good. The mint of his toothpaste mingled with something more tangy-raspberry or some kind of soft fruit he'd breakfasted on. The rest was pure Nairn.

Aela was lost, unable to do anything but ardently respond as her hands slipped around his deliciously warm chest, the insanity of it escaping her till she felt Nairn's agonized gasp against her lips. She felt the tremors of his desire, and his flaring erection at her stomach, but she also felt the sheer ache of his ribs at her nerve ends for her grip of his torso was still too tight. His face leeched color, his breathing erratic and troubled. Breaking free, her embarrassment was as heated as her voice.

"Nairn. I told you we can't do this!"

His body wasn't ready for more stress even if his emotions and rigid arousal cried out for it. She had to suppress her own overpowering desire or make him need another hospital visit if she didn't back away. She was no feeble or delicate woman. The lifestyle she'd led had made her what she was, a strong woman, with hands and muscles to match. And now she'd met Nairn Malcolm she knew her passions were strong too. There was no choice, though; she had to back off.

The lie she produced was so hard to voice, it nearly crumpled her to her knees. "I told you already I don't want this. I don't do passing flings. And you don't date employees!"

Nairn's hand reached out and brought her mouth close again, recapturing her lips. Though it lasted mere moments, this time the kiss was tender. It still demanded a response, a response she wanted to give yet she knew was wrong. "No! We can't do this." Pulling free from his grip, she retreated out of the room and flew down the corridor like a bat out of hell.

His faint cry echoed along the corridor. "We can, Aela. We will."

Clothes a haphazard throw on she bolted for the stables. Having made up her mind she could wait no longer to launch into an affair with him the timing was all wrong. He wasn't fit for making love to anyone and wouldn't be for some time. Knowing that didn't stop her feverish mind from perfecting the best approach to make love to a body with two plaster casts and extreme sensitivity around the torso. How perverted did that make her? But she wasn't sure she cared any more.

It was regrettable Lanera had no huge prairie to gallop out her demons. On the positive side there was a horse available she could use.

After her ride, and some light tack cleaning, she headed down to Mariskay for lunch, to avoid Nairn yet again, having made her apologies to Kirsty. Her meal had just arrived at an outside table of the harbor restaurant when Ruaridh appeared. It was so coincidental Aela knew Kirsty must have phoned him.

"How come you're here and my son isn't? What's he up to today?"

"No idea. Left him to his own devices." Masking the pain from her statement wasn't easy.

"So Nairn's giving you the cold shoulder?" Ruaridh's question was serious.

"We're being polite and businesslike, Ruaridh, which is how it should be. How it must be!"

She was amazed when Ruaridh invited her to go out in his catamaran. How could she refuse, desperate as she was to learn how to navigate them, to do her transporting jobs well? It was much easier than the learning curve becoming a detached employee to Nairn Malcolm.

Nairn was asleep on one of the huge couches in the great room, his full length stretched out, on her return to Garvald Castle. She'd missed him all afternoon; how stupid was that? He was so handsome in repose. None of those ugly frowns marred his attractive face, no lines fanning out from his lips indicating disapproval; any residual bruising faded to a faint yellowish tinge. She wanted to capture his curving lips and taste them. Prudence won, though, and she crept out instead.

"I'm not quite asleep," Nairn called, but she could tell she'd wakened him by the sleepy pitch of his voice. Sexy. So sexy.

"Sorry, I tried not to wake you," she whispered, warmed not just by his tone but by his intense scrutiny of her skimpy shorts and camisole.

Nairn's movements were sinuous as he worked himself upright. A pair of swim shorts was all he wore, though she was sure he hadn't been so rash as to use the pool. "Had a nice relaxing day?" His inquiry was casual, but his eyes were hooded.

"Lovely." She didn't quite know how to respond to him, he was being so nice.

"I told you the day was yours, but if you don't have any evening plans, would you mind driving us both down to Mariskay for a meal?" His inquiry was apologetic, followed by the admission he'd told Kirsty she'd not need to cook on the Sunday evening.

"I'm happy to drive you down, though you don't have to include me in your dinner plans."

"The truth, Aela?" The rise to his feet awkward, he dominated her airspace once he was standing. "If you're with me I'll not be accosted by well-wishers every two seconds. You could save me from such a fate, surely?"

The teasing grin accompanying his request was a deal breaker. How could she resist? "Your ego wouldn't need polishing a little, would it?" she jested, amazed at his arrogance, yet having learned how well thought of he was she didn't doubt there would be people who'd stop by asking after his health.

She wasn't wrong.

The meal was not at all romantic as there was a constant interruption of people asking after him. The tension between them lightened till Ruaridh arrived as they started on their desserts.

"Aela! I'm so glad to see you." Ruaridh swallowed her in a big bear hug. "So you've given up the chariot, Nairn?" Ruaridh launched in without preamble when he straightened back up. "Feeling much better?"

At first, Nairn continued to fork his chocolate pistachio mousse with determined precision. "Thought I was." His reply was cryptical since he didn't look at Ruaridh. "Now, maybe less so." All Ruaridh did was grin.

"Aela? Got personal things to talk to you about. I forgot to tell you this afternoon," Ruaridh declared after a few minutes of general chitchat. "Maybe we could meet tomorrow night after work?"

With startling speed their waitress was signaled, the bill paid and in double quick time Aela found herself outside the restaurant. No coffee. No further chat to Ruaridh. Not even a proper goodbye because as soon as Nairn had tossed down some banknotes on the table he limped toward the door. Aela had made her apologetic goodbyes to a grinning Ruaridh.

Nairn didn't speak at all on the way back. Blowing hot and cold with her seemed to be his favorite pastime. He was so unbearably rude to his father, she hadn't a clue what'd caused it, but she couldn't condone his manner.

Unlocking the back door she preceded him inside, feeling around for the hall light switch. In her wake Nairn declared he was heading for the office, his eyes lingering on hers for much longer than ever before when she turned back to him, a question there she couldn't interpret before he bid her a clipped goodnight. He wasn't angry. His silent question was almost-disappointment?

It took her unawares when he whirled back and pinned her to the wall, the full-body collision a surprise to them both when he grunted in pain. The swift hard kiss was devastating, demanding a response she was all too eager to return, but it was too brief, since before she'd time to even realize what was happening, he lurched away, his breathing an alarming rasp in the hush of the silent house.

Aela touched her fingertips to her bruised mouth, bemused at first, and then angry he could rouse her so easily with his aggressive and contrary attitude. She couldn't pretend not to be affected by the blasted man. But what he wanted she couldn't seem to give him, at least she didn't think so since he kept walking away.

****

Aela experienced the full force of Nairn's dynamic personality when she presented herself in the office just after eight a.m. Monday, the beginning of the traditional working week. Traditional for some—Nairn's week proved to be a little different.

"Miss Cameron." She'd begun to dread the formality of her surname. "We're leaving by nine o'clock. I need to do a day trip to my London headquarters. Already checked weather and landing conditions, and maintenance in Glasgow has the jet on standby."

Aela almost blew a gasket. They had planned this but later in the week when he might be fit to do it. "Are you loco? You could barely manage a few hours in the floatplane on Saturday, so what the friggin' heck makes you think you're ready for a trip to London and back?" Nairn's one-eyebrow lift was impressive, but Aela wasn't fazed by it. "All the healing you've done to date will be for nothing, you stupid prat!"

Since Nairn wasn't put off in the least by her censure she stomped to her computer and powered up, muttering dire warnings—all ignored.

Nairn detailed his usual flying procedures that she made a hasty note of for future reference. His mood was light, yet she didn't quite trust it. Why, or what, would make him so changed from the angry man of the evening before?

"For this first trip would you prefer a chartered pilot to take us from Glasgow to London? Now, don't get your hackles up! I'm asking because I also need you in the capacity of my PA immediately after the flight."

Aela's frown must have shown she wasn't sure how to interpret his inquiry. On the one hand he could doubt her expertise, yet on the other he could be thinking about her energy reserves as she juggled the different jobs. Either way, this was a first test of her stamina and of her capabilities. "I'll be fine with all the transportation, and with my role as PA."

"Glad to hear it." Nairn nodded, then detailed the calls they each had to make before they left, and the correspondence needing completion before leaving.

Around 8:45, Nairn declared he was off to change out of the ubiquitous dressing robe. Scooting off herself, she donned her one and only suit.

Ten minutes later he was at the office door wearing an unbuttoned short-sleeved white shirt and a pair of black cargo pants, one leg unzipped to the knee. A striped tie lay across his arm on top of a formal suit jacket of soft black cashmere. She heard an irritated exhalation of breath as he lurched into the office.

"I'm going to have to call up that extra clause on your contract."

Aela's eyebrows rose in inquiry from the delicious sight of his bare chest; she hadn't a clue what he was talking about.

"It's too difficult to fasten all these small buttons, and there's no way in hell I can tie my tie."

Her surprised chortle couldn't be suppressed. "You expect me to tie your tie? How do you know I can?"

"I've every confidence in you."

"Do you need to be so formal?" she asked, tamping down the rush of yearning, amazed in his present circumstances formal clothing was necessary.

"I always wear a tie at the London office, and I'm not going to change that because of a blip in my health." His eyes strayed down to the cargo pants. "This is as close as I can get at the moment to cover my legs, though I assure you, I do need the tie."

Aela spent the next few minutes getting to grips with her churning attraction as she deftly fastened his buttons, re-zipped the leg of his pants as far as it would go over his cast, again ignoring the visible sign of attraction he pretended wasn't happening. Tying a tie was easy since she'd worn a tie at school and knew how to do it, except tying it for Nairn meant very close proximity to her heavily breathing boss.

Nairn reached forward to hold onto her shoulders, just for stability of course. Ignoring the pressure of his gentle squeezing and the whisper of his lips when they got closer to her hair she bent her head. No, they hadn't touched her.

Liar, again!

She pulled the knot up into place, her fingers purposely caressing his neck before she smoothed down his collar. The breath she huffed on purpose onto his stretched up adam's apple made his skin erupt into little goose pimples. The swift fall of his mouth on hers wasn't a surprise either. It lasted only seconds but was...incredible. Hard. Stirring. Seeking. Arousing. Too short.

Over.

Nairn's fingers curled on her shoulders as he put her away from him, his sigh loud, so close to her ear. "Enough. Thank you, Miss Cameron."

Nairn found Aela's ministrations excruciating. Being so close to her bent head was killing him. His good hand twitched, wanting to drag itself through her waterfall of intense shiny hair. His mind strayed to the question of how he could use Aela to fill that sneaky little clause, which now had more connotations. How precisely could she help him with other needs due to his lack of mobility?

For the first time in days he felt more in control.

During the little valet session he'd told Aela that Ruaridh had popped in already but had stayed a very short time. He'd been particular about her reactions to the information, glad when he detected nothing more than a small regret on her part that she'd missed him. He felt quite cheery when they began their journey.

Chapter Fifteen

"Almost in Glasgow," Aela shouted to Nairn. "So, was that spectacular or what?"

Nairn's dry answer blasted her ear. "Not down yet, so I guess a nine and three quarters."

A little after ten o'clock they were moving away from the hangar where the floatplane was berthed. Aela laughed at Nairn's comment. They sat atop one of the powered baggage carts while it chugged them along to Nairn's jet. She had warned the ground crew that this time Nairn might just need a little shunt between planes. Glasgow to London was the next leg of the journey, and she just couldn't wait to get her hands on the jet controls. She'd been conscious of the way her skirt rode up her thighs as she'd used the foot controls in the floatplane but decided not to make an issue of it knowing Nairn was affected by her proximity, as much as she was by him. She was now attuned to his never diminishing crinkling tent.

Nairn's jet was a delight to fly, a newer version than any she'd flown before. Too soon she followed instructions from air traffic control in London for descent, and after that handed the plane over to maintenance crew. Her next challenge presented itself; the greatest so far since flying had been a pleasure. Another Range Rover awaited them, Aela expected to drive it to the London office. She'd spent five days as a tourist in London when she'd made landfall in the UK, and knew London traffic was vastly different from Lanera. Her boast about being competent with any transport Nairn might require had just boomeranged back and bitten her on the butt. Yet, she could do it. She would.

Nairn hobbled down the jet ramp, swearing profoundly. It was followed by an apology. "Sorry. I didn't think ahead enough to ask if you'd rather have had a driver get us to the office." When both of his feet were on terra firma he smiled at her then explained, "I'm so used to doing all this myself I haven't broken it down to individual transportations."

She made sure her grin looked confident. "My driver's license allows me to drive in the UK, and we've sorted out insurance details. With directions I'll get us where you want us to be, so long as you don't expect me to scoot around like a London cabbie—there's no way I could do that!"

Nairn's answer was good-humored. "I don't expect you to be familiar with London streets. Soon, though?"

His smile wasn't just around his mouth, his deep blue eyes twinkled a smile just for her, and the day seemed to get brighter.

The drive was daunting. Thank heavens for Satellite Navigation! The posh voice was very clear and helped her negotiate the route. All she'd to do was concentrate on driving on the left and wend her way through the traffic throng. Soon she parked in a dedicated bay at an impressive waterfront development, which housed Nairn's main office building and two warehouses.

His glance settled on her as she set the parking brake and turned off the ignition. "Not too late to back out, Miss Cameron."

Aela knew very well what he was doing, but she wouldn't change her mind anytime soon. Their eyes clashed as she shook her head. "Nice offer, thank you, but I'm here for the duration and in this quest just as much as you are now, sir. Shall we get to work?"

Stepping out of the car, she slung their laptop cases across her shoulder, fisted his walking aid, and booted her door closed before she went round to hand Nairn the metal cane.

"Don't say you didn't have your chance!" His jaw was set, a steel glint in his eye as he maneuvered himself out of the car.

The swift kiss he planted on her when he straightened up wasn't really a surprise—it was inevitable. Need had been building all morning. That it was rapid was a disappointment for she would really have liked a very long tasting, but the car park outside his office was definitely not the place.

"If you're sure about not deserting, then let's get on with it."

"I don't feel like abandoning you today, sir." She zinged the automatic locking device and opened the entrance door to the offices. "A problem shared is a problem halved? Isn't that what they say?"

He still appeared uncomfortable with the idea of her being with him. "So I've heard, but my problems shouldn't be your problems."

Their entering the building created quite a stir.

"Mr. Malcolm! You'll need the elevator today." The entrance level receptionist gushed as she hastened over the tiled foyer to summon the car. "I didn't know you'd had an accident."

"Sandra, this is my new PA, Aela Cameron. She needs a security pass. Organize it, please. Field all my calls through her direct line, and send Robert up to my office right away!"

Aela had barely time to note the doors with clear insignias for Nairn's different companies, Lanwater: Traders; Dry Gear; and Whitecaps.

"Personnel and Payroll Departments on this side," he barked at her. "The link door leading to the warehouses is the one at the far end of that corridor beyond the security office."

A bright purple head popped out of one of the offices, noted Nairn's injuries and made a hasty retreat. "Mr. Malcolm's here!"

The comment was no doubt intended to be a stage whisper, yet they heard it clearly. Aela could well imagine the flutter inside the office. She guessed as soon as the elevator was in motion his health issues would spread like wildfire before they even reached his top floor office suite. As they exited on the top floor Nairn ushered her into the Gale Breakers office and made introductions. She'd already spoken with the woman on the phone so there was marginal familiarity.

Nairn spent no more time than necessary on updates from Lanera then led her into his small Technical Division. It housed a computer department and a room serving as a base for his small team of technicians.

"Nairn Malcolm, what the hell have you done to yourself?"

Aela was surprised by the informality of the question being asked by a female seated at a large bank of computer monitors. The woman's head bobbed as she tut-tutted, appearing highly amused by Nairn's state of health.

"Good morning is all the greeting I need today, Miss Faulds!"

Nairn smiled at the woman who was still chuckling and muttering to herself about idiots who should only sell and not try out all the products.

"Ginny Faulds, meet Aela Cameron, my new PA."

"Glad to see you got lucky about something, Mr. Malcolm!" Ginny chortled, the stare she sent Aela's way quite blatant.

Nairn looked from woman to woman, his grin wide. "You know something? I believe I did, Ginny."

Aela had no idea of the relationship between these two people, but they were very comfortable with each other as Nairn got a brief update on the department's progress.

Robert, the security guard, was already waiting in Nairn's office by the time they entered.

"There's nothing at all, Robert?" Nairn sounded frustrated, the lack of evidence a disappointment he couldn't seem to mask.

Robert confirmed he'd looked at the security tapes, along with police officers, and nothing from the previous Thursday, when the tank problem was discovered, appeared suspect. He clarified the tapes from the previous two weeks were still being checked, the police matching up movements with personnel who were legitimate around the area. "The warehouse staff has been interviewed but nothing has transpired from that."

With no new information to process, they sat down to work. In some ways Aela found the office situation easier. As PA, she had her own front office. Nairn occupied a spacious corner office overlooking the Thames. Now, she wasn't aware of his dominating presence every second on the opposite side of the room, but it did mean buzzing him often before transferring some of the constant calls coming up from the main switchboard.

A couple of hours later, she buzzed him yet again. "Warehousing just rang about the new two-clip buoyancy aids for kayaking." She checked her notes. "They think you should assess them before they're dispatched to Adrenalinn Adventuring, Tallinn, Estonia. Someone in warehousing doesn't sound happy about them."

Almost before she'd finished speaking Nairn hobbled toward her. "Let's go. It's time for you to meet Adrenalinn Adventuring staff and visit the stockrooms."

She'd been surprised nobody from the floor below had made any kind of excuse to come and talk to him, but then again, with a grin she had difficulty suppressing, she guessed why no one had bearded the grouchy ogre's den.

They exited the elevator on the floor below, Aela trekking behind as Nairn got into a good lurching rhythm and entered a large office with a dozen littered desks, manned by clicking staff in rapid communication with customers. Nairn stopped at the desk of Robin Ellesmere, the Manager of Adrenalinn Adventuring, introduced her and asked for an update on the buoyancy aids in question.

"The spring clips are harder to operate than those from our last manufacturer. In extreme conditions they might be too difficult to deal with, but I don't have the practical kayaking experience you have, Nairn, to be sure about them."

"When did you place the order?"

"Stella organized it about a month ago. Remember you requested a bigger front pocket than those on the previous design?"

Nairn nodded. "Sure, but I don't remember okaying this manufacturer."

"I'd need to check, but I'm pretty sure Stella got a better deal on this batch, so long as it was a bulk order, that's why it went through."

As Robin answered Nairn's question he pointed out an example for Aela on a brochure to bring her up to speed.

Nairn nodded acceptance of Robin's reservations over the goods in question. They were going to climes that were often very cold at times, and deficiencies couldn't be contemplated. "I'm taking Miss Cameron on a tour of the warehouses, so I'll look at them when I'm there."

Nairn lurched away from Robin, passed the next desk, which was empty, and moved on. Aela was quite used by then to his terse announcements as he introduced her to the rest of the staff, but she detected a tension that didn't seem related to his injuries or to the staff's concern for his welfare. Nairn scanned around as though he wanted to avoid something...or someone.

"Stella isn't here today?" Nairn asked Robin.

Aela knew from personnel lists Stella Grainger had joined the company some months before as Assistant Manager of Adrenalinn Adventuring.

"She's down at payroll. There was an issue about the wages and conditions for the staff at our bungee site in Perthshire."

"I've heard nothing of it."

Nairn's brow was creased. Aela had already realized he hated to be out of the loop about anything, though delegation meant he was only informed about the larger issues.

"Want me to send her up to you later, Nairn?" Robin's chuckling request was accompanied by twitching of his eyebrows, a suggestive twitching she wasn't meant to miss. Robin's hearty laugh accompanied Nairn's silent exit.

Aela wouldn't pry; it was none of her business. Nairn had told her he didn't date employees, and even if he'd forgotten, or lied, it was still nothing to do with her. A slow tour of the rest of the premises followed, where she was introduced to the staff

Nairn knew his business intimately and had a good rapport with his workers. They were respectful; no animosity toward him—in fact there was a general camaraderie. So, who on earth had been sticking knives in Nairn Malcolm?

The journey around the warehouses exhausted Nairn. His brow furrows deepened with every move forward, although she knew him well enough to recognize he was unwilling that his employees should see his debilitation. But if he was as well liked, as it seemed, why were the incidents happening?

Nairn interrupted her slight distraction. "Miss Cameron! We'll take a sample up to my office. I'd like to have another think about it, John."

John Reid, the warehouse manager, passed a floatation vest over for her to carry.

"Maybe someday I'll get a chance to try one of these out," she said as she hitched the buoyancy aid over one shoulder. "I fancy kayaking in Estonia, but I never made it so far north in Europe."

John's friendly replies were cut short by Nairn's declaration that they were done and were returning to his office. As they headed back along to the elevator, she sighed. The ogre was back. An incommunicative Nairn occupied the elevator car alongside her.

His voice buzzed through the intercom a while later. "I'm through with the buoyancy aid. Could you take it back to the stockroom, please?"

A blatant inquiry if he'd remembered his pain killers resulted in one of his condescending black glowers. Time to make a strategic exit, but first she went in to collect the vest.

"Call in to the Adrenalinn office, please, and give Robin this file for counter-signature." Nairn's request was accompanied by a suppressed grunt as he stretched his arm a little too far, his last words gagged.

"Not a problem." Aela's answer was blithe, amazed at his stamina but bugged by his determination to act normal when he clearly wasn't. "It's way past time for you to chew down some more happy pills and take a break, sir, but I don't suppose you're going to listen to little ol' me." Another black glower was the answer as she picked up the buoyancy aid and slung it across her shoulder.

There was no way she was waiting for the

elevator when Nairn wasn't with her. She skipped down the narrow staircase and elbowed her way in the Adrenalinn Adventuring office door. A blur of russet hair flashed past, almost knocking her down as she made an awkward negotiation of the buoyancy aid in one hand and the now cascading file of papers in the other. Someone was in a hurry! But Aela wasn't and she was going to take some time out from Nairn.

Using Robin as a fount of knowledge, she spent some time clarifying issues she was still unclear about.

Returning the buoyancy aid was her next priority. Thinking about the way to the warehouses, she stepped onto the lower staircase leading to the ground floor. A few skips down, her foot slipped off the step; her whole body launched itself clear into the air, feet first, and she landed with a spectacular whoosh on the bottom step, right on top of the buoyancy aid which had somehow managed to end up under the small of her back. The air was punched right out of her lungs, her head whacked back like a whiplash on the concrete step behind it, and her legs sprawled out in an ungainly loll.

All within sight of anyone, and everyone, who was, at present, in the entrance foyer.

"Miss Cameron!" Sandra's shriek as she ran across from the front desk penetrated the haze around Aela as she felt her faculties flip back into place again. "What on earth happened?"

A flurry of people appeared in an instant. Once the adrenaline stopped pumping so hard she realized short of having a bump on the back of her head she was otherwise unhurt. Assuring them everything really was in good working order had no effect— their concern for her was overpowering. There was no doubt she'd have her own bruises appearing to match Nairn's, but they'd be in places he wouldn't be seeing. Thank goodness for the buoyancy aid. It hadn't exactly floated her to the bottom, but it had saved her lower back from being pulverized by the bottom step.

"Sandra!" Robert's gruff tones hissed in her ear as he helped her to stand. "Don't let anyone go up that staircase, and get Miss Cameron to a seat right now."

All Aela wanted was to be up in the office she'd been having a little escape from. Embarrassed by her tumble, she hated the solicitous fuss.

"Someone, take this back to the warehouse now, please!" Robert indicated Aela's burden as he bent to examine the bottom step of the staircase.

Margaret, Head of Payroll, prized the buoyancy aid from Aela's tight grip and assigned it to one of her staff before she helped her toward the soft seating near the front door.

"I'm fine. I'll just get back up to the office and sit there," Aela summoned a hearty laugh to minimize the tense concern.

Margaret insisted on escorting her into the elevator and up to Nairn's office suite.

"I'm fine." Aela dredged up a reassuring smile as she sat at her desk. "Look...I'm sitting!"

Nairn appeared in the doorway as she entreated the woman to go back down to her own work. "Is there a problem, Miss Cameron?"

"She took a tumble on the staircase, Mr. Malcolm. Claims she's fine but I think a doctor should look her over." Margaret clucked like a mother hen.

"No doctor!" Aela was adamant.

"Thanks, Margaret. I'll deal with Miss Cameron."

Chapter Sixteen

"Bloody hell, Aela! What happened? Are you really all right?"

She winced as she lowered herself onto the chair at his desk. "I guess you could say I found an unusual method of descending your staircase."

"Jacket off!"

"What?"

"Take off your jacket, pull up your top and let me see your back."

Ignoring his high-handed way of asking, Aela complied knowing his concern was justified. She slid around in the seat as she hauled up her top, baring her back for his examination. The phone buzzed alongside them, but Nairn ignored it.

His voice came out muffled as he twisted himself around to see the damage. "Thank God, there's no actual bleeding, but it's grazed and quite bruised." His fingers were gentle as he probed the area around her lower spine. "Feel that?"

"Sure, but it isn't so bad. Honest!"

Aela was much more conscious of the fact his fingers were a tender caress on her. Her skin prickled in awareness, all too brief though, since his fingers removed themselves from her back. She shivered as she pulled down her blouse again. Anticipation squashed as soon as it had begun for Nairn had started an agitated lurching around the room.

"How the hell did it happen?"

She told him about slipping, then landing on the buoyancy aid and how it bore the brunt of the impact with the bottom step.

Nairn's swearing was vehement; no surprise there. The phone buzzed again.

"Will you answer, or shall I?" Her inquiry was calm for she realized just how upset Nairn was by her tumble.

As she put her jacket back on, he picked up the phone and dragged around his plaster cast till he seemed to remember how awkward that was. Aela had a hunch his words to Robert were not the ones he really wanted to vent. "Yes. Call the police now."

The phone thumped down on its cradle. He groped his way back to his chair and sat down with a struggle, his breathing back to being labored again because she knew he'd overdone some of the moves in ensuring she was in his office and checked out. "Robert wants to talk to me."

"Okay, I'll be out in my office." Moving to rise, Nairn's bark stopped her.

"Sit right there. It concerns you, Aela!"

"Things are just getting better by the minute," she huffed, knowing she wasn't annoyed with him— far from it. Although he was very angry, he wasn't angry with her, and the concern in his gaze swamped her.

Robert's update wasn't a good one. "Grease of some kind. I'm guessing something simple like petroleum jelly, but it was slathered thickly enough on the edge of the step to make it effective. I've cordoned off the staircase till the police arrive."

"Shoes!"

Nairn's request was a bark, though Aela knew what prompted it. Slipping off her heels, Robert-the healthiest of them, bent and lifted them up. All three had a look together at their undersides. She'd walked off the grease from the sole, however, there was still a solid smear of it on the arch of her left shoe.

"Could it have got on the stair by accident, by someone dropping something?" Aela asked.

Nairn wouldn't be convinced about an accident theory. Neither would Robert as his phone bleeped.

"The police are in reception, Mr. Malcolm. I'm going down to meet them, but Detective Woods is on his way up to interview Miss Cameron. I suggest you leave your shoes off; he should take a look like we've just done."

Having taken a statement from her, Detective Woods would have liked to take her shoes in for evidence but since they were her only footwear, he took a sample of the grease. After handing them back, the detective went off with his uniformed colleagues to interview every staff member in the building. Aela wasn't sure she wanted to wear the damned pink shoes again but they were all she had, and being realistic...the shoes were not to blame.

Nairn hobbled to the window as she sat again. He turned back and stopped by her chair, his hand thumping the desk, the violence of it startling her. His blue eyes implored, his voice determined. She could sense the anger held in check by the twitching of his neck muscles. "You've got to go now, Aela. You've not even been here one day, and the bastard's hurt you, too."

"Nairn Malcolm!" Aela was furious, as indignant as he was when she stood up to match his height. "You're not listening to me. I'm not leaving you." Grasping the hand pumping a deadly rhythm on the desk beside her she drew it to her front, flattening his fingers across her heart with her own. "This person will be found. And this will all stop, but believe me now..." She dropped his fingers and took his face between her two hands, her eyes scant inches from his, seeking his endorsement. "Look at my lips, Nairn. No friggin' way will I give in to threats!"

168

His eyes closed, Nairn's forehead dipped to rest on hers. He was exhausted, distressed and so angry she felt he was going to explode. With careful movements, she supported his strung-out body, her arms sliding around his back to banish some of his tension, her fingers caressing tight bowstrung muscles. After long minutes she felt him relax a little.

The kiss she started was gentle at first, a confirmation of sorts of her decision to stick with him, but it soon escalated into fiery need. Their tongues shared, tasted, gave...devoured. When the end came their foreheads touched once more for long moments while Nairn's breath eased, then he slid out of her grasp, his gaze unlike any they'd shared before. Anxious? Yes. Concerned? Also yes.

But so full of guilt.

"I should be comforting you, Aela. You're the one in the firing line today." The blue of his irises darkened, regret changing to a much deeper emotion as his lips gently sought hers and fed on them. It was sweet, tender and quite beautiful. Their lips clung for ages, Aela not needing the passion of before, but drawing beneficial sustenance from Nairn. His eyes became an indisputable entreaty when he whispered, "I can't let you be hurt again."

Aela bit back a negative response as she slipped from his arms. It wasn't going to be easy to make him believe her so she was deft in changing tack, forcing a brisk tone. "Nairn. The police are still downstairs making their enquiries. There's nothing I can do about leaving you right this minute. I'd have to get myself back to Lanera, in case you've forgotten that little fact, so sit down, please. We're going to carry on doing your business till the police come back in here to give us their updates."

She knew Nairn wasn't happy with her decision. It wasn't simple to continue to work, yet she drove the pace—while the detectives were questioning the staff no one was allowed to leave the building, anyway.

The police authorized a doctor's examination for Aela as soon as they declared the incident a malicious attempt to harm. X-rays were not thought to be needed, but the assertion was Aela should go to an Emergency Department should any change occur in her mobility, or should she have any tingling, or changes to the feeling in her legs.

Nairn wasn't convinced about the doctor's decision.

"Nairn Malcolm. Would you just listen to yourself? You're neither my mother...nor my father, but you are one helluva big pain in the ass! I do not need to go to a hospital."

The tender kisses they'd shared faded into memory, as though they'd never occurred.

The grease was dispatched for lab testing, but the police were in accordance with Robert: it likely was some kind of petroleum jelly, the kind found in medical kits. There were loads of those kits at strategic places around the buildings, accessible to the whole staff. Not exactly good news for pinpointing the exact source.

The conjecture over why it happened took less time to establish. If Aela was injured, unable to ferry Nairn around, then Nairn would be confined to base—back to square one.

Too many people, it would seem, had been party to the information Aela had flown his jet, and had driven him to the office.

Way past nine p.m. they were still in the London office, though everyone else had long since exited the building—apart from security and those working night duty. The return journey Nairn planned had not transpired, but nothing had been mentioned yet about a stay-over in London. He hadn't rested at all:

relations between them were still glacial. She'd refused to leave him so many times he'd stopped asking. He'd also stopped speaking to her, except when absolutely necessary.

Logically she knew why he was doing it but it wasn't what she wanted. She wanted him. She wanted his tender caresses, wanted his fiery ones even more. But again he'd backed off from their intimacy, developing relationship...whatever. She didn't know what to call what was happening between them.

Aela would have to get herself booked into a hotel and get Nairn to his London apartment, yet thinking about the effort required made her groan. Wincing as she rose from her chair she knew her back was fine, but her butt cheeks had not got off so lightly. A determined grin spread as she met Nairn coming through the connecting door, her inquiry clashing with his.

"I'm booking myself a..."

"Bring round the car, please. I'll wait in the lobby."

He tottered past her to the elevator without giving her a chance to say any more. Knowing he was back to almost passing out again, she gathered up their laptops. Chiding him for neglecting himself seemed such a waste of energy. And now it smacked of maybe just a bit too much like the pot calling the kettle black.

After she plotted the route to his London apartment he reeled off a telephone number, his eyes already closed.

"Tell Richard we'll need a meal as soon as we arrive."

The classy block of apartments wasn't far away, thank heavens.

"We're here, Nairn."

His sleepy eyes met hers and he smiled a

genuine smile just for her, a smile that rocked her bones before he looked around and acknowledged his surroundings.

Nairn's housekeeper, a dapper white-haired man of around sixty, ushered them inside the apartment. Much to her surprise she was shown into a bedroom for her use and in no time at all Richard had them seated at the dining room table with a meal in front of them. Almost too tired to eat, she was conscious of Nairn's fatigue. The limited amount of bruising she had made her empathize more acutely with his extensive injuries.

They ate in silence because Nairn seemed distracted. Not morose—disturbed. She sensed guilt sat heavy on his shoulders, but she'd had more than enough of it. Her tone was harsh, intended to break through his abstraction. "Nairn. Would you cut the bloody guilt trip? I'm fine."

"Are you sure?"

Again, convincing him wouldn't be easy. "The doctor checked me thoroughly. My butt feels like a friggin' punching bag, but I've enough padding to take it. My injuries will heal long before yours."

"I guess I'll have to take your word for it." A weak smile accompanied his next quip. "I suppose I'm not getting to see all your bruises up close?"

"No way!" Aela gurgled as her head wavered a negative invitation.

Nairn declared he was going to bed, instructing her to be ready for breakfast at eight a.m., after which they'd return to the office. "Will you still be here, Miss Cameron?" The formal name put her back in her place.

"You can bet your life on it, sir!" Her mock salute gained her a dozy grin from him. "I keep my promises."

She was annoyed by his neglect of his recovering body, yet was in awe of his stamina. All she wanted to do was drop into bed and sleep the sleep of the dead, but she still had a predicament. Nairn had clothes, and basic necessities stored in the London apartment. She had nothing, apart from what she was wearing, since he'd categorically declared they were making a day trip.

Asking Richard for directions to the nearest store operating twenty-four-hour-trading she was told anything could be acquired by placing a few phone calls, even at such a late hour. For some reason his assured answer disturbed Aela; it smacked too much of him kitting out Nairn's lady friends on previous occasions. Not appealing at all.

"Good heavens, that's not necessary." She tried not to sound judgmental. "Could you just direct me to a store which can provide basic supplies?"

Richard mentioned a large supermarket nearby stocking almost everything, his scathing tone indicating they didn't cater to anyone of quality, but he relented sufficiently to say he would arrange for a porter to accompany her. Only a short walk away, using local pathways was quicker than going by car.

"You have porters downstairs?" Aela's eyebrows shot up for it wasn't a hotel.

"Of course, Miss Cameron. These serviced apartments can organize anything our owners might want, and that requires twenty-four hour porter services."

Before she left Aela ensured Nairn could get properly undressed before bed. "Mr. Malcolm is totally exhausted right now, he might need assistance with fiddly buttons. Could you help him without awakening the ogre?"

Richard glided toward Nairn's bedroom. A discreet knock on the door came before he declared he'd sorted out alterations to Nairn's suit trousers as requested, and could he lay out a suitable choice for the morning? True valet style.

Aela smiled at the panache, but Nairn's problems weren't hers—she had enough of her own to sort out!

Chris, the porter she found downstairs, couldn't be more than sixteen. Delighted to help, he accompanied her to the store. "If you don't mind, Miss, it'll be best if I wheel your purchases for you," he declared, grabbing a shopping cart.

The purchases Aela intended to make were going to be items of a very personal nature. However, the cheeky grin on the porter's face said it all, as did his next words.

"I've shopped with my older sisters. I know how to turn the other cheek. No worries there, miss."

Aela hated shopping, knew she'd be out of the store as soon as she found the basic necessities, but the clothing racks and lingerie section displayed plenty of choices. Though low budget items they would do well enough, and since her backpack back at the castle only held casual items she kitted herself out with a selection of business attire. Having gained the help of the fitting room assistant her shopping cart filled up quickly. In a record twenty minutes they were approaching checkout, Aela brandishing a credit card.

"Chris? I need a suitcase. Do you think there might be such a thing here?"

Chris beamed for he knew exactly where the luggage was situated.

Much as she'd wanted to drop into bed earlier she enjoyed the little sojourn with Chris, who was a well-informed young man about the neighborhood.

****

Nairn blinked in admiration of the woman who stepped into his dining room. Leaving aside the newspaper he'd spread open at the side of his cleared breakfast plate he gave her his full attention. Aela was indeed still here. She was a woman who lived up to her promises. And how! The woman was stunning. He'd said it before, and he knew he would say it again, many times, if he got the chance.

The day before she'd been wearing the flirty little silky suit she'd interviewed in but now she looked so elegant, clad in a suit of black pin-striped with cream. The yellow silky-knit top hugged her luscious breasts so close he wanted to hold them in his hands and feel the richness of them. In two healthy hands. A deep moan rumbled for that wouldn't be for a while yet. A pair of black court shoes were suitably business-like. He missed the sexy pink ones already, but he guessed what she now wore was more practical. She was so beautiful he ached. His aches were one thing; he couldn't contemplate Aela getting hurt again.

Where had she acquired the clothes? They'd brought no luggage with them the day before.

Although he'd had previous lovers stay the night in his apartment he was certain none had ever left a work suit like the one Aela was now wearing. In fact no previous lover had ever left anything personal, for they'd been fleeting contacts, their clothing never remotely like business attire.

The day before had been so fraught with anxiety, it hadn't occurred to him a stopover might present problems. Aela hadn't quibbled at all when it'd become obvious they'd have to stay in London. His London wardrobe was better equipped for business clothes than the castle, so he'd not considered any inconvenience to her.

Yet, somehow, she'd managed to kit herself out very proficiently. He wasn't sure how he felt about this capable woman, apart from lusting after her luscious body. Now a bruised body. That thought pained him nearly as much as his own real aches.

"Good morning."

Aela's breezy greeting warmed as much as her

beaming smile, Nairn belatedly realizing he'd been gaping without returning a dickey-bird. It was Richard who greeted Aela with a smile as he held out the chair, and seated her at the table.

"Good morning, Miss Cameron. I see your evening stroll went well," Richard said.

A stroll? Last night? Nairn flicked open his newspaper to the next page, his ears perking up. In London? His apartment wasn't in the suburbs, and it was always busy around his neighborhood.

Richard continued. "Please permit me to say I was too scathing—your choices look superb. May I assist you with some coffee or tea, Miss Cameron?"

After a solicitous flapping of her napkin into place Richard smiled again, a smile Nairn had rarely seen during the five years the man had been his employee. He watched the exchange with mixed feelings. It appeared Aela could charm any male over the age of puberty. He'd never seen Richard so attentive to any of his previous guests' comfort. Although Aela was clearly the most beautiful woman he'd ever brought to the apartment, previous lovers hadn't exactly been ugly.

"Coffee please, and thanks for your help last night. Chris was a wonderful escort."

Aela's warm recognition earned another smile from Richard.

"Chris?" Nairn made his inquiry sound casual as he noisily turned another page, one-handed, but the sudden churning in his gut unsettled the breakfast he'd just finished.

How was it possible for her to have met someone last night after the stressful day they'd put in? Someone had maliciously harmed her! Was the woman bionic or something? She'd gone out on the town without him, seeing how incapacitated he was? Even after her own accident? What the hell else had she done with this Chris? Her escort for the night?

While he'd been sleeping the sleep of the dead? In the next room?

Nairn was growing sick of all the questions spinning around his bothered brain.

Aela had said she was afraid of nothing. And it seemed she was. Capable, very capable. He told himself he could shed the guilt and not even think about putting her in harm's way again. Quiet seething consumed him; a totally different kind of fuming from the day before. Retreating into his paper, he didn't see a single word in front of him. That stubborn trait of his shut his mind down. Analysis of this sort wasn't his style.

"Mmm...Chris."

Aela's expression looked quite dreamy when he chanced a glance. Only the one.

Chapter Seventeen

When Nairn's fingers tightened on the paper he was gripping like grim death, Aela realized how he'd misconstrued her statement.

"Very skilled Chris was, made my evening so memorable."

A vein pulsed at Nairn's neck, indicating just how tense he was, demonstrating just how much he was trying to control his temper. But perhaps it was something else? She wasn't entirely sure, but she liked the idea he might be in a bit of a jealous huff.

"I'm fine today, just in case you were about to inquire, sir!"

Nairn's preoccupation with a particular article seemed intense so she judiciously tucked into her breakfast. The short exchange served its purpose, though, for he mentioned nothing about her leaving his employment.

A tense silence reigned all the way to the office, which suited Aela just fine since navigating the traffic was enough to think about in the morning rush hour. She had an idea he was worried in case another incident might happen, but she'd resolutely ignored his prompts that he could get a taxi and go alone. Not happening, she'd said, and Nairn had relented. Reluctantly...and moodily.

Later that morning she was glad she'd splurged on a range of new clothing since plans changed yet again.

"Miss Cameron!" Nairn's bellow through the open office doors rivaled the chiming of Big Ben. "In here, please."

Count to ten...and then again!

Aela drew in a deep breath, summoned a polite smile and picked up a sharpened pencil. Fingering the point, she mentally assessed which part of Nairn's already bruised torso could take a nice little jab. He was being a pig again. He'd taken to hollering her into his office, disregarding the indicator on the telephone system.

She decided not to challenge why he was dispensing with it in favor of bawling her name, and focused instead on ignoring his bad temper because, since breakfast, it hadn't diminished. When he didn't even bother to look away from his current work, she refused to get riled as she strode up to his desk. The fingers of his left hand stabbed away at his keyboard, his abrupt instruction drifting up to her from his bent head.

"Book a hotel in Muscat for two nights, Wednesday and Thursday."

Aela couldn't help her enthusiastic response. "Muscat, Oman? How lovely! Another place I've never been."

Her attempt to lighten their interaction went down like a kite without wind. His acerbic comeback was distinctly unfriendly when his expressionless mask faced her.

"Did I say you would be going too, Miss Cameron?"

Professional *faux pas*! Her throat was suddenly dry, her face hot, a weak smile pursed her lips, but she refused to be baited any further by his continued blank stare. "Got it. Book for how many? Just one room...or a suite for your...harem?"

Nairn flashed a dark sardonic glance before dipping back to his keyboard. "I do prefer a suite, Miss Cameron."

"We're talking Wednesday week?" When Nairn made no move to give further information, she persisted, "The date, please?"

Not as polite as she should be but Nairn's attitude wasn't well-mannered either. He barely made eye contact for more than a nano-second. And horrible at that!

"I'm talking tomorrow, Miss Cameron. For possibly two nights. Which part of that didn't you understand?"

"Tomorrow? You're joking!" Skepticism tumbled out. "Come on, Nairn. You're not fit for such a long-haul flight."

One look at Nairn's tight jaws was more than enough. A little backtracking might just be the order of the day. "Okay! If you say you're friggin' fit, you're fit! It's your broken ribs that'll be against that seat for hours."

His intent focus was on the desk in front of him; a pen slid around and around the fingers of his left hand as though he was about to blow a fuse. Or maybe he was just readying the pen for a direct hit at her? She knew not to expect any kind of agreement, but also refused to be cowed by his attitude.

Less than four weeks to work. She did a furious mental count—only three weeks and one day. She could manage to keep going for such a short time, but her lip wouldn't stay buttoned for the duration. Far too much to expect. "Know any good hotels in Muscat, with palatial rooms and multiple beds, sir?"

Nairn's head rose slowly as he rattled off the hotel where the business meeting was taking place—a hotel he'd used before.

"Any other details I should know about, sir? Anything else I need to organize for your trip?"

Nairn's reply was toneless, devoid of eye contact since he stared out of the window.

Prince Hasson, a potentate who was developing a coastal resort area in his Arabian Gulf state, intended to order a fleet of two-seater jet-skis, and had heard of the new version Gale Breakers had recently brought onto the market. Prince Khalid— their current customer—had recommended Gale Breakers. It was far too good an opportunity to defer till later, Nairn declared, no matter what his present health requirements might be. He was going, regardless.

Aela jotted notes during his monologue, her concentration jolted when his phone rang.

"I must see what John Reid is talking about, Miss Cameron. Let's go."

She trailed after Nairn like the proverbial collie dog. What wasn't part of the job were the collisions he created, caused by his inability to stride properly, though that hadn't happened the previous day. She'd bumped into his back too often when his abrupt halts to reposition the walking aid startled her. It seemed he expected her to have some sixth sense about his hitches.

"For cripes sake, Nairn! Give me some warning, please, or I'll be mowing you down like a bloody combine-harvester!"

She felt tight as a drum as she shouldered her body free of his to punch the elevator button.

He'd set up an embargo—neither of them would go anywhere around the building without the presence of the other. At first hearing Aela had balked at the infringement to her autonomy but then relented when she realized just how fearful he was over her safety. Her use of the staircase had been categorically banned.

Aela forced the day to get better, knowing she had to do something about their frosty relations or she'd burst a blood vessel. Nairn mellowed a little when she enthused about Chris's fabulous porter-cum-escort services on their way to the stockrooms, but the news from the warehouse was again disconcerting. Nairn's mood dipped again.

Stock control had just taken delivery of breathable drysuits, for diving activities, at the newest Lanwater Whitecaps site in Ireland. They were due to begin operating the following week. John Reid showed them that all one hundred drysuits were of the same XXL size, instead of a range of sizes.

"I'm going to throttle the bastard who tampered with this order!" Nairn's anger blasted off him, as surging and violent as the waves could be in the Northern Atlantic.

The incident was again a petty mistake, not life threatening. Yet who had changed the order at the last minute the day before, by telephone, was unclear. The manufacturer had been used before so they'd had no concerns with changes made to the original order. Nairn seethed, and grumped back in his office suite. Aela found a hasty retreat her best option. Minimizing physical contact with him for the next few hours, her office desk was a haven.

Late afternoon he surprised her. Buzzing her through, his tone was affable. Mmm... Suspicious. Aela's immediate reaction was to be on her guard.

"Do you need time to go shopping, Miss Cameron?"

"Shopping?" She was mystified. "Why would I need to shop?"

"For going to Oman. Perhaps you need...toothpaste, or something." Nairn's tone sounded laid-back.

"I'm going to Oman? With you?"

Her questions were cautious, her mind reeling, replaying their earlier conversation. Nairn was up to something. The returned sexy twinkle in his eye indicated he was teasing. Attraction revved up again. The dratted man made it happen so easily she could scream. She welcomed a return to more intimacy but not at her expense, if he was making a mockery of her.

"Yes, of course, I'll need my PA."

"But you..." His enigmatic smile made her decide not to complete the sentence, realizing he'd been winding her up. However, she wouldn't be trapped again. "Should I book myself a room at your hotel, sir?"

"You booked a two-bedroom suite, didn't you?" At her nod he continued, "You'll use one of them, Miss Cameron, and I'll make good use of the other."

Aela felt he was being obtuse, still not giving a proper answer. She remained dogged about their travel arrangements. "Do I need to pick up anyone else for the flight? Maybe a female friend to tide you over till you meet up with your ever-so-ready-harem?"

Her face was as innocent as she could make it, though that wasn't saying much because subterfuge wasn't really in her make up. Subtlety wasn't either.

One eyebrow raised itself just a hint as Nairn met her gaze, neither of them giving an inch. Eventually he spoke, a low hum purring around her ears, the merest hint of a grin escaping him, a cheeky sparkle lightening the blue of his irises. "No, Miss Cameron. It will be just the two of us, and, of course, my discreet flight staff. Since you're determined to stay employed by me, you'll come too."

The frost melted. A little. The sexual heat climbed quite a few notches as his darkening gaze lingered and held. Back to fluttery. She contemplated how she could arouse him just as easily, and play him at his own game.

It was no surprise, though, when he got in the last word. "Naturally we'll be busy on the flight."

His attitude for the rest of the afternoon and evening was hard to gauge. He was polite, yet under the surface, sexual tension simmered again, a bubbling and brooding combustible heat of desire that Aela found more and more difficult to suppress. She avoided glances, avoided unnecessary touches. Sort-of. Nairn didn't. Collisions seemed to have become part of his norm, his straying pats and attentive strokes she relished but tried to pass off as insignificant. Though they weren't!

She didn't think he was trying hard enough to keep his distance. The deliberate clash in the hallway of his apartment as they were headed to their own bedrooms was far too fluky as his hands came to rest lightly on her shoulders. Soft midnight-blue irises caressed her, right down to her toes, the expression on his face so caring it made her dissolve. It appeared he had just as much trouble as she did with sticking to their friends-only agreement.

"Well, it seems we've survived the day with no injury, Aela."

"Apart from these latest bruises, you mean? And a hundred little others during the day, sir?"

Her smile belied her censorious words as his hand caressed her shoulder. She sneaked her arms gently round his middle, barely touching though what she really wanted to do was hug him to pieces for his little caresses of the day had been so disturbing...to her resolutions.

Nairn's smile of regret was matched by his tone. "All the contact I can have, Aela Cameron."

"Really?"

Nairn's lips touching down were not a mistake at all. They were a direct response to her tease. It was a kiss of promise that went on and on, Nairn changing the angle, their tongues greedy for each other. Aroused almost immediately, Aela was wet with desire when Nairn's mouth slid away from her. His lips were not the only thing sliding, though, for he'd lost his balance and was tipping over. Her frantic clutch got him upright, but his yelp of agony was again alarming.

Nope.

Nairn Malcolm was not healthy enough yet for frenzied lovemaking. She went to bed feeling...let down? Definitely frustrated as hell!

Aela's aunt had always claimed that sleep was a great healer. It seemed she was right. Sort of. It was as though nothing sexual had occurred the previous evening.

****

Drawn up in the mercurial tornado that was Nairn, they were flying to Muscat a little after seven a.m. Breakfasting, and leaving the apartment had been a rush because Aela had almost slept through her alarm call. Their dash to the airport was a cajoling josh, Nairn calling her all manner of sleepyheads as she zipped the car along, traffic at that early hour still light. A nice simmering banter continued between them—more than friendly, more of a cozy mutual sharing.

In her role as PA, they worked through the first four hours, during which Nairn's fear for their welfare seemed to have diminished. Aela guessed this was because the perpetrator of the incidents was unable to do anything personally to them. Adamant on being present during extremely thorough flight checks, the flight staff was miffed, but Nairn was a good customer.

Aela relaxed. Although she'd been brave enough the day before, she, too, was concerned over their joint wellbeing. After lunch, a pained looking Nairn prepared to spread out the laptops and business papers again.

"Not going to happen, Nairn Malcolm." Insistent as she reached for his pain-killers, she shook two into her palm. "Rest time!"

Nairn grumbled through a mouthful of pills. "I never rest on flights, Miss Cameron."

Her reply was sweetness and light. "No, but you're not normally sporting all these injuries. I've already rubbed my sore little butt down with anti-inflammatory gel, so I'm fine." Firm tones brought his wandering gaze back to her face. The overt groan and sexy leer she ignored. "My face is up here, sir! I can't conduct the business talks myself so, if you don't want it to turn into a fiasco, a little rest might be in order."

Little resistance from her workaholic employer surprised her, beyond muttering for the first few minutes after his chair was reclined. The jet didn't have a dinky little bedroom, a disappointment on embarking, but Nairn cheered her up with a sexy gleam, and by saying he tended to charter those on longer flights.

Aela felt wonderful. Lips feathered around her mouth, captured her lower lip and nuzzled it, caught her too rapid breaths and absorbed them. The kiss deepened. The nibbles at her lower lip moved to the upper. A delicious minty tongue sneaked into her mouth and explored, all around, sucking her tongue and thrusting, a mimic of the sexual act she wanted so much. Her thighs quivered, the whole area tingling and filling with a rush of blood. Satisfaction was just out of reach. She was sure that a little more of the arousing attention would bring fulfillment. She moaned. Fingers slid over her rock hard nipple, pinching, and teasing. She quivered and shuddered. Delicious. Boiling. She was afire.

An arm gently nudged her awake. Her reluctant eyes opened to focus as she squelched the lingering low-down stimulation that had her thigh muscles squeezing tight. The table in front of her was spread with paperwork.

"You've had your rest, Aela," Nairn crowed. "Back to work now."

Her eyes took time to adjust as he moved back

out of her vicinity and booted up his laptop.

Jittery. That's how she felt. The sensations in her dream had been so real. She stole a glance at Nairn's lips. Glistening? She looked down at her still very aroused nipples and tingled even more. Had he been fondling her? Nairn smirked like a horny teenager who'd got laid for the first time. Mmm... Too suspicious. Too much like the cat that'd just had a sneaky taste of the cream.

Another couple of hours sped past. Satellite communications were a delight—usually—but Aela wondered if maybe reading a dull in-flight magazine would have been a better bet. Business was the order of the day. Unremitting business. Yet contrarily their interaction was enjoyable, sexual stress back to an anticipation that bubbled.

Toward the end of the flight, Nairn turned to her, his face warped into to a tight mask, their comfortable mood totally zapped. "Miss Cameron?"

Looking up from the information she was scanning, she found him staring at his cell phone as if it had just bitten him.

"My father wants you to get in touch with him since you haven't returned his calls."

"Pardon me?" Why was he so upset over Ruaridh trying to reach her?

Nairn's tone was contemptuous. "Ruaridh's sent text messages you've not responded to, so he's requested I ask you to call him."

He pocketed his cell and proceeded to ignore her.

She'd switched her phone off before takeoff. A quick call to Ruaridh confirmed he'd managed to track down the son of her great-grandfather's sister on the nearby island of Mull. Ruaridh had been calling on and off over the last few days giving her a progress report on his findings so she knew the relative he referred to. "Oh, lovely, Ruaridh. Yes, I'll meet you the minute we're back on Lanera."

The rest of the flight was almost silent. Nairn was in a black mood she decided not to encroach on. She couldn't understand his attitude at all because Ruaridh was a lovely man.

Aela was moderately familiar with high-class hotels, but the one they'd booked into stole her breath. It had been built as a palace for an Arabian Prince, but now functioned as a regular hotel, except during special conference times once or twice a year when important dignitaries descended there to thrash out political and international issues.

Arriving at dusk was the absolute best way to appreciate the impact of the splendid building—a startling white against huge dark and craggy mountains soaring behind. Strategic floodlighting created an incredible setting that was both romantic and enthralling. Huge palms were planted in columns like majestic sentinels guarding the entrance, swaying in the soft breeze beside the fountains and shallow ponds that fronted the whole exterior. Magical. An Arabian Nights visualization, passionate and sensuous.

At the heart of the hexagonal tiered block was a huge marble atrium with areas discreetly sectioned off by lush planting and Moorish screens. The upper floor walkways circled around the heights of the atrium and led to the accommodation areas behind. Many floors up, the domed ceiling was made of delicate stained glass, the starlit sky just visible, twinkling here and there in places, but Aela had no time to peruse it further than a cursory glance.

She checked them in since Nairn was in serious flag mode—still by her side, but in an awkward prop against the marble desk. In minutes they were whisked up to their luxury suite by an efficient desk clerk, a bellhop trailing behind with their luggage on the most ornate gilded cart she'd ever seen.

"Just time for a quick clean-up before the

meeting downstairs at nine," Nairn prompted as he negotiated his way behind the desk clerk who displayed the first bedroom, the décor redolent of traditional Omani architecture with its fret-worked panels and patterning on the blue and white walls. "This one has your name on it."

An attempt at levity? Aela thought maybe, but Nairn's voice sounded very tired.

"Do you need me tonight?" she asked, not sure what was expected of her since it was eight-twenty p.m. local time.

"Of course!" Nairn looked perplexed by her question. Aela could read his expressions quite well now—he most likely had intended to brief her earlier but their communication breakdown had put the scuppers on that. "We're having an initial drink in the Piano Bar where we'll begin the consultation before eating in the main dining room. I'll expect you to take note of any necessary details."

"Then business attire will be suitable for me?"

Having seen the hotel patrons in the foyer, she'd deemed that business attire was not the order of the day for the women.

Nairn's eyebrows rose as though he'd never even considered what she should wear. "I suppose it will have to do, unless you happen to have a little black number in the suitcase you magically filled last night."

Aela's thoughts were pretty mutinous. Her spending spree had been on business related apparel. Nairn followed the bellhop into the second bedroom where his bag, packed by Richard and full of altered clothing to accommodate his casts, was deposited. Clearing her throat, beckoning the desk clerk she pressed a discreet tip into his hand, saving Nairn the embarrassment of fumbling around. She did likewise with the bellhop, who beamed at her.

Excusing herself, she declared she'd be ready in

half an hour, but not before. Slipping out of the suite, Aela rode the elevator to the mezzanine shopping level. The tinkling sounds of a soft harp being plucked in the foyer filled the interior and created a peaceful ambience, soothing and unhurried. But Aela no time at all to appreciate the excellence of it as she sped into the small corridor housing several expensive boutiques. Pulling out her credit card, she swooped along the racks.

Ten minutes later, she was upstairs and in the shower. At one minute past the expected time to meet Nairn, she was in their elegant salon. He wasn't there, but his vehement cursing informed her he was having difficulty getting dressed.

"Aela!" he bellowed. "Get in here, please, and help me with this bloody tie!"

Her eyes met with a horrendous mess when she opened his bedroom door. The expertly packed case had been raided. Clothing was strewn all over the bed, or was cascading onto the floor. Nairn stood in front of a mirror wearing a partially buttoned formal shirt, a tie drooping around his neck. Dark suit trousers were sliding down his legs, his good hand fumbling to hang onto them while he failed to zip and hook them.

"Got a little problem here, sir?" she responded serenely, stifling a full-blown grin before she sped to help him recover his dignity. Not meeting his eyes, she ignored his blasted tirade of profanities. Obviously Richard had worked wonders in organizing new trousers sufficiently wide to pull over the cast, but the hooked fastening at the waist needed more than a one-handed approach.

She couldn't deny the rush of feelings engendered by Nairn's closeness. Neither could she remain unaware of his clenched jaw and rising arousal while her deft fingers pulled his pants up and into place. Touching him was inevitable as she fastened the clip. His breathing was ruffled, though she knew very well it had nothing to do with rib pain. His head was bent toward her when she completed the process. Heat emanated from him in waves. She straightened up, her head bumping against his chin before she fixed the tie.

Aela looked him squarely in the eye and calmly berated him, steeling herself not to drown in the blue depths glistening there, a fierce need having replaced his temper over his infirmity. She smoothed the necktie in place. The pure Nairn scent of him was almost too much.

"Next time, just ask. Let's call daily business dressing part of my job description. Remember the little clause about *during your incapacity*? It includes cuff links."

The sexy glint softened to an even deeper blue yet she couldn't quite gauge what he was thinking. His lips swooped onto hers in a brief yet satisfying kiss before she could evade it. No anger—just need. His arms were gentle, cradling her as the kiss deepened. Heat escalated, and a hunger so overpowering buckled her knees. It was just enough to bring her to her senses.

"Nairn. I'm here to help you with those little things you can't do yourself, that's all," she chided.

"Exactly." Nairn's gaze twinkled with mirth.

Seconds later she was slipping his widened jacket sleeve over his arm cast, though how she did it at speed was a miracle, because her own arousal was spiked to dangerous levels. What she really wanted was to rip the clothes off him and take full advantage of his partial incapacity. The man made her so needy! Having straightened the front of his jacket in place, she faced him, handing him the walking aid.

"I think you'll do, sir."

Nairn's gaze was relentless as one finger tilted

her chin up. "My name is Nairn. Call me that when we're alone." The sizzling desire still blazing from his eyes lit an inner candle in her. "Will I only do? Aela?"

She barely heard his words as his mouth touched down, demanding another much longer kiss. Nothing in the world could stop Aela's desperate response. She melted into him, her mind as numb as her body under his greedy lips. She wanted it to continue...and continue. When he drew away, she was dazed.

He cleared his throat, his head shaking as though to dispel a dream. "You have no idea what you are doing to me, Aela."

Two good fingers slipped across his lips, removing her clear lip-gloss. With intent focus on her eyes, he shared his banked heat and then wiped the fingers across her mouth, as though returning her kiss. She could do nothing but stare, her lips burning.

"Let's go, Miss Cameron."

Business took priority.

Lovemaking on the back burner.

They waited for the elevator. She heard Nairn's indrawn breath as he took in her dress. "You are stunningly beautiful. Once again you floor me, Aela Cameron. Not a little black number, but a...ssssexy dark red one. So, you did have something in your suitcase."

She took his compliment in stride. "I didn't. The hotel happens to have some very well-stocked boutiques."

"If you bought that here, then I definitely must reimburse you. Your salary package obviously needs to include an evening wardrobe as well as a day one. Give me any clothing bills you incur for our business needs."

"For exceptions, maybe, sir. Otherwise I'll seem

like a kept woman, and we wouldn't want your accountants to think that, would we?"

Before she hastily repaired her lip-gloss in the copper mirror of the elevator car she feathered her fingers across Nairn's mouth. "Just a little still there, sir. Wouldn't want you to be embarrassed."

Nairn's hearty chuckle vibrated around the small compartment.

Chapter Eighteen

"Good evening!"

Aela preceded Nairn into the intimate Piano Bar. A voice rang out from a nearby alcove seating arrangement. Two men sat there—the only occupants of the whole area. One of them, lounging wide on the curved banquette, Aela reckoned to be Prince Hasson, his headgear an indication of his rank. The prince's aide sat to his side, on a separate stool, his laptop resting on the table. As the prince's greeting rang out the aide jumped to his feet and gestured them forward.

"You have to be Nairn Malcolm. There can't be too many men of your description here tonight." Prince Hasson spoke from the couch using perfect English. His words addressed Nairn, yet his focus was elsewhere.

The prince's gaze lingered far too long on her chest. She was immediately put on her guard. A gut-feeling sparked. Something told her a professional approach to her wasn't what he had in mind.

Introductions completed, Aela sat as requested by the prince in the middle of the u-shaped couch, large enough to seat eight people, though Nairn needed to remain at the edge to extend his leg cast. Prince Hasson, seated opposite Nairn, had not risen during the formal greetings. His dark looks were handsome, yet he exuded a false charm that Aela detested.

A waiter appeared at the flick of a long finger. "Miss Cameron. What would you like? To drink?" His smooth tones, she realized, were meant to seduce since his eyes had not removed themselves from her discreet cleavage. She was, to all intents and purposes, fair game to him since her introduction was as Nairn's PA, not his girlfriend...or wife.

Masking her feelings, she avoided direct eye contact, believing it wasn't the done thing. "Sparkling water, please."

Aela needed to keep her wits about her; she had a hunch the man would take liberties. Efficiently powering up her laptop she settled to take notes.

As they discussed the possibilities Nairn could provide, Aela was aware of his increasing tension. He had to be exhausted, of course. They'd already put in a long day. The fingers of his good hand clenched around the table edge, his jaw growing progressively more rigid, as though it was a strain to talk. There was a bit of teeth clenching going on that she didn't understand since the conversation was urbane, business-like, as Prince Hasson inquired about small changes to specifications.

Her own role was purely secretarial, since she wasn't familiar enough with the nuances of the newest jet-ski designs, although she remembered seeing an example during her whirlwind tour of the boatyard.

Her hunch proved to be true. Little by little Prince Hasson slid alongside her. The urge to shake him off was immense, but with her teeth set, she ignored him without being impolite. She wanted to whack him when his wandering arm curved around her shoulder to rest on the seat back. Sliding closer to the table, she sat so erect she felt her back would surely break with the rigidity. The shivers rippling her frame had nothing to do with temperature, or excitement, at his proximity. Loathing was too trite a word for how she felt. Her natural instinct was to use some choice words and tell him to take a hike! Of course she wasn't expected to make any eye contact with the prince, so she couldn't even give him the back-off eye she'd perfected over the years.

Protocol was a bitch!

Nairn was furious. Why hadn't he thought about the scenario that was being enacted right in front of him? Why hadn't he factored in the implications of bringing Aela to this late evening meeting? He cursed himself blind for being so short sighted and stupid.

He detested it when the prince settled within touching distance of her, ostensibly to see the display on her laptop better, even though his own secretary had the same screen for his perusal. It had been impossible not to note how the prince's eyes lingered on Aela. Impossible not to note the predatory gleam in the potentate's eye as he appreciated Aela's beauty. Impossible not to realize how easy it was for the prince to have his wishes fulfilled at the flick of a finger. A woman like Aela was a tasty morsel for the prince. Nairn had heard, through the grapevine, of the prince's predilections for picking up beautiful women for the night.

Aela was beautiful. But she wasn't for the prince.

It mattered she was uncomfortable; he'd put her in such a vulnerable position. For years, when Brian was his assistant, he hadn't had to be aware of any such thing, but that was no excuse for not thinking ahead. Her restless resettling on the couch warned him she wasn't happy about the Prince's changes of position, either.

When his potentially lucrative client's fingers strayed again to brush against her hand, as she moved on the touchpad, protective instincts Nairn didn't know he had rose to the fore. It was even worse when Prince Hasson's arm crept over the back of her body and all but caressed her hair.

Nobody should be touching his Aela in such blatant fashion. His temper spiked when she recoiled at the Prince's drifting fingers a fleeting touch at her neck. He had no wish to offend an important client but he wouldn't sit there any longer and watch Aela being pawed.

Not a moment too soon, they were informed their table awaited them. In the dining room, he was unsurprised to find a whole section had been cordoned off, and the Prince's security detail discreetly hovering around them.

The hotel was not a usually a business venue, the live music quartet a charming and lulling backdrop to the low-lit romantic ambience. Other patrons, just visible, were mainly couples in splendid attire, enjoying a meal at leisure. Nairn was glad to see Aela wasn't out of place in her purchase from the boutique; it easily matched the gowns of the women present.

Between mouthfuls of food, Aela made penciled notes as he directed, but Prince Hasson's leering of her continued no matter how much he deflected his royal highness's attention. The arrangement of the seats at table meant Prince Hasson wasn't right up close to her, but his examination of her person was so overt, Nairn remained furious.

Every now and then, when Aela had to look at him for confirmation on something, he sensed her rising resentment. Determined to end the discussions as soon as possible he set a furious pace in the negotiations. By the time their coffee arrived, Aela looked as strung out as he was feeling. He felt beyond exhaustion, emotionally tattered in a way he'd never before experienced, so much so he wondered if he'd be able to maneuver himself into the elevator and up to bed.

He deftly wound up negotiations, relieved when Prince Hasson agreed to an eight a.m. breakfast meeting to finalize the last few details. But he fumed as the prince bid them goodnight, lifting each of Aela's hands in turn and kissing her knuckles, holding onto her fingers too long. Thankfully Aela neatly fielded it all. The invitation to continue personal relations with her was so barefaced. Prince or not, he'd had enough truck with polite protocol.

"Get the elevator, please, Miss Cameron!"

Nairn managed a curt goodnight to his client. Inside the elevator car, Nairn again cursed the maniac who had caused his body to be in such a state. Extreme fatigue warred with sexual frustration. He wanted to make love to Aela all night long, but he was so damned pathetic that dragging himself to his room looked too much of a challenge.

Aela buttoned her lip, disgusted with the prince's sleazy moves and annoyed at Nairn's presumption she should blindly obey his curt orders. She hadn't flirted with the Prince, not once! Riding in the elevator was an excruciating affair—Nairn limp on the walking aid, the grim ogre was definitely back.

Inside their suite he snapped, "Breakfast at seven. We've a lot to discuss. Goodnight, Miss Cameron."

Aela was glad to escape, dog-tired and furious. She had no idea why he was so angry. She'd tried hard to be competent and professional.

Hanging her dress with some care, in case it was needed again soon, she removed her bra and shrugged into the thin silky robe she'd bought in the London store. Her minimal makeup had just been removed when she heard someone banging on the outer door.

A glance through the peephole showed Prince Hasson's aide waving a piece of paper. What on earth could he want now? They'd made their goodnights only a short while ago.

She opened the door just enough to slip her head around. "Can I help you?"

The aide handed over the slip of paper without a word, not making eye contact of any kind. Aela scanned it quickly-Would she care to have a nightcap with the prince in his suite?

She was sure her eyes must have bugged as she swallowed down a nasty reply. The prince's assistant looked so bland she felt sure it was a commonplace errand as she handed the note back.

"Please inform Prince Hasson that Mr. Malcolm and I are about to go to bed now, and must decline the prince's invitation." She tacked on a belated thank you as she snicked the door closed.

When she turned and collapsed her seething body against the door she faced an equally angry looking Nairn.

"You asked for room service?"

Aela's resentment took flight. "No, I did not. And I didn't ask to be propositioned by that sleazy prince either."

She stomped to her room too furious to say anything else. Pulling the pins from her hair she yanked a brush through it but it only made her head ache. A deafening curse, accompanying a loud crash, stopped her grooming.

Good God, what had happened now?

Nairn was flat on the floor at the side of the bed, his trousers in a tangle around his feet, his plastered leg lying at a horrifying angle. She didn't really mean her screech to be so loud. But it was. "You stupid man! All you needed to do was ask for help. You can't be so annoyed at my incompetence you'd endanger your own health!"

Disentangling the trousers and wrenching them behind her, she straightened his leg. Biting her lip in sheer frustration at her outburst, and at the heart-beating concern he might be hurt even more, her hands cradled his face, her eyes beseeching. "Do I need to call a doctor, Nairn?"

Pained blue irises gazed up at her, darkening to the deepest, softest blue while she sniffed, the merest tweak at his lip calming her frantic heartbeats. "No, Aela. Just my pride that's hurt, but I'd appreciate help getting off the floor."

Her arms cradled him as she helped him sit on the edge of the bed where she loosened the tie and unbuttoned his shirt. Kneeling between his legs to remove his gold cufflinks, his head was so close the exhalations of his strained breathing ruffled her hair. It was a torment to peel the shirt down his arms and off at the wrists. Her shaking palms hovered over the waistband of his boxer shorts, incapable of proceeding further, yet desperate to stroke the rigid flesh beneath. Denying herself what she knew awaited there was such an ordeal.

She felt the whisper of Nairn's fingers when he gently combed the strands covering her cheek before he urged her head up. His lips found hers in an urgent collision of teeth and soft flesh. An agonized groan escaped her, their blistering kiss deepening. Her need all-consuming, she almost breathed for both of them. How could she deny this? Nairn's mouth searching hers was relentless, his tongue seeking entry to the soft interior of her mouth when she opened up without question.

She enjoyed Nairn's taste before his fingers traced the bare skin of her shoulder, opened her robe, and slid down to mold her bared breast—the gentle cupping and squeezing shooting a bolt of pleasure straight to her core. His tongue explored hers as his deft fingernails plucked her nipple. She loved when his lips feathered her cheek, her chin, and trailed a dipping path to a throbbing breast. Her hands framed his head as he paid attention to the soft underside, nipping and swirling till he moved up to cover her nipple, sucking gently at first, then with more pull.

She gasped as the heightened sensations drove her to the edge. Aela presented the rest of her body for his exploration. Pulling the robe to her waist, he lavished the other nipple with the same care before his mouth moved back up her neck to her parched lips. His hand grasped the back of her robe, groping for a way to get it off.

"That little clause, Aela?" Nairn's plea was a low urgent rumble at her ear. "Help me get this off, please?"

Passion escalated. She was beyond denying him anything. Standing, she opened the tie at her waist and kicked the robe clear when it pooled at her feet. All she was wearing was a tiny thong and the sparkling pair of heels she'd bought in the boutique.

"God Aela, you are too beautiful for words," Nairn groaned and struggled to his feet and pulled at his boxers. "Help me get these off, please. It takes me ages one-handed."

His predicament lightened the frenzy—just a little.

Slipping to her knees again, she pulled the elastic waistband free and slid the silk down to his feet. Encouraging him to sit on the bed's edge a few deft moves removed the underwear.

"You dazzle me, Aela." Nairn's voice deepened to a growl as he pulled her into the V of his legs, where she allowed herself to be devoured yet again. He kissed and kissed her, holding her carefully with the arm cast, till he'd used up her breath as well as his own. He teased her nipple and tugged at her thong down in a deft one-handed movement as far as he could. "Bloody wrong arm to break, Aela, but I'm dying here. Take it off."

As he tilted back on the bed she slipped off her thong before she crawled alongside him. Nairn's left hand feathered her breast and slithered down her body to nestle in the clutch of curls below.

"Too long. I've waited too long, Aela." His fingers glided along her as she squirmed and panted.

"Yes, Nairn." In her sheer haze of lust she surged closer to him. She'd never felt whipped up into a maelstrom of passion like this before as she rode his fingers unmercifully. Couldn't believe it was happening. Couldn't credit that she loved it.

"Nairn?" Seeking even more...

Nairn was in utter agony.

The angle he was at tortured his broken arm. His ribs were aching, his arousal was on fire, but he wouldn't give in till Aela splintered. Satisfaction for himself would have to wait. Acknowledging his limitations was part of it, yet more important, he had no condom—probably couldn't even open one.

Ignoring his own agony, he slipped first one finger, then two inside her, and kept up the rotating pressure of his thumb on her most sensitive flesh. Her orgasm was close, but he'd experience enough to know the ministrations of his fumbling left hand weren't going to do it. Shushing her whimpering protests when his hand left her, he coaxed her toward the edge of the mattress. Shunting to the edge himself he slipped to the floor, and spread her legs with his shoulders.

"Nairn?"

"Trust me? Let me..."

His leg cast stretched out behind him as he half-sprawled, his lips and tongue continuing what his fingers had started. Ignoring his own agony—he wasn't sure how—in seconds Aela burned and burst like a fire-curtain.

Elbowing back onto the bed alongside her he pulled her to him, mindful of the casts, her heartbeat thudding against his chest, her tremors easing. A single tear slid down her shuddering cheek and dropped onto his skin.

"Aela? Did I hurt you?" He used his fingers to smooth the moisture trace away from her cheek. His mouth followed with gentle kisses till she stilled.

She gasped into his neck. "I don't know what to say, Nairn. It was...I've never had an orgasm like that before."

"But you liked it?" Pulling her head up, he sought the truth from her. Her eyes looked...pained; he felt her draw back from him.

"I definitely liked it, but now I'm so guilty. You've not..."

"Don't I know it? But you can help." He plundered her mouth again, pulling her hand down to his pulsing arousal. "Aela, I don't have a condom." He kissed her hungrily, showing her how to squeeze and caress him. "So do this." He guided her hand, teaching her what he liked as he continued the onslaught on her mouth. She was a quick study. Soon, almost too soon, he felt himself roaring out, spilling onto the delicate skin of her stomach, screaming inside with the pain of breathing. Pain it seemed almost everywhere else now, except his spent erection.

The irony of it didn't escape him.

Physically he hadn't been ready for this, but they'd taken the edge off their hunger.

Maybe.

They slid into the most comfortable position they could manage and lay wrapped together. Nairn sensed when Aela drifted off to sleep. She didn't stir when he crawled out of bed to down a dose of pain killers; accepted him back under her arm like a mewling kitten when he edged alongside her.

Before the pills kicked in with their magical sleep properties, he tried to work out how to keep his hands off her delicious body, for a while longer, till he recovered a bit more. He was damned if he'd do shove-by, makeshift love with Aela again. The next time he'd show her just how proficient he was at bringing them both to a mutual climax. His groan he squeezed back into his throat—a new erection wanted most desperately to be inside her. How the hell he would manage to not pounce, he couldn't envisage.

Chapter Nineteen

Aela stirred on top of the pile of clothes Nairn had strewn over the bed, his arm a protective bar across her naked hip. She touched her face and realized the boxer shorts' elastic was imprinted on her cheek. A glow warmed all around her, a smug satisfaction over what they'd shared, but there was an undeniable shame as well. Sliding away, she removed what she could of the debris without disturbing him, and then draped the cover over his motionless form. She fisted her clothes, and then, like a thief in the night, she crept into her room.

It took ages before she fell into an exhausted slumber. Guilt wracked her for having caused him so much pain, yet all he'd seemed focused on was her satisfaction.

Later, when she surfaced again her conscience bothered her even more. She shouldn't have allowed it. What they'd shared had been an escalation of her craving; it was a yearning run riot, and it hadn't even been the full meal. If they made love properly, she wasn't sure she'd be able to walk away in three weeks with her heart and soul intact. He was coming to mean far too much to her...something no other man had ever done.

She had to distance herself.

Yet how could she say no to a short fling with the best lover she'd ever have, because though limited in what had happened the night before, she'd had too tempting a taste of what Nairn Malcolm was capable of. And his body wasn't properly healed!

It had to stop now.

Business only.

She showered and dressed on automatic pilot.

"Aela?" Nairn's lighthearted plea reached her as she walked past his bedroom door. "Can you help me, please?"

Oh God! It was going to be much harder than she thought. Mentally bracing herself for the inevitable she drew deep breaths before walking into his bedroom. "Good morning, sir."

"Sir?"

Nairn's eyes lost their happy welcome. He held his tie outstretched for her assistance. Pretending nothing had happened between them, without meeting his eye, she silently helped him fasten his trousers, touching at an absolute minimum. When he was properly dressed, she faced him, forcing her tone to be even, and impersonal, though her heart felt gutted. Every single word hurt.

"I don't want to talk about last night except to say it was my fault, and it won't happen again. It was a mistake. I don't need a lover. We need to get back to our professional only relationship. Friends maybe, but definitely nothing else."

She could no longer maintain eye contact when his jaw firmed, and a vein started pulsing at his neck. Far from blushing this time, she felt blood drain from her face as his eyes grew antagonistic, shutters slamming into place. He viewed his neatly sorted appearance; lips tightening to a slit his words were clipped. "I hear you. Thanks for helping me dress. I'll not ask too often."

When she bent to gather discarded clothing he stopped her, his hiss urging her upright again. "No need. A valet will pack during our breakfast meeting." He held her shoulders, his fingers trembling with tension, his anger seeping into her. "I can see you're regretting last night, but we need to work around this."

Shrugging out of his grasp she turned away unable to face his pleading. "No! We don't! I'm sorry." Taking a shaky breath a whisper was her best. "I did want what we shared last night, but it can't happen again. I'm sorry to disappoint you, I'm going back to Canada soon, and I don't want a fleeting relationship."

Rushing to her room, unchecked tears dripped down her cheeks as she ensured her case was ready for collection.

The strain was horrendous as they rode the lift down to meet with Prince Hasson. When the prince was called away soon after their meeting started, Aela was barely able to contain her glee. She'd had more than enough of the potentate's inappropriate attentions.

They departed after the aborted breakfast meeting and headed for the airport. It was a very long tense flight, their interaction terse and minimal, the strain so bad Aela contemplated jacking in the job when they arrived back in London. If that was to be the pattern for the remainder of their days, she wasn't sure if she would be able to survive the Arctic relations between them without having a nervous breakdown.

She had work to keep her going, though, during the flight back to London and, typical of Nairn—she knew him well enough already—they even had time for a short visit to the office on their return.

"Too late to head back to Lanera tonight," he declared around eight-fifteen that evening. "Alert Richard, please, that we'll be staying over."

By then Aela hadn't expected anything different. They'd both maintained controlled attitudes. It was what she told herself she wanted, but she missed touching him, kissing him. Hell, even properly speaking to him. Missed him!

****

Indifferent interaction between them was detestable, but it was how they played it the next day as well. Into the office early she slogged on till around two p.m. when Nairn buzzed her.

"I've a client meeting in half an hour. Bring the Range Rover to the door for me, please."

"You don't have a lunch meeting on your diary, sir."

"Change of tense, Miss Cameron. I didn't. But since I just made the appointment I now do have a meeting. Do you have a problem with that?"

Apart from the posh voice of the navigation system, stony silence accompanied them on the short journey, till Aela pulled up in the car park of the office building.

"Do I need to be prepped for this meeting, sir?" Determination to be professional reeked from her, maybe a little too much because she hated the impenetrable wall between them.

"You'll cope. I'm here to negotiate a better deal for the newest advertising campaign for Adrenalinn Adventuring. Robin Ellesmere was primed to attend, but he's gone off for emergency dental treatment. That's why this meeting wasn't on my diary."

Aela refused to apologize for her manner. Their cool relations were his fault just as much as hers, but she was careful not to allow her feelings to be noticed by the advertising executives. As she was coming to expect, the meeting was successful from Nairn's perspective, though it did take a couple of hours. By the time they were through, though, some of their antipathy had melted—not totally relaxed, but not at odds either.

Nairn was describing an earlier ad campaign as she drove along the slow lane of a busy divided highway on their return to the office.

"What is—" Nairn broke off when his butt began juddering on the seat.

"Brace yourself!" Aela yelled as her finger flicked on the left indicator, the nearside of the car shuddering even more to the right underneath a yelping Nairn.

Aela yanked her foot off the gas pedal. Defensive driving techniques she'd learned years before got their first proper airing. She was wrapped in traffic. Car in front; one behind; another in the next lane alongside. A glimpse at the rearview mirror told her the car behind was too close for sudden deceleration. Harsh braking was no option anyway.

"Hazards!" she yelled at Nairn.

Nairn angled forward and punched on the hazard button in the middle of the console. Before sliding back in his seat again he flipped down the visor at his side of the car for a rear view.

"He's too bloody close, Aela!" he warned.

"No. Look. He's slowing down."

Adrenalin pumped fiercely as she guided the convulsing car over onto the hard shoulder, thanking the almighty the driver behind had got the message as soon as the hazards flashed, but he was still a hairsbreadth from her fender as she cleared the carriageway.

Struggling to keep on a straight course, Aela's grip was indomitable till the car eventually grated to a halt. Setting the parking brake she braced her forearms on the steering wheel. Her whole body was still vibrating, though thankfully the car wasn't any more. Her head twisted around to look at Nairn before she collapsed back in her seat.

"You okay?" she muttered, a nervous smile erupting. "Bejeezuz! Thought we were done for, there."

His eyes flickered, his mouth twitching before he groaned. "You sure are a cool customer under pressure. What the hell happened?"

Aela didn't care to analyze. The adrenaline was

still pumping high and all she wanted was to devour Nairn. Unclipping her seat restraint she grabbed his face and took his lips in a kiss robbing both of them of their senses. Still on a roll, she snatched another. Nairn needed no prompting to control the next as his good arm crushed her to him.

Sanity slowly returned. They were not in the safest of places to be conducting any kind of lovemaking, or an affirmation of life. Slipping free of his grip, her chest heaving, Aela grinned. "We are still alive, aren't we?"

Admiration, gratitude, barely banked lust…and something else, really intense, radiated back to her. When he eventually spoke his voice was the deepest whisper. "Yeah. My…oh…so competent PA. More alive than you know." His knuckles stroked her cheek.

For an eon Aela stared. Nairn stared back. Neither moved. But the car did from the buffeting blast of other vehicles whizzing past.

"Don't you dare move yet, Nairn Malcolm! Not till I make sure it's safe," she ordered as her pulse settled, just a little.

A swift check of the side mirror told her when it was clear to open the door. Staggering her way around to Nairn's side, she checked the state of the car.

The front wheel under Nairn was in place though only barely, and was pitched at a precarious angle. Exactly what was wrong with it, she hadn't a clue. The tire seemed to be intact. Nairn wasn't sure either when he gingerly removed himself from the car and stood alongside her. Both, however, thought it much too coincidental to be just one of those things. The Range Rover, Nairn explained, was less than a year old and had never had any malfunctions before.

Vehicles gusted past them as they gaped at the

wheel, but since the Range Rover displayed no appearance of an accident other road users drove along on their merry way.

"I get the impression a change to the spare tire is not what this needs." Aela waited for Nairn's response to her question as he pulled out his cell phone.

"We're not touching this at all. It would be normal to call the emergency road services, but I'm thinking a bit of advice from Detective Woods won't go amiss on this one. What's your opinion, Aela?"

Easy to concur.

Detective Woods was categorical. They should sit tight and await the breakdown services. The Range Rover would be towed for a thorough inspection by the garage services being used regularly by the local police. He would send transportation to get them to wherever they wanted to go. Detective Woods wasn't treating the incident lightly.

The hard shoulder wasn't the most comfortable place for Nairn to wait but there was no choice; remaining inside the vehicle wasn't the best place to be either. After what seemed like a very long fifteen minutes a bright yellow breakdown truck drew up behind them.

"Looks like a problem with two of the wheel nuts," the mechanic muttered after he had squatted down and had a first inspection of the wheel. "We'll know better after it gets a good investigation back at the shop."

Aela stood back as the man got to his feet and brushed off his fingers on his already greasy coveralls.

I'll just take some snaps of this, sir. Standard procedure now."

The mechanic disappeared inside the cabin of his truck, and returned with a camera. After taking some general photos Aela watched him take detailed ones of the wheel area. The Range Rover was just onto the tow-truck ramp when Detective Woods arrived in an official squad car. He didn't look too impressed at first as he came alongside them and squinted at the car up on the ramp.

"I'm getting the feeling you need a babysitter, Mr. Malcolm." His words were softened by a small smile.

Aela wasn't sure whether to be miffed by his statement, or to ask who he recommended.

"I don't think a bodyguard could have done any better than my competent Miss Cameron," Nairn grunted as Detective Woods went off to confer with the mechanic.

The hot look Nairn sent her way scalded Aela's nerve ends, warming her to her center, much more than any complimentary words could ever do.

On Detective Woods' return he confirmed the mechanic's preliminary diagnosis. Something had likely caused damage to the wheel nuts. "More paperwork for me to shunt around, Mr. Malcolm, but don't worry, I'm sure you're not on a suicide pact with this new PA of yours."

It appeared as though it was yet another botched attempt to ground Nairn...and Aela as well. Results of the car inspection would take time.

Aela helped Nairn fold himself into the rear seat of the squad car, then squeezed herself in alongside. By then sanity had fully returned, their frantic affirmation of life past history.

"My apartment, please, if it's not too much trouble," Nairn requested of the police driver, his voice dispirited more than exhausted.

Six-thirty was really early to be home, but Aela agreed a return to the office wasn't worth it. They could as easily continue in Nairn's study.

Strung out with the events of the day, it wasn't

too difficult a decision to hit the sack early, her resolve to resist Nairn having strengthened again. No sex. Business only.

Nairn was far too worn out anyway. "My sore bits need a little TLC, Aela. How good are you at body massage?" Nairn's weak grin followed her as she turned for her room.

"Useless, sir!" she quipped, walked back and gave him a swift peck till she realized her resolve hadn't even lasted seconds. She evaded a second kiss for he hadn't even the strength to reach out his good arm and catch her. "But I'm pretty sure Richard could arrange a real masseuse in a blink for you. Want me to ask?"

Separate rooms.

Nairn's genial laugh echoed in the hallway.

****

The next morning. Saturday. Aela was stumped by Nairn's bold statement on entering the dining room. "Eat breakfast quickly, please. A cab's on the way to take us to the airport."

Though told nothing the night before she wasn't too surprised when Nairn declared she was flying him to Estonia to check the setup at the Adrenalinn Adventuring base. A few hours later Aela had them successfully landed at the airport in Tallinn and straight on to meetings at the base. Routine stuff.

"I won't need you for the rest of the afternoon, Miss Cameron. I've arranged to meet with a representative of the Tourist Board." Nairn's declaration after their lunch at the center was a surprise. He was too good at arranging things without giving her information, or consultation. The atmosphere between them had been congenial during the morning, but now he didn't want her?

"You won't need me for notes...or something?"

"No. But I do need you to go the check-in desk. There's something you need to pick up."

213

Like the good little PA she was, Aela trotted to reception to find he'd surprised her again! Nairn had arranged for her to be included in the afternoon kayaking tour around the waters of Tallinn.

Fabulous.

The ancient marine castle of Tallinn was astounding as Aela paddled her way around the bay in a two-person kayak, a center instructor behind her. The strong sunshine reflected off the water, the old medieval town a fascinating backdrop. The stone fortifications, turreted walls and parapets made such an impact from the water her smile seemed never ending. The old prison buildings were just as fascinating. The whole tour was exhilarating!

Four hours later, she struggled out of her buoyancy aid as Nairn hobbled up to her.

"Impressed?" Nairn's midnight blue eyes twinkled.

Aela could barely answer, so fired up with the pleasure she'd just had. "Totally incredible. I must come back sometime, and do the two-day kayak tour to the island of Saaremaa."

She eventually dropped the buoyancy aid onto the counter top, the assistants hanging the returned suits on the racks and stowing the other gear in behind. Peeling off her sticky neoprene-sided boots she dumped them too before she turned to Nairn and gave him an unconscious hug of thanks. "You've no idea how at home I felt paddling out there on the water. Peter the Great's walled city is incredible, unlike anything I've experienced, and to see it from out on the bay like that was...heaven."

Nairn's arms clasped her. Even more heaven, but his next words shattered her comfort zone. "Sorry to burst your euphoric bubble, Aela." He grinned down at her, those eyes of his a teasing glimmer. "I need you to tell me right now. How easy was it to unclip?"

Eyes hit the ceiling. "You used me as a guinea pig?"

Nairn's answering laugh said it all.

Aela couldn't believe it. Nairn had given her such a fabulous experience...yet had used her at the same time—the devious sod! Still, she couldn't stop the mirth rising. "You watched me, didn't you? So you know just exactly how much I fumbled, Nairn Malcolm. And it's only the month of June...not September when it's much colder!"

On their way back to London that evening, Nairn confessed to wanting to give her a taste of northern Europe. And he had to have someone reliable give him the low-down on the clips on the buoyancy aid. A firm glow settled around her. She loved it that he thought her reliable. That he had virtually engineered the trip for her enjoyment gave her such a buzz. She wasn't sure she'd ever meet anyone like him again.

She forgave his subterfuge but resisted his playful advances when they got back to his London apartment, shrugging off his straying hand as she rose from the dining table. The atmosphere between them had been light, less of the sexual tension, though it still hovered. The fact that no suspect incidents had occurred that day had made Aela fear less for their safety; no doubt it had lightened Nairn's mood as well.

"A couple more weeks of being your employee. Let's just focus on that, sir!"

"What if I don't want to focus on that, Aela?"

Her laugh echoed in the hallway as she closed her bedroom door. Fourteen, maybe fifteen days tops, still to go. The old prison at Tallinn flashed before her. A prison sentence, indeed. Difficult to go to her lonely bed.

Aela's dreams were full of...

A confined, happy...prisoner.

Chapter Twenty

Entangled in work, they spent the next toilsome days at the London office. Any minor glitches they put down to usual operational errors, nothing untoward, thank heaven. Yet it seemed the whole office, and warehouse staff, were walking on eggshells. Unfortunately no evidence had been uncovered to prove the accidents *were* anything more than accidents.

Aela was glad Nairn kept her so busy because it meant no time to brood on what she was beginning to fear might have been too hasty a decision on her part. Keeping her distance. From Nairn. But the time of the month had descended along with hormonal temper surges, so having sex with Nairn was a moot point anyway.

His health was improving, his ribs much healed, but he was back to being polite. Not cold. Just controlled. He'd obviously decided she was a lost cause and had put seduction out of his mind.

Well. Not really.

She knew he still wanted her, but now it seemed he was better than she was at repressing the yearning. Sometimes he shuttered his smoldering looks when she intercepted them. At others, he let her know exactly how he felt. Didn't attempt to hide his crinkling tents. Or manufactured collisions when he stole fleeting kisses. Or when he put his arm around her as they studied documents, or shared data on his screen.

It was infuriating when he caught her ogling him. He grinned back. Or winked. Even blew her air kisses! The man was insufferable, but exhaustingly gorgeous. She would never meet anyone like him ever again. That same thought...again. It made her stomach plummet. But she'd resolved to have no fling with Nairn Malcolm.

"Two short hops to organize for tomorrow." Nairn was, as usual, succinct.

They'd stayed put in the London office for a couple of days Aela reckoning it was par for the course they were off again—and truth be told, she was excited by the prospect of being on the move.

"The Netherlands first for a meeting in Rotterdam with a Hot Air Ballooning company representative. I'm negotiating to add ballooning to our repertoire of European activities. Ever done any balloon trips?"

Aela's smile was huge. "Just one! Floated over Ayers Rock and the Australian desert for a bit out at Alice Springs. It was one of the highlights of our Australian leg of the world trip. We splurged out a heap of dollars, but it was soooo worth it! Can you imagine drifting up in the hazy grey-blue alongside the MacDonnell ranges? Then, when the muted colors of pre-dawn seep into the oranges of sunrise, the kangaroos bounce across the rugged landscape." Aela sighed dramatically with the recall. "The birds were pretty fabulous too."

"Well, I've got to say in Europe ballooning is more at the vagaries of weather conditions, but I'd like to get my fingers in that particular pie too!"

She was amazed that he remembered so many things she had said or done when they'd first met. "You've done some ballooning?" she asked.

"A bit like you. A totally memorable trip over the Kalahari in Africa, but I've ballooned in other places too."

Aela poised her pencil ready for details. "Ah...the joys! But back to organizing. Rotterdam, then fly back to London?"

"Not quite." Nairn was back to an enigmatic deep-blue twinkled expression and mischievous tone. "When the Rotterdam meeting is over, we're moving south to Paris to meet with guy looking for investors to support a new facility he wants to build."

"Paris?" Aela's squeal of excitement could probably have been heard all the way to L'Arc de Triomphe. Nairn grinned at her enthusiasm.

"Ever heard of Bun-J-Ride?"

"Can't say I have."

"It's a cross between a bungee jump and skiing—or cycling—off a ramp over a valley, or a canyon."

"Whoa! Sounds...scary!" Aela's eyes twinkled at the vision, although her one and only bungee jump had been a bit daunting. "And then back to London tomorrow night?"

Disappointment probably peppered her gaze but she couldn't help it. Paris was such an exciting prospect to visit.

"No. We'll stay over in Paris since the second meeting is not till 4 p.m. and I have no idea how long I might want to thrash that one out."

Aela had spent three days in the Netherlands, mainly around Amsterdam and Den Haag, and managed to zip through quite a few of the tourist attractions, adoring the quaint style of everything there, including the canals. She'd love to see more but another fleeting visit appealed a lot.

But Paris?

****

The flight from London to the Netherlands was short—the airspace extremely busy. Vigilant concentration was required as she followed landing procedures at Vliegveld Zestienhoven, near Rotterdam. Their first meeting was conducted efficiently, Nairn ecstatic that ballooning looked on the cards within a couple of months.

Flying to Paris was much the same as the earlier flight—busy European airspace again. Once they landed, and were out of Le Bourget Airport, an arranged car sped them to their destination. Aela was delighted about that. Driving Nairn around Paris didn't appeal, even if they did drive on her customary side. Everything enthralled her as they whisked past numerous landmarks.

The meeting went on till eight-thirty, Nairn only concluding when he'd negotiated the best deal. Aela took notes, referencing when required. Nairn's grasp of French impressed her. Although the talks were largely in English, at times the client couldn't find the words to describe the experience he wanted to set up. Nairn's fluent French filled the gaps, ensuring translation for Aela when needed.

What a guy!

Exhaustion had crept in by the time they were ushered into their hotel suite. She could only imagine Nairn was hanging on to his last energy by the thinnest of threads. Opening the door to their small balcony her gasp went uncontained. "Oh friggin' heck! Would you look at that?"

Directly in front of her was the Eiffel Tower. Since dusk was only just falling, the view over the city was incredible. So incredible it brought a lump to her throat. "You've done it again! You've stayed here before haven't you? You knew we'd have a view like this?"

Nairn hobbled out onto the flagstones to join her at the railing, his arm draping her shoulder, his fingertips tingling her skin. He turned her to him and dropped a soft kiss on her lips. It lingered...till it ended in a soft whisper as Nairn turned her to face the vista before them. "Never stayed in these suites before, but I've been on a lower floor, so yes, Aela, I did expect to get a good view when I told you to book this place."

The balcony was the perfect spot as dusk fell, the temperature still pleasant to be outside, so tempting to flop down and savor the view for hours. Showering and gearing up to go downstairs, or out to another restaurant, seemed too exhausting for words. Again Nairn took her breath away.

The candlelit dinner he'd pre-ordered for the small balcony table was something else.

Enchanting. The setting was so magical Aela seriously struggled to keep her distance from the charm of Nairn Malcolm. Though shattered, he gave her a verbal guided tour of what they could see as they ate.

Room service discreetly cleared away, leaving them with the fascination of a perfect Paris evening. Aela didn't want it to end, but Nairn was beyond whacked. He hadn't complained yet she could tell his chair, though normally comfortable for most people, wasn't supportive for a still healing torso. He'd already taken his pre-sleep dose of painkillers and they were kicking in with gusto.

"This is too beautiful for words, Nairn. I don't think I can tell you how much I appreciate what you've done."

Nairn's reply was sleepy. "You are the beautiful view, Aela. Glad to be able to provide the rest."

"Come on, Mr. Masochist, time for bed." Dropping a tiny kiss on his forehead, she grasped his hand. Nairn's tired eyes glowed in the semi-darkness. Lust, hope, and...something else, was there, yet the grimace when he got to his feet was more telling. Her arms cradled as she ushered him through the doors and on toward his room.

"Have I wasted money on this suite, Aela?" Expectation, tinged with a measure of resignation, was in both tone and heated glance.

"Naughty, naughty of you, sir. Told you before.

Friends, Nairn. I'll help get you to bed, but that's it. No extras. Remember?"

No demur resulted when his lips stole a lingering kiss. It was so hard to keep to the infernal resolution she'd made—impossible not to respond, but the soft kiss had little oomph in it. Nairn swayed in her arms. Reluctantly, she peeled herself away and shuffled him to the edge of his bed before she removed his solitary shoe, his lips still nuzzling any body part they managed to land on.

"Going nowhere. You need rest or I'll be flying you onto some hospital helipad for emergency resuscitation."

"Bet you can give me all the emergency resuscitation I'll ever need."

She evaded marauding hands as she unbuttoned his shirt and pushed him back onto the bed to remove his trousers.

"Come on, Aela. You know you want me."

No way was she removing the boxers. Nairn was already asleep as she slid his body under the covers. Looking so peaceful she couldn't resist the kiss at his cheek.

Huge bed.

In seconds she was naked except for her cotton panties, and she was in alongside him.

Aela awoke the following morning to feel a warm hand squeezing her breast. Nairn nuzzled her shoulder, his erection bobbing against the small of her back. Unfortunately she could also feel the rigid plaster cast around his arm for it was wedged between them. It was the work of seconds to turn around and kiss him senseless. His warm hand continued to caress her body, working its way south as his lips plundered hers, but she knew making love properly couldn't happen yet-she was the one who wasn't ready. This time, she decided, would be all about Nairn's satisfaction.

He protested at first when she broke off the kiss, protested even more when she slipped from his grasp. His protests lost their vehemence, though, when her lips found his throbbing flesh...and didn't leave before he had the sexual release she'd determined on.

Afterward, she evaded Nairn's declaration that he'd make sure she was satisfied too. Making light of it she scooted from the bed and collected her clothing before he could detain her, her head shakes quite definite. "Not even going to take a rain check, sir! That mistake was my very own, but as I said before, it won't happen again. PA only, remember?"

Time was in her favor, literally. They had to rush to be at the airport for the take-off slot they'd pre-booked, and she needed another day or so for her period to be over, but Nairn didn't need to know that.

Relations between them were...odd for a while. Again sexual tension escalated far too many times, but there was also a strange withdrawal. Aela cursed herself for creating the awkwardness between them. She'd given him the opportunity to have sex with her, and she now regretted it. Not because he'd not satisfied her, it was because he was coming to mean too much to her. She couldn't bear to do the fling thing and say goodbye. She was in the grip of retreat, yet again. Sex with a fully healthy Nairn was not something she'd be able to voluntarily walk away from.

She'd no idea why Nairn should be embarrassed by their morning in Paris escapade, but she felt he was. Molten gazes and lingering brushes of hands still happened, but at other times Nairn seemed uncomfortable, averting his eyes quickly whenever she looked at him. The strain was only relieved by exhaustion for they were both working flat out.

Two mornings later, Aela walked through to

Nairn's office and switched on the speakerphone. The Glasgow Police office. Security tapes from the hotel car park had been examined, they had evidence Nairn needed to view when he was next in Glasgow, though it wasn't urgent. On its own it wasn't conclusive enough but might prove helpful. Aela listened in as, a clearly disappointed, Nairn agreed to meet with them as soon as possible, explaining that business would keep him in London for another few days.

Again it was late when she got Nairn back to the London apartment. Food and separate beds. It had been a repeated refrain for days. All she'd allow for they skirted thin ice again. She'd fielded his intense looks during the day; sensed he craved her as much as she craved him but they'd avoided physical contact, reining in their passion on the few occasions their fingers brushed. Their lack of contact was killing her.

The yearning grew even more.

****

"Who's calling please?"

Aela maintained a professional tone even though she felt anything but gracious since she and Nairn were at loggerheads again. Just short of four-thirty p.m. it had already been a long day and that 24-hour-a-day contract had been no joke.

"It's taken me ages to track him down. Put me through now."

Aela winced and waited for her name. Another of Nairn's bloody women!

"You must be a new hire from the filing floor so I'll excuse your ignorance. My name's Thaliana."

Through the open office door Aela saw Nairn popping painkillers into his mouth, swallowing them down with a swig of water.

"One moment, please." Putting the call on hold, she walked to his office door. "I'm transferring a personal call, sir. Don't ask me who for she's not enamored about speaking with new hires." She deliberately returned to her desk loudly informing him over her shoulder, "By the way, your caller doesn't like to be kept waiting."

Aela smacked the appropriate button to transfer and set about her next task, scolding herself for getting annoyed; reminding herself the woman was no concern of hers. She was only Nairn's employee for a getting-smaller number of days, and she personally wasn't going within ten feet of him again. Even as she thought the words, she knew how much of a lie they were. Her mood darkened as the afternoon waned.

Just short of seven p.m. her irritability crested, she needed to lay down the law or she'd surely combust. "I'd like to finish soon, sir." She forced her tone to be impersonal, yet decisive. "If you don't want to return to the apartment now, I could organize a taxi for you if you want to wait longer."

Nairn's glare could have stripped varnish. "Ten minutes. Then we'll go."

Their drive to the apartment was totally silent. Whatever caused Nairn's mood was as murky as her own.

He seemed on edge when they entered the apartment, his eyes hedging as he spoke. "Have the evening off. I've made plans. I don't need you till after breakfast when we'll leave for Lanera."

Though he didn't specify it appeared he'd made a date with Thaliana. Aela only had herself to blame if he turned his attentions to another woman, but she didn't have to like her decision.

Determined not to be distressed by Nairn's nasty dismissal, she donned her best semi-casual clothes and made her way downstairs where the concierge ordered a cab to take her to a Greek restaurant she'd seen advertised during her brief stay in London. At the time, she and her backpacking friends had avoided the expensive restaurant, but now it was the perfect boost to her spirits.

After a solitary meal she lingered over coffee and ouzo, enjoying the traditional Greek dancing on the small dance floor. It was noisy, friendly and energetic—just right to lift her spirits. Advances by some handsome young men she rebuffed easily, but did allow herself to be persuaded by her server to join in when snaking lines danced together. It was fun enough to pull her out of her gloomy disposition over deliberating what Nairn might, or might not, be doing with the sultry-sounding Thaliana.

Just past midnight she returned to the apartment and buzzed for entry, and was surprised when Nairn answered himself instead of Richard, although he was clearly dressed for bed. On opening the door his intense scrutiny was accompanied by a Neanderthal grunt.

He'd not seen her change of clothes earlier, had not seen the sparkling orange vest top and black satin trousers she was wearing.

"Been painting the town red, or should I accurately say orange, Miss Cameron?"

"Yes sir, probably just like you have! I've had a lovely evening, thank you, sir, but I'll be ready whenever you want me in the morning to make our way back to Scotland."

"That was the plan, Miss Cameron, though if you hadn't been out partying all night," he unfairly stated, "you'd already know we're heading to Barcelona instead. I've appointments there tomorrow."

Aela refused to feel irresponsible. He was the one who insisted she have the evening off, which although she'd enjoyed, had been solitary! He could easily have called her cell to give her the update. So why hadn't he?

"I'll be ready whenever you want me." Her voice was efficiently clipped as she bid him goodnight. The man made her so mad...but she still wanted him, none the less.

****

Whenever he wanted her? Nairn cursed quietly to quell the rising torment. He wanted her all the time. The little tastes of her hadn't nearly been enough, and the need was now back to unmanageable. Yet instead of grabbing and ravishing her he growled at her disappearing back. She didn't want him as her lover—had made that clear in Paris.

"Breakfast at half past four. It'll take at least forty-five minutes to drive to the airport. The plane will be readied for your six o'clock take off slot which I organized, myself, this evening."

Aela closed her door with a definite thump, but it didn't offend him. His door thump was even better, but he was swearing at himself, not Aela.

The fact she was safely back at his apartment didn't cancel out the anxiety he'd felt during her absence. Alone and wandering about in London. He'd expected her to have Richard get her a meal; had expected her to remain in his apartment. Had expected...hell, he didn't know quite what he'd expected her to do, but it certainly hadn't been go out and enjoy herself—looking the way she did!

Looking that way, any man who saw her must have been drooling over her. His good fist banged the wall. But she had come home, thank heavens, to his apartment, even if she wasn't to be his.

He'd had a bloody awful evening. He'd agreed to meet Thaliana for dinner, a stupid gut reaction to Aela's rejection, but as a diversion it hadn't worked. On three past occasions, Thaliana had been amusingly sexy and temporarily available, the way he liked women. Short-term fun.

Thaliana had been sympathetic to his injuries, in some ways touchingly concerned, yet it had taken only a few minutes with the woman for Nairn to realize he didn't want to be with her. He wanted Aela. And only Aela. Except Aela wanted nothing to do with him.

Aela responded to his kisses, he was sure her desire for him was just as great as he felt for her, yet she didn't want him.

He cursed himself for being so inept during their attempted lovemaking in Muscat. Although she'd climaxed, his clumsy fumbling around must have sickened her! Paris was worse. She'd not even let him near enough to try again in Paris.

He yanked off his dressing gown, cursing the state he was in both emotionally and physically. The need for Aela gnawed, and he was no longer thinking short-term. What about her, though? When he forced recall of her actual statements, all she'd said was she didn't do flings. He was sure now a short fling wouldn't do it for him either. Could she have meant she would want him long-term...like maybe very long term?

Such a concept had never before crossed his mind. No previous woman had ever prompted such thoughts. Did it mean he more than just liked feisty Aela Cameron? Maybe was in love with her? He wasn't sure, but he did know he'd never felt such yearning; and he'd never respected, or had such a high regard for any woman before either.

Proving to Aela they could have a longer-term relationship wouldn't be easy. The black cloud descended over him once again. But tomorrow was another day. He'd have to bide his time a bit longer and plan—temper—those urges. But he would win her over.

Chapter Twenty-One

Four-thirty a.m. found them snatching a quick breakfast and coffee. A few hours of sleep had done very little to bolster Aela's confidence in confronting Nairn, yet she determined to be competent as she drove them to the airport. He was pleasantness personified; the fuming rage of midnight had vanished.

Confidently flying Nairn's jet, she was pleased he'd stayed outside the cockpit. That way, she didn't have to talk to him. After handing over to ground crew in Barcelona, they climbed into the waiting taxi, Nairn orchestrating the conversation neutrally as he organized the day's meetings, his attitude so positive it made her sick.

His night with Thaliana must have cheered him up. Aela hated the very thought of it. Her mood sour, she hoped she kept resentment from her tone, but wasn't too sure about it, or, in her misery, too concerned either. He was a bloody android! How else could the unfeeling tyrant seem so smug? She was the one who had pulled the brakes on their lovemaking, but he didn't need to rub his conquest with another woman in her face!

Aela had visited Toledo and Madrid but hadn't gone anywhere near the coastal cities of Spain during her backpacking trek. And she'd not stayed in anything like the stylish hotel he'd had her book them into. After an early check-in to their suite, Nairn declared some rest time before their eleven a.m. meeting. Too strung out to relax, their tense interaction almost suffocating, Aela took the opportunity to go on a short walkabout close to the hotel.

The buildings around her were utterly amazing. Some were incredibly fanciful concoctions with pink-checkered facades and magical balconies that had to be for show only, for they seemed too impractical to be otherwise. Other buildings appeared just plain weird in their architectural style. Many had strong Islamic overtones in the turrets and long narrow windows, the streets a mish-mash of whimsical styles. The balconies of one particular building reminded her of face-masks, the kind worn at regency masked balls, though she was unsure of why she thought that. The Casa Batllo...according to the sign. She resolved to pick up a guidebook for more information.

The sun shone making the air pleasantly warm. Her grin widened as she moved on and found something just as exciting at the next corner. What an incredible city!

The last working days had been so fraught with tension it was a relief to be free of Nairn's overpowering presence for a while. And free from the specter of sabotage, although thankfully there had been no further incidents. Focusing on the views, she pushed aside gloomy thoughts.

Fabulous little tapas bars and small boutiques peppered the streets as she whisked around at warp speed to make the most of her short break. She wasn't normally impulsive, but she couldn't resist the dazzling gown displayed in one window. The sheath was a deep, sensuous petrel blue-green. One shouldered, it had delicate beading around the molded bust line. The back was non-existent with the exception of one slender cross strap. Not long afterward, she was back in their suite clutching the cellophane-wrapped garment. Contrasting ankle-strapped heels and a tiny clutch bag hung from one hand. Her credit card had another serious dent in it, though her savings account in Vancouver would cover the purchases till Nairn paid her generous salary.

Another package lay deep in her purse—an impulse buy from a drugstore she passed on the way back to the hotel. Her hesitation over what kind of condoms to buy had nothing to do with language problems, a wild guess had been her best. So not like her!

Flopping on her bed she exhaled, excitement still tingling. Who was this new woman?

Aela had existed for more than six months with a backpack full of inexpensive practical clothes and for no logical reason she'd just blown hundreds of euros on a dream dress she might never wear. Being in Nairn Malcolm's orbit was turning her head, but she'd needed an outlet for the intense frustration consuming her.

Aela decided later the mad spending-spree had been worth it because they spent hour after hour in tight negotiations with two different sets of clients. Their eleven a.m. meeting lingered through a late lunch, concluding around two. By then it was Spanish siesta time, though they didn't have one. Up in their suite, Nairn prepared her for the next meeting starting at four. After the second round of talks, they stepped in to a small tapas bar next to the hotel. Over a quick glass of local wine and a selection of mouthwatering tapas, Nairn declared another rest time for, Spanish-style, their next dinner meeting wouldn't start till ten p.m.

Though the meetings were hard work, the tension had dissipated and a much-relaxed atmosphere was the state of affairs.

"It's only just after six. If you're not too tired we could maybe do a tour of Barcelona for the next couple of hours."

"If I'm not too tired? You're the one who must be shattered, Nairn Malcolm, but it's a very tempting suggestion."

Aela told him about the buildings she'd had a brief glimpse of.

"You're talking about the Antoni Gaudi buildings." Nairn laughed at her expressions of delight. "Pretty impressive, huh?"

He insisted she must see more of the architecture, for she'd only seen the tiniest bit. It wasn't too difficult to persuade Nairn touring around in a taxi wouldn't be nearly as exciting as going around on an open-topped City Tour bus, even if they could only go inside. "They're tremendous value, Nairn, and the commentaries are packed with great information."

An official tourist bus stop was, in fact, right alongside their prestigious hotel, since it was situated in one of the main plazas.

Nairn maneuvered himself into the empty back seat where he could stretch out his leg cast. Although they didn't take advantage of the hop-on hop-off facility, Aela loved the couple of hours spent touring the city, and even allowed herself to be persuaded to go on the top of the bus at strategic points during the tour, egged on by Nairn who promised she'd get a better view of the fanciful Gaudi buildings, and the multitude of church spires adorning the skyline.

They were leaving the restaurant after their late dinner meeting when Nairn read a text on his cell. He flagged a taxi, the grim ogre back again. "My mother is meeting us at our hotel for breakfast before we head back tomorrow."

When she suggested she'd breakfast alone and meet him afterward, Nairn's refusal was categorical. "You'll be there, Aela." His tone brooked no options.

"Why?" She looked at the line of his tense

mouth, and the anger flashing in his eyes.

"Ruaridh has, apparently, been singing your praises." His teeth looked almost glued together. "My mother has insisted she meet you."

Again Ruaridh's name was enough to send him into that thunderous black pit. Nairn soon stomped off to his own room, the cast thumping the wooden floor.

****

Caitlinn was a chic woman in her mid-fifties, superbly well-presented for eight a.m. From first introduction she was unfailing in her manner, and friendly. She asked Aela interested questions about her background, her world travels, and her current status as Nairn's PA. Then she asked about Aela's intentions to visit her Scottish relatives with Ruaridh. Nairn looked confused as well he might for, as far as Aela knew, he'd been told nothing of those intentions.

"When I can arrange an afternoon off I'll organize a visit," she told Caitlinn. "I've got family photographs on a flash drive that I intend to print out. I'm hoping someone will recognize my grandfather and family."

She found Nairn's interaction with his mother difficult to judge. They were comfortable with one another in a strange, yet detached, way. His mother rebuked him for not meeting up with her often enough and he in turn berated her for not visiting Garvald Castle either. Caitlinn then retorted he was never there long enough for her to visit. "You have to know Ruaridh is very taken with you," Caitlinn gushed as they said their goodbyes. "I'm sure I'll be hearing more about you in the near future."

Aela was mystified that Ruaridh had even talked about her during a conversation with his ex-wife. Caitlin's last comment was meant to be a whisper for Aela alone, but was loud enough for the whole restaurant to hear. "Ruaridh looks forward to you joining the family! Now, I believe I can see why."

Aela felt blood rush fiercely across her cheeks.

It was a huge relief when they bid Caitlinn farewell and headed to the airport. Communication between her and Nairn was sparse; he suffered yet again another mood change. A single glance, or a tiny brush of their clothing, or fingers, set off a desperate longing, which she wanted to alternately ignore and succumb to. Never had any man confused her feelings as much as Nairn.

The days were passing, though.

Early next morning Aela drove Nairn to the office for a quick visit before their return to Lanera. She couldn't say why but he seemed edgy, unsettled.

"I don't need you to come in with me!" Nairn's statement was a surprise when they arrived at the car park-and yet, somehow it wasn't. "Take time off. Go walkabout. I'll text you when I'm ready to head for the airport. No longer than an hour, two at most."

When she asked if something was wrong, Nairn barked at her so vehemently she backed off.

Although she felt redundant and quite cast off, accepting his bald dictates, she sped off to visit a nearby street market. It was an intriguing mixture of flea market, world-trade food stalls, and stalls with new products. After spending a pleasant though distracted hour browsing around she found a seat at an outside café for a coffee. There was just time enough to appreciate it before heading back to collect Nairn when he sent her a text message. She couldn't explain the flood of relief, happy her role had shifted to being his chauffeur once again. It had nothing at all to do with being needed by him.

Scolding herself was easy. Self-delusion was the pits.

Nairn's heart shifted when Aela arrived for him,

glad he'd made the decision to keep her out of the office, out of harm's way. Gut instinct had unsettled him earlier, alerted him in some weird way that she'd once again be in danger if she entered the building. Yet during his short time in the office he'd found absolutely nothing to confirm those feelings, but was convinced his decision had been the correct one. Temporarily pissing her off was better than she be dead.

There'd been too many people solicitous of her health. Most he knew were genuine, but he was now so suspicious it was hard to decide who was trustworthy. A few ill-judged comments about Aela having an easy job with extra time off he quashed, with no mercy spared. Especially the semi-ribald comment Robin Ellesmere made about him having ridden his new work-horse so hard he'd exhausted her. Robin had been joking, he knew it, but his comment had been heard by the whole Adrenalinn Adventuring office. He hadn't appreciated the acid look on Stella Grainger's face when he asked her how a particular work issue was progressing.

Aela was in the car waiting for him, safe and well, as far as he could determine, though her neutral look wasn't inspiring. Next he had to face the prickly problem over their return to Lanera. It couldn't be postponed any longer. He remained irked by his mother's parting comment of the day before, yet couldn't bear to have a bust-up with his father over any woman.

He couldn't wait to be back at Garvald Castle, his ribs and stookie leg be damned! The lingering embarrassment he'd felt after their encounter in Paris had gradually dissipated. He'd felt so useless, almost impotent in his inability to properly make love to Aela like he wanted to. And the only way he could stop himself from groping her right now was to remain cool, like she was, as he made an awkward climb into the car.

The flight from London to Glasgow Aela accomplished with her usual competence, her sheer delight evident to Nairn as this time he squeezed onto the co-pilot's seat. Handing the plane over to maintenance crew in Glasgow he bid Aela organize a taxi to a nearby hotel where they could lunch, too hungry to wait till they arrived on Lanera. Of course his wants were more than food, but satisfying one out of two hungers was what he had to settle for.

He ensured the conversation during their meal was pleasant, though suppressing his escalating feelings was excruciating. He really, really wanted this competent, gorgeous woman. Aela remained civil, with that artificial friendship thing she had going, making him even more determined she would be his.

The floatplane trip to Lanera wasn't accomplished so textbook-easy. No sooner had Aela checked in with air traffic control than she was apprised of a potential problem as Nairn listened in on his earpiece.

A raging inferno in a disused Victorian warehousing block on the outskirts of the city, close to the airport, was causing major flight traffic problems. Many commercial and domestic flights in and out of the passenger and freight airport had been cancelled, others rerouted where possible because a huge pall of dense black smoke had drifted up and over a wide area. Aela was given clearance if she took a huge detour. The detour itself wasn't a problem, but the weather update for later wasn't good. A storm front approached from the Atlantic and would affect their flight by the time they got closer to Lanera. She chewed her bottom lip as the information was relayed to them. He could see her concern wasn't about flying the plane, rather more about how he would cope with the ride.

"I've every confidence in you, but if you don't want to do it we'll stay in Glasgow."

"I've had many a scary flight in British Columbia when the weather has suddenly gone down the toilet. I'll be fine piloting so long as you think you'll cope."

Aela evaded the drifting black clouds sweeping up from the southwest, hitting severe turbulence as the weather front made its mark. "I'm making another wide sweep, Nairn, to avoid this low drift. Brace again," she shouted over the growing noise of the battering rain.

Nairn's discomfort was extreme. Adrenaline pumped through his body but he imagined, as pilot, it would course through Aela even more. Her concentration never faltered, though, as she controlled the floatplane. As they got closer to Lanera they were being buffeted by Atlantic winds. Aela relied on her experience to keep the little floatplane level, adjusting the height more often than during a normal flight and balancing it constantly.

"Nairn!" Her cry was faint over the noise of the howling wind and pelting rain. "I'm going to have to go down on the other side of Lanera, then I'll taxi round to Mariskay, but it'll be rough."

The vibration juddered up her arms to her locked-in-place shoulders as she clutched the controls. Her expression looked as tortured as he felt. If he'd wondered before if she was concerned for him, he definitely knew it now. Concern for his health was in her eyes, yes, but he hoped the rest he could see meant what he wanted it to mean, something stronger, like affection. Or...love?

"Can you bear it, or should I try landing on Mull instead?"

His good arm braced against the dash as buffeting turbulence jolted them. For a healthy person, the instability would have been a mild tremor but with his condition, it was something else. As pilot, Aela would have been concerned for any passenger in his condition, but he knew her concern for him was doubled when she often flicked her gaze his way. He was in agony, he just wanted the damned flight over, but he didn't want to make it any harder than it was already for Aela. He just wanted to be home safely, able take her in his arms and kiss the hell out of her!

"Land on Lanera waters." His teeth were grinding together, but he couldn't stop it happening. He attempted a smile, knew it was weak as dishwater. "I'm fine."

One thing he wasn't lying to himself about was the fact very soon he was going to tell this woman exactly how he felt about her. He loved everything about her. Her looks. Her generous spirit. Her courage. Her empathy. Her competence. God Yes! Right at that moment he really, really loved her competence!

With incredible skill Aela landed on the far side of the island in heaving waters so high at times the waves sloshed over the wings, breakers he wasn't convinced he'd tackle himself. Although only late afternoon the summer sky was so slate-dark it was like night; the angry grey-caps surging up and around them, their height dangerously close to submerging them. The rain battered the glass windshield, a momentary blocking of the way ahead till the wipers did their job.

"Brace again, Nairn!" she yelled over the horrendous noise. "This isn't going to be smooth." Her words were no sooner uttered than the floatplane lurched, a dangerous list in the high winds. "No worries, Nairn! I've got it under control!"

How Aela managed to keep it steady he hadn't a clue, but it would have been beyond his own experience. The craft vibrated, a violent and relentless buffeting, as she taxied around the headland to Mariskay harbor. The storm lamented, the rain bombarding them with even more force from that direction. Having radioed ahead the automatic roller doors of the boatyard opened for them as Aela made the harbor entrance where she bumpily-bounced the little plane up the slip and inside out of the weather.

"You still with me, Nairn?" Aela grinned. He knew her adrenaline was pumping wild around her-for his was no different.

His smile was weak, his pain-wracked body having given in to the relief they were home. Not dry by any means...but home. And Aela was safe. "Jeeze! That beat the hell out of a boring ride, Aela."

She drove the floatplane into an empty bay. When she killed the engine he grasped her one-handedly and kissed her soundly before she could do anything else. His first greedy kiss led to another, and another heated kiss, before a noisy knocking on the side of the door jolted him from his absorbance. His release of Aela was reluctant; curses flew at the interruption.

"Someone's trying to tell us something," she chuckled in his ear as she unbuckled and prepared to exit, then waved merrily to the bystanders who had watched their entry, and their ardent embraces.

"Just get me home without any more delay, woman." His impassioned plea was matched by the eagerness he could see in her sparkling eyes. "I want to devour you...but not here."

"Mmm, sounds delicious. But don't worry, Nairn Malcolm, you're in good hands. I'll get you home in one piece."

Aela saw to the plane checks before leaving the boatyard, since in the current weather the floatplane would remain there till conditions improved.

Keeping his eyes off her proved impossible as Grant, one of the boatyard employees, drove them the couple of miles back to the castle. If her expression was anything to go by Nairn knew Aela was just as keen to get back as he was.

"You go on in and get the kettle on right now!" Aela chided as he got out at the back door. "Grant will help me with the bags."

Chapter Twenty-Two

The minute Aela opened the castle door it was obvious something major had happened inside.

"Nairn!" She heard the woman's delighted greeting well before she saw a tiny blonde vision do a jaunty skip down the nearby spiral staircase and rush forward to hug him. "I've got those bedroom needs sorted out for you," the woman trilled.

"Mhari."

Aela inwardly groaned. Another of his bloody women. Been there done too many times! Side-stepping their enthusiastic hugging she rushed along the corridor, wishing she'd got well out of range for Nairn's words to his visitor cut her to the quick.

"You lovely woman. Get me to the bedroom without delay!"

Aela didn't want to hear any more as she sped to the office apartment where she dropped her case and flopped, with no ceremony, onto the bed. Nairn's words repeated till she was ready to scream. She even surprised herself by drumming her hands on the mattress, a fevered beat that lost control. He'd been with Thaliana nights ago; he'd just kissed her senseless on the floatplane, and now here was the ditzy blonde called Mhari? Did the man never stop?

Eventually she raised herself off the bed, needing a diversion to pull her out of her fug. Latent adrenaline from the extremely difficult plane ride warred with emotional frustration. Nairn Malcolm was a temporary boss and not a long-term player. Of course a long-term player wasn't what she was

looking for either...

A half hour later, the pool suite Jacuzzi bubbled around her, her furious swim having re-energized rather than exhausted her. The pulsating gushes had only a marginal effect in warding off the horrible images she was creating—images of Nairn with the bubbly blonde wrapped round his eager body. She wiped his large bed out of her mind and focused on the gurgling noises around her.

Gastown gurgles came to mind. In a deliberate attempt to banish Nairn Malcolm she thought of the famous gas-driven street clock in Gastown, her favorite street in Vancouver, even though it was a tourist haven. Home. She'd see it soon. She should have been buoyed by that thought, but it was...depressing.

A while later, after another twenty furious laps, she was exhausted and having a second shot in the Jacuzzi. A prune wouldn't look any more wrinkled, but by then she had resigned herself to her role as PA, chauffeur, and whatever else. Except the whatever-else would never be diminutive blonde bunny, not without a serious doze of chlorine, and some leg chopping. It was amazing how difficult it was to huff under the bubbles of the Jacuzzi.

"Aela?"

She was astounded to see Nairn enter the pool suite.

"Sorry to disturb you."

He didn't look sorry. He was staring as she dipped in and out of sight in the bubbling foam. She wore a bikini, but still he looked agitated. He checked his watch, and then groaned. Loudly. "Just came to tell you we need to leave at seven-fifteen for Mariskay. I've booked a table at the Ship's Inn for seven-thirty."

He dragged his gaze away, momentarily closed of his eyes, then whirled away.

Instinct told her his first reaction to her almost naked body had been sheer hunger. Now he was at the door, using the walking aid so well he seemed hardly incapacitated at all. She lay back and closed her eyes, willing her unruly body to stop yearning. Who was eating with him in Mariskay? It crushed her to ask his retreating back; but that professional conscience kicked in-she felt she had no choice.

"Nairn?" He turned slowly, his eyes darting askance. "When will you want me to come back and collect you?"

He whipped back in her direction. "Come back? Why would I want you to do that, Aela? You'll be eating there with me." His mouth formed a grim slash as she rose from the froth and walked toward him. He looked angry; his brows were drawn into a frown as though something had just occurred to him. "Unless you've managed to make alternative arrangements already?"

"No, I haven't, but I thought perhaps you meant your visitor, Mhari, would be eating with you."

"Mhari?" Nairn looked genuinely perplexed. "Why would Mhari want to eat with me when she has a husband and child at home to eat with? Aela, if you'd waited long enough to be introduced you'd have found out Mhari was the architect I employed to reconstruct Garvald Castle four years ago."

Her shame was muffled as she dipped her head onto her chest. The significance of his words kicked in. "I'm sorry. That was so friggin' rude of me."

Nairn lifted her chin. His searching look in her eyes made her even more embarrassed. Oh piffle! That darned rush of blood scalded her cheeks, she felt on fire again. This man made her so...mad!

"Aela? Were you jealous of Mhari?" He didn't wait for an answer, or a denial. He took her lips in a soft, caring, but all too brief kiss. She wanted it to go on, and on, but she dragged her eyes back to his

delighted blue ones. The demand for her complete focus snared her to him. "Mhari's original plans for the reconstruction of the castle included a small service elevator. The construction work and mechanics were already done when I came back from one of my trips. I was an arrogant shit. I pulled the plug on it, deeming it would be unnecessary."

She thought Nairn sheepish as he continued, "I didn't like the anachronistic look of its metal door in the corridor because, as you can see, we've tried hard to give the castle a feeling of age, even though it's all a facsimile. I thought the shiny steel door spoiled the continuity in the corridor and made the place look like a hotel."

"A hotel?"

He cuddled her close, his fingers tracing a light pathway up and down her spine. "I was being bloody-minded and unreasonable. At the time, I was living out of a suitcase, sometimes in bijou hotels with dinky little elevators, and I didn't want that here in my home. Even though Mhari put up some resistance, I insisted she had the doors removed and false walls put in place, instead of removing the interior structure entirely."

Aela squirmed closer. "So, all the innards were hidden and easily uncovered?"

Appreciating the heartfelt groan seeping from Nairn, she rubbed herself sinuously against the parts of him that showed they were interested in her attention.

"Yes. But let me finish my story, woman." He nudged her hips back just the tiniest bit. "In view of my recent incapacity, I realized how wrong I'd been and asked Mhari to get it operational as soon as possible."

Aela found herself dragging her lips across his for another soft kiss before whispering, "What time is it?"

"Doesn't matter, for it's never going to be enough." Nairn's answer was drowned as he developed the kiss further. A few minutes later he disentangled himself. "Now I wish I hadn't made the dinner arrangement to meet with Ruaridh."

"You'd rather stay here?" Aela knew her own answer to that one.

"Oh God, yes, but I must talk with my father. Can't postpone it any longer."

She tried to convince herself to stop being swayed by his drugging kisses as she went to her room to dress. At seven-fifteen, she was at the back door. Nairn wasn't in the bedroom on the ground floor. It had been cleared of his presence; the room was starkly bare and tidy. The subtle new developments had just been worked out when she heard a soft hiss, the deep bronze door not looking too out of place with the décor in the corridor.

Nairn exited his grin exultant, his kiss a fierce plunder. Aela went all hot…again.

"I'm not often wrong, Aela, but I was about this little beauty! It's small, though I did specify Mhari had to make sure it could take a proper wheelchair. There's no way I will be so ill-prepared again."

Aela knew her inquiry lacked punch when he ushered her toward the door. "Food?"

Nairn nuzzled again for a bit before he exhaled. The poignant sound was not caused by his ribs this time. "Got to go, Aela. Can't put this off any longer."

She was unclear what he meant. He surely wasn't just talking about hunger.

Dinner was marvelous, although Ruaridh had cancelled. Nairn seemed to be edgy about it, but Aela wasn't fussed for there was a strumming tension building between them that she couldn't wait to be resolved-back at the castle. It was no great surprise when Ruaridh joined them as they were having coffee.

"Aela!" Ruaridh's bear hug of welcome almost crushed her. "It's good to see you back."

"You too." She gave him a little peck on the cheek.

"Don't even think of hugging me too, Father." Nairn's sarcastic quip blasted, phony emphasis being put on their relationship as he glowered at Ruaridh. "I've a bone to pick with you."

Ruaridh's answering grin gained the laugh he'd intended from Aela. "Only one? You must be slipping, my lad!"

"What was in your mind, old man, foisting your ex-wife on me in Barcelona?"

Ruaridh's grin was even wider. "That's no way to refer to your dear mother, Nairn."

Aela accepted Ruaridh's hand-patting before he continued. "I hope it wasn't too much of an ordeal, Aela, meeting Caitlinn?"

She polished her tact. "Caitlinn was very nice and keen to find out lots about me. Thank you very much, Ruaridh."

"Nosy was she?" Ruaridh's chuckle reverberated across the room.

"Mother was her usual domineering self, driving the conversation where she wanted it to go." Nairn's eyes remained on her as he added, "It was very enlightening, Aela, to find out both my parents seem to know much more about you than I do."

Ruaridh shook his head. "You just don't ask the right questions, lad. When you learn to do that you won't be left behind."

"Well, tell me, then?" Nairn pinned her gaze, seemingly refusing to rise to Ruaridh's bait. "Have you got lots of family skeletons you're hiding from me?"

"I don't think so, but I won't know till I meet them." She truly found the situation amusing though the dissent between father and son was still unfathomable.

"Fancy coming out with me tomorrow, Aela, if Nairn can spare you for a while?" Ruaridh's tone was mirthful as he turned to include Nairn in his innocent gaze. "I've hunted down your great-grandfather's nephew on Mull. There's also another cousin of his still alive, and they'd both love to meet you." Ruaridh then quoted the names of the people he'd located.

"I found records for those names on the internet," Aela cried, now sure they were the correct Camerons, since Cameron was a fairly common name in the surrounding area.

Nairn couldn't refuse to give her the time off to go sailing with his father; how could he deny her anything when she was so enthusiastic?

He felt such an idiot.

He'd been blind jealous of Ruaridh, but the phone calls and meetings made good sense now. Ruaridh definitely liked Aela, but now the jealous haze had cleared a little—just a little. His father's regard for Aela was that of a concerned friend, and nothing more. Relief washed through him because he no longer had to suppress the concept of alienating his father over a relationship with her. Of course, he still had to make her believe she was the one for him. He knew that now.

They spent a while chatting to people who came by to get an update on his health, though at the same time it was clear Aela was being checked out.

To his total chagrin, she told everyone her visit to Lanera was temporary, emphasizing her short-term contract, and was so enthusiastic when relating her plans to do her Masters course back in Vancouver. An added bonus, she said, was Ruaridh helping her contact long lost relatives.

Though she wasn't ignoring him, he found sitting beside her was unbearable.

As Aela drove him back to the castle he reviewed his own plans. Her contract was still extant, but for how long? Rapid calculations made, there was a handful of days left to convince her she could be his lover for more than a fling. But he had to tread carefully and not scare her off again.

Light and friendly, putting no immediate pressure on her was the tactic he decided on. Probably for the best, since his body still wasn't up to the gymnastic bouts of sex he wanted with this stunning woman. Being ready was just around the corner, though, his near-permanent arousal would just have to wait.

In the castle hallway he kept his invitation cajoling as his lips took hers for brief, but strangely satisfying, little kisses. "Would you care to try out my new elevator with me...to make sure I'm satisfied, before I reach my bedroom...and my huge...bed?"

Clearly Aela knew how to parry teasing. "Not happening tonight, thank you, sir. How about I really do take a rain check?"

Before he could recapture her lips, she sped away to her own quarters. Unfortunately, running after her was not yet in his repertoire. Cheeky tease! The reference to a rain check he filed away as a very positive step forward. Prior to dinner, he'd been so sure she was as desperate to make love as he was, but since then, she'd backed off.

Patience was bloody hard to summon, but there seemed little choice.

****

The next day dawned clear and hot, perfect for the floatplane flight to Glasgow for Nairn's early hospital appointment. Once again he was chameleon-like, back to being just friendly. Aela determined to be the same. What else could she do?

The consultant gave the green light for weight

bearing on Nairn's broken leg saying everything was healing nicely, and his cast was redone with a proper walking cradle. The new lighter-weight plaster stretched from below the knee to his toes. Nairn needed to bend the knee again and gradually get the muscles flexing properly. A different lightweight walking aid replaced the heavy crutch he'd been using. Nairn was over the moon when he hobbled out to her, his limp was fast and furious!

His arm cast had also been changed to a lighter weight support, freeing his fingers. When he reached her, regardless of the watching consultant, the kiss he gave her almost knocked her for six. It went on, and on, and heated the waiting room to furnace hot. A discreet cough behind them reminded her where they were.

She couldn't miss the twinkle in the doctor's eye when he, quite loudly, stated, "Give the ribs a chance, Mr. Malcolm. Or perhaps I should book you both into a recovery room?"

Nairn made a new appointment for a few weeks hence when the plaster casts would be removed, then they bid their goodbyes. His mood was euphoric. It seemed it wasn't just the casts that were lighter; his whole demeanor seemed lightened too. His jaunty hobbling had Aela striding to keep up as they headed for their waiting taxi.

An interview at West End Glasgow Police Station was their next venue. Minutes after their arrival, Aela found herself sitting alongside Nairn in front of a bank of monitors, one of which displayed the hotel car park security tape the day of his motorbike accident. The detectives had included her in the showing explaining that although they'd no real expectations of her recognizing anyone they felt she should view since they suspected she'd also been targeted as a victim at Nairn's London headquarters.

The grainy images were hard to discern; careful viewing being advised. Nairn concentrated on the freeze-framed images of a man and woman. They'd exited a car in the bay adjacent to his motorbike.

"Do you recognize either of these two people?"

Aela heard Nairn's breath exhale as he answered the detective. She recognized the tone already-Nairn was frustrated with himself. "The man I don't recognize at all, but there's something familiar about the woman, though I can't pinpoint it."

Nairn was bothered even more when the footage was repeated because the man did seem to be tampering with the bike. The car had been parked cunningly close, the back passenger door left open deliberately. The woman partially obscured the view of the camera, but the opinion of the detectives was the man was maliciously interfering with the bike's front wheel.

Nairn's disappointment grew even more acute by the end of the interview. The woman, he repeated, was elusively familiar. The detectives concluded the tapes could be used as evidence later to prove malicious intent to harm, but only if further evidence was uncovered. The police warning them to remain on their guard, since a motive for the bike tampering had not yet been established, sent Nairn into the pits of hell.

It was easy for Aela to sympathize with his impatience since it was clear the threats to both of them had been spitefully intended. Calming Nairn's rants was a challenge because he was again berating himself for putting her in the firing line. Yet again she refused to leave his employment. Nairn's euphoria on leaving the hospital had distorted to a sunken gloom.

Thorough checks were undertaken before the floatplane took off; there was no way she was flying an aircraft that had been fiddled with. The extra time she took didn't seem to matter to Nairn given that he was preoccupied, intensely frustrated and disappointed. At times during the flight his introspection was unbearable, and her advances to lighten his mood were either met with gruff answers or stony silences. What she could do, however, was be a competent pilot, and thankfully the short flight was accomplished smoothly with none of the drama of the previous day.

Ruaridh called after a late lunch at Garvald Castle. Was she free go to Craignure, on the island of Mull, that afternoon? Nairn readily agreed. Too readily.

She didn't know whether to be peeved or joyful about getting out of his range when he grunted his afternoon work could be done without her. She whipped out her flash drive and made printouts of her collection of family photographs then fled. Her ancestry quest was what she'd come to Scotland for, not to get embroiled with a moody lover who ran hot and cold.

The visit was a revelation because Aela found the old man bore physical characteristics akin to her Uncle Harris. The tone of voice and the deep rumble of his laugh were uncannily alike, but the man's lilting accent was a big difference. She was saddened to realize her own father might have looked just the same if he hadn't died while still a young man. On the positive side, her elderly relative was able to identify and name a few of the people in her photographs, telling her his female cousin on another small island nearby would be much better at remembering the family stuff. The visit ended with Aela promising to return soon to meet up with other family members. She hoped she'd be able to keep to the promise, though her days as Nairn's general factotum were diminishing. Her gut clenched; she was going to miss Nairn so badly.

On their return journey Ruaridh relinquished the wheel for her to pilot them back to Lanera. Brilliant! Her spirits were buoyant by the time she reached the castle.

"Back down to London tomorrow," Nairn informed her as she entered the office. "Just a quick hop, though. I'm going to my corporate lawyers to sign the agreements with Prince Hasson."

"Will he be there?" She wasn't sure she wanted to be there if he was.

"Don't expect so. His legal team should arrive with his signatures already in place."

The rest of their interaction was lukewarm, polite...

Except for the many times Nairn seemed to bump into her, or touch her hand...or shoulder. And the looks, the searing hungry looks were the worst before he turned away and hobbled off.

Chapter Twenty-Three

Next morning's cloud levels and wind conditions prevented them from going to Glasgow by floatplane. They instead traveled by catamaran with Aela at the controls. It was exhilarating, even if the journey south took a bit longer.

The day was successful, thankfully without the presence of Prince Hasson. Aela cherished transporting Nairn, and mentally patted herself on the back as she felt she'd been competent in her PA duties as well.

But for the rest, she wasn't so sure. Their interaction wasn't unpleasant, merely tepid. Now, on their return journey she was desperate for some sort of resolution, or compromise. There were hardly any days of her contract left.

Surely she could contrive something?

There'd been no overtures to resume any kind of sex with her. Nairn seemed to have taken her at her word. Some unnecessary touches, yes, but no stolen kisses. She should be glad, since it was at her own behest. But she was frustrated...and exasperated.

As one colleague to another, Nairn coolly applauded her expertise on landing at Glasgow Airport, having encountered some unexpected turbulence over the Scottish borders, but during the sea trip back to Lanera, he melted into a friendly companionship, jabbering away like a bubbly jock. Aela could hardly credit him but wasn't going to, literally, rock the boat because he was just so...annoyingly stirring. Sexual tension was strung between them like a trip-wire waiting to be breached. One tiny glance was all it would take for the smoldering to warm, and warm, and escalate into full-blown fire.

Aela was coming to understand how Nairn's fevered brain worked—since that was what it seemed to be. Problems were thrashed out in moody silence, followed by some conclusion he personally could live with, and then the sun appeared from behind his black clouds. His mercurial moods infuriated her, but at least she now felt she had an inkling of what drove him. The specter of the sabotage still sat heavily on him as they discussed it, and she accordingly cut him some slack. Returning his friendly overtures about other topics of conversation she couldn't prevent her reaction to him. She didn't want to repress the sexual urges that strangled her with every touch...or look. Unfortunately, she was piloting the catamaran, and was physically challenged.

"We're here, Nairn," she said on their arrival at Mariskay harbor in the almost-dark. They couldn't possibly have made such a long day trip if it hadn't been the month of June when daylight was at its longest. Full dark didn't descend till well after eleven p.m.

On wobbling and exhausted legs, she piled them into the awaiting Range Rover. Bed. What a lovely concept, she thought as she switched on the car headlights.

Nairn wasn't prepared to wait any longer to get closer to Aela, really close, but first he needed to touch base with developments. He hadn't been near the computer, or phone for hours.

Deliberately.

The last hours of their travel time on the catamaran he'd spent asking Aela everything under the sun. Her childhood; living with her Uncle Harris after she'd been orphaned when her mother suddenly died when she was thirteen; her favorite things; her time at university; her schooling. Anything and everything that occurred to him. In turn he fed her any answers she requested. It had been a magical time of discovery. They'd laughed and shared, and bonded in a way they hadn't before.

He stopped at the office while Aela went on to the apartment telling him she'd dump her jacket and make a bedtime drink for them. Minutes later, he tracked her down in her bedroom to announce that they had to fly off to the Caribbean the following day. She was flopped on the bed, her discarded jacket hanging off the edge.

"The Caribbean? Jeeze Nairn, you don't piss around, do you?" Aela groaned.

"Woman! I'm paying you for twenty-four hours a day…" Grabbing her hand he prized her off the duvet cover.

"Yeah! Yeah! I know, body and bloody soul!"

Nairn grinned at her phrasing.

"Okay. You got me! Where should I book, and for how long?" she asked.

Guilt crept in at the fatigue in her voice, struggling as she was to rise from the bed. "Aela." He grasped her hand as she passed him. He pulled her to him, loosely sliding his arms around her waist. "I know you're bushed, but think about it, we've already worked out that this possible contract is now the most likely reason my company, and both of us, by the way, has been targeted for bleeding mayhem."

"Are you trying to flush them out?"

He meant his answer to be evasive. He didn't want to alarm Aela in any way. "You know I contacted them last weekend for details of the meeting. They were the ones who postponed it, and now their confirmatory e-mail has come. The meeting is definitely on for this Friday." She had penciled in the consortium's two future possibilities. The first opportunity was for the Friday coming, now only two days away. "We are going to this meeting, and we aren't going to arrive too late for it. We leave tomorrow morning."

Aela slipped out of his arms to get things organized, yawning. "Where do you suggest staying?"

He rattled off the hotel where the meeting was being held, unable to suggest any others as he'd never been to the Caribbean before. He left the booking choice to her for a stay of three nights while he volunteered to make them their hot bedtime drink.

He appeared back at the office, two mugs precariously propped on his right cast, to find Aela flopped across her desk, her head cradled on her arms, her eyes closed. He only just managed to decipher her mumbled, "Okay. Weather's good. Leave early."

He closed down her computer, hobbled to the apartment where he placed the two mugs on the table in the small sitting room, then returned for her. "Come on wonder-woman-who-ain't-quite any more! Time for bed." He hauled her up from the seat in a one-arm hug and wobbled her unresisting body down the hall and into the apartment sitting room where he gathered her into his arms and kissed her. No demands—pure sensation. "Thank you, Aela. You are one highly competent woman. All day long you've done my bidding and haven't complained once."

"I haven't?" Aela muttered into his shirt.

"Well, nothing that really mattered." His lips captured hers for a sweet and claiming kiss then he stretched for a mug and presented it to her. "Drink your hot chocolate."

Picking up his own drink, he urged a salutation. "*Slainthe*, Aela!"

Clanking their mugs together, eyes closing, she sipped.

"Come on," he declared a few silent minutes later, even before they had finished drinking. He couldn't wait any longer. He stumbled Aela into her bedroom and started to unbutton her shirt, fumbling one-handedly with the fiddly fastenings. "That clause again, Aela, my competent woman?" Nairn growled into her neck as he found a spot she really liked him to nuzzle. "Get rid of these clothes for us."

"Nairn?"

She clearly wasn't denying him anything, nothing at all as she unbuttoned his shirt first and slid it off his shoulders.

"I can't wait for your body next to mine any longer, Aela, even though we're not going to have mind-blowing sex."

"We're not?" She looked ready to capitulate even though she was beyond shattered.

"No. Tonight we need to sleep together in the proper sense. Please don't say no. I need to wrap myself around you."

They crept into bed naked, Nairn cuddled around her, sort of, as his much lighter leg cast would allow. He was aroused. She wriggled her bottom against the length of him, exhausted though she was.

"Aela?"

"Mmm..." Her sleepy response accompanied another directed wiggle.

"Don't suppose you've got a condom handy?" His question accompanied some vague neck-nibbling, and a few marauding fingers.

A short stretch to the bedside cabinet produced one and Aela had it in place in seconds. A few magic touches, and some deeply soul-searching kisses, were all it took for Nairn to be sure Aela was ready to receive him as he easily slipped in from behind.

Together they set up a gentle rhythm, a slow and languorous build-up, but it couldn't last long. The climax creeping upon him escalated the second his fingers reached around and found the perfect stroking spot. A few really strong thrusts from him was all it took for Aela to shatter around him. He followed a few thrusts later, his cries a mixture of satisfaction...pain.

Slipping free Aela turned around and kissed him. A slow kiss to soothe his hurts as it still had been torture. He'd thought his ribs were healing well. His weak grin went a long way to assuage any repentance.

"Pathetically pedestrian, eh? Couldn't resist you though, not any more." Sleep claimed him. His last coherent thought was that she was so...special.

They'd have better sex in the future; he wasn't at his best. Didn't matter for now. He watched her little grin relax.

She woke before Nairn, just short of the six a.m. alarm chirp. There was no doubt at all in her mind now she wanted to be with this incredible man on whatever terms he was willing to make, for as long as he wanted her. She denied it no longer. She loved him. Had for weeks, probably right from the very first stolen kiss. Whatever time was left of her contract she resolved to include joining with Nairn's body at every opportunity.

She was showering when he called out that he was going up to his own room and would be ready to head out in fifteen minutes. Her tuneless whistling filled the shower cabinet as she rinsed the suds from her hair, thinking of the huge bed in the master bedroom suite. And the fabulous shower stall, big enough for two...up there. A girl could dream. Sometime though?

Fifteen minutes later, her suitcase was packed with a combination of business gear and casual items from her neglected backpack.

The burr of her cell phone stirred her from her introspection. Nairn. "I need you."

A grin broke free seeing the brief text message. Was he luring her to his lair? Or was it just that sneaky little clause again? Didn't matter. He needed her. Didn't just want her—he needed her. Such a small change of word, but Aela put a wealth of meaning into it.

Clothes were strewn all over the bed, again, items he'd yanked from his dressing room rails, but packing them into his case had still proved a setback. Avoiding his straying fingers and lips, she packed for him, telling him to behave.

"Heaven's above! Why am I such a workaholic? Why don't we just stay at home?"

"You're paying me to help you be one, Nairn Malcolm, so keep your clever fingers to yourself, and let me get us out of here."

He reciprocated her laughs and smiles, but groaned at her bossiness as she swept up the case and made for the door. He caught her before she got very far. "You're a torture, woman. Why did I pick such a competent assistant? You should just agree with me and let me have my evil way with you."

Aela let his kiss deepen till she herself could stand it no longer, easing away and urging him to move on. "You're the one who made the decision about this trip. I'm going to do my bit now, sir, and get you there on time." She nudged him into the spanking new lift, softening her jokey chastising by dangling a neat little carrot. "Get your butt in there and keep your pants zipped. For the time being, behave. And if you're a good boss man, I'll maybe give you a kiss tonight."

"Tonight?" Nairn's grimace told her what he thought about her plan before he snatched another kiss in the few seconds it took for the lift to descend.

"You're a witch. Tonight is far too long away."

They were down to Glasgow and then on to London in good time for their long-haul jet, piloted by Nairn's charter service. The connecting flights had been textbook easy so it wasn't too arduous for her to launch straight into the arrangements for the coming business.

Any brushing of hands or eye contact weren't inadvertent at all. They warmed her thoroughly. She craved even that small measure of contact. Sometimes it was more. Nairn couldn't seem to stop himself from taking lingering kisses in between explaining the details.

"Romala Hotels are building new complexes all over the Caribbean and doing corporate image refurbishing in most of the existing ones they've gathered into their portfolio. They'd heard about the package I put together for the first Malaysian deal, liked what I'd done, and since they're looking for something similar, their agent contacted me to suggest I put in this bid. It's a tight schedule for you to learn it all, but here's how we're going to do it..."

Aela beamed at his use of "we". A figure of speech, but it bonded them even more as they worked on the presentation. His fingers often lingered on hers as he passed some documentation for her perusal. Or his eyes sought her out and loitered when a question occurred. Or when she needed clarification on some particular point she, in turn, really just wanted to watch his lips explain it further. They were interim connections: sexual tension and steaming passion on a low simmer.

"Go and lie down, Aela," Nairn cajoled when her head drooped for the third time. He was taking a call from Lanera and she was ostensibly ready to take any notes. "There's nothing I can't manage myself here."

It wasn't a curt dismissal; he was concerned

about her welfare. Caving in, she laid on the neat little airplane bed.

The feel of Nairn's lips on her brow stirred her. So comfortable, pillowed in the crook of his good arm. When he'd joined her wasn't important; he was wrapped around her, and that was all that mattered. Nairn's silent gaze warmed and rippled all the way through her; it spoke of fast and furious sex in the future. Mutual satisfaction of the soft and sweet, as before, was all Nairn was fit for, but she wasn't complaining.

She gave him another light kiss before his eyes closed. She let herself drift again knowing her smile was happy, and more than a little bit smug.

It was a short hop from the airport on St. Vincent, to a nearby island. Aela had booked them into the same hotel as the business venue.

She was itching to have her fingers on the controls of the small plane. A little way below them the Caribbean glistened, the water taking on darker hues of blues and deep greys as dusk descended. The setting sun, almost vanished for the day, cast a strip of golden flame across the lightly rippling waves; a few ethereal cirrus clouds hovered alongside the blazing orb their edges backlit with white-hot fire. Aela felt a deep sexual excitement build as Nairn's thumb caressed lazy circles on her sensitive lifelines.

Their hotel complex was even more stunning than in the internet advertising, each villa having its own discreet butler service. Aela gulped at the decadence of their stone-built villa, the outside dining gazebo itself a fabulous structure. She gulped again for she hadn't realized just how much of a romantic getaway it was.

When the beaming porter introduced the accommodation it wasn't quite what she thought she'd reserved. There was only one bedroom with a super king-size bed and a convertible couch in the living area.

Although they'd shared a bed the night before, and on the airplane, no way did she want Nairn to think she'd set it up.

Chapter Twenty-Four

Nairn ushered the porter to the door, pressing a large tip into the man's hand, stating they'd need no further butler service at present.

"Aela, it's perfect." Nairn avowed when the porter's back retreated from view.

His lips crashed onto hers with no doubt at all in his kiss. Her own response was no less frantic. Dazed, she realized they had rocked each other toward the bed and he was removing her blouse. One-handed, again, but not too much of a problem since she sped up the process. She was so ready for this, so hungry for this man's touch and still amazed at her reaction to him. Nairn's whispers at her neck, the nibbling of his lips, declared he was beyond ready, the lovemaking of earlier only having kick-started their appetite.

Bending down to pull off the last item, Nairn's almost see-through white boxers, Aela's anticipation increased. He was fit to burst but any momentary hesitation over how they were going to make love she squashed—she couldn't wait another second-they'd work it out. He pulled her to her feet, their lips crashing together.

Aela's loud groan when Nairn eventually locked onto her breast probably startled the tropical birds outside, the thrilling attention sending a contraction of desperation straight to her core. Her eager whimpers tempered his frenzied lovemaking; his clever tongue became a soothing ache; his fingers seeking to assuage the need between her legs. He'd gotten so much better at arousing her with his left hand. In seconds she shattered, her breath literally sharing his. Her knees buckled; a frantic clutch at him for support. An unrestrained chuckle lightened the fierce hunger between them when Nairn turned her so the back of his knees touched the edge of the bed.

"I'm going to sit down before I fall down, for this Sir Smash-Em-Up is not going to crush you to death."

A gentle push from her had his torso down on the bed.

"You're going to have to guide me a little bit here."

Kissing her way down from his lips, under his chin, she nibbled a pathway down his chest to his belly button. Nairn announced he was in heaven as her hand circled him, telling her any discomfort would be worth it, although if she kept up her massage it would be over far too soon.

"Condom, Aela. Has to be now. Right pocket."

Aela ignored him, her mouth taking over. Moments later his hands slammed down onto the bedcovers, his cast missing her by a fraction as he squirmed out of her grasp and bellowed, "Bloody hell, Aela! You've got to stop."

"Sorry. I didn't mean to hurt you."

"Not hurting. Just can't take any more."

"You want to stop?"

"No way! I've been aching to have you. I'm fine; just get the bloody condom on."

The color had leeched from his face so Aela knew he was lying.

"We can't do it like this, Nairn. It's too soon."

"I'm dying here, Aela. Please? I just need to support myself better."

How could she ignore his desperation...or his inflamed erection bobbing a merry tune? Suppressing a giggle at the situation she fumbled for the protection, smoothing it in place as he maneuvered himself into a semi-recumbent position, taking the weight of his body on his braced forearms. Groping for the pillows she padded them all around him. His heartfelt groan amused her all over again, the look on his face incredible since he was half laughing, half agonized. Though totally desperate to have sex with her, he seemed as amused by the situation as she was.

"It's time. Climb aboard."

"I'm not sure about this, you stupid man! On your head be it if you kill yourself." Aela giggled her way across his groin, arranging herself above him, squashing his arousal before she slicked him home.

Nairn's bellow was again a mixture of pained laughter and sheer yelping, his eyes squirming. "Jeeze woman! Definitely on my head! Hurry up, please, before I explode!"

"I'm...oh my...it's..." At first she slid up and down slowly, acclimatizing herself to his girth, her breasts tantalizingly positioned for his mouth to pay tribute to, though that was easier said than done since Nairn was not capable of bending up to feast.

"Is this okay, Nairn?"

Nairn was incapable of answering; all his energy was focused on holding back his climax. His eyebrows twisted, beads of sweat ran down his temples, his pupils defocused in a different sort of drunken haze—it all made Aela grin again.

He wasn't quite so far gone, though, because he surprised her by giving a serious thrust, his good leg forcing his body upward. "You're an evil woman, Aela Cameron, but don't you dare stop what you're doing or..."

Aela clenched muscles making his grimace widen even more, and increased her pace. "Or..."

"I-I'll increase your working hours...a...aah!" His groan was again so loud Aela swore the birds outside stopped their birdsong.

Slow and easy wasn't going to cut it though, Aela could see the strain it was putting on Nairn even when she was doing most of the work.

"I can't wait for you, Aela...but I want you to come, too!"

She had to make it happen quickly. Bending down to him she snagged his mouth, her tongue mimicking their movements, bringing herself to a new height as Nairn's thrusts grew longer and firmer. On one last aggrieved shout, Nairn found his own release then melted into the bed, his eyes defocused with utter pleasure. "My god! I knew I really loved you, woman! But I think I'm dying."

Aela grinned and removed herself, then rolled him properly onto the bed, lifting his leg cast up into place.

"Fabulous. You are so good at this, wonder-woman-and-general-factotum that you are!" Nairn smirked, a weak smirk but contented like a Cheshire cat.

"And here I thought I was useless at sex." Aela's chuckle rumbled in his ear.

"What the hell do you mean?" His pained expression made her laugh even harder as he stared at her, their noses touching.

"I mean I don't have any prior experience in pleasuring a man this way, Nairn Malcolm. You'll just have to forgive my lack of finesse."

Nairn's breath was thready, still recovering in strength. "You've never had sex on top before? I can't believe that, Aela Cameron. You're no shrinking virgin."

His words sounded mildly accusatory but she forgave him when he grasped her hand, twined her fingers through his own, and set their linked hands over his heart.

"I'm no virgin, as you well know, but I've only

had a couple of lovers before you, and we weren't adventurous."

"How come so few? You're so beautiful I can't believe lots of men haven't tempted you into the sack." He lips pecked at her neck.

"Oh, plenty tempted me, but Jed scared them off. Guess I chose badly, the ones I had sex with were only interested in getting to home base with no detours, and weren't interested in the cheerleader getting a thrill." She laughed at the memories.

Nairn's fingers stiffened against hers.

"Jed?"

"Jed. My cousin, Jed!" She was miffed he'd not been listening the night they'd made the sail back to Lanera for she was sure she'd spoken about Jed quite a lot.

Nairn seemed confused. "Jed's your cousin? The one you grew up with?"

She nodded back wondering what had led to the misunderstanding. "Yes, my Uncle Harris is Jed's dad. I told you."

Nairn captured her lips in an addictive kiss before he eventually broke off, a grin emphasizing his relief. "No, actually you just kept referring to your cousin. You never named him Jed."

"Well, in a nutshell, Jed's my protective cousin who's only a year older than me. He takes the family thing too seriously, was the older brother I never had, scaring off wannabe adventurers he didn't like the look of. But I wasn't too bothered since all through my teens I was a happy tomboy. I wasn't pushing for a relationship with anyone."

"Aela!" Nairn gurgled. "Never in a million years were you a tomboy!"

"I told you I didn't do girly stuff with females. I grew up so tall I wasn't like them anyway. I was always mooching around the hangars. My mates, all boys of course, and I went around like a pack of jackals feeding on the older pilots and maintenance crew. Their knowledge was our quarry. They fed us well with know-how till it was time for us to be trained up ourselves."

"Okay, I believe you about that!" Nairn's expression still didn't look too convinced about the rest.

"The guys made passes, but they knew I meant business when I rejected their overtures." Aela's laugh in his ear was a full-blown guffaw as she deliberately held eye contact with him. "Jed taught me well, so you'd better watch out, Nairn Malcolm."

"You'd assault me?" His teasing query raised her eyebrows.

"I wouldn't kick a lame man when he's down..."

She didn't get to finish as his fingers tickled her ribs and set her squirming which in turn made him groan as a new erection burgeoned against her.

"Your pathetic story, woman. I really want to hear it."

"Okay, okay. I was almost twenty before I launched myself onto the sex scene. I was tired of being the only virgin student around."

"Aela!" Nairn's grip tightened protectively around her. "It should only be time if it's what pushes your buttons."

"Yeah, well. In retrospect you're so damn right. I did like the guy at first, but we both got a bit drunk and staggered back to my student room. The minimum of clothes barely off, we fell onto the bed. He opened my legs and pushed in, grunting and moaning, swearing at me because I was so tight. Heaving and whining he told me I was useless and pushed at me."

"The bastard raped you?" Nairn clutched her to him, cradling her into his chest.

"No! That wasn't the problem."

"It wasn't?"

Aela could see confusion gripping Nairn.

"He came immediately. My legs were covered in his semen. He staggered off, and I never spoke to him again."

"So for all these years you've avoided sex, having had such a pathetic first experience?"

"Jeeze, Nairn, I'm twenty-seven."

Nairn slipped his fingers under her chin and lifted her face, so easy to melt in his soft blue depths. Encouraged by his tenderness she continued. "I've had two engagements, and another opportunity to get over my first experience."

She smiled when his brows rose at the engagement word. "Number one: macho guy, ice hockey player, kind, funny, caring. Thought it was a game when I resisted his sexual overtures. I'm ashamed to say I kept him at bay for a couple of months, even though he proposed to me after the third week. He was desperate for me."

"I understand that." Nairn encouraged her to continue, his lips nibbling her sensitive earlobe.

"I thought at the time he was the one." She gasped as Nairn's mouth traveled further, whispering around the tops of her breasts.

"So, what happened?"

"We eventually had sex." Nairn's grip tightened around her as if talk of other lovers didn't please him but his lips moved off her skin. "I hated it, Nairn. I hated his intimate touches. The whole time I lay there thinking, when will this be over?"

Silence fell. Nairn's attentions faltered, the ministrations of his fingers pausing till she continued. "We had sex a handful of times, our split up was acrimonious. He called me unpleasant names, but I felt I deserved every one of them. For a very long time I really did think I was the frigid tease he accused me of being."

"I'm going to guess the next engagement was no

better?"

Aela couldn't help the laughter convulsing her, not surprised Nairn couldn't comprehend her. Before she continued she kissed him soundly and purposely set his hand back on her breast. "Number two engagement didn't get as far as sex. Not even after months of dating."

Nairn looked incredulous. "Was he a eunuch or something? What the hell was wrong with the guy?"

"Twelve years older than me, I didn't enlighten him when he assumed I was still a virgin."

"And?"

"His ex-wife came back into the picture." Hearty grins bracketed her lips as she nibbled at his fingertips. "I was toast from the second she reappeared, and totally glad to be so!"

"So no more attempts at lovemaking?"

"One more guy. Same result as macho hockey player. I hated the intimacy and decided it was something I could easily live without. I dated a lot over the years but never more than a few nights out."

"No one night stands?"

"God no!" Aela was horrified at the idea.

Nairn swooped down for a sweet and loving kiss.

"Nobody felt good..." Aela eventually gulped, "...till you."

"Darling woman, I'm so, so glad to hear that."

Nairn's next kiss was not so sweet. It was predatory and set her pulse racing. She'd heard people talking about their heart bursting with love but had scorned the phrase. Now she knew for she was overflowing with it.

"Aela," Nairn whispered, his voice hesitant but reassuring. "Will you let me make love to you and help you learn?"

"Oh...yeah!" She couldn't answer coherently but covered his lips in a crazed kiss.

Nairn softened her haste and kissed her lips, her eyes, her cheeks, her chin—everywhere. He slid down awkwardly on the bed encouraging her to do the same, kissing her collar bone and onto her breasts where he lingered there for some time.

"Nairn, I love you touching me."

He moved down her abdomen to the thatch of dark hair where he paid the area a lot of attention too.

"Merciful heaven! Yes, Nairn…so good." By then she had a good idea of what he could accomplish and liked it very much. Her encouragement was all he needed to send her over the brink.

Rolling himself clumsily off the bed he pulled a condom from his other pocket. The easy bit.

"Over to you, Aela."

She started at his lips and continued downward. "You feel wonderful and taste…" She laughed again. "I'm not at all sure what you taste like but you're gorgeous, and I want more of you."

The teasing could only last so long. Protection was donned and they kissed again and touched and…loved slowly with hands and lips. Spooning her, he lay on his good side and slipped in. A nice steady rhythm was as much as Nairn could cope with, but both had satisfactory climaxes.

She pondered other possibilities as she drifted off to sleep; her clutch of Nairn as though she feared he might disappear. Out of her life.

No. She wouldn't think about that. That was the future. This was the now.

Chapter Twenty-Five

Nairn struggled out of a sleepy haze not sure what the noise was. Another gurgle. His laughter muffled onto the rumbling belly.

"Aela! Wake up!" He nudged as he slipped away and struggled up. "Food."

Sleepy brown eyes blinked at him as she struggled to consciousness, her upper body rising from the mattress. "Food? Sounds good."

He nudged her again. "Dinner, Aela. But first we need to wash off the smell of ssssex."

"Yeah!" Her lips curled up appreciatively as he bent down to give her a peck of encouragement. "Scrummy ssssex!"

"You might be fine, you insatiable sex goddess, but I stink just a bit too well!"

Aela's gurgle of laughter inspired a bout of tickling till she called for truce.

Laughing, and lingering a little, Nairn allowed Aela to give him a sensuous washcloth bath using the toiletries provided in the sumptuous bathroom. Afterward he informed her, with some vehemence, it was great to smell of something other than baby wipes!

Eventually dressed, they wandered out along the twisting pathways of the complex lit by tall flickering flambeau to find somewhere still serving food. They barely tasted the superb fare. Nairn wasn't interested in his meal, and he didn't think Aela was either, but they needed sustenance.

For ages, into the wee small hours, they enjoyed each other, mostly touching, lots of kissing, and talking, for Nairn needed recovery time.

By then Nairn had no doubt he wanted to be with Aela for many more fun events, but he kept that knowledge to himself. Although she'd given in to her desires, and had relinquished some sticky principles, he still wasn't sure how long-term she might be thinking.

****

Just short of noon they headed to the lunchtime venue so entwined they were almost one body, compensating for Nairn's cradle and walking like a three-legged race.

"Whoa! Did you see that woman?" Nairn stopped at an intersection of pathways and whipped around so quick Aela's laptop case almost slipped from her grip. She hadn't a clue who he was talking about because there were plenty of scantily clad women to claim his attention. "The redhead skipping along there!" Nairn pointed along a pathway to the side of them.

"No, I didn't see her, sir. I was far too busy supporting you."

She gave a playful punch at his good arm, but he was still staring at the pathway the woman had taken. Slipping from his hold she stood right in front of him. "Nairn? I'm not enough for you? You're chasing another skirt already?"

Nairn came out of his reverie, his full focus on her. On an Aela who wasn't happy because humor had faded. "Don't be daft, woman. I'm never ever going to get enough of you." Swinging her into a fierce embrace he kissed her lingeringly then clutched her hand and shook his head as though to clear his thoughts. "It was nothing like that at all."

Aela forced full eye contact with a still mystified Nairn. "So, what then?"

"It looked like Stella Grainger."

"Stella? Assistant Manager of Adrenalinn

Adventuring? Why on earth would she be here?" Aela queried, and then shushed his muttering. "She must just remind you of Stella."

Nairn looked rueful as he stared in the direction the woman had vanished to. "I hope to God it's true. Although you've yet to meet Stella, I regret ever employing her. The woman's a menace."

"A menace?" Aela was quite shocked. Nairn usually had only good things to say about his workforce.

Nairn scraped back the hair from his brow and cursed. Loud enough to cause a flutter of birds to rise from the nearest tree, and an older woman nearby to give him a non-verbal glaring reprimand. "Let's just say she came on to me almost from the first minute she was hired. I made it clear at the time I wasn't interested in dating her, but the woman's a piranha. Every time she had to update me she'd slink into my office and try again."

Aela's giggle made him frown.

"You don't believe me?"

"Oh, Nairn! I truly believe you. How could she not want to seduce you? You're a gorgeous man. That's what Robin Ellesmere was alluding to?"

He swatted her backside to move her on along the pathway as he added, "Yep. She even tried on a business trip to some sites in Northern Europe. Claimed her room had been double-booked and she'd need to share my suite, even though she knew the second room was already occupied by Brian!"

Aela grasped his arm, stopping their progress, her smile fit to break her jaw. "She never did! So unbelievable." A little niggle told her she'd done something similar with their present booking, but it was convenient to ignore it.

"Don't I know it? The stupid woman was miffed when I rebuffed her again for the umpteenth time. Brian thought it the most hilarious thing ever."

Nancy Jardine

Nairn was exasperated even telling her the story.

"What happened then?" Aela could only imagine how awkward the trip had been.

"I got her a room in another hotel and only met up with her when strictly necessary. You can imagine how that went down like a gas-less balloon."

"I can see Stella got to you, but forget the woman and concentrate on this bid."

She put his mind at rest by squirming under his shoulder and set them off down the path to the designated meeting place in the central complex building.

****

Though Nairn felt his deal seemed favorable, the client made it clear no final decisions would be made till other personnel were consulted. A second meeting was called for the following morning at ten. He'd anticipated hitches; the reason he'd stipulated a hotel stay of three nights. Using the hotel's business centre work occupied them till dinner. He'd held himself in check all afternoon, wanting to devour Aela's delicious body every second, his customary dogged dedication to business stretched to the absolute limit but truth be told, his energy reserves would survive another afternoon bout of lovemaking, but not an evening as well. Nightlife sounded preferable.

Aela was showering. Nairn drooled as he washed himself down at the vanity, his imagination jumping ahead a few weeks when he'd be taking her hard and fast against the shower wall at the castle. So aroused he was sure Aela must hear his groans as he exited the bathroom, for he was determined they'd eat first.

The restaurant was just as fabulous as the one the previous evening, a mariachi band entertaining as they wended their way around the tables. Nairn experienced an unaccustomed feeling of total bliss:

good food, good wine, but best of all, Aela. In his mind there was no question. She mattered to him. A lot.

Conversation was spattered with questions about each other's travels as they filled in details unknown about each other until they sipped the last of their wine on an outside terrace, watching the water softly lap on the beach, listening to the sounds of the Caribbean, some manufactured and many of them the natural animal sounds around them.

For Nairn it was magical.

In the warm cocooning darkness they didn't talk at all for a while. Feeling so at one with Aela his fingers caressed hers as she nestled into the crook of his good arm. Then, inspired by their surroundings, he related experiences he'd had at beach locations around the world, encouraging Aela to add her own.

Inevitably the narratives took on the proportions of angler's tales where they landed whoppers—except in both cases they had had the hair-raising experiences they related.

"I think I did a quadruple flip..."

"Whoa! Time for a respite, Nairn Malcolm, Adrenalinn Adventurer. Too much information for a wimp like me. You could have broken your neck. This wakeboarding sounds too scary for words."

Wakeboarding, he told her, wasn't provided for on the island, the wave quality not generally present in that part of the Caribbean. He got the impression Aela was relieved to hear it.

"Stop! Bathroom break before you go on any more." She slipped away from him.

Aela recapped Nairn's daring experiences as she wended her way to the restroom. Deep auburn hair joined her dark hair in the wide mirror as she washed her hands. The woman glanced away, the way total strangers often do, as she shook off her hands and scuttled for the nearby hand dryer, her head in profile.

Aela washed her hands, very slowly, as she observed the stranger. There was something she recognized, and it wasn't just the woman had very eye-catching, long and curling deep red hair. Her profile was distinctive. She had a slightly hooked nose, wide plump lips and her eyebrows were plucked to the point of almost being non-existent, which made her eye sockets seem larger than they really were.

That was it!

Aela bent her head, squelching the bile-ridden anxiety rushing up from her gut. Stalling till the redhead exited the bathroom, she then made her own slow departure. The woman had been glancing back toward the restroom, Aela could tell from the angled bounce of the long hair, though the woman was now darting around the corner.

Aela needed to see the woman's face again, a full-front view. It might just be she was imagining too much.

At the corner her circumspect peek was just in time to see the woman enter the Piano Bar. Aela crept along to the nearest window. Though small, the bar was heaving, patrons sitting, or standing around, conversing over the trill of excellent piano playing.

The redhead approached a guy seated opposite the door, her lingering kiss an almost frantic clutching, the interaction indicating familiarity. Aela gasped seeing the man's face. Earnest talking and nodding to the entrance door of the bar followed as the woman squeezed down beside him. Aela surveyed their intent talk for a few minutes. Both looked bothered; upset and angry.

What the hell was going on?

She sped back to Nairn, her mind in turmoil. "Back to the villa," she whispered all but dragging him away.

Laughing at her haste Nairn complied till he realized it wasn't because she was dragging him back to make mad passionate love to him. "What's wrong?"

"Not here!" Aela hauled him along the walkway.

By the time Nairn hobbled the short distance to the villa she knew he was spooked by the darting looks she'd been making over her shoulder.

"What's got you in such a tizzy, Aela?"

Standing between his spread legs she cuddled him, secure in her grip, her words seeping into his shirt. "You were right. The redhead is Stella!"

"Stella Grainger? But you haven't met her, how can you know it's her?"

She lifted her head to face him. "A redheaded woman came into the bathroom. She didn't recognize me. Though..." She reflected on how quickly the woman had turned away from her at the vanity, and then the darting looks the woman had made to the door of the Piano Bar. "Maybe she did? I'm not sure. But I recognized her."

"I'm too thick, Aela. You're not making sense."

"Nairn, she's the woman on the surveillance video in the Glasgow hotel car park. I'm sure of it."

"What?"

"It's the eyebrows. She's got very distinctive eyebrows, almost plucked to nothing, and she's got a very noticeable hooked nose."

When confronted with that information Nairn had to agree. "But the woman in the car park had short hair, nothing like Stella's mane."

She grabbed his hand and linked fingers. "Had to be a wig. But that's not all. I followed her to the Piano Bar. Her companion was the man we met today. She was all over him, and their kisses were familiar!"

"Hold on! Which guy are we talking about?"

277

She knew her information was getting weirder by the second. "Remember when we finished the client meeting? We left the room and were still talking ten to the dozen when we rounded the corner?"

"Sure. The short guy you knocked over didn't appreciate his file folder being tipped out, didn't appreciate you being so pumped up with excitement over what we'd achieved."

"I'm sure he's the guy the redhead met in the bar."

"And?"

"Nairn. Think! Our meeting was in a private room hired by our client. Most people come here for leisure, and don't wear business suits, or carry business paraphernalia like that guy."

Nairn said he couldn't fault her logic.

"I helped pick up his papers then he went into the room we had just vacated."

"You're thinking he was a competitor who had an appointment after us?"

"Yes."

"Connected to Stella Grainger?"

Unfortunately they both agreed the man seen at lunchtime was nothing like the one who had tampered with Nairn's bike. That guy had been a tall beanpole. The one at lunchtime, no more than five feet eight or nine, was stocky.

But if she was correct the implications were horrible. The culprit of Nairn's mishaps was right on their doorstep—Stella Grainger. What kind of trap were they in? Her head bent to his chest again, her palms making gentle circles round his spine.

Nairn had difficulty believing it could be Stella Grainger. "Too far fetched, Aela. Why would she be here?"

What did the woman have to gain by following Nairn to the Caribbean? Aela had made the booking the night before they left, and no one at his London office knew they were coming here. Prior knowledge of Nairn being on the island didn't seem plausible, or make any sense.

Or, Aela wondered, was it the man who'd lured Stella to the Caribbean?

"How can we find out if it really is Stella?"

"Mike Van Heyden might know who the guy is."

Their questions overlapped each other.

Aela let Nairn explain.

"Mike Van Heyden was initially bidding for this contract as well. He's snowed under with work; I heard he'd withdrawn, though he might be aware of who else is still bidding."

Mike, a friendly rival of Nairn, told them two other companies were still in the running. Nairn knew one, though not the other.

Short of ten p.m. local Caribbean time, almost two a.m. in London, Nairn dialed his office, knowing someone was always on duty. He was delighted to find Ginny was working night shift. Aela hugged him tight to listen in. He had to stay safe. Even if she became the target again she was determined Nairn would not come to any more harm.

The news was disturbing. Stella Grainger had tendered her resignation three days previously, and hadn't appeared at work since then. Robin hadn't contacted Nairn about it because he'd guessed Nairn would be glad to see the back of the woman. Where she was now was anybody's guess. Aela stopped Nairn's agitated pacing by the best method she knew. The kiss to soothe soon became one of desperation; Aela awed by the strength of her feelings for the man wrapped around her, a man of integrity she knew did not deserve any of what had happened to him. Gradually frantic became calm, their foreheads nudging as Aela's heartbeats regulated.

"Can we check Stella's whereabouts on the days of the incidents?" she asked.

Stella hadn't been in the London office on the day of Nairn's motorbike accident. No real surprise since it was a Saturday, but she had been present when the other incidents occurred.

"Where was she working before she came to Adrenalinn Adventuring?"

"It'll be on her file." Nairn vaguely remembered Stella telling him she'd worked as an events coordinator in a hotel.

"That's why she was hired, then? If she'd a background in the leisure industry?"

"Yes. She'd good experience organizing events and activities."

"Did she work for a British employer?"

Nairn couldn't recall, but he'd a feeling it was an international chain. Grabbing her hand he dragged her to their laptops. "We need to go back to the business centre."

Chapter Twenty-Six

A short delay ensued till the business center was opened up for them; Aela realizing money does grease palms when necessary. Once their connections were organized Nairn's searches began. Typing one-handed on his laptop, the fingertips of his broken arm punched numbers into his cell. Connection made he switched hands to lift his cell to his ear.

"Hello again, Ginny."

Nairn's smile broke the tension she hadn't realized was gripping them. Nairn requested Ginny access Stella's personnel records. Brief conversation. Succinct.

"Won't Ginny think it odd us asking for this information? Can you trust her?"

"Sure do! Ginny's tight lipped about everything—knows I'd only ask for something like this if it's really important."

Nairn declared he'd look up details of the other two competitors for the current Caribbean bid.

A short while later Ginny had emailed the information—a crushing disappointment because it seemed they'd gone down the wrong line of inquiry. Stella had never worked for either of Nairn's two competitors.

Aela's eyes lit up though when she looked at Nairn's information. "Nairn! The outfit you'd never heard of before is based in Miami. I know Miami is huge, and it might be another red-herring, but it's the same location as Stella's last employer."

They passed on their hunches to Detective

Woods, Ginny having been asked to locate a photograph of Stella and e-mail it to the police department. Till further investigations were made, they could do nothing else. Aela wasn't surprised when Nairn declared he would attend the next meeting with the client, regardless of the proximity of the maniac who'd put him in plaster, and who'd likely also harmed her. In spite of whatever machinations Stella Grainger and her accomplice were up to Nairn told her he was going to win the contract fair and square—or not at all. Aela had no qualms about that, or with any of his plans.

****

Nairn cradled Aela's naked body in beside him and exhaled loudly. What else could they do but go to bed? They'd exhausted all possibilities and in truth, he was completely pooped.

"Aela?"

"Mmm..."

Her sleepy voice answered him. He kissed her nose, her cheeks, and then her lips-a mere whisper. "I'm sorry I've involved you in this."

"Don't say that again! I want to be with you." She drew closer, rubbing herself against his growing erection. Her voice was quiet, but vehement, as she punctuated her words with fierce kisses down his neck and torso. Kisses reeking of possession. Her possession of him! He loved every single one of them. He loved her.

"Don't you dare try to push me away," she repeated.

Their coupling was faster and more furious than before, ribs be damned, Nairn pulling her to the edge of the bed to accomplish it. A pile of pillows neatly stacked, and him standing, the arrangement had given his casted leg sufficient leverage.

Afterward, Aela cuddled him, their torsos gleaming with mingled moisture, her smile a mile wide. "Hells teeth! So fabulous, Nairn. Remind me to try that position again."

Nairn beamed before crawling back up the bed where he spooned her into sleepy oblivion. "Wish I'd thought of trying that arrangement before."

"Short cast, okay, long cast...absolutely n..." Her voice drifted off on the last syllable.

****

Paranoid though it might seem, he insisted they breakfast on the fruit, which was already in their villa. They drank the canned fruit juice from their mini fridge and used the coffee provided. He wouldn't risk anything being tampered with if they ordered room service, and he'd no plans to leave their suite too early. They remained constantly vigilant till it was time to meet with the client at ten a.m.

At the meeting he clarified a few more points in his bid with the Marketing Director and reviewed the pricing structure. Again it seemed the meeting went well, though the results were not expected immediately.

"Shall I book the next available flight to St. Vincent?" Aela asked as they returned to their villa.

Nairn squeezed her arm, the arm he was already clamped onto. "No, my workaholic P.A. We're not budging our asses from this island! We both need rest. We're booked in for one more night, and we're staying one more night, regardless of Stella Grainger and her sabotage." Nairn laughed at her raised eyebrows. "We'll still watch our backs!"

Of course their rest period only started after they checked in with both police departments. No developments yet was a disappointment, but not unexpected. Contact with the London office was brief, Nairn afterward, surprising Aela by declaring a mini-holiday, though their phones would remain switched on.

"I bet you've never taken a real holiday in ages, Nairn Malcolm." Aela teased him as she whipped off her clothes to his utter delight.

Then she not so delightfully put on a bikini and skipped out to the pool leaving him shouting his frustration as he lounged on the bed.

Still careful of their safety around the villa, he improved their repertoire of what was sexually possible, but what wasn't in doubt was his need to be close, to be really close to Aela. Nobody was going to harm his woman during his guard duty—and Aela declared she had his back equally well covered!

Deciding to eat out that evening took some deliberation, but since there was no way Nairn would entertain anyone delivering poisoned food, he reckoned it safest to be random patrons at the first restaurant they came to. They walked along the widest and most well lit paths and took every care they could, seating themselves amongst the throng rather than being on the periphery. He didn't want to even glimpse Stella Grainger again...or her sidekick.

Back at their villa he concluded that if Stella had been maliciously trying to stop him from winning the present Romala bid, then the danger phase had to be over. It was incredulous to believe Stella would have gone to such devious lengths to prevent him from being successful with the Romala Corporation. He slipped into bed with Aela; exhausted, but the happiest he'd ever been.

Nairn woke first determined that the beautiful woman in his clutches would never be free of him. While Aela slept on he contacted hotel reception and arranged a surprise for the woman he now knew he loved more than life itself.

"Get up, lazybones!" He greeted her from the side of the bed, bouncing a pillow at her head before he reached forward and kissed her lingeringly. "You are so beautiful, you tempt me so much," he mumbled, his hand slipping down to cup her breast before he teased her there with his mouth. He knew he disappointed her when he pulled away and sat up.

"You're dressed already? Why didn't you wait for me to wash your hair properly?" Her hands reached out and fingered his dripping locks since all he was able to do was dunk his head in the washbasin.

"No. I'm not going to be diverted by your fabulous hands. Get up. It's time to rise."

"You already are!"

Aela reached down but he whipped the pillow across his groin. "Not going to happen, woman. Get dressed right now."

"Slave driver," she mumbled scrabbling to her feet and heading for the shower. "Who are we meeting now?"

"Nobody." Nairn followed, unable to resist patting her bare behind because he constantly needed to touch her luscious body. "Dress comfortable casual. Shorts would be good, bikini underneath and wear soft sneakers, not flip flops."

"Such orders, sir! Going to brush and braid my hair too?"

The noise of the shower drowned his mumbled threats of exactly what he'd be doing with her soon.

"Promises! Promises!" Aela chirped, reaching for the soap as Nairn beat a hasty retreat because the sight of her glistening wet body almost...almost had him canceling his plans.

A few minutes later she joined him at their gazebo table, her glass of juice already poured, because he knew already it was how she preferred to start her day. After a simple breakfast, Nairn reached for her hand. "Given the choice, what would you most like to do today, since we have six hours before we head back to Barbados for our London flight?"

As Aela pondered he hoped and prayed he'd read her correctly over the days he'd known her. Her pretended huff was spoiled by her big grin. "My first choice would be to jump back into bed and make love to you."

The smirk he felt spreading across his face wasn't discouraged by her waving finger.

"No, no, no. You made me get up, so my next choice would be to spend some time flying over these fabulous islands, over this sparkling sea and discover the delights of the landscape from a little way up. Absolute heaven and a total dream, I know, but you did ask."

Nairn pulled her onto his one good knee and put his arm around her, his large hand splayed across her breast, giving her a gentle squeeze as he pecked at the lips he couldn't resist. "How about we go for a limp on the beach instead?"

Aela actually looked eager to join him in a lurching hobble. "Good plan. Let's hop the beach."

As they walked the length of the pool Nairn heard the approaching drone of a seaplane engine. It coasted to a halt in front of them as they reached the beach.

Aela looked suspicious as she turned to confront him. "You didn't?"

Her glee was unmistakable when he simply replied, "I did."

Her answering whoop and bear hug almost toppled him onto the sand. Ouch! But it had been worth it to see her delight.

A magical few hours were spent exploring the area, Aela having had a fast induction from the pilot who handed over to her, giving her details for local flying. Nairn itched to get at the controls himself but the next best thing ever was to have Aela fly him around. His competent woman of many talents. He now loved them all. Definitely loved her.

He bided his time though. She wasn't quite ready yet for him to declare his intentions.

Nairn's cell phone chimed.

"Get the call for me, Aela?" he mumbled a while later as he wielded his battery driven razor. Packing was almost completed for their departure.

Aela popped her head inside the bathroom door and relayed the call was from New York. An established client of his on the Eastern seaboard wanted further water sports upgrades, an extension to the order of kayaks successfully supplied only six months previously.

"Great news. Tell him we'll detour to New York tonight and meet up with him tomorrow." He grinned at her.

"Excuse me a moment, please."

He heard Aela respond to his client before she put down his cell and scooted back to the bathroom door. Her next words were a stage whisper at him. "Nairn Malcolm! Do you ever stick to travel arrangements already made?"

"No sense in going all the way home to come back to the Big Apple in a couple of days." He repositioned the razor for a different angle of sweep to get under his raspy chin. "Don't fuss, woman. The order will be signed off after one meeting. Make it eleven a.m. at his New York office if that's good for him."

He continued, leaving her to arrange it, and was haphazardly packing up when she returned with an update. "Client can't make eleven, asked for nine. I know it's early, but I agreed it since it's the only time he can make it tomorrow. Otherwise it would have to be three days from now as he's heading off somewhere."

"Good thinking." His good hand smoothed on his shaving cooler, the woodsy smell redolent of lime

and cedar Aela seemed to love so much she couldn't resist a little sniff, followed by a peck at his cheek.

"Will you be staying at your New York apartment, or shall I book somewhere else for you?" She pulled away from him before he could start something they didn't now have time for.

"The apartment." He grabbed her and kissed her soundly. "Call my housekeeping service and have it made ready. Number's on my cell. They'll freshen it up and stock the refrigerator."

"Did I tell you I've never been to New York?" Aela grinned as she bracketed her hands on his cheeks, forcing his attention. His blue eyes lingered on her lips. "Are you going to tease me this time about whether or not I'm coming?"

"Say no more, woman! You're definitely coming. And you're definitely sleeping in my bed."

This time their kiss lasted a lot longer. Aela's sensory system kicked up in anticipation, but her practical brain ruled as she teased herself away from his clutches, and turned away. She felt the whispering touch of his hand trailing a pathway down her long hair, grasping it back to him, sniffing its fragrance.

"My woman. You're definitely my Snow White," he murmured, soft and sexily. "I love...your hair!"

Aela's heart blipped then slowly regained its rhythm. She thought he'd been going to say something else...for a second time. They'd been having a fabulous affair, but that's all it was, and she had to remind herself of it. All she'd have, if she was lucky, for a few more days. Gulping down a difficult breath she sidled well away from him, her hair eventually dropping from his light grasp.

"We'll stay three days. I've nothing really pressing on the calendar, have I?"

"You always have something pressing, Nairn Malcolm."

"I do. I certainly do," he chuckled as he again reached for her. "But I don't want you driving me around New York. Order my usual limo service."

"Don't you trust my driving?"

His arms snuggled her tight against him. "I don't even trust myself driving in New York. New York drivers scare the shenanigans out of me."

She squirmed against his groin, purposely growing it some more. "I don't think anything ever scares you Nairn."

"You'd be surprised." His look was odd. Wistful. Almost sad.

****

The insistent trill of the alarm startled both of them from deep slumber.

"Shall I book your ride now?" Aela mumbled a few minutes later as she slurped down a quick coffee from the drip machine that had been pre-programmed. Propped up against the countertop in her underwear, she'd had a really quick shower, but Nairn was still stumbling around naked in a sleepy daze. Yet even with plaster casts, he was the most gorgeous hunk of man she'd ever clapped eyes on. It had taken such a short time for her to be comfortable with his nakedness. She would miss it so badly. The coffee suddenly tasted vile.

His answer was dozy as he cradled his coffee mug, his eyes slumberous, but now with more than tiredness, irrepressible sexual promise was banked in the blue depths as he answered. "Sure. So long as you come and help me button up quickly." He toddled off to the bathroom to wash and dress, yawning so widely Aela wanted to join in.

As Nairn expected, the client meeting was straightforward, and brief. Aela's job was easy as Nairn negotiated a good price, which would net a sizable profit.

His office was their next stop. Twenty-seven

stories up in a huge tower block it was only one large room. Two out of five desks were currently manned, the staff of five servicing the office on a 24-7 basis. Aela appropriated an empty desk opposite Nairn, and for the first time in days they had to be circumspect. Employer and employee.

Aela found her glance straying to the other two women, wondering if they could sense the sexual vibes she constantly felt radiating between her and her boss. Nairn, she was glad to see could compartmentalize because he didn't seem to find it too much of a strain as he caught up with a lot of USA news first, then he went global.

Around four-thirty p.m., he looked up from the pile of correspondence he'd been working through. He fingered a card on heavy vellum he'd just removed from an envelope. Aela wasn't sure how to interpret the little smirk sneaking around his mouth.

"Shania?" Nairn's enquiry sounded slothful as he turned to the woman who dealt with his Adrenalinn Adventuring business. "Is there anything in particular you need my physical input on tomorrow?"

"Nope." The young woman shook her neat bob of dark hair. "We've had no problems with any of our bookings recently, and since we didn't expect you to be here I've no appointments made for you."

"Great!"

Nairn's return smile looked decisive. He closed down his laptop then added the paperwork to his carry case. "Tomorrow, Miss Cameron and I are going to do some sightseeing."

"We're going sightseeing?" She wondered if his declaration had just catapulted her into some category which wasn't quite P.A., but since he was preparing to leave the office she began to pack up her own gear. "What do you think you'll be able to cope with, Mr. Malcolm?"

"Don't be so dismissive, Miss Cameron. I'm game for a lot of things I'll have you know."

Aela bit her lip to prevent the huge satisfied smirk she wanted to produce. Didn't she know what he was capable of? Squelching the truthful comment she wanted to disclose-for it definitely wasn't the place-she answered, "Like what, sir?"

"How about we do New York by City Tour bus? Or maybe a boat on the Hudson? Something not involving a walk and I'll be fine."

He smirked as he shoved a pile of unwanted paperwork into the recycling bin beside him, and then turned to his employees.

"As these fine workers will tell you I've not often been to the New York office, and I've not done much in the way of sightseeing myself!"

"You're having me on!" Aela quipped, preparing to leave. Her flashing eyes dared him to deny her words. "You spent a year at Harvard Business School. You're not going to tell me you didn't take a few little body swerves from Cambridge to New York."

"Ah, but way back then my priorities weren't sightseeing, Miss Cameron."

Nairn's cheeky answer, twitching mouth and gleaming blue eyes made her blush. He rose clumsily, rebalanced his cradled foot, clutched the vellum card in his hand, and made his farewell-short and sweet. "I'll see you two ladies next time I'm back this side of the Atlantic."

Aela gathered up their belongings and held the door open.

"Back to my apartment first. I've a dinner engagement tonight." His announcement was accompanied by a jaunty wave of the card.

"If that's what I think it is, Nairn, have fun!" Shania called to his retreating back as Aela made her rapid goodbyes.

At the bank of elevators she pressed the button to summon a car. "You have a dinner engagement tonight?" She hoped her reply didn't sound as unenthusiastic as she felt.

"Yes." Nairn's smile was inscrutable, but she noted it also held the desire he'd had to conceal all day.

"A business dinner?"

"Not exactly." His appraisal of her mouth was becoming more sexual by the second.

"Nairn Malcolm, you are so maddening when you do that!" She gently nudged his good arm.

"Do what?" he asked innocently, snuggling up close.

"Innocent you aren't!" Her tone chastised but also showed she loved his teasing. "Do I need to do anything for you?" She groaned at the thought of maybe having to be his chauffeur. He couldn't possibly be squiring around some beautiful woman he'd pre-invited? Could he?

"Just look your beautiful self, Aela."

The elevator car was so full their conversation halted till they reached the lobby of the building. She took up the threads again as they went out to flag a taxi. "No answer, Nairn. Is it business dress, or casual?" She waited but no answer followed. "Black tie?"

"Definitely black tie."

"How exactly am I supposed to produce that for you at such short notice?"

"I have more than one tuxedo at my apartment. Don't fuss about it." Nairn's chuckle deafened her ear as he leaned over to smooch at her neck. He refused to say more as they piled into a cab—seven New York blocks way too much for his hobbling.

"How long before you have to leave?" she asked stifling a sleepy yawn as she placed their laptops on the dining room table after reaching his apartment.

"Before we need to go. You'll attend this event too, you lovely woman."

Nairn grabbed her round the waist and nestled into her neck as he pulled out the band securing her topknot and fingered her ebony soft hair.

"I've been dying to do that all day. And this..." he murmured, nuzzling the exact spot behind her ear, sucking the lobe and tonguing it in the way he knew highly aroused her. "And this too..." He gently squeezed her breast.

"How long, Nairn?" she asked, arching even more of her chest into his welcome hand.

"A seven p.m. cab will do. The hotel isn't far away, but...say a half hour for traffic." His mouth was now devouring her as he sidled them out of the sitting room. "Jeeze woman! You must know I'm dying for you."

Aela dragged off their clothes, set her alarm for six p.m. knowing if she fell asleep they'd be snookered, and tumbled with Nairn onto the bed.

Chapter Twenty-Seven

Nairn looked up from the dress shirt he was attempting to button. Aela was a vision in a barely there floaty gown of blue-green. The one-shouldered creation was beaded here and there, emphasizing her cleavage. It cinched in at her narrow waist then shimmered to her ankles, just above a pair of extremely high, delicate shoes.

"Aela," his voice croaked as he reached for her. "You're so beautiful you steal my breath. I don't know how you do it but you surprise me every day. You are one hell of a competent woman."

His reverent kiss could have escalated into much more if Aela hadn't drawn back with a chuckle and stepped out of his reaching arms.

"Time to go, lover. You agreed to this dinner engagement so let's get on with it."

"Okay, but you're a selfish woman to deny me so! My fingers are worse than useless now. Look at them shaking with sexual frustration." He waved them laughingly in front of her, tendering his gold cufflinks. "You're going to have to satisfy that little clause again."

"Get on with you," she chided further as she buttoned him up, allowing him only the tiniest peck on her cheek as she yanked him into the tuxedo stretched to the limit over his casts.

Nairn knew exactly what he wanted to get on with. Once again she absolutely floored him. He'd expected her to wear the little red dress she'd worn in the Middle East, but like a conjuror she'd produced the incredible gown she was now wearing.

When had she had the opportunity to shop? His demands on her time had made it seem impossible.

"Where did you produce this sexy dress from?"

"I'll maybe tell you later." His bow tie was fastened in a blink.

****

Aela glanced around the New York venue at a room full of splendidly attired patrons. Nairn's introduction of her as his partner, followed with a by the way she's also my PA and chauffeur at present, seemed to claim her as his woman. A warm glow settled around her heart. It had more of a permanent ring to it since the word temporary didn't feature. At all.

Her impulse purchases in Barcelona were perfect for the glittering occasion. Dinner was tasty if not ground-breakingly exciting, Aela finding it easy to relax as she conversed with people nearby—associates of Nairn. After the meal was cleared, the charity pledging over, soft music filled the room.

"Dance with me?" Nairn's head indicated the already jam-packed dance floor.

His request made her hoot as she pointed to his leg cast. "You can't dance."

"Then let's shuffle." Dragging her from the seat he towed her onto the dance floor and held her tight. Swaying, just swaying, to the slow, sexy jazz throb. "I couldn't wait to feel your arms around me. You're driving me crazy, you lovely woman."

His lips hovered around her ear, close but not quite touching because it was a very formal event. Yet their bodies were plastered together, almost literally, and definitely emotionally. Aela couldn't stop her laughter from bubbling up as she felt something very hard nudge her stomach. She tortured him by wriggling even closer. A few minutes into the dance Nairn's groan almost deafened her.

"This was a big mistake. I can't do it."

"I told you so! I knew it would be too much for you." Aela's scold was softened by her quick peck on his cheek.

"Sway-dancing's not the problem. Holding you like this I've acquired a third stookie. Get me out of here without anyone seeing it, please. I'm an invalid after all."

"Your associates aren't going to buy that."

She grinned at his woefully pathetic look, but he was undeterred. He whipped her round, tucked in at her backside and shunted them off the floor. Aela knew her laughing drew more than a few looks as they made their hasty goodbyes.

****

Tourist pursuits were the order of the following day. The hop-on-hop-off City Tour bus was lazily perfect for more than four hours. This time they did a little bit of hopping. Stopped off to take in a few of the well-known sites up close. Ate hot dogs from a street vendor. Lapped up rapidly dripping ices in the early July heat.

Much more exciting though was their speedboat ride on the *Beast* which whizzed on the Hudson, Aela having had to work really hard and grease a few palms to convince the pilot Nairn really was capable of managing! She wondered what could top it after their ride was over, but Nairn wasn't yet done for they finished up with a tourist helicopter ride over the city at dusk.

Breathtaking!

They collapsed back into the apartment clutching a Chinese take out meal. All they wanted was to be on their own, away from the incredible crowds.

Later they were tucked up in bed languidly watching a movie. A refreshingly cold dry white wine was still sitting in a cooler, having been sipped only a little. They'd already made slow love, craving on a constantly bubbling simmer. Nairn's hand stroked her breast, gently squeezing it as his lips feathered her forehead, her head tucked snugly into his neck.

The peal of his cell was unwelcome, but it had to be important. Only on pain of death had the office been given leave to call. Reaching over for it she heard Nairn's groan as he glanced at caller ID. "Only a call from Detective Woods would make me stop ravishing you right now!"

Aela shifted out of his arms so he could answer properly. Pouring some white wine she watched his face as he received an update. "You picked Stella up at Heathrow Immigration?"

One sided conversations were frustrating, Aela reading between the lines as the call continued till Nairn slid his body up and sat with his back propped against the wall. Sliding alongside him, Aela listened as he flicked the volume higher.

Detective Woods explained further. "It appears she was so unnerved by bumping into Miss Cameron at the resort, she scurried back to London."

Aela snuggled around him as Nairn asked, "The man was with her?"

"No, sir. Her fiancé went back to Miami, apparently very disappointed in Grainger. Claimed she'd bungled very badly since you'd made it for the interviews. It seems they'd been confident you weren't going to make it to the Caribbean."

"This guy, John Sanders, is her fiancé?"

"Correct, sir. Grainger and Sanders both worked for the same employer in Miami, till around nine months ago. Their relationship fizzled out when Sanders decided to strike out and create his own company. His aim was to acquire contracts for hotel water sports upgrades—much like you've been bidding for, sir."

"Stella Grainger returned to the UK?"

"So she informs us."

"Not particularly supportive, was she?" Nairn's question was scathing.

Detective Woods sounded derisive. "It appears from her statement the lady in question was interested in having a financially sound future, Mr. Malcolm."

It was no surprise to Aela that she had targeted Nairn as her future well-heeled husband.

Detective Woods related months passed before Sanders took up with her again while he was in London on business. By then Nairn had rejected Stella's advances so many times she'd given up on him.

"Sanders managed to convince Grainger his company was thriving, and would soon be rolling in big money if he got the Romala contract," Detective Woods explained.

Nairn's voice was glacial. "What made the nasty bitch decide to take revenge on me?" Aela heard Detective Wood's voice catch a little at Nairn's vehemence.

"Sanders heard about the Romala Hotels possibility at the same time you did, and he regarded you as his only competition." The detective continued making a clear attempt not to sound judgmental. "It appears Miss Grainger liked the idea of Sanders making the profit, rather than you."

Again Detective Woods cleared his throat before continuing. "During her confession she was very happy to tell us you continually spurned her advances." Aela could almost hear admiration in Detective Woods voice. "A determined woman, sir."

Beside her Nairn grunted into the phone. "She's a bloody piranha!"

"Beautiful, but somewhat deadly, I have to concur." Aela could tell Detective Woods was quite enjoying the conversation though still careful to keep within the bounds of professional conduct. She snuggled even closer to Nairn.

"What about my bike accident? And the other incidents?"

"She has confessed to messing up orders; organizing the computer virus; setting the fire; and later on paying someone to sabotage the electricity supply. She confessed she was most put out those delaying tactics didn't have the effects she wanted, for she thought you would be too busy sorting them out to be on the move. Since you were still forging ahead with the Romala contract, she decided something more drastic had to happen. Sanders was in Miami so she coerced her young brother to tamper with your bike, unquestionably malicious intent, but it seems designed to stall you rather than kill you."

"What about the accident to Miss Cameron?"

"A spur-of-the-moment tactic to put your chauffeur out of operation and thereby keep you from traveling around."

"And my Range Rover problem?"

"Again, spur of the moment sabotage. She'd heard Robin Ellesmere organizing his emergency dental treatment. It was easy enough for her to follow you to the Ad Exec car park."

"Bloody maniac! So what exactly did she do to my car?"

Aela held Nairn's fingers before he yanked out all of his hair, and did a little bit of the finger massage she was getting very good at.

"Well, it seems her ingenuity and her bravado were a little bit thin by the time she got to your parked car. All she could think about was loosening the wheel nuts in the hope you might have a little problem when you drove off."

"Yeah! We certainly did. She almost damned well killed us!"

Nairn was almost boiling over. Aela, again, had to do more massage magic but not only to his fingers. Detective Woods was on a roll though and wasn't finished.

"It appears the car park was busy and she only managed to loosen two of the nuts, a little bit. Since she was using the wrench from her own car it didn't fit properly. It was sufficient to mangle them a bit and they eventually loosened at the worst possible moment for you. The mechanic's opinion is they may not have slipped like they did if you'd been driving at thirty M.P.H. The fact you were doing sixty to seventy miles per hour created enough vibration."

"So, with all of that, surely you have enough evidence to charge them?"

"Yes, sir, we do, for Grainger, her brother and the electrician friend. Sanders, unfortunately no, since he was not in the UK when the incidents occurred."

Sanders had left Stella and her brother carrying the can.

"Stupid…nincompoop!"

Nairn was scathing beyond belief when the call ended. "To think such a deranged bitch could put me off bidding with those unhinged tactics!"

"She obviously knew diddly squat about you and your relentless work drive, Nairn Malcolm!" Aela cheekily added more in an attempt to bring down his blood pressure. "You know, I really do think she must be a bit deranged. It's incredible she could have been so infatuated with you she needed to take out her revenge in such fashion."

Startling her with his speed Nairn rolled her over and tickled her ribs. "Are you saying I'm not worthy of infatuating over?"

"Wanting your positive attention, yes sir, I can understand," she squealed as she batted out of his playful reach. "But infatuated? No. Who'd want to be so taken by you, Nairn Malcolm?"

"Are you saying you're not the tiniest bit infatuated by me? Or want to be taken by me?"

Aela was certainly taken off guard when she remembered her initial thoughts on first seeing him at the castle wall. Taken by the sexy wild highlander? She'd achieved that...and never wanted it to stop.

Nairn pinned her to the bed and kissed her soundly. Then started to nibble and tickle again. "Don't I make you do passionately irrational things?"

"Hands off," Aela warned because he had indeed found her most vulnerable tickling spot. "Get back to your side of the bed!"

But Nairn was now in a mischievous mood declaring no one was out there plotting to harm them or kill them! The relief was hard to believe. In turn Aela no longer felt Nairn was under threat. He continued to tickle her along the bed till she cried, "Stop!"

He clamped her down again and took his fill of her lips till out of breath he slumped over on the bedcover.

"I'm definitely infatuated by you, you gorgeous woman, for you make me do passionately irrational things, all the time, my darling!"

His eyes closed as he regained his breath. Had he just declared more than a passing fancy for her? Called her darling, again? But she still wasn't sure how serious he was. She dared not break the mood, found an answer in glibness. "Well, you'd better be nice to me or maybe I'll get irrational like Stella Grainger and do something ridiculously horrible."

Nairn looked at the merriment on her face and knew her statement for what it was.

"I'll tickle you back," she whispered her fingers theatrically reaching for his ribs. She tried it to his chagrin, for it was still difficult for him to laugh heartily. She aimed for compromise.

"Okay. Let's see. I'll not scratch under your plaster when you itch, even if you beg. Or, I'll refuse to help you with fiddly buttons and stuff."

Their laughter echoed around for quite a while as they got creative again.

The next day when their return flight was an hour or so out of London Nairn had Aela pack up their work. She complied readily, searching his face for signs of exhaustion but found none, for, as par for the course, they'd been working all through the long flight. She sat back in her seat when all was cleared away and looked at him, just looked.

Locking her hand tightly in his Nairn's question came out of the blue. "How much do you really want to do your course at UBC?" His eyes were earnest.

He'd just thrust reality right back on her doorstep. Only a few days of her contract to go. Her answer was slow in coming, and very guarded, as he threaded his fingers more tightly through hers. "I've been thinking about doing it for years—the next step in my business career." Suddenly she couldn't face his eyes, could only fixate on their linked hands.

"So, if there was a similar course in Glasgow, or London, would you consider doing it there?" Nairn sounded a little odd.

What was he asking? They'd had a fabulous few days, but although she knew in her heart he really liked her he had never indicated long-term, or said he loved her.

But then she'd never said it to him either.

"Full-time it would take at least a year," she answered, dropping his hand.

Could she have occasional contact with him knowing full well the way business drove his life? She'd be busy studying, for sure, but she'd never see him.

No.

The price of not knowing where he was, and who he was with, was too high a price to pay. How could he ask this?

She'd heard people saying their heart had been hurting over a guy and thought they'd been exaggerating. They weren't. Her heart hurt so much she was surprised she was still sitting there. Turning to him she met his eager regard.

Hope was in his eyes she'd say yes, that she'd stay in the UK. She'd already capitulated and given in to him in their short-term fling, but she couldn't contemplate a half-hearted longer attempt at being his lover to be discarded at a later date when it was no longer convenient for him. Her heart wasn't only hurting...it was breaking.

Nairn knew he'd won when he saw the disillusionment in her gorgeous glistening brown eyes. He didn't want to ever cause her pain, but he had to be sure what they shared wasn't temporary for her. He had to be sure she really did love him, and she wasn't just in the throes of a passionate end-of-world-trip fling. He wouldn't, couldn't, allow her gulped words to put him off his ultimate goal.

"No, Nairn. I'm not going to stay on in Glasgow, or London, and do an MBA. I'm sorry I can't do it." Tears formed and hovered on Aela's beautiful eyelashes before the first one silently slid down her cheek. A cascade followed as she sobbed her heart out.

"Oh God, Aela, don't cry!" He crushed her to him, and then with his finger he forced her chin up and kissed her eyes clear of tears. "Do you love me then, as much as I love you?"

"You love me?" Her sobs became big huge gulps. "You can ask what you just did and then you say you love me?"

"I love absolutely every single thing about you.

You are the loveliest, sexiest, most desirable wonderful lover, even if I have to teach you everything."

He took each finger and kissed it separately before claiming her lips in a long satisfying kiss. Their shared laughter shattered any tension. After he broke for necessary breaths, he started cataloguing again. "You're also the most capable, clever, organizing, sometimes cheeky, bossy woman I know—except for my mother! But in spite of all those faults..."

As Aela swatted him with her hands he saw her eyes fill up again. "Nairn Malcolm, you are the most devious sod, ever! You came first in the scheming manipulator class, second only to Stella Grainger!"

"Don't say my name and hers in the same sentence. Not ever. I didn't mean to make you cry, or hurt you, but I had to be sure you weren't just using me for a few days last fling." Grabbing her he held her close to his chest. "I can't live without you in my life. I want you by my side forever as my wife."

He punctuated the next flow of words with nipping kisses around her chin and eager lips. "My lover, my PA, my sometimes chauffeur when I'm too tired to fly or drive myself...or when you're too bossy to let me have a go."

Aela climbed on top of him and pinned him to the airplane seat, swamping his mouth with her own, grinding herself against his rock hard arousal.

"If that was a proposal, you insufferable man, I'm going to say no until you get down on your knees and beg. That was the worst one I could ever imagine." To prove it she kissed him till he was breathless.

"Aela you wouldn't do it to me in my incapacitated state, would you? I might not be able to bend both knees properly for at least another three weeks."

"Oh, well, you could try?" she teased, capturing his lips and nibbling just the tiniest bit.

Nairn slid to the floor his leg cast at a precarious angle and held her head securely. "Aela, would you please be my wife, for ever and ever?"

"Nairn, I already feel I'm your woman, but yes I would love to marry you because I know I'm going to love you forever."

"My woman!" he joked, kissing her senseless. "Do you know what you do to your poor defenseless love slave?" Struggling up he dragged her by the hand...

The trilling noise of his cell phone made Aela groan. "Hells teeth!" she laughed. "Detective Woods again?"

It was.

"Detective Woods?" Nairn's face was a picture of discomfort as he flicked up the speaker. Aela made to sit on the other chair but he drew her close enough to share, close enough to slide his fingers to places she loved them to be. "Yes!" Nairn cleared the sexual haze from his throat as he attempted to listen. "We wondered how they could possibly have known about it."

He was referring to the fact Stella and her brother knew the whereabouts of Nairn's bike that memorable Saturday.

"Well, Mr. Malcolm, walls definitely have ears."

Detective Woods was in full flow again, the man obviously liked this denouement part of his job, as he updated. Aela nibbled Nairn's neck as she listened in, making sweat begin to bead on his forehead.

"Grainger was in Marsha Hilborne's office the Friday before your accident and heard of your plans to use your bike."

Nairn felt Aela's clever little fingers travel down his torso to his throbbing crotch. A little deliberate flick sent his voice spiraling. "Really!"

He brought the tenor of his speech down, swatting her persistent little hand away. He was amazed. Amazed at Stella's cunning, but even more amazed Aela continued to torture him while he was conducting this particular phone call.

"While Brian Dalkin updated Marsha Hilborne on your travel plans Grainger heard everything on the speakerphone."

Nairn turned the tables on Aela by catching her hand and pinning it to her breast, squeezing and molding it under his own. Barely able to follow the conversation he blinked hard as Aela started to caress herself.

Detective Woods continued blithely unaware of their preoccupation. "Grainger ferreted out your hotel meeting place and time details."

Aela stripped off her top and bra, flinging them to the side as she started on the zip of her jeans. Nairn felt his blood surge. "And?" he asked baldly, to rush the conversation on.

"Grainger gathered up her young brother, got them on the first available flight to Glasgow on the Friday evening and they were waiting in a hired car when you arrived at the car park on the Saturday."

There was a little silence, almost, as Nairn watched Aela turn around and present his rear for him to ogle as she slid her jeans down her...fabulous...long legs.

The almost was a little squeal of a throat clearing as Nairn adjusted his own jeans.

Detective Woods added jauntily, "I'll let you get on with whatever pressing needs you and Miss Cameron have, sir, now you have those last details."

Nairn heard the clear laughter in the other man's tone as he thanked him profusely, switched off the phone, and threw it onto the nearest seat. "Fifteen minutes left, woman!"

"Fifteen for what?" Aela cried as he hauled her

into the little screened off area and launched them onto the small bed, the sudden flip of turbulence not to blame, not to blame at all for his increased heart rate.

"Get these clothes off me. I'm desperate for you."

"And I'm desperate for you, too, my very own Sir Smash-Em-Up! That I love so much."

A few moments later Aela whooped. Nairn grinned at her, a happy, contented—still a little bit pained grin as she flopped down on the bedcover alongside him.

"Do you think you'll ever stay put in one place for any length of time, Nairn Malcolm?" Aela's voice was sleepy. Satisfied and dreamy.

"Twenty-four-hours-a-day-for-a-lifetime forever is what I'm engaging you for, Aela Cameron. Why would I want to stay put anywhere?"

"Know any good doormat companies?"

A happy sigh escaped them both.

A word about the author...

Born and raised in Scotland, Nancy Jardine loves to include her native country in her writing whenever possible, even if it's just a brief mention.

She lives with her husband in an area of Scotland that's steeped in history. Ancient monuments, castles, and beautiful countryside are all on her doorstep, which is convenient since researching history—ancestry in particular—is a hobby she indulges in when not writing.

Lucky to have travelled to many places around the globe, she finds the locations give inspiration to her writing. Experiencing fun things to do with her extended family is something she never tires of!

Website: http://nancyjardineauthor.weebly.com
Blog: http://nancyjardine.blogspot.com

Thank you for purchasing
this publication of The Wild Rose Press, Inc.
For other wonderful stories of romance,
please visit our on-line bookstore at
www.thewildrosepress.com.

For questions or more information
contact us at
info@thewildrosepress.com.

The Wild Rose Press, Inc.
www.thewildrosepress.com

To visit with authors of
The Wild Rose Press, Inc.
join our yahoo loop at
http://groups.yahoo.com/group/thewildrosepress/

Lightning Source UK Ltd.
Milton Keynes UK
UKOW040252180712

196163UK00005B/3/P